A Woman's Flame

A Historical Novel About a Woman Who
Paved Her Own Path

Alex Amit

Alex Amit

Contents

Chapter One

Vienna, August 1910

An old building in the impoverished part of the city.

"Wally, take your things and get out of here," she yells at me while opening the wooden closet. The two of us stand in the small bedroom we all share. Its walls were once painted gray, but now the plaster is peeling, revealing ugly red-brick stains. "You're already sixteen. You can take care of yourself." Her hands quickly grab the only two dresses I own from the simple rope inside the closet and toss them onto the old wooden floor with a sharp gesture. "Considering what you've done, I'm certain you'll manage on your own," she continues to yell, her fingers removing my neatly folded shirts from the shelf and casting them onto the floor as well.

"Mom, please, stop," I whimper as I kneel and try to gather my scattered clothes off the floor, grasping them with one hand and pressing them to my chest. My other hand tries to pull a white camisole she had thrown on the wooden floor, but Mom moves and steps on it with her old leather boot. As I pull it with force, I hear the sound of the delicate fabric tearing. Why won't she listen to me?

"You and your big mouth have no place in this house," she continues to speak loudly as her hands threw all the clothes left in the closet, tossing them onto the iron bed in the room. It's my sister's and my bed. We snuggled on it every night, covering ourselves with an old woolen blanket.

"It's not my fault. It's because of him," I grab the shirts from the bed and ball them up in my hands with the others. What will I do with the torn camisole? Now all I have is the one I'm currently wearing.

"Don't talk back," she shouts and looks at me for a moment before turning again to the closet and searching for the remainder of my clothes inside it. "I knew this would happen. There's no place for you here in this house," she slams the wooden closet door, ignoring my little sister, Marie, who's crying. She clutches mother's leg, her little toes wiggle over Mom's torn leather boot. Marie keeps screaming loudly, her face red and wet with tears. "I've got enough mouths to feed," Mom keeps shouting as she turns her back on me and walks into the kitchen. Marie rushes after her, screaming and clutching tightly at the hem of Mom's simple gray house dress.

"But he fired me," I cry and stand up, with my clothes in my hands. I rush after her to the kitchen, which is separated from the bedroom by a dirty brown curtain. Hilda and Antonia, my two other younger sisters, aged nine and ten, sit silently in the kitchen on a brown wooden chair and hug each other. Their big blue eyes follow Mom and me, tears pouring down their cheeks.

"You always have an excuse for everything. It's your fault. You need to learn to keep your mouth shut. You're good for nothing. How will I feed them without your money?" she bends over and slaps Marie, who's still holding onto her dress, "Enough, Marie, no more crying," she yells at her, but this only makes her cry more and run to the chair where Hilda and Antonia sit in silence. She clings to the chair's legs as if they were a lifeline at the heart of a storm stirring in the middle of the steamy and cabbage soup-reeking kitchen.

"Please, Mom," I approach her from behind, trying to hug her despite carrying all my clothes. "I'll find another job," I can smell the sour scent of her sweat absorbed by the simple dress she's wearing. She stiffens, takes a wooden spoon and stirs the soup in the iron pot on the small stove, used for heating and cooking. Mom doesn't respond to my embrace and continues stirring, trying to shake me off as if I were an abandoned puppy. Why is Marie crying and screaming so loudly? I try to caress her head and calm her down, while my other hand still clutches onto my few clothing items. But Marie continues to scream, her yells echo throughout the small house, and her face turns red.

"He'll fire me too because of you," Mom turns to me and tries to hit me with the wooden spoon. "I should have hit you harder when you were a child. I don't want to see you anymore. What right did you have to yell at him? What do you think? That you're the first woman who's been cast away by a man? And you, shut up already," she slaps Marie again, as she continues to scream and grabs Antonia's leg, her chubby fingers holding on to her with all her might.

"Please, I'll be a good girl. I'll do whatever it takes. I won't talk back anymore. I'll shut up next time," I whimper and step back. All I can see is my sister's big eyes staring at me while my Mom's sweaty hands push me back as she continues to shout, "I shouldn't have married your father. Now he's dead and left me with nothing but you and debts. And now you're just another mouth to feed. If you think you're allowed to resist a man, then it's time for you to manage on your own. The streets are waiting for you," she grips my hand tightly, causing me to let out a cry in pain, as she opens the brown wooden door of our apartment and forcefully pushes me into the stairwell. In a swift movement, she bends down, picks up the clothes that fell from my hands on the dirty parquet floor, throws them into the hallway, and slams the door shut. I hear the iron slide bolt securing the door on the other side.

"Mom, please, I'll be a good girl, don't throw me out. I'll let him do what he wants to me," I yell and cling to the door, pounding on it with my fists, ignoring the pain as my hand scrapes against the rough wood, peeling off the paint. Through the closed door, Marie's incessant crying reaches my ears. The clothes fall from my hands as I hit the door, but I don't care. I have nowhere else to go.

"What's going on? You're always so loud," the neighbor from the adjacent apartment peers through the crack of her door and shouts at me. "What's all this?" she examines the clothes scattered in the stairwell, "Do you think you're allowed to throw around your clothes here? The stairwell belongs to all the tenants." She approaches me, and steps on the clothes strewn about.

"I'm sorry, Mrs. Steiner," I turn to her and wipe my tear-streaked cheeks, and sniffing, "I'll collect them, don't worry." I kneel on the hallway floor, ignoring scraped and sore hands. Bending down at her feet, I quickly gather my clothes. My wounded hands leave small blood stains on the white fabric of my torn camisole.

"I'll report you to the landlord," she says in a hushed voice. "It's time for him to kick you out of here. I'll tell him you've been sleeping in the stairwell." She turns and walks towards the door of Mr. Bauer's apartment on the same floor. She knocks on it. What is she going to do? Is she going to tell all the neighbors?

"Please, Mrs. Steiner, no," I say, looking up at her. "Please do not involve Mr. Bauer." I fear he'll come out and shout at me too. He always gives me nasty looks when we cross paths in the stairwell.

"I always knew your family would cause trouble. A family without a man to look after them always causes trouble," she says as she continues to stand by the door of his apartment, waiting for him to open the door.

"Please, don't," I collect the clothes and press them to my chest, pinning them to my body so they don't fall while I slowly stand up.

"I'll make sure the landlord kicks you out," she turns around after a moment and walks back to her apartment. She enters it, and slams her door shut.

"Mrs. Steiner, I'm leaving!" I shout after her at the closed door as I hurry down the stairs, being cautious not to stumble.

I head out to the street, hoping they won't evict Mom, Hilda, Antonia, and Marie from the apartment because of me. It's been two years since Dad passed away and we moved here. I've been missing him for two years. Now I'm all alone in an alley.

I walk down the narrow alleyway and wipe my cheek. *Walk, walk, don't think, just keep on walking.* My hands tightly squeeze the pile of clothes, and my fingers run through the fabric, feeling its softness. What will I do? Where will I go? Who will take care of me? Perhaps I should go back and beg Mom to let me in? Why was she so mad after he fired me? I keep walking and notice two children in torn clothes playing on the street with a ball made of rags. The most important thing is to leave this place, get away from all the constant yelling and crying.

I walk out of the alley and into the street, passing a knife sharpener and two older women standing next to him, their gaze fixed on me. The knife sharpener stands next to the wooden cart, holding a large knife, running its blade against the whetstone, creating a sharp, metallic sound. I notice his thick mustache and brown eyes as he stares at me. The two women, clad in brown coats, stop chatting and look at me. Their eyes linger on my tear-streaked cheeks, and the bundle of clothes pressed to my chest. I walk away from them to the other side of the street. They will probably gossip behind my back in a few seconds, but it no longer matters. My gaze casts downward, I continue to walk as fast as I can, looking at my shoes and the gray cobblestones. I can sense their eyes, staring at me. Only the metal screeching sounds of the knife against the whetstone follow me like a wounded dog's pained howl, as I slowly walk away from them.

I stop further down the street near Mr. Walner's fabric store. Slowly, I approach the shop window and look in, pressing my face against the cool glass. I notice him inside the store talking to a young and unfamiliar girl. He's gesturing to explain something with his hands. I should keep on walking. If he turns to look in my direction and notices me standing outside, he'll come out and shout at me as he did this morning after attempting to do what he did to me. I clench my thighs and tremble, take a few steps back and breathe heavily. However, my feet feel as though they're rooted to the pavement, and I can't turn my gaze away from his shop. The name "Walner" is written in bold black letters above the glass door, and the display window features a multitude of colorful fabric rolls. My attention is drawn to the blue roll with tiny flowers, similar to the one he requested me to place on the large wooden table in the center of the store earlier this morning. The shop was empty of customers when he commanded me to cut a piece of fabric, then invaded my personal space, leaned over my shoulder, and tried to do that... thing.

I breathe heavily and find that I can't move, even though I have to keep walking. Regardless of what had happened, I shouldn't have started shouting as I did. I should have kept my mouth shut. I must learn to shut up. I hardly breathe and close my mouth, still looking at the shop window and the figures inside the store. Mr. Walner had a distinct scent of tobacco. He buys it in small metal boxes, specially delivered from England. I close my eyes. I can feel that smell burning my nostrils, even though he is on the other side of the glass, far away from me. Clenching my thighs, I caress the clothes in my hands, pinching them tightly until my fingers ache and I want to scream. But I'm determined to keep my mouth shut.

"Watch out!" I hear a shout and open my eyes, looking to the side. The loud clattering of hooves fills the air as two brown horses pulling a carriage gallop in the narrow street towards me. I hastily move to the side. They gallop past me, their well-groomed fur glistening in the afternoon sun as they pull a closed black wood carriage coated with shiny varnish. I hear the whip as the coachman, seated high on the front seat, cracks his whip and shouts at passers-by to move out of the way.

I lean against the hard stone wall, scraping my back as I try to avoid the passing carriage. I grip my clothes, and catch a glimpse of a distinguished lady wearing a fancy hat sitting inside the carriage. Her gaze is indifferent as she observes me. But when I look down again at the cobblestones, I notice one of my dresses that had fallen from my hands, now lying in the street. The horses trample it, and the carriage wheels roll over the yellowish cloth, staining it with black streaks.

The carriage rushes on, and I hurry to pick up the dress lying in the street. I tuck it under the other clothes in my hand, ignoring the mud stains. I can hear the horses' hooves slowly growing distant, and all the passers-by resume walking down the narrow street. They ignore me as I continue to aimlessly wander without knowing where to go, looking for a place to spend the night. Soon the sun will set, and the street will be empty.

"Hostel for Girls," says the sign above the entrance to a building on Hafnersteig Street. I walk through the wooden door that was painted in gray oil and is now wet from the raindrops that have started to fall.

"May I help you?" a woman asks as I close the heavy door behind me and step inside. She positions herself behind a brown wooden reception desk at the entrance. I look at her under the dim light of a single lamp hanging from the ceiling. She's in a dark brown dress, but as I approach her, I notice the fabric has a square pattern. I walk towards her and shiver. The hostel lobby is as cold as the street outside.

"I'm looking for a place to stay for a few nights," I observe small wooden boxes behind her. Some contain folded papers or keys.

"I know you," she stays behind her desk, her eyes surveying me, "you're the Neuzil family red-head. Your mother works for Mr. Walner. What happened?" her eyes linger on my hands still clutching to my wrinkled clothes. "Were you thrown out?"

"I need a place to stay for a couple of nights," I repeat. What can I say to convince her?

"What did you do? Why were you kicked out? Did you do something immoral?" she walks around the counter and stands in front of me. "We don't accept that kind of behavior here." She reaches out and touched my bundle of clothes. "You don't seem like you have good manners."

"No," I answer her quietly, lowering my gaze, "I didn't do anything immoral." I take a step towards her, but she takes a step back. She won't take me in. My gaze focuses on her old black boots. They laces are tightly tied. For a moment, the stifling smell in the hallway reminds me of Mr. Walner's breath when he leaned over and touched me. "I'm a good girl," I add, looking at my old shoes that wet from the rain. I'll keep my mouth shut. I won't shout. I'll be sure to always smile and learn to be silent.

"It's one Krone for two days, payment in advance," she continues to stare at me.

"I don't have any money, but I'll find a job and pay you back," I said in a hushed tone, glancing at the dim hallway and the winding stairs leading to the second floor. I must find a place to sleep.

"You can give it to me," she says and pulls my hand so forcefully that all the clothes in my arms are scatter on the floor. I take a step back, but she continues to hold my fingers, trying to seize the silver male signet ring on my finger.

"No," I loudly exclaim, "I can't give you that." I keep shouting and desperately pull my hand back.

"Where did you get it? Did you steal it? You look like a thief to me," she whispers and draws her face closer to mine while maintaining a firm grip on my hand.

"It's mine. I didn't steal it," I protect the ring with my other hand, clenching it tightly until my hand aches. The heavy ring is too big for my thin finger and can easily slip off. I must protect it.

"So, where did you get it?"

"That is none of your business."

"You must have stolen it. You deserved to be kicked out of your home. Three Kronen."

"What?" I ask and continue to shield the ring with my hand, trying to step back and free myself from her grip. She's hurting me.

"I'll give you three Kronen for it. You can sleep here for a week," she finally releases my hand, walks away from me, and returns to her position behind the counter. "You won't find a better deal."

"I can't," I bend down on the stone floor. "I'll find another way to pay you," I swiftly gather my clothes. It was my father's ring, my only memento of him.

"I don't accept any other form of payment," she scoffs mockingly. "Only cash in coins or bills. The type of payment you can offer is not acceptable in this establishment. That must be why you were kicked out. I'll ask Mr. Walner next time I visit his shop."

"Have a nice evening," I say as I pick myself up, clutching my clothes and rushing out of the hostel. I push the heavy gray door with my shoulder and step out into the rain. I'll find some other place.

The cold of the night prevents me from falling asleep. Even though it's still summer, a cool wind starts to blow, and it rains heavily. I sit shivering under a freight wagon parked in one of the squares. All my clothes are bundled in my lap as I shield them from the rain and wet pavements, glistening in the yellowish light of the distant street lanterns.

Why did you have to die? I whisper to myself, my fingers trace the cold metal of Dad's signet ring. Why did you leave me alone? I wrap my arms around myself, trying to keep warm. But no one answers me. Only a stray cat, drenched by the rain, hesitantly approaches me and stands under the wooden cart at a safe distance from me, slowly begins to lick its wet fur.

⁓

"Wake up," I open my eyes and look around, trying to remember where I am. My whole body aches. "Wake up," the voice says again. I look up and see a woman in a simple dress and a dirty coat leaning toward me, shaking my shoulders. "You'll freeze in this cold. You have to find a place to stay," she says. Her silver hair is covered in an old woolen hat. Her hair seems to be streaked with gold as the early morning sun illuminates the small square. Where am I?

I survey my surroundings. Market carts are arriving one after the other. The vendors stop their horses, stand and talk to each other, sway from side to side to keep warm in the chill of the early morning. Meanwhile, I gather the clothes around me. I used one of my shirts to cover myself at night to keep warm. I had to. My muscles ache from the cold. I look for the cat that approached me last night, trying to get warm; but it's nowhere to be found. Only my torn camisole, the one I tried to cover us with since we were both shivering from the cold, remains discarded on the gray cobblestones of the square.

"Take it," she says, and I notice her reaching out and offering me a slice of bread. I take it, slowly chewing it. My stomach aches with hunger. I haven't eaten since yesterday. "Do you understand me? Are you an immigrant from the East?" she asks me emphasizing each word. I shake my head.

"I'm from here," I answer while taking a bite from the slice of bread.

"You need to find a place to stay. The police seize homeless people at night and throw them in detention," she says as she stands up and leans against the cart that sheltered me during the night. I can't see anything but her legs and hear the sounds of the wooden crates being unpacked. I need to move on and keep looking for a safe place where I can rest my head. I slowly collect my clothes and emerge from under the cart to the square, groaning from the pain of my cramped muscles as I struggle to stand and almost lose balance.

"Take this," she says and hands me a burlap sack that she pulls from the boxes on her cart, "for your clothes, so they don't get dirty."

"Thank you," I express my gratitude and hold the coarse fabric, shoving my crumpled clothes into it. "Thank you for your kindness," I repeat before I begin walking away in the awakening market. I'll look for a place for myself. The movement will keep me warm.

"Go to the hostel on Schultergasse Street," she says. "There is a kind woman there who will assist you," she continues as she turns her back to me and arranges the wooden boxes on the cart.

"You are a good woman," I say to her, but she continues unpacking her crates and doesn't turn around. It's time for me to leave. I give her one last look, walk among the peddlers, enter one of the side allies, and sit down. I gnaw on the slice of bread. I don't want to go to the hostel, the woman in the hostel will probably be just like the woman I met yesterday; she will try to steal my ring. I resume to gently caress it.

I return to the square and wander amidst the stalls, looking for someone who'll be willing to give me another slice of bread or something to eat. I'm starving. However, at noon, I can no longer continue walking. Some peddlers look at me with suspicion, as if I were a thief, just waiting to snatch a vegetable from their stall when their attention waned. My legs ache, and I sweat under the scorching summer sun. I'm afraid to sit in the corner, lest I be caught by one of the policemen patrolling the market. I can easily spot them from a distance as they pace around in their black helmets stamped with the gold insignia of the Empire.

"Take it," a saleswoman says to me and hands me a potato.

"Thank you," I hold it in my grimy hand and take small bites, trying to quell the hunger in my stomach. As I eat, I continue searching with my eyes for any policeman. What will I do when evening falls again?

The sun begins to set, and the peddlers pack their carts. Some tether their horses to the wooden wagons, load the empty crates, fold the cloth umbrellas that shield them from the sun, and leave the square. I remain standing in one of the alleys overlooking the square, I watch as it empties and the silence replaces the market sounds. The woman who gave me a slice of bread in the morning had also disappeared, leaving me to walk alone amid the empty square. A cold afternoon breeze sweeps through the alleys causing me to shiver. Finally, I give up and turn down an alley towards Schultergasse Street.

The heavy wooden front door of the hostel looks identical to the one I had seen the other day. The raindrops glistened on the oil paint as they did yesterday, and it had the same shiny and smooth brass handle. The only two differences were the door's color – brown instead of gray and the name of the establishment written above the door.

My hand lingers on the brass handle, flutters against it as I debate whether to go inside or turn around. Perhaps I should return to the empty square. Maybe someone had left their wagon behind and I could hide under it until the morning.

"Are you coming in?" I hear a voice and look up at a young woman standing next to me. She seems a little older and taller than me, and looks at me with a smile on her face. Her blue eyes survey me. I try to comb my unruly red hair with my fingers.

"No," I reply her and take a step back, my gaze fixated on her lips painted in bright red. Mother had always said that only certain women wore lipstick and forbidden me from using it on my lips. However, I noticed that respectable customers wore lipstick at Mr. Walner's shop.

"Have a nice evening," she smiles at me, opens the door, walks in, and disappears into the dark corridor. The brown wooden door slams in front of my face with a thud.

I grasp the brass handle again, feel the smooth cold metal. But a moment later, I change my mind and take step back. I must try to look more mature.

At the corner of the alley, I bend down and find a sharp stone. I nick my palm with it, ignoring the pain. I carefully apply the drops of blood to my lips, savoring the blood's rusty taste. I tightly clench the palm of my injured hand around the jute cloth, hoping the bleeding will stop. Then, facing the wind, I wait for the blood on my lips to dry. I'm ready.

My fingers comb through my wild red hair, trying to arrange it as best I can. I stand in front of the brown wooden door, wiping the tears of pain from my cheek. My wounded hand still hurts. Once again, I grip the brass handle, take a deep breath, look down, and enter the dark corridor. The peddler who gave me a slice of bread in the morning said that the place was run by a good woman who would help me.

꧁ ❧ ꧂

The entrance hall to the hostel appears the same as the one I was in yesterday: dimly lit by a single lamp hanging on the wall, a reception desk manned by an older woman, small wooden cubicles behind her, some of which contain papers or keys, and an entrance to a back room.

"Good evening," she says politely as she scrutinizes me, examining my hair and dirty dress. She bends down, and for a moment, I think she's going to ignore me. I consider turning around and finding another place to stay. But then she stands up, takes a silver box out of a small bag, pulls out a cigarette, and lights it for herself. "Did you come looking for a place to sleep?" she looks at the burlap sack pressed against my chest. He silver hair is tightly pinned, and she has thin lips and blue-gray eyes that resemble pebbles.

"Yes," I reply, looking straight into her eyes, even though it may be considered impolite. In any case, I know she will kick me out when she finds out I have no money. The taste of blood on my lips bothers me, and I resist the urge to bite them and remove the blood.

"How old are you?" she looks back into my eyes.

"Old enough," I finally look down, unwilling to tell her my age.

"You're not," She says, "this is no place for girls like you. You should look for somewhere else."

"I have nowhere else," I answer her quietly and continue to look down, not wanting her to see my teary eyes.

"Do you have any money?" she blows the cigarette smoke into the damp hallway, filling the air with the pungent smell of tobacco. It's customary to write in the newspapers that women are not allowed to smoke. Mom also used to say that. She used to say that smoking is a man's pleasure and it soothes them.

"No, I don't have any money," I finally answer her and look up.

"Sorry," she inhales from her cigarette, "I don't give rooms for free."

I turn to leave and head for the door, but then I stop. I have no other choice. I need a place to stay. I won't survive any more nights outside in the cold. Winter will soon come. "I have this," I walk over to her and place my father's signet ring on the counter, slowly slipping it off my finger, feeling the cool metal against my skin one last time. Maybe that's what he wanted, for me to use it when I had no other choice.

"Did you steal it? Get out of here. I don't allow thieves here," she looks at me.

"I didn't steal it," I look back at her. I don't care what she thinks of me anymore.

"So, where did you get that ring?" she scrutinizes me as if trying to see if I'm lying to her. Still, I look at her right in the eyes, and after a moment, we both lower our gazes and look at the ring on the dirty wooden counter, sparkling under the yellowish lamplight.

"It's mine," I fight the urge to snatch the ring and walk away. I place my hand on the wooden counter, at a touching distance, ready to act. I mustn't trust this woman.

"And how did you get it?"

"It was my father's. He was a teacher," I examine her bright eyes and silver hair. Will she be willing to purchase it?

"And what happened to him?" she raises her gaze from the ring to me.

"He's dead. It's worth five Kronen," I answer quickly. I'm willing to haggle.

"So your father was a teacher? Do you know how to read and write?" she inhales from the cigarette and blows the smoke in my direction.

"Yes, madame."

"Young lady, listen to Ms. Bertha, you don't belong in this place," she leans back against the small wooden boxes behind her but continue to look at me. She doesn't chase me away, nor does she make an attempt to grab the ring placed on the counter between us. My hand rests on the counter, ready to protect the ring if she tries to take it.

"Four Kronen, final price," I say, reaching out for the ring. Where will I go if she refuses to accept it?

"I only accept cash," she puts out her cigarette in the bronze ashtray on the counter. I look at the crushed brown cigarette butt against the delicate bronze designs of flowers and butterflies.

"Thank you, Ms. Bertha, have a good evening," I take the silver ring, turn my back to her, and walk towards the door, wiping my lips with the palm of my hand. Tears well up in my eyes. I'll be fine. I'll be fine.

"There's a pawnbroker at the end of the street," I manage to hear her before I close the heavy wooden door behind me and smell the cold evening air, a welcome contrast to the suffocating air inside.

"Eight kronen, that's what I'll offer you for it," the pawnbroker examines the signet ring with his thick fingers. He turns it over, puts on his glasses, and closely inspect it. "Make up your mind quickly; I'll be closing in a few minutes," he shifts his gaze to the gold watch hanging high on the wall amidst the metal and wooden cabinets.

"It's worth more," I look at my ring resting in his palm. I want him to ask me where I got it from and about my father, but he doesn't.

"Eight kronen, no more, and I'm doing you a favor. It's not gold," he looks up at me, lingering on my lips. He has a black mustache that's starting to turn silver, and I struggle to recall his name, though it's written in black letters on the sign outside the store, marked by three gold balls hanging above the door, the symbol of pawnshops.

"I agree," I nod. What would Dad think? Would he have embraced me and commend my decision?

"You have a year to pay me back fifteen kronen; otherwise, I'll sell it. The ring is mine after a year and a day, and I'll sell it as per the law," he closes his fingers around my father's ring, and I nod again, though I'm still somewhat uncertain. What will I do without it? I watch as he turns his back to me, takes out an envelope from a drawer, places it on the wooden counter standing between us, and writes something on it in neat handwriting. He slips the ring into the envelope. His pink tongue licks the envelope, sealing it carefully. I watch as he places it in one of the drawers in the large wooden cabinet behind him. Iron bars separate us, allowing only a narrow opening for my hand to reach through. He takes my father's ring.

"Excuse me, sir," I say to him.

"Yes?" he turns to me, but the envelope is no longer in his hands.

"Never mind," I look at the large wooden cabinet full of drawers. I shouldn't have given him the ring. I should have found another solution.

"There you go, eight kronen," he places the metal coins on the wooden tray between the iron bars. He also hands me a note written in neat handwriting beside. There's a number and a date on the note. "A year and a day. After that, I'll sell it. Do you understand?" he asks, his blue eyes fixed on me. I don't respond. I swiftly grab the silver coins and the note from the wooden tray, hastily leaving the small shop. I'll find a way to get the money. I'll get the ring back.

"You're back," she says when I enter the hostel again. I approach her reception desk and wordlessly place a Kronen coin on the wooden counter. The rest of the money and the note are safely tucked away in a hidden pocket in my dress. I stood in the alley and quickly put them there, hoping no one would pass by and see me. "I didn't think you would come back," she adds after a moment, but I don't answer her. I look at the corridor and at the light of the gas lamp illuminating the stairs leading to the upper floors. I'm so tired.

"Come with me," she walks out from behind her counter and starts walking towards the stairs. I follow her, holding my bag of clothes, and look around at the waiting area in front of the stairs. There are two old floral fabric couches on either side of the room, and beside one there's a mahogany wooden coffee table. I notice an ashtray on the table, as if expecting someone to arrive. The sound of her footsteps climbing up the stairs makes me quicken my steps, and I hurry to catch up with her. She wears a long dark green dress, and I get a glimpse of her black boots with each step she takes.

"Come on, girls, don't waste the whole evening getting ready. You're beautiful just the way you are," she walks quickly to the bathroom at the end of the corridor and scolds two young women standing there. They're wearing white camisoles with a lace trim and are talking to each other. "Come with me," she turns and says to me, and I follow her until she stands in front of one of the doors in the corridor and knocks on it, "Christina," she knocks on the door again, "Open the door, Christina, I won't wait for you all day."

"Just a moment, Ms. Bertha," I hear a voice from inside, and after a moment, the door opens. Through the crack of the old wooden door, I see a young woman with disheveled golden hair and ample breasts peeking out. She's in a nightgown and black stockings, one of which is slightly torn.

"What do you want?" she looks at Ms. Bertha and then shifts her gaze to me, surveying me with her green eyes. She appears slightly older than me and about the same height. "Who's she?" she asks, her gaze fixed on the bag of clothes in my hands.

"Meet your new roommate," Ms. Bertha opens the door wide and enters the room, passing Christina. "Come in. I don't have all day," she says to me. I follow her and enter step through the narrow door, brushing lightly against Christina, who remains standing, gripping the door handle and not moving aside to let me in.

I take a look around the small room. Its walls are painted a faded yellow, and I notice the peeling plaster forming peculiar shapes on the wall. There's a tiny window above the bed, a wooden closet on the side, and a dressing table with a mirror in the corner.

"These are your shelves," Ms. Bertha opens the closet, shifting Christina's clothes to one side to make room for mine. "You'll be sharing the closet and the bed. I assume you're used to it," she says without waiting for a response. I glance at the single iron bed, which takes up almost the entire room, leaving up cramped. Since my young sisters were born, I've grown accustomed to sleeping like this. Every night, we would huddle under the covers, and I would hug and comfort them. What will happen to them now? I look down to conceal my teary eyes.

"You said I could have a room to myself," Christina says, walking past me. She picks up one of her dresses from the floor and places it on the wooden chair near the dressing table.

"For what you're paying me, be thankful I'm giving you any work," Ms. Bertha retorts, slamming the closet door. "And be nice to her. She's still a young girl."

"Yes, Ms. Bertha," Christina replies, turning her back to both of us. She bends slightly and examines her face in the dirty mirror hanging on the wall above the small, cluttered dressing table. "I promise to treat her kindly," she says as she combs her light hair with her fingers with slow, deliberate motion. Even though it's disheveled, I still find it beautiful, like a cascade of wild oats in the breeze of a spring morning.

"What is your name?" Ms. Bertha turns to me.

"Walburga, ma'am, but everyone calls me Wally."

"Walburga, welcome to my hostel. Payment is due weekly; otherwise, you'll be thrown out to the street. No delays and no discounts," she examines me with her gray-blue eyes and doesn't smile.

"Yes, Ms. Bertha," I stand before her in the stuffy room. I will survive. I will find a way to pay her.

"The shared bathroom is located at the end of the hall. You'll need to get along with the other girls, including Christina."

"Yes, Ms. Bertha," I glance at Christina, who leans against the wall, watching us with her hands folded over her night-gown.

"And whoever doesn't comply with the rules of my hostel can always go back to the street," she adds, walking past me and standing by the open door.

"Yes, Ms. Berth. I will be obedient and behave well," I say and lower my gaze. I have to succeed.

"Christina, get ready. It's already evening. You can't sit in your room all day," she says and turns, walking out of the room and disappearing down the hall.

"Yes, Ms. Bertha," Christina answers her, but I'm not sure if Ms. Bertha hears her.

"Thank you for letting me stay in your room," I say to Christina.

"No one let you stay in my room. She forced me," Christina replies as she passes by me, the fabric of her nightgown brushes against my body. She stands in front of the closet, opens the doors, and returns her clothes to the shelves that Ms. Bertha cleared. "You'll have to settle for this," she says to me after a few moments, and I see that she left me only one shelf. "I've been here longer than you, and I'm older, so I deserve more space."

I don't answer her and sit on the iron bed covered with a wool blanket, looking at the small wooden window covered with a yellowish stained curtain.

"This is also my side of the bed," she continues.

"Sorry," I reply and get up, and move to sit on the other side. Why is she so mean to me? What did I do to her?

"This is my room, not yours, just so we're clear," she says and sits on the other side. I hear the creaking of the bed springs, but I don't respond. I simply turn my eyes to the other side and look at the yellowish wall, still gripping the burlap sack tightly until my fingers turn white.

"You're such a child. You shouldn't cry about everything," she says after a moment.

"I'm not crying," I continue looking away from her, my gaze fixed on the wall. I don't wipe my eyes. "And I'm not a child. I'm sixteen. I'm an adult."

"You need to show her that you're mature and not afraid of her, or else, she'll take advantage of you."

"I'll show her," I mutter and wipe my cheeks. "I'll show her, and she won't kick me out of her hostel."

"It's not really a hostel," Christina says mockingly, but I don't care. I keep staring at the wall, wiping away my tears.

"Enough, don't cry. In a few days you'll get used to this place."

"Thank you," I say to her and look in her direction.

She gets up from the bed, takes the burlap sack from my hand, and places it in the closet on my shelf. "Welcome to Bertha's Girls' Palace, Walburga, also known as Wally," she smiles at me.

"Thank you, Christina," I smile back at her and lean against the peeling wall. I will think about everything tomorrow, not today. Today I found a bed in this hostel for women.

Chapter Two

The Women's Hostel

The room is dark at night. I lie in the iron bed with Christina and can't fall asleep. The touch of the woolen blanket itches and feels unpleasant. I try to stay as close as possible to the side of the bed, avoiding any accidental contact with Christina's legs. I can hear her slow breathing. Her head is placed next to my legs, and mine is next to hers, so we try to make the space less crowded. Back home, I used to comfort Hilda and Antonia when we huddled together at night and couldn't fall asleep. I would sing them lullabies, assuring them that everything would be fine. But here, I'm afraid to even turn around and touch Christina, fearing she might get mad at me.

Occasionally, I hear noises or muffled laughter in the corridor, and I turn my head to look at the narrow slit of light under the door. Christina mumbles something in the dark, but I can't make out her words. At least I managed to find a place to stay for a few nights, but what will I do next? Was I wrong to shout at him? Maybe I should have let him touch me and kept quiet, pretend that nothing happened as he groped and leered at me. I can still feel the lingering touch on my thighs, and it makes me shudder. I should have ignored him, continued spreading the light blue fabric with flowers on the big table as he requested, and not turned to him in panic and nicked him with the scissors. Why did I do that? Now I'm left with almost nothing.

I turn slowly in bed and gaze at the dark ceiling. I have seven Kronen coins left, they're tied in a small cloth bag close to my body. I have only two dresses, two camisoles, one of them torn, one shirt, one skirt, a thin coat, and two pairs of socks. I'll be fine. I must succeed, find a job, and find someone who will care for me. Despite the warmth under the blanket, I shiver. What will I do if I can't find a job and run out of money? I hug myself gently, careful not to make any noise. I imagine Dad telling me a bedtime story like he used to when I was a child, and I was afraid of the dark.

Later, I slowly move the woolen blanket, get out of bed, and stand in the dark room, feeling my way towards the closet door. My fingers find the handle and I open it, retrieving my clothes-loaded burlap sack. I haven't had a chance to arrange my clothes yet. Carefully, I sit back on the bed, lying down slowly to avoid making any noise and waking Christina. I tightly clutch the burlap sack, holding it close to my body as I cover myself and press my cheek against the coarse fabric. I find comfort in feeling the roughness between my arms. I continue to look up at the ceiling in the darkness, imagining Dad hugging me and his two blue eyes looking at me with love, assuring me that he is protecting me.

"Wake up," someone pinches my leg the following day and I open my eyes. Where am I? "Wake up, carrot head, get out of bed. I need my room," Christina pinches my legs again, and I close my eyes and open them again. This is not a dream.

Gray daylight penetrates from the small window, seeping in through the dirty curtains. I look at the open closet door. Where is my bag of clothes? I sit up in a panic. As I look around, I spot my bag lying on the floor at my feet, and remember. It took me a long time to fall asleep last night.

"Rusty, get out from my bed and leave the room," Christina snaps as she gets up from the bed and sits on the small wooden chair in front of the dressing table. She opens a small box, and looks at herself in the mirror.

I put my bag of clothes back in the closet and leave the room, wearing nothing but my nightgown. I wish Ms. Bertha would have set me up with a nicer roommate.

All eyes of the women waiting outside the bathroom watch me as I approach and stand last in line, looking down. There are five or six women dressed in lace nightgowns, all older than I am, and none of them have red hair. I run my fingers through my hair ends as I examine my bare feet on the cold wooden floor.

"Are you Bertha's new girl?" one of them asks me.

"Yes," I answer her, looking up.

"She definitely likes young women," another says, and they all laugh. I lower my eyes again. Some of them are wearing simple but clean shoes, and others are only wearing socks.

"You should try hydrogen peroxide," one of them says.

"What for?" I ask her.

"For your hair, it will make it blonde," she answers me, "Men love blonde hair."

"Thank you," I reply and touch the red hair scattered over my shoulders, not wanting to tell her that my father also had that hair color.

"I'm Erica," one of them stands beside me and smiles.

"Thanks, I'm Walburga, but everyone calls me Wally," I move a little closer and smile at her. She's slightly older than me and has brown hair and brown eyes. She smiles back at me; her lips are thick and pink.

"Come on. We are waiting here outside. We don't have all day," one of the women shouts to the girls in the bathroom, "and we have a new one called Walburga, but everyone calls her Wally," she continues to shout to the girls inside, and they all laugh.

"Don't mind them. They're always like that with new girls." Erica says, giving me her hand. I feel her warm fingers and smile at her. I don't care if they laugh at me.

"You're back?" Christina asks me when I later enter the room, but I ignore her and turn to get dressed. She is still sitting at the dressing table, wearing a cream-colored lace shirt and a pleated skirt rolled up on her hips. I peek in her direction and

29

examine the garter socks on her feet. Why do the other girls think I'm Ms. Bertha's new girl?

Christina ignores me. With a pink brush, she gently collects lipstick from a small silver bowl on the table and applies it to her lips. I look away from her and put on my dress. I need to find a job.

"Have a nice day," Christina says as I finish putting on my shoes. She gets up and spreads perfume in the room from a glass bottle, filling it with the sweet scent of roses.

"Thank you, have a nice day too," I respond before heading out into the hallway, looking for Erica. However, she is not there; only two other girls are watching me and whispering. I hurry down the stairs towards the entrance. Is Erica one of Ms. Bertha's girls too?

⁓⚬⚬⁓

I briskly walk out of the small alley of the pension, passing through the square where the carts gather. It's still early, and only a few buyers are meandering through the market while vendors engage in conversation with each other. I search for the woman who gave me a slice of bread yesterday, but she's nowhere to be found. Instead, I pause next to a vendor by a basket brimming with ripe red apples. Should I buy one now or wait? Money is tight, so I decide to push through my hunger for the time being. I continue walking, leaving behind the mix of smells - horses, spices, and the tempting aroma of hot pastries from the bakery on the street corner. I'll find something to eat later on the main street.

As I make my way, I notice elegantly dressed men in black suits, donning top hats, stopping at a newsstand to buy newspapers, glancing through the latest headlines, or simply strolling between fancy shops and cafés. Carriages laden with goods pass by in the center of the street, guided by waggoners urging the horses to move a bit faster. I resist the alluring scent of coffee wafting from the nearby cafes, but eventually, I give in to temptation and stop to buy a pastry. I savor each bite of the sweet pastry, licking my fingers as I walk. Perhaps I should have bought food at the market where it's cheaper, instead of squandering my money like this.

Near the Ring Boulevard that surrounds the old city, where city walls once stood but were demolished to make way for newer buildings, I stop and watch the tram as it speeds along the tracks, while horses carrying carts cross its path. I observe the tram moving away. I don't have enough money to ride it. So, I continue walking towards the Opera house, despite the scorching sun hitting my head and the sweat on my back. I notice women in floral summer dresses, wearing white gloves and holding lace parasols, chatting with each other as they stroll down the boulevard. They look at my simple dress as I approach them. Feeling self-conscious, I lower my eyes and keep walking.

Taking a moment to rest near the Opera House, I admire the row of fancy carriages lined up in the square. The clean horses stand patiently, waiting for passengers to arrive. Suddenly, a new automobile passes by, filling the air with engine rattling and the pungent smell of gasoline. I observe the uniformed driver sitting upright, expertly navigating the black automobile through the boulevard, amid the pedestrians, trams, and horses; each hoof clicking on the cobblestones. The street leads to the new neighborhoods and the opulent homes of the city's wealthy population.

Their houses lie across the ring boulevard, sparkling with cleanliness, adorned with large windows. As I approach, I stand in front of the first building, admiring the stone flower decorations along the windows. I then move towards the servants' side door and knock on its black surface. I need a job.

"Yes, please?" A woman opens the door and stares at me suspiciously. She is dressed in servant clothes, her gaze fixated on my hair.

"I'm looking for a job. I'm hardworking," I say, observing at her clean black and white uniform.

"Wait here," she instructs me and closes the door after she scrutinized my dress and old shoes. I remain standing on the street, watching the driver positioned next to a shiny black automobile parked in front of the main entrance. He's dressed in a dark green uniform and diligently moves around the car, polishing its copper headlights with a leather cloth.

"Do you have any references?" the servants' door opens again, revealing an older woman in a gray dress who examines me, paying attention to my shoes and simple attire.

"No, ma'am, but I'm hardworking and ready to do any job," I stand up and look at her.

"You cannot come into this house without references," she slams the door shut, leaving me out on the street. The driver, still focused on his task, doesn't even glance my way. How can I get references?

Afternoon sun rays spread the tree's shadows across the boulevard, resembling giant monsters painted on the pavement as I walk quickly, passing the trams and carts that keep moving. I couldn't find a job in any of the houses I tried. In most of them, the maid at the entrance refused me outright, and they didn't even bother to call their housekeeper to see me. At least one kind woman gave me a bowl of soup to eat, took me into the kitchen of a luxurious house, and chatted with me for a few minutes while she poured me a bowl of delicious lentil soup. When I thanked her, she also gave me a few slices of bread to take with me. What will I do tomorrow?

In the alley, I avert my gaze when passing the iron-barred glass window of the pawnbroker's shop and quicken my steps towards the hostel. I am determined to find a job tomorrow.

"Good evening, Walburga," Ms. Bertha observes me from behind her counter as I walk through the door. "Where have you been all day?"

"Good evening, Ms. Bertha," I reply, standing and surveying the surroundings. The air is suffused with cigarette smoke, and a man smoking a cigar occupies a sofa in the entrance room. "I was looking for a job, Ms. Bertha," I add, still standing and observing the two girls sitting on the other sofa. One of them is also smoking a cigarette. They're both dressed in cream-colored lace dresses, smiling at the man and keeping their legs crossed.

"Did you manage to find a job?" Ms. Bertha asks me, and I turn my gaze to her, no longer looking at the girls who are caressing their thighs with gentle movements.

"No, Ms. Bertha, nobody wanted me," I reply.

"That's how it is in the streets, Wally," she lights a cigarette. "Keep looking. Eventually, someone will want you."

"And what if no one will?" I ask her quietly, straightening the fabric of my dress that covers my thigh. I regret asking that question. I'll find a job tomorrow.

"Don't worry, girl," she smiles at me from across the counter, "in the end, all the ones that no one wants end up at Bertha. That's what I'm here for," she blows the cigarette smoke into the air, "Bertha is always here to provide a warm bed and a job for all the women who no one in the world wants." She comes out from behind the counter and approaches me, stroking my arm for a moment as if examining me, "Gita, Magda, you have a job," she turns her back and talks to the girls. They smile at the man sitting in front of them, and after a moment, they both get up from their sofa. Slowly walking, they cross the room and sit beside him. They look like stray cats slowly walking toward a fat, tasty fish thrown at them from the fish shop. Ms. Bertha walks toward them, caresses the waist of one of the girls, bends over, and whispers something in the gentleman's ear. He smiles at her while continuing to smoke a cigar, with the two girls positioning themselves on either side of him.

I have an unpleasant feeling in my stomach, and I start walking past them towards the stairs.

"Wally, your room is taken right now. You'll have to wait," Ms. Bertha stops me, holding my hand.

"Yes, Ms. Bertha," I answer, looking down. I don't want to watch the girls and the gentleman. Does she want me to go outside? What does she expect me to do? To be like the girls down here? I smile awkwardly and sit on the sofa in front of them, the heavy scent of his cigar fills the air. I press my legs together tightly, feeling clumsy next to them. Where do I put my hands? Should I put them on my thighs like they did before? I look up at them and try to smile, even though I want to close my eyes and take a deep breath.

The man examines me and exhales smelly smoke from his cigar. He signals to Bertha, and she approaches him. I nervously watch them as they whisper. Are they talking about me?

"Wally, wait upstairs, not here," Ms. Bertha instructs me, and I get up from the sofa and walk to the stairs. I tightly grip the metal railing until my fingers turn white. Keeping my eyes closed, I climb up to the second floor, feeling my way with my feet and taking a deep breath with each step.

Once I reach the second floor, I lean against the wall beside Christina's room. Occasionally, I hear sighs and the creaking of bed springs. I have to wait.

Two other girls pass and laugh, and I look down at my shoes. After they are gone, I go to the chair at the end of the corridor and sit on it, waiting for my room to become available. What about Erica? Is she also now in one of the rooms whose doors are closed? My fingers gently caress the smooth wooden handles of the chair. I have to find work tomorrow.

35

"We are not interested," the maids say to me one after the other in the following days, as they close heavy black doors in my face.

"Thank you," I reply and go to the next building, only to be rejected again.

Every morning I arrange my hair and dress as best as I can in Ms. Bertha's hostel, and every afternoon I return slowly, sweating from the summer sun or soaking wet from a drizzle.

I stop for a few minutes next to the Opera house, and stand near the horses tethered to the carriages, awaiting their passengers. I gently caress their necks and noses, feeling the softness of their warm fur.

"Get out of here. You're disturbing the horses," one of the coachmen yells as he menacingly raises the whip. I raise my hand to shield my face from the painful whipping, but he reclines in the coachman's chair at the front of his carriage, observing me as I slowly back away, careful not to turn my back. I have nowhere else to go but Ms. Bertha's hostel, even though my room will likely be occupied until nighttime, and there are gentlemen in the reception room at the bottom of the stairs. I walk down the wide street toward the alleys of the city center, observing the ladies in their summer dresses passing me by. What will I do without a job?

My fingers brush against the silver coins in the inner pocket of my dress. I'm hesitant to leave them in the room in the hostel room or give them to Ms. Bertha. I don't trust her.

I stop walking and look at a display window of a corset and pantyhose shop. What would it feel like to wear such a lace corset? Does Christina take it off when she's with a man in the room? I feel the fabric of the simple camisole I'm wearing and trace the hem of my dress with my finger. What would it be like to be with a man? My fingers brush against the coins in my pocket again; I have four Kronen left and they will soon run out. I take one last look at the shop window, and the white lace corsets hang side by side and resume walking down the street. I will manage. I will find a job. However, after a few steps, I abruptly turn around and enter the shop; I have never stepped foot in such a luxurious store before.

"How can I help you?" a lady older than me, dressed in a purple evening gown with a tightly fastened black corset around the waist, addresses me.

"I'm just browsing," I answer and blush. Satin corsets hang on the hangers around me; so exquisite and beautiful. One day I'll own one too.

"This is a luxury store. There are no cheap things here for women like you," she retorts, stepping closer.

"Thank you," I blurt, hastily opening the glass door, rushing out of the store, and starting to run.

Run, run, run. The people on the street stare as I run past, but I can't bring myself to stop. My legs lead the way and my body aches from the exertion. What will I do in a few days?

Only when I reach the knife seller's wooden cart do I finally stop running. I stand there for a few minutes, panting, trying to catch my breath. I need to see my family, to ensure they're alright. I'll explain that I never intended to disappear like Dad did.

I walk down the shaded gray alley and keep my distance from the entrance to the building. I hear children's voices from the stairwell, but I'm afraid to approach. What if Mrs. Steiner complained to the landlord and they got evicted because of me? What if these are children of another family who moved in? I think I recognize the voices of Antonia and Hilda, but I'm not entirely sure. I wipe the sweat from my forehead. I have to go inside.

"Wally," Antonia runs out of the stairwell and hugs me.

"You're back," Hilda follows her, wrapping her hands around my waist so tightly, nearly knocking me over.

"Yes, I am," I hug them back and apprehensively look up at the building. Where is Mom?

"And you won't leave us again?" Antonia wipes her tears as she clings on to me.

"How's Marie?" I stroke her hair and change the subject.

"We take care of her," Hilda proudly replies. "We even feed her porridge when Mom is not around."

"And where is Mom?" I ask them. "Is she at work?"

"Wait, I'll call her," Hilda says, disappearing into the stairwell.

"Hilda, no," I call after her, but Antonia hugs me and prevents me from running after her. "Hilda, come back." I call out again.

"Are you back for good?" Antonia looks up at me with tear-filled eyes.

"Antonia, listen to me," I bend down and reach into my secret dress pocket, taking out two coins, and placing them in her hand, closing her fingers tightly around them. "This is for you and Hilda in case you ever need it," I say nervously, glancing at the building's entrance. "I promise I'll be back."

"Are you leaving?" she starts crying.

"Keep these coins safe, don't lose them," I hug her, tears streaming down my face.

"Get out of here," I hear shouts, and Mom emerges from the building, holding little Marie with one hand and tearful Hilda in the other. "Why did you come back? For them?" She yells at me, releasing Hilda's hand. "Did you come back to take them with you? I heard you've been looking for places in girls' hostels. Is that what you want? To turn them into prostitutes like you? Take them!" She pushes Hilda in my direction, and the little girl stumbles and falls on the cobblestones, bursting into tears.

"That's enough, Mom," I yell at her. As I help Hilda up to her feet, the tears pour down my cheeks.

"Go away! You're a whore, don't corrupt your young sisters!" She screams at me. "Would you like to hear what I had to do so Mr. Walner wouldn't fire me?" She approaches and tries to hit me with her free hand. I break free from Antonia's embrace and run away, ignoring the stares of the people in the alley who have stopped to watch us.

Run, run, run, don't think, I'll manage. I'll find a place to stay. I'll come back for Hilda, Antonia, and Marie, keep running, don't stop.

"Good evening, Wally," Ms. Bertha says when I enter the hostel, breathing heavily and covered in sweat. However, I don't respond.

"Miss Walburga, where are your manners?" She steps out from behind the reception desk.

"Good evening Ms. Bertha," I reply and walk past her while she watches me. The girls sitting in the entrance room also gaze at me, whispering amongst themselves. I wish I could join them, I don't want to be alone. But Ms. Bertha will probably ask me to go upstairs. Men will likely arrive soon. I climb up the stairs to the second-floor bathroom to wash my face and then wait on the chair in the corridor. Maybe Mom was right, and I should work for her.

"Christina," I whisper later that night. The room is dark, and we both lie in bed, her legs next to my head and my head next to her legs. I have to ask someone. "Christina," I whisper to her again, feeling the woolen blanket against my nightgown.

"What?" she whispers back to me.

"Have you been at Ms. Bertha's hostel for a long time?"

"Much too long," she answers, and I fall silent.

"Christina?" I whisper to her again.

"What, Wally?"

"And how did you get here?"

"Does it matter?"

"What is it like to do it?" I finally ask, looking at the crack of light seeping in from under the door. Will she give me an answer?

"Do what?" she asks after a while.

"What you do here with the men," I blush in the dark.

"You won't understand. You're too young for that," she replies.

"I'm not young. I'm sixteen," I say. I want to know. Mom never talked to me about it. She'd yell at me that I had to keep my legs shut and be obedient. After Mr. Wallner tried to touch me there, she shouted at me. She said that I tried to seduce him with my smiles and I would end up being a prostitute. It didn't help that I denied it. She didn't believe me.

"You just do it," Christina replies after a while.

"And is it pleasant?"

"It's not about it pleasant or unpleasant," she whispers.

"So what is it about?" I press my legs together and then slightly open them. Does it feel different down there? Do the men touch her there? Lena, one of the workers at Mr. Wallner's store, blushingly whispered to me that it's different for men and women.

"You're kicking me," Christina says. "Move aside," she gets up, and I hear the bed springs creak as she rolls over and gets back into bed, her face next to mine. I can hear her breathing so close to me.

"So what's it like when they come to visit you?" I whisper to her once more.

"I try to get them to be nice to me," she responds quietly, "and to be polite." I can feel the warmth of her body through her nightgown.

"Do you have many gentlemen friends?" I ask. Does she have more than one?

"Yes," she laughs bitterly, "I have many gentlemen 'friends'. You're such a child. You understand nothing."

"I'm not a child," I assert. "I'm here by myself at Ms. Bertha's place, and I can handle myself." I don't mention that I haven't found a job yet and that my money will soon run out.

"I thought I could handle myself too."

"And what happened?" I ask, hearing her breathing quietly.

"I ended up staying here, at Bertha's, asking her to take care of me."

41

"And does she?"

"I wanted to be a countess, but I chose to be one of Bertha's girls," she responds, avoiding my question and trying to tickle me playfully.

"I wonder what it's like to be a countess with servants." I smile in the dark. Countesses probably wear beautiful dresses all day, and never go hungry.

"You're still young. You should get away from here before she offers you to work for her."

"I will run away, I promise," I say, looking at the dark ceiling and gently caressing my stomach. I skipped dinner today. How can Christina do that with them? I tightly press my legs together, feeling her feet touching mine. "Did you try to run away?" I ask her.

"It doesn't matter. You shouldn't be here. Just find a place to go."

"Does it hurt?" I ask her, gently caressing the wool blanket and shivering. I have so many questions.

"It doesn't hurt if they're kind. Good night, go to sleep already," she replies, turns around, and falls asleep.

"Good night Christina," I say, thinking of Ms. Bertha, who agreed to accept me in her hostel, waiting for me to fail and become one of her girls. I'm afraid of this place, but what can I do? I'm hungry.

"Ms. Bertha," I go down the stairs early the following day and approach her counter. However, the counter is empty.

"Yes, Wally, what do you need?" she emerges from the back room after a moment, holding a book.

"Ms. Bertha, I want to work for you," my stomach is aching.

"That's it? You've finally decided to listen to Ms. Bertha? How long have you been looking for a job?" her eyes scan my torn camisole. I didn't have time to mend it.

"Two weeks," I reply, looking down. I need her help. I'm hungry, and I have no other options. I didn't eat yesterday.

"You were certainly more determined than my other girls, but it's no surprise that you didn't find a job. Who would want to hire a girl with red hair like yours? It doesn't inspire confidence," she remarks, closing the book she's holding. "I told you that all girls end up working for Bertha," she adds, taking a cigarette from a box placed on the counter and holding it in her hand. "What kind of job do you want?"

"Whatever you can offer," I reply, running my fingers through my red hair, attempting to fix it as best as possible. Perhaps Christina will lend me one of her corsets, so I can be more like her.

"I have enough girls right now. They'll resent me if I add another one," she explains, lighting her cigarette. "Besides, I don't think you get along with them anyway."

"I'll manage on my own," I say with determination, turning away and heading towards the stairs. I don't want Ms. Bertha to see me crying. Quietly, I enter Christina's room, closing the door behind me. I sit on the bed in the dark. Christina is still asleep. Soon, I'll get dressed and go out to look for work in the market. Maybe someone there will give me something to eat.

"Wally," I hear Bertha's voice a moment later, and a knock on the door. Does she still want to hire me? I freeze in place, unsure if I should open the door.

"Come on, Walburga, I'm not going to wait here all day," she impatiently knocks again.

"Answer her already. She wants to talk to you," Christina urges me.

"What Ms. Bertha?" I crack the door open and hide behind it.

"Do you really want a job?" she scrutinizes me.

"Yes, Ms. Bertha," I answer, feeling the coldness of the metal door handle.

"I knew you would say 'yes,' you're a smart girl," she remarks, glancing down at my fingers holding the door slightly ajar.

"Show me your hands," she instructs, and I extend my hands through the opening, spreading my fingers. Does she want to check if they're clean?

"Excellent, now clean your clothes properly," she continues, pointing with her foot to a stainless steel bucket and a gray bar of soap placed at her feet, "and clean yourself too." With that, she turns and goes down the stairs as my gaze follows her.

"What did she want?" Christina sleepily asks.

"She told me to go wash my clothes and clean up. She wants me to work for her," I reply.

"Welcome to the palace," Christina says when I sit on the creaking iron bed. I want to lie next to her and hear comforting words, but I'm too embarrassed to admit my fear. I continue to comb my red hair with my fingers in slow motion while I watch the silhouette of the wooden cabinet, which appears almost black in the weak morning light. I know I have to go. She's waiting for me with work. In the dim light, I retrieve my dress from the closet, grab the stainless-steel bucket and soap placed in the hallway, and head towards the bathroom at the end of the corridor. I rub my dress firmly in the cold water until my fingers turn red.

"Is this your best dress?" she says when she sees me coming down the stairs.

"Yes, Ms. Bertha," I reply and look at the floral leather couch in the reception room. In the morning light, I notice stains on it.

"Remember, they are wealthy men. You have to be nice and politely answer whatever they ask you," she steps out from behind her wooden counter, scrutinizing me with her gray-blue eyes.

"Yes, Ms. Bertha," I nod and look down, my body still shivering from the cold. Who are these wealthy men?

"And you have to do what you're told, no questions asked." What if they try to do something to me? How will I keep quiet?

"Yes, Ms. Bertha," I reply, gazing at her silver hair. My dress is still damp as I barely had time to dry it over the iron stove at the end of the corridor. All the girls in the hostel use it to dry their underwear.

"Be sure to lower your gaze. They expect you not to look at them at all. Stop touching your dress. It's not dough," she reprimands, swiping my hand away from the fabric. "Stand with your back straight, hands behind your back, and your eyes down. You have to make yourself invisible. I don't know how you're going to do that with that terrible red hair of yours."

"Yes, Ms. Bertha," I quickly fold my hands behind my back and stand still. I am determined to do whatever it takes to make them like me. Who are these people she's referring to? Are they gentlemen?

"And if they ask you a question, you give them the answer they want to hear," she continues to examine me, walking around me slowly.

"Yes, Ms. Bertha." I hear her footsteps behind me. She must be examining my clasped hands and my nails. I made sure to clean them.

"I hope they don't mind that you're red-haired. Where did you get that ugly hair color?"

"From my father," I keep looking at the floral sofa and resist the urge to play with the ends of my hair. I hate my hair color. I hate being so different.

"I hope they'll accept you," she says. What does she have planned for me? I start walking back towards the stairs.

"Walburga, where are you going?" she scolds me, and I stand there, looking away to hide my tears.

"Walburga, look at me," she returns behind her counter, bends down, and pulls something out. The smell of cigarette smoke fills the air as she rises with a cigarette between her lips. She approaches me again. "Walburga, stand up straight."

Her fingers hold my hair tightly as she braids it, pinning it to my head. I sigh as the pins scratch my scalp, "It's best to cut this carrot hair," she says, "but we'll have to settle for this. Maybe they'll agree to accept you like this."

She takes two steps back and examines me again from my redhead hair to my old black shoes. She reaches out her hand and adjusts the collar of my dress. "You're ready."

"Thank you, Mr. Bertha," I whisper, feeling as sense of unease crawling up my thighs. What will they do to me down there?

"Walburga, did you say you could read and write?" her fingers quickly run down the sleeve of my dress, and she removes an unruly strand of hair.

"Yes, Ms. Bertha," I reply quickly, tempted to tell her about my father, who was a teacher and taught us to read and write by the stove in the kitchen before we arrived in Vienna, back when I still had a father. But I sense that she isn't interested in my personal history.

"Listen to Ms. Bertha. You don't show it. Men don't like women who can read books. They're afraid of them," she warns, going behind the counter to write something on a piece of white paper. She then tucks it into an envelope and hands it to me, along with another note containing an address.. "Go to this address and give them the note I wrote for you. It's in the palace area, past the ring boulevard."

"Yes, Ms. Bertha, I will not show them that I can read."

"Pay attention," she looks me in the eye. "If the maid at the door asks you who the letter is from, you say you don't know. You are only the messenger."

"Yes, Ms. Bertha," I look at the closed envelope with a man's name written on it. I breathe slowly. I'm afraid of going.

"Walburga, what are you waiting for? Go already," she takes the cigarette out of her mouth, turns, and returns behind her counter. I rush out of the hostel, gently closing the heavy wood door behind me while holding the envelope tightly. I will do whatever this gentleman asks me and I won't scream.

I stand in front of the brown wooden door on Elisabeth-straße. The building's pristine walls are painted grayish-white. I look at the delicate flower ornaments above the large white windows. I tightly hold on to the envelope that Ms. Bertha gave me. I'll do it. I'll think of something else when he does that to me.

I approach the large wooden door, ready to knock on it.

"The door for the servants is in the back," someone says. I turn and see a driver in a dark green uniform standing next to a shiny black automobile. He has a visor hat on his head, and he looks at me angrily.

"Excuse me," I say and hurry to the servant's door at the back of the building. I ring the bell and wait patiently. I need to run away, but I'm afraid of Ms. Bertha and desperately hungry.

"Good morning. What do you want?" a woman in a black dress opens the door and looks at me. She wears glasses with a thin frame and her hair is tied up in a bun.

"Good morning, my name is Walburga," I can't find the words to continue.

"We don't need any workers, and we don't have food for the poor," she starts to close the door in my face.

"I have this," I hand her the closed envelope.

"From whom is this letter?" she asks, turning the envelope upside down.

"I don't know, ma'am," I blush. "I'm just the messenger."

"I'll ask the master. Wait here," she gives me one more look and slams the door in my face.

I stay there as I wait for her to return and try to catch my breath. What could Ms. Bertha have written in that note? I nervously fumble around with my own fingers until they are hurt. Will she come back?

"The master told me to let you in," she opens the door and looks at me. "Do you have lice?"

"No, ma'am."

"Follow me," she lets me in, and I follow her into a large room filled with covered in boxes of vegetables and fruits, jars of food, and sausages hanging on hooks from the walls. She keeps walking, and we pass a kitchen larger than the entrance to Bertha's hostel. Two women in aprons are working there. Further on, there's another spacious room that looks like a waiting room. At its center stands a simple dining table surrounded by cupboards.

"Put this on," she goes to one of the cupboards and hangs me a simple, clean, black dress.

"Should I go up to him? To the master?" I hold onto the dress she gave me. I will do whatever he tells me to do. I will.

"By no means," she replies. She takes out a stainless steel bucket and mop from one of the cupboards. "You must not address the master or the lady unless they address you. I'm the only one who will instruct you where to clean and give you tasks. Lunch for the servants is at twelve o'clock sharp. Now, follow me."

"Yes, ma'am," I take a deep breath, grab the bucket and mop, and follow her. I'll work hard; nothing will prevent me from doing my very best.

Chapter Three

The Lacquered White Door with Golden Decorations

"Wally, after you finish cleaning here, please move on to dusting the Chinese porcelain jugs," the housekeeper says, and I nod, continuing to go over the bookshelves with a thin cloth. I have been working here for two weeks as a maid in the big mansion.

Gently, my hand wipes the dust off the family photos in the silver frames placed on the mahogany cabinet. One by one, I pick up the photos and examine them from all sides, ensuring they are shiny and spotlessly clean. The housekeeper is very strict about cleanliness. I pause for a moment, gazing at a yellowish photo of the entire family. The father is dressed in a suit, his dark mustache protruding, while his wife sits upright at his feet, wearing a cream evening dress. Their two children are dressed in private school suits and stand by her side. I have never seen their children, not even the master of the house. Only the lady, whom I once noticed passing me one morning, holding a folded lace parasol. One day, I too will have a parasol like that. I smile at the lady in the picture. My friends, the ladies, and I will sit in a café and savor Sacher Torte.

"Wally, are you done here?" the housekeeper asks me, and I hurry to put the picture back in its place. Has she been watching me for a long time? Did she notice that I was admiring the picture instead of working?

"Yes, ma'am," I turn towards her and straighten up. She always wears a modest black dress. I make sure to look down, fixing my eyes on her polished black shoes.

She stands next to the cabinet I had just finished cleaning and runs her finger over the frames and the shiny brown mahogany wood, checking whether I had cleaned them to her satisfaction. She has been inspecting my work like that for the past two weeks.

"Follow me," she finally says, turns her back, and walks upright. I grab the bucket and quickly follow her.

She climbs up the grand staircase from the main entrance to the second floor, crosses the corridor, and approaches the lady's room. I haven't been there since the first day when she had showed me the house. Without knocking or waiting for permission, she opens the lacquered white door with golden decorations. I follow her inside, and she closes the door behind us with a gentle click. "Clean the floor. Make it shine."

"Yes, ma'am," I respond and get down on my knees, starting to rub the light, smooth wooden floor with a rag. I hear her footsteps moving away behind me, and the door clicks shut.

I raise my eyes and look at the large room. Two expansive windows allow the morning sun to penetrate through embroidered floral sheer curtains. Besides the windows, there's a spacious dresser, two brown leather armchairs, and a wooden chair with a small coffee table. But there is no bed here. The lady probably sleeps in another room.

I resume looking at my red fingers, clasping onto the damp rag, panting with effort of scrubbing the floor in the quiet room. After a while, I hear the door open, and the sound of laughter fills the air. It's the lady's voice, and she seems to be talking to someone. I quickly focus my gaze on the parquet floor and continue moving on my knees toward the corner of the room. Does she know I'm here? Should I get up and leave the room? What should I do? I look down, watching my red fingers tightly gripping the rag.

"Is this room good enough for you?" she asks.

"This room is perfect. I like the morning light in here," the man answers her. Have they noticed I'm here?

"And where will I sit?" the lady asks him.

"Here, I want you to sit here," the stranger replies. I hear his footsteps and the sound of a chair being dragged in the room. My eyes remain fixed on the floor.

"I demand nothing less than perfection."

"I'm certain of that. You, my lady, are simply flawless," he replies, and she chuckles. I'm not allowed to eavesdrop on their discussion. I keep my gaze on my fingers, tightly clutching the rag against the parquet floor.

I hear his footsteps move away and leave the room, but after a while, he returns, carrying something and placing it on the floor. Glancing up briefly, I see a large easel and a stretched canvas being positioned in the center of the room, in front of the chair. He's standing with his back to me. The man is big, dressed in a brown suit, and has short, curly hair that used to be red, now turned brown. He appears to be about the same age as my father was. I must not look at him; if the lady complains, they might fire me. I continue to examine his short, untidy brown beard, that has yet to turn gray. What color are his eyes? The lady stands before him, wearing a light green taffeta dress adorned with delicate flower designs, her hands on her hips. I have to look down and continue working; I'm just a maid. However, I can't help myself and keep stealing glances at them, silently observing the fabric of her dress and the suit he's wearing.

"Will this dress fit?" she asks as she twirls around, the dress fluttering like leaves dancing in a summer breeze. She looks so beautiful and regal. I sneak another glance at her. Her dress has a low neckline, and her bosom appears to nearly burst out of her bustier. I'm unable to avert my gaze. When she gazes at the painter again, it seems like she notices me for a split second, but she doesn't say anything and returns her attention to him, smiling. I blush and lower my eyes gaze once more. I wasn't meant to look at her.

"This dress is perfect for the painting."

"So now it's your turn to get dressed," she replies and giggles.

I can't resist looking up for a moment and see him walking behind a decorated wooden screen that stands at the side of the room. He is not the man in the photo I had seen earlier.

Should I get up and leave? I wasn't told anything. I clutch the rag firmly in my hands.

"Please don't peek," he tells her, laughing. A moment later, when I look up, I see him standing beside the easel, no longer wearing a suit but instead donning a blue painter's smock, which is smudged with paint stains. He bends down to a large leather bag at the foot of the easel, pulling out brushes and paint tubes from it. I notice his gaze fixed on the lady as she approaches him in small steps, her dress almost brushing against the brushes he holds. He has blue eyes.

"Maybe the master can draw my portrait from this angle," she whispers as she bends down.

"Perhaps the master of the house won't like this angle for the painting, and you won't be able to hang the picture in your living room," he responds, and she laughs again. I scrub the parquet floor vigorously, ensuring the wood is shiny and clean.

"Maybe I should show you a different angle. Wait," she says to him, and I hear her footsteps on the parquet floor. When I peek for a moment, I see only him and her hands behind the wood curtain at the end of the room, next to the dressing table. "You are the painter. I would like to hear your opinion before we start."

"The clothes you choose should complement your fair skin tone," he answers her.

"Don't worry, it'll fit," she laughs. "Can you ask the maid to leave and go clean the smoking room?"

He turns and gazes at me as if he has just noticed me for the first time. I'm on all fours on the floor, and raise my head in his direction. His blue eyes stare at me, as if I were a stray cat seeking a gentle pet, and he offers me a small smile. He appears so imposing, and I feel so small as I kneel on the floor. However, I don't wait for him to instruct me to leave. I promptly get up, collect the rag and the stainless steel bucket, and walk slowly out of the room, keeping my eyes lowered as I exit. Gently, I close the white door behind me, the one adorned with golden decorations.

"Christina," I whisper to her late at night. We're pressed against each other in the iron bed. "Christina."

"What, Rusty?" she whispers back.

"Have you ever been to an art exhibition?" I ask her. Since this morning, I can't stop thinking about the artist wearing a blue painter's smock.

"Art exhibitions aren't for us, lower-class women," she says.

"I saw a painter today," I caress the wool blanket.

"Where?" she sits up, turns around in the bed, lies down next to me, and covers us again with the wool blanket.

"In the house where I work. When I was cleaning the lady's room, she had a painter over to paint her. She laughed and went to change clothes for him," I recall the lady standing behind the decorated wood screen.

"Believe me, he didn't just want to paint her," Christina laughs.

"How do you know?" I ask her. Did they do it too? I press my legs together tightly, feeling uneasy.

"Because they come here too, not only to fancy ladies' houses. What do you think? That they don't visit Bertha's hostel?"

"What do they do here?"

"What all men do when they come here, they're no different from the others."

"And they paint the girls?"

"No, Rusty, they play with us and then throw us away. They only paint the respectable ladies."

I want to ask her what she means by 'playing with us,' but I am ashamed and remain silent, listening to her breathing in the dark. "He also went to change his clothes. He changed into a smock," I say after a while, picturing him walking around the room like a big bear wearing the blue smock.

"He must have wanted to be prepared for what he was going to do with her after he finished painting her," she laughed.

"And that's what all men want?"

"They don't come here just to look at us and smoke cigars. Trust me; they want us for only one purpose."

"At least Ms. Bertha looks out for us," I say after a while.

"Ms. Bertha doesn't look out for anyone. Ms. Bertha looks out only for herself. She likes these painters, invites them here to choose girls for themselves," she whispers. "They pay her for that. Ms. Bertha is probably taking money your work in the house of the rich woman who undresses in front of painters," Christina continues to whisper while I gaze into the darkness and listen to her breathing. "If Bertha doesn't get money, she doesn't lift a finger. It's time for you to grow up and become a woman. Stop being so naïve," she concludes, turning away from me.

"Good night, Christina," I say to the darkness, but she doesn't respond. I stay awake and stare at the dark ceiling. I won't be like Christina. One day, I'll find someone who loves me and will take me out of here, just like the lady with the painter.

⁂

"Wally, go clean the lady's room," the housekeeper instructs me a few days later. I nod and make my way to the lady's room. I gently knock on the closed white door, waiting for her permission before entering. I'm not allowed to enter otherwise.

"Come in," I hear a voice from inside.

I step into the room and gently close the door behind me. The lady is sitting with her back to me, facing the dresser at the other end of the room. She gazes at her reflection in the mirror while combing her black hair. Her modern cream-colored morning dress reminds me of the attire worn by women who stroll on the boulevard, holding parasols in their gloved hands to shield themselves from the summer sun. I lower my head, turning towards the cabinet by the window, and carefully place the stainless-steel bucket on the parquet floor. I should start with cleaning the big window. With a wet rag in hang, I press the rag against the cool glass, but I can't resist stealing occasional glances at the lady sitting in the room.

The painting I had seen a few days ago seems to have vanished, leaving only the decorated wood screen standing in the corner of the room. The lady continues to apply her makeup in front of the mirror, seemingly oblivious to my presence. On the wall behind the wood screen hangs a large painting of a field of flowers framed in gold, which stands out against the yellowish wall. I remind myself to focus on cleaning the window and resist the urge to sneak glances at the painting. It's adorned with spots of red, yellow, and green. I hope the lady doesn't turn around and catch me stealing glances at her from time to time. Tearing a piece of old newspaper given to me by the housekeeper, I slowly wipe the window glass with it. The housekeeper mentioned that the lead in the newspaper's print makes the glass shine. As I glance outside the window, I see women strolling down the boulevard, holding white lace parasols. In their cream-colored dresses, they resemble white summer butterflies floating among the gentlemen wearing brown suits and top hats.

"Go down to the driver and tell him to be ready. I'll be leaving in a few minutes. Tell him I need him to take me to the suburbs, to the painter's house," the lady instructs me. I quickly put down the torn newspaper.

"Yes, my lady," I hastily leave the room, heading down the side stairs to the first floor.

"He's not here. Look for him outside, near the entrance," the cook tells me, and I rush out, exiting through the side entrance to the sunny street, and circle the building.

The driver stands by the family car with his back to me, dressed in his green uniform while holding a brown leather cloth, and cleaning the car's shiny brass front fenders.

"Excuse me, sir. The lady wanted me to tell you that she is going to the painter's house in the suburbs in a few minutes," I inform him, trying to catch my breath.

"Thank you. You can return to your duties," he replies, opening the car door and removing the tarp that covers the leather seats. I take another step closer and look at the automobile. It looks like a black metal box mounted on white rubber wheels. In front of the driver's seat, there is a round steering wheel, a handle, a strange clock, and a few more buttons. I take another step closer and touch the small handle of the chrome car door, feeling its coolness.

"Don't touch anything," he scolds me and approaches the door, turns his back to me, and slowly wipes off my fingerprints with his brown cloth.

"Yes sir," I reply, turning around and hastening back to the side door, Before I do, I run my finger along the side of the car, feeling the smoothness of the shiny black painted metal. What must it be like to drive such an automobile? I can hear the sound of my footsteps on the cobblestones of the quiet street as I circle the building, heading for the side door. I hardly got to ride a horse-drawn carriage.

As I walk along the corridor on the second floor, I spot the lady coming towards me, dressed in her summer attire and wearing a wide hat adorned with flowers. I quickly move close to the wall and glance down respectfully, unable to resist stealing a fleeting look. Her beautiful black hair is pulled back and her lips are painted. Near the main staircase, she pauses to chat with the housekeeper, her gloved hand resting gracefully on the curved wooden banister.

"Wally, what are you looking at?" the housekeeper scolds me after the lady descends the stairs. She noticed me staring.

"I apologize, ma'am," I answer awkwardly and rush back to the lady's room, eager to complete my cleaning tasks. This time, there's no need to knock on the door for permission to enter.

I press my face against the clean glass and observe the driver hurrying to open the car door for the lady. She nods in greeting as she sits down, while he closes the door and takes his place behind the wheel. Is he taking her to the same painter who visited here a few days ago?

The car starts and drives down the boulevard, disappearing between the horses pulling carriages and the slowly moving tram cars in the center of the road. I turn my attention back to the room. What should I clean now?

There's a lavender dress hanging on the pink chair next to the dresser. I pick it up, gently running my fingers over the fabric. Back in Mr. Walner's store, we used to sell such fabrics to the wealthiest women. He's personally attend to them, allowing us to serve only the simpler clients. How would it feel to wear such a dress? I slide the cloth over my cheek, relishing its softness. In a dance-like move, I walk to the center of the room, holding the dress, pressing it to my body, and standing in front of the large mirror. "One day, I too will have a dress like this," I whisper to my reflection. "One day, a famous painter will come to my house and paint me." I try to arrange to straighten my red hair with my fingers; I must look perfect for the painting.

There's a hairbrush on the makeup vanity, but I dare not touch it. My hands are holding the jar of reddish blush powder.

Beside it, there's a bowl with real lipstick and an application brush lying temptingly. What would happen if I were to apply some on my lips? I look back again at the closed door. The housekeeper would surely fire me if she finds out.

At the end of the workday, I make my way back to the hostel. On my route, I can't resist stopping by the window of the corset shop I had entered before. With a cautious glance around to ensure no one is watching, I bend down, scratch the lipstick from the inside of my shoe with my finger, and gently apply it to my lips as I lean closer to the glass. The taste of the lipstick is unusual, but it's not as bitter as the blood I had once used on my lips when I first arrived at the pension. I smile at my reflection in the window and continue walking down the darkening street.

"Good evening, Ms. Bertha," I say quietly and look down. I hurry past the stuffy reception desk and find that the waiting hall is devoid of men, and none of the girls are sitting on the floral sofas either. The lingering smell of Bertha's cigarette smoke fills the air. I'll show my lips to Christina; perhaps she won't think I'm a little girl.

"Wally, what is that on your lips?"

"Nothing, Ms. Bertha," I say and place my hand on the stair's banister.

"Wally, come over here," she calls out to me, and I turn around, walking towards her. I should be allowed to wear lipstick; I am grown up now. "Did you put on some lipstick?" she examines me while holding a cigarette between her fingers.

"Yes, Ms. Bertha," I reply, watching her closely. She is not my mother.

"Come closer," she instructs, leaving her counter, and placing the cigarette in the ashtray.

"Yes, Ms. Bertha," I stand still before her. She is slightly taller than I.

"Wally, you are not allowed to wear lipstick," she says firmly, reaching out and holding my chin, grabbing it tightly.

"But...Ms. Bertha," I try to reason with her, feeling the discomfort of her fingers on my chin.

"Take off the lipstick," she says, releasing her grip, but still scrutinizing me.

"You let the other girls wear lipstick," I say quietly, lowering my eyes.

Ms. Bertha returns behind the counter, takes a drag from her cigarette, and looks at me for a long moment, observing my lips and simple dress.

"Listen carefully, Wally. You're still too young, and I'm the one who decides and makes the rules here. Anyone who doesn't like it is welcome to live on the streets, running away from policemen who search for homeless people like you at night," she says, blowing cigarette smoke into the hallway.

"Yes, Ms. Bertha," I reply, turning and ascending the stairs. I will prove to her that I am mature enough to wear lipstick.

⚬⚭⚬

"I keep seeing you sitting on that chair in the corridor," one of the girls in the hostel taunts me. "What happened? Did

Christina replace you with a man?" she walks past me, and I remain seated in my chair, waiting for Christina to finish with the man in our room. I don't want to go out for a walk on the street. It rained earlier, and the entrance hall is filled with men and girls, enveloped in cigar smoke. "Sit close to the door and listen. You might learn something," the girl turns back and says before heading towards the stairs. I follow her with my gaze, expressing my annoyance by sticking my tongue out at her back. Her semi-transparent dress flutters around her, resembling the foam of a waterfall. Among the girls in the hostel, only Erica and Christina are kind to me. Christina might have no choice, and Erica occasionally talks to me when I sit by myself in my chair.

Do the gentlemen respect the girls when they come to visit? My fingers caress the handle of the chair. One day, when I'll be all grown up and famous, I'll have a man who respects me when he visits my room. But it won't be here, in this hostel. I'll have a large room, just like the lady's, with large windows and a beautifully decorated wooden screen.

I bring the chair closer to our room and sit on it once more. Through the thin wooden door, I hear the creaking of the bed springs and occasional sighs. My fingers absentmindedly trace the stitches of my simple dress down to my legs. Blushing, I feel the fabric gently caressing my thighs. Suddenly, a door opens in the corridor, and a man emerges, buttoning up his shirt. As he walks past, he examines me. I hasten to place my hand in my lap and lower my gaze, waiting for him to disappear down the stairs. But to my dismay, the door opens again after a moment, and Erica steps out. "Move a little. Give me some room," she says, and I scooch in the wooden chair, allow her to sit next to me. She has thin legs, not like mine. I feel clumsy compared to her.

"Ms. Bertha sent you to stay here again?" she smiles at me as she adjusts the black garter over her leg. I watch as she rolls up her lace dress and pulls the garter belt down over her thighs, asking for my help to attach it properly. "Copper, can you help me attach it? It keeps coming loose."

"Did he treat you with respect?" I inquire as I kneel at her feet, gently holding the smooth garter stretched over her thighs, attempting to attach it to the metal clip on the garter belt.

"I make sure he's comfortable," Erica smiles, "and if he's comfortable, I get what I want."

"And what do you want?" I sit back beside her, moving closer.

"It doesn't matter. I can get anything I want from them," she laughs, "and they still pay me for it. They believe they are in control, but they don't realize that I'm the one who holds the power."

"Ms. Bertha thinks I'm still too young," I confess, glancing down at her exposed thighs, partially covered by the black garters.

"Copper, of course you're still young, but soon you won't be, and Ms. Bertha won't decide for you," Erica reassures me, getting up from her chair. "Let's go for a walk in the city. Give me a few minutes to get ready, we can slip past Ms. Bertha." She disappears into her room, returning shortly after, "let's go," she pulls my hand as I get up. We both make our way down the stairs. I choose not to mention the rain from earlier. This place suffocates me, and I'm eager to be away from it.

"Erica, where are you going?" Ms. Bertha stands up from the sofa at the entrance and approaches us. "Erica, this gentleman might want to see you," she turns to look at a thin man dressed in a blue suit and a beret, sitting and waiting patiently on the sofa.

"Ms. Bertha, Wally is not feeling well. I have to take her to buy medicine," she answers.

Ms. Bertha suspiciously examines us, but says nothing and sits back in front of the thin gentleman.

"See?" Erica laughs as we walk through the rain-soaked alleys, "We can get everything we want. We just need to know how," she suddenly starts running between the raindrops, and I follow her, trying to stay dry. After a while, we find shelter in one of the alleys, waiting for the rain to stop.

The small square is covered in puddles, and only a few vendors remain. They finish loading their wooden crates onto carts, occasionally tending to their horses, draped in coarse blankets to shield them from the cold. The patient animals stand with their noses buried in sacks of millet, waiting for the day's work to conclude.

"Wally, don't wander off," Erica calls out to me as I approach one of the horses. I halt my attempt to caress its nose and instead resume walking, following her towards the Hofburg Palace. As we draw nearer, we pause by the fence at a safe distance from the imposing gate and the vigilant soldiers standing guard. We both grip the iron fence, holding onto the black metal bars while we gaze at the opulent carriages and modern automobiles parked outside. The vehicles look foreign to me, their absence of horses and constant noisy engines making them appear strange. I find comfort in the familiar sound of horses' hooves echoing on the cobblestones.

"One of the gentlemen I know has an automobile like these," Erica remarks. "He told me that one day, he would take me for a ride."

"One day, we will be countesses at a grand ball," I declare, freeing my hands from the iron fence and moving away from the palace. One day, someone will promise to take me for a ride in an automobile.

"A handsome prince will invite us to dance," Erica answers me.

"Let's go," I say, breaking away from the fence and heading back down the dimming street.

"Where are you going?" Erica asks and starts to catch up to me.

"To pick out dresses for us," I chuckle and take her hand, "how can we attend a ball without a proper dress?"

Not far from the palace, we stop in front of an upscale fabric store. Step by step, I approach the window, pressing my face against the cool glass, creating a small oasis of light and color in the gathering dusk. Inside, an array of fabric rolls in various hues beckons to us. The materials resemble a vibrant spring meadow, with shades of light green, turquoise, and gold woven together like flowers. Gripping the hem of my gray dress, I pull at the coarse fabric, imagining myself as a dignified lady, ready to be swept into a dance by a prince.

"I'll choose a light green dress," I whisper to Erica.

"I will choose a dress in shades of gold," she presses her face to the window next to mine, and I hear her breathing.

"It'll have a plunging neckline, accentuating my figure," I share in hushed tones, "just like a lady."

"Mine will have a white lace collar, concealing my breast from anyone but the duke, late at night, in our boudoir," Erica declares.

"I'll dance all night," I declare, twirling around with my arms outstretched.

"More tea? Mrs. Wally?" Erica approaches me mimicking the action of pouring tea with her raised hand. "Two cubes of sugar, or perhaps just one?"

"What do you think about this delightful painting, Miss Erica?" I gesture toward a charming café nearby.

"In a moment, Miss Wally, I'm currently entertaining a few ladies with sacher torte," Erica declares.

"I'll dance all night with a true gentleman," I proclaim, extending my hand to an imaginary partner and letting my feet carry me in rhythmic dance steps. In the fading light of the setting sun, I watch the ethereal pink fabric displayed in a nearby window, adorned with delicate rose motifs. My movements become bigger, and I spin faster, attempting to make my dress flutter like petals in the wind.

"Wally, careful you'll fall," Erica calls me, but I don't stop. My feet quickly move on the wet cobblestones another spin, careful not to lose my balance. And yet another spin, my gaze fixed on the twinkling lights of the nearest café, resembling a brilliant chandelier adorned with stars. Another spin, and I feel my breath quicken.

"Miss, are you alright?" I hear a man's voice and open my eyes, momentarily dizzy. My hands search for something to hold on to, and I find myself gripping onto a walking stick held by the man who addressed me. "Miss, are you alright?" he asks me again, and I look up at him, panting.

He is a respectable, elderly gentleman, dressed in a three-piece suit and holding a cigar.

"I apologize, sir, everything is fine," I release my grip on his walking stick and examine his white beard and round glasses, feeling myself blushing.

"She was just dancing in the street," Erica tells him, moving closer to me and taking my arm.

"Decent girls don't dance like that on the streets," he watches me for a bit longer before tipping his hat in a polite gesture. He takes a puff from the cigar in his hand, then proceeds to walk toward the café. He enters the bubbly hall, disappearing from my sight. I can hear the murmur of conversations and laughter inside.

"Let's go, Wally," Erica urges me. "By now, Ms. Bertha must be searching for us. There's likely a gentleman waiting for me back at the hostel."

"I'm coming," I say, but my gaze is still fixed on the lights of the café and the people in it. I won't be a maid my entire life. I will find a way to get out of Ms. Bertha's hostel.

Two weeks later, when I return to the hostel after work and walk through the reception area as usual, keeping my eyes downcast, I notice him.

At first, I'm unsure if it's really him. He's dressed in a dark blue suit, not the painter's smock he wore when he visited the lady's room. He's seated on the floral sofa, leaning back comfortably. His large frame seems at ease here. I pause and glance at Erica and two other girls on the opposite sofa. Erica smiles at me, her hand moving slowly as she combs another girl's hair with a copper-colored brush adorned with pink flowers.

"Walburga," I hear a whisper and turn to see Ms. Bertha standing next to the sofa with the painter. She's wearing her usual black dress and holds two teacups. "Walburga," she nods at me, gesturing that I should keep walking towards the stairs before she bends down to offer the painter one of the teacups. I watch his big fingers holding the delicate porcelain cup with great care, as if afraid to break it into pieces. Will he remember me if he notices me? I study his blue eyes and brown beard, standing there awkwardly. My gaze is fixed on his large hands as they bring the teacup to his lips, and then sips from it. Dad also had a beard.

"Wally," Ms. Bertha whispers to me again, her gesture guiding me towards the stairs. The painter places the teacup in his lap, his gaze turning towards me. Why did I let my red ugly hair down on my way from work? I keep standing there, wanting to grab the ends of my hair and put them in my mouth. My hand reaches up and grasp at a couple of strands.

"Wally," Ms. Bertha scolds me, and I lower my head, hurriedly walking towards the stairs that lead to the second floor. My cheeks flush with embarrassment. Did he recognize me? When I place my hand on the railing, I turn around and get a glimpse of him. His blue eyes stare at me, and he smiles. Ms.

Bertha is also looking at me, she's enraged. I continue up the stairs. Why does she keep treating me like a child?

Cristina is not in the room. I stand in front of the mirror and examine my red cheeks, pinching them hard to deepen the crimson shade. I yearn for him to recognize me. Is he similar to my Dad? Even the lady trusts him. I close my eyes and picture his blue eyes, the ones that were watching me just a moment ago before I was sent back to my room.

The bed's springs creak as I sit down on the iron frame. I untie my shoelaces, forcefully throw my shoes onto the wooden floor, and enjoy the sound they make upon impact. In a few moments, he'll choose another girl, not me, to take care of. I lie on the bed and stare at the ceiling. What does it feel like to have a man on top of you? I wish I could be the delicate teacup he held in his hands.

I sit up in bed and quickly unbutton my dress. I need to hurry. Then I open the closet and gaze at my solitary clothes shelf. Christina doesn't let me use more space. She says I haven't been here long enough to deserve another shelf of my own.

Gently, I caress her lace corsets hanging in the closet, feeling the soft fabric beneath my fingers. For a moment, I hesitate about what to do, but now is the time to decide. This is my chance.

I reach for a white corset, quickly putting it on and tightening the laces as best I can. My breasts aren't as beautiful as Erica's or Christina's. They're smaller, not as full. I pause for a moment. What am I doing? Christina will be furious if she finds out I took her corset. But it doesn't really matter. He'll never choose me and care for me.

I untie the corset and carefully return it to the closet, wiping my cheeks from the tears. All I have is my plain dress. I put it on and run a brush my red hair in a few swift strokes. How can I make my breasts more noticeable? I grab some socks from the closet and stuff them into my bra, trying to make them seem larger. Lipstick? Maybe there's a bit left inside my shoe from the time I took some from the lady. I attempt to scrape the remnants of lipstick from the shoe, but there's hardly any left. Despite my efforts to apply it generously and pinch my lips hard, they remain pale and bright, almost their natural color.

Will Christina notice I used her lipstick? I open her small round silver box, which sits on the makeup vanity, but I can't find the brush she uses. After a moment's thought, I gently dip my fingertip into the soft lipstick and apply it to my lips. I gaze at myself in the mirror, the red lipstick stain a bold contrast against my lips. What have I done? I feel so inadequate compared to the other girls. But does it even matter anymore?

In the corridor, before descending the stairs, I stop abruptly. I was so excited I forgot to wear shoes, and my bare feet on the wooden floor seem incredibly plain. Do I have time to turn back and retrieve them before he chooses someone and claims her for himself? Downstairs, the sounds of conversation and laughter mix with the scent of Ms. Bertha's cigarette smoke.

Step by step, I descend the stairs with my gaze fixed downward, heading toward the sofa where the girls are seated. I know that everyone is watching me, but I press on, ignoring Ms. Bertha's hushed calls of my name and avoiding her gaze. But when I reach the floral sofa, I realize there's no space for me to sit among them. I stand awkwardly, feeling my cheeks heat up once more. Erica smiles at me as I nervously tuck a strand of my hair in my mouth. What should I do? I have a strong urge to run back to my room, but my feet feel as heavy as a sack of coal in winter, and I can't move. In the end, I lower myself to the floor at the feet of the other girls, attempting to conceal my hips and legs beneath my dress, only my bare feet exposed. I lower my gaze with embarrassment. Then, I feel Erica's soothing caress against my hair. She slowly and gently starts to brush it. My gaze remains humble, focused on the painter's brown shoes. How I long for him to rescue me from this place, to escape the watchful gaze of Ms. Bertha.

"Who is she?" I hear him asking. Could he have recognized me from the lady's house? I lift my gaze slightly and observe Ms. Bertha leaning in, whispering something into his ear, though I can't hear what she says to him. After a moment, she looks at me again, and I lower my eyes, but she doesn't command me to leave. I feel the touch of the hairbrush on against my hair as Erica continues to brush it.

"She's resembles a young fawn," I hear the painter say to Ms. Bertha.

"Mr. Klimt, she's still young. She's new here," Ms. Bertha replies.

"Young fawn, could you look at me?" he shifts his gaze to me, and I slowly meet his eyes. Leaning forward on his sofa, he peers down at me, his stare resembling that of a curious bear investigating me in the grass.

I smile back at him, and become very aware of my painted lips. Why did I paint them? My finger instinctively moves to wipe the lipstick off and it brushes against my lips. Erica's gently hair brushing continues to soothe me. Once again, Ms. Bertha leans toward him, and whispers to him. I can't hear his response, but know I shouldn't be here. I should stand up, run to the second floor, and lock myself in my room.

"Very well," he turns his attention back to Ms. Bertha, conveying something to her. I wish he'd keep looking at me.

"Leisel," Ms. Bertha signals with a nod, prompting one of the girls to stand before Mr. Klimt. He rises and takes her outstretched hand. "Monica, Erica," she continues, tapping her hand, and they both rise and disappear upstairs.

My gaze follows the painter, Mr. Klimt, as he slowly climbs the stairs to the second floor, holding Liesel's hand. I remain seated on the floor, my eyes following Ms. Bertha's black boots as she approaches and stands above me. I can feel the cold floor under my bare feet.

"You can get up. Show time is over," she informs me once their footsteps have faded on the stairs.

"What do you mean, Ms. Bertha?" I keep holding the ends of my hair between my fingers.

"Wally, I have a hostel full of girls. You're not the first, nor will you be the last, trying to play games out here," she stands over me. "Go back to your room. Another gentleman is expected soon. I don't want him to find you lingering here."

"I'm sorry, I just wanted to be like all the other girls," I say. I won't tell her that I want someone to take me away from here.

"Wally, you're not a little girl anymore. It's time you stopped acting like one." She comes closer, bends, and slaps my hand holding the ends of my hair in my mouth.

"Yes, Ms. Bertha," I respond, rising to my feet, and heading toward the stairs to the second floor. I'll sit and wait on the chair in the hallway.

"Oh, and Wally," she calls out as my hand clasps the railing.

"Yes, Ms. Bertha?" I stop and look at her.

"Your little performance worked. He wanted you."

"What do you mean?" I look at her. He chose another girl. He didn't pick me. Does he want me now too? For a moment, a cold wave of fear washes over me.

"He wants you to come to his place tomorrow evening with Erica, who combed your hair so neatly."

"Thank you, Ms. Bertha," relief replaces my anxiety. I'll do whatever it takes for him to notice me. I'll find a way out of this place.

"Wally," she looks at me.

"Yes, Ms. Bertha?"

"You won't get from him what you think he'll give you," she says and turns away. She walks to the counter, takes a brown cigarette from a silver box, lights it, and blows out the smoke in a slow, deliberate manner.

Chapter Four

The First Portrait

"Do you have nothing else to wear?" Ms. Bertha walks in circles around me, scrutinizing me as she does every morning before I go to work. But it's afternoon now, and I've already returned. I stand before her with anticipation, clad in my plain dress.

"No, Ms. Bertha, this is my best dress."

"Maybe a belt could help?" Erica suggests, coming down the stairs to join me. She carries a fragrance of sweet roses. When I returned from the lady's house, she had just finished taking a bath in the stainless-steel tub in our shared bathroom. I watched her pouring hot water on herself from a bucket she had heated on the stove earlier.

"No, a belt won't be enough. She needs a new dress," Ms. Bertha answers, pulling my hair tightly into a bun. Her fingers insert hairpins into my hair, and I try to suppress wince. "And more modern shoes, too," she continues, speaking almost to herself, while cinching my dress laces so tightly that my breath momentarily falters. I look down at my old shoes. Perhaps I'll have enough time to go upstairs and apply some grease to give hint of shine.

"Eventually, she'll be one of us," Erica laughs.

"She's still too young for that," Ms. Bertha replies, her blue-gray eyes assessing me as if inspecting sheep under her care. She looks like a German Shepherd closely guarding a herd of sheep. "Erica, turn around so I can take a look at you," she finally steps back and looks at Erica.

"Am I presentable?" Erica smiles and twirls, her dress flutters like a yellow summer butterfly.

"You should leave now before I regret letting you go and gentlemen start to arrive, wanting you all for themselves, Wally. Do you have Mr. Klimt's address?" Ms. Bertha asks.

"Yes, Ms. Bertha," I confirm, reaching into my dress pocket to ensure the note bearing the address she provided is still there.

"Let's go, Copper," Erica wears a wide-brimmed hat decorated with a ribbon and takes my hand, leading me toward the front door. "Goodbye, Ms. Bertha," she smiles at her. "We won't be out too late."

The rain that had fallen earlier has stopped, and the last rays of the autumn sunlight up the quiet alley. We walk down the street hand in hand, passing an old horse slowly pulling a supply wagon. I stop for a moment next to the pawn shop, and peer through the barred window. How long has it been since the day I had given him my ring? I try to recall. That day feels like a distant memory, even though so little time has passed.

"Wally, we need to hurry," Erica pulls my hand, and we head towards the main street that leads to the palace and the Ring

Boulevard. We pass a lamplighter standing by a streetlight, holding a ladder. This part of the city still hasn't got electricity. The palace however, and the nearby streets, do have power, and the people turn on the lights simply by flipping a small switch.

A shiny black automobile drives past us, its engine purring like a fat farm pig. The driver honks twice, signaling for us to clear the road. I glance at the lady seated at the back next to a gentleman. Her neck is adorned with a diamond necklace, and she looks ahead, not acknowledging our presence. I stand in the street, watching the car drive away toward the palace.

"We would buy a necklace like hers with the money we'll get from the painter," Erica chuckles, and a cold wave washes over me, freezing my feet. What will he expect from me? What if Mom was right and I'd turn into a whore?

I release Erica's hand and watch the lamplighter as he moves to the next light, places the ladder on it, and climbs quickly. I should return to the hostel. What if Ms. Bertha is right, and I shouldn't trust him? On the side of the street sits an older woman begging for alms. Night will soon fall, and she will have to hide from the police.

"Wally, we're going to be late," Erica's voice calls from a distance, prompting me to run toward her. I reach her, panting. I won't end up like that woman. I'll be a lady, seated before a painter, not a servant scrubbing parquet floors in a luxurious house. I'll wear an exquisite dress and host distinguished gentlemen in the parlors of my own home, where they'll smoke fragrant cigars and engage in debates about politics and the emperor's accomplishments against the Serbian nationalists.

We run up the main street towards the tram, passing clothing and fabric stores adjacent to a patisserie. Outside the patisserie, an automobile bearing the empire's symbol is parked. Two individuals in blue uniforms load cakes from the patisserie into the vehicle. One day, I'll enter that patisserie, order a slice of lemon cake, and relish the renowned sweetness everyone talks about.

"Excuse me, I apologize," I say to a gentleman in a suit, holding a folded newspaper, as I narrowly avoid colliding with him. We sidestep to let an open carriage pass. He offers a nod, and we continue our rush. We can't afford to be late. At the boulevard, we quicken our pace and catch onto the slowly moving tram on the rails. Gasping, we manage to board the crowded car. I squeeze between men in suits returning from work, Erica standing with her back to me. Positioned between an older man in a top hat with a gray mustache, who's captivated by her golden hair, and a younger man engrossed in an open newspaper. "Emperor Franz Josef threatens to send troops against the Serbian nationalists," I manage to read the newspaper's headline. Shifting my gaze past Erica, who exchanges smiles with the older man, I recall Dad's words, 'Women shouldn't delve into politics,' as I used to attempt reading newspaper articles on our living room table as a child. I need to smile more. Christina says men appreciate women who smile.

"Ticket please," the ticket collector addresses me. I hand over a coin reluctantly, parting with it with a touch of sadness. I don't have enough money, but I'm left with no choice but to take the tram. The painter's house is on the outskirts of town, and it's getting late.

We disembark long after the yellowed Schönbrunn Palace and start walking. The streets here are wider, and the houses have fewer floors, usually one or two. The cobblestone streets have transformed into an unpaved dirt road. Occasionally, we pause at a house entrance, double-checking the address against the note I'm holding. Finally, we come to a stop in front of a black iron gate. Behind it lies a flower-filled garden and a pathway leading to a one-story house. We've reached the painter's house.

***

It's growing dark outside. I pull on the gate handle, hearing its creak as it opens, and we stroll along the gravel path leading to the white house. My hand is tucked into my dress pocket, where I caress the note with the address. I'm tempted to loosen the pins that gather my long red hair and braid it.

"Meow..." I hear a plaintive howl and look down, spotting a white cat with black spots that's rubbing against my leg and yowling.

"Hello, sweetie," I bend down and stroke its soft fur as it continues to press its head against my palm.

"Wally, come on," Erica whispers to me. I hear the soft footfalls of her shoes on the gravel path amidst the flower bushes, but I linger to stroke the cat, relishing its soft fur. My nervousness makes it difficult to continue walking.

"Meow..." the cats yowls once more, and as I attempt to calm myself and lift it into my arms, my gaze shifts toward the door, and that's when I see him.

He stands near me, close to Erica, donning a broad blue smock reminiscent of the one he wore back then. Panic courses through me, and I instinctively take a step back, the plump cat snugly cradled in my hands. I hadn't noticed he had stepped out of the house.

"May I?" he approaches me, and reaches out for the cat.

Without saying a word, I pass him the cat. His fingers briefly brush against my palm as he takes the feline into his embrace. A warmth emanates from his large hand, causing a shiver to run down my spine, though the cool evening breeze might also be responsible.

"Cat," he informs me, his gaze examines my hair and face.

"I apologize for the abrupt intrusion," I speak quickly, my cheeks heat up. Only Erica knows how to handle the situation and smiles at him.

"Cat, its name is 'Cat,'" he tells me, stroking the cat nestled in his arms. He turns and starts to walk down the gravel path between the bushes and trees. The cat rests securely in his muscular arms. "Please, come inside," he tells us without looking back, prompting us to follow him.

I follow them inside, and Mr. Klimt patiently waits, closing the front door behind me as I stand and take in my surroundings. The house differs greatly from the residence of the Lady I serve. The spacious room is painted white and its simplicity is remarkable. The walls lack the bookcases or gilded mirrors that adorned the other house. Opulent carpets, grand statues, and delicate Chinese porcelain are conspicuously absent. The ceiling light is a modest lamp rather than an opulent, glittering chandelier. The only contrast to the pristine white walls is found in the black-painted door frames.

Mr. Klimt releases the cat, which leaps from his hands and vanishes into one of the rooms. Without uttering a word, akin to a shepherd strolling through a field, confident the herd will follow, Mr. Klimt continues across the polished and luminous parquet. We trail after him, passing through an open black-painted door into an even more expansive room—could this be his studio?

Several easels, each bearing paintings in various stages of completion, stand to the side. Adjacent to them rest wooden boxes brimming with brushes. I study the incomplete paintings and manage to identify the Lady in one of them. Her proud and exquisite visage is already rendered, along with her ebony tresses. Yet, her attire is still unfinished, and the canvas is adorned with yellow and gold square brushstrokes.

"Mr. Klimt, should we position ourselves there?" Erica asks him and points to the big bed in the corner of the room. It's draped with a black-white striped bedspread. Is this the reason for our invitation?

I search for the cat. Even though I know it's irrational, I can't bring myself to look into the painter or Erica's eyes. I could simply locate the cat, cradle it, and caress its velvety fur, everything would surely be alright. Will Erica protect me?

"Whatever feels right to you, make yourself at home," Mr. Klimt smiles at her. "I'll be right back," he leaves the room, and

I remain standing in the center of the room. I look at Erica as she takes off her shoes and sits on the large bed.

"Copper, sit down," she says, gesturing me to sit next to her. But I stay put in the center of the room, and keep searching for the cat. I'll feel safer if I stay standing.

"Are you alright?" he enters from the other room and asks me. He changed into a different smock. It was simpler and stained with paint; it was probably the same smock I had seen him earing in the Lady's room. I must follow Erica's lead.

"Yes, everything is fine," I try to smile at him, "I just wanted to see your paintings," I gaze into his blue eyes. He is much older than me. I shouldn't be afraid of him. I should trust him as the Lady does. It was my decision to arrive at his house.

"Please sit on the bed so we can begin," he places his large palm on my shoulder, and I feel the warmth of his fingers as he guides me to the bed. His hand's warmth calms me. He will show me what to do.

"Should we undress?" Erica asks him. "Wally, can you untie my dress?" she promptly turns her back to me without waiting for an answer. I untie the laces of her dress' bodice. "Thank you," she smiles at me, quickly removing her dress. She stands there, in nothing but her camisole and stockings. "We're ready," she informs Mr. Klimt as she unbuttons the top of her camisole covering her fair skin, freeing her breasts.

"Place your hand on your thigh," Mr. Klimt instructs her. "I'll show you," he approaches and takes her hand, positioning it precisely where he wants. All I can hear is their breathing. What should I do? Should I act like her? This is what is expected of me, but I feel that I do not belong here. It's as if I'm standing and watching myself from the room's entrance.

"Don't move," he instructs her, and walks away towards the easel, places light brown paper on it, and begins to draw. Erica smiles at him and remains in a frozen position. What about me? Does he expect me to undress before he draws me? Why won't he talk to me? Why doesn't he give me instructions? I yearn to take part.

I move closer to the bed, nearing Erica, almost making contact, feeling awkward in the dress I'm wearing. I need to undress. My fingers attempt to untie the laces, but I can't manage it, nor can I ask Erica for help. The painter instructed her not to move. What about my shoes? Should I take them off? I look up at him. He is focused on Erica, his hand holding the pencil and moving swiftly. Occasionally, he glances at me as well, but Erica is the one who captures his interest. I search for the cat with my eyes. If only I could hold it, I would relax, but it's nowhere to be found. I remain seated on the bed, dressed next to Erica, averting my gaze from her exposed, white breasts. He won't invite me anymore. Neither will he place his hand on my shoulder and instruct me to assume the correct position, as he did with Erica.

"Thank you," he says to Erica after a long time, "you can get dressed."

"Can I see the painting?" she stands up and approaches him. She doesn't bother closing the buttons of her camisole. I watch as she walks barefoot, her beautiful breasts swaying with each step. I'm too embarrassed to see the painting.

"It's a sketch, not a painting," he replies. "Would you like to see it?" he addresses me. His blue eyes observe me, and I feel uncomfortably short of breath, despite the spacious, tidy, well-lit room. I shake my head in refusal and move to stand by the door, feigning interest in searching for the cat. He chose her over me. Why couldn't I undress like her? What chance do I stand against her captivating breasts and the smile she's directing at him? She touches his arm affectionately as he assists her with dressing. She turns away from him, allowing him to tie the laces of her dress.

"I'm glad you came, Erica," he places his hand on her back and escorts her to the door.

"Thank you, sir," she replies.

"Good night to you too. You didn't even tell me your name," he turns to me, standing so close that I have to look up.

"My name is Walburga, sir, but everyone calls me Wally," I say. He doesn't smell of cigarettes.

"You are *Fuego*, my little fawn," he caresses my palm and leans down to kiss my cheek, as is the French custom. "The word 'fuego' means fire in Spanish," he whispers in my ear while leaning down to kiss my other cheek. "You are like a fire waiting to be lit." I feel his warm lips fluttering on my cheeks as if they were the strokes of a loving hand, and I want to cling to his lips. I'm so embarrassed.

"Thank you, sir," I open the door and rush out into the cold air of the garden, feeling my face redden. From behind, I hear Erica bid him goodbye and start walking on the gravel path after me in the dark.

"Wally, can you come here for a minute?" I hear him say.

"Yes, Mr. Klimt," I turn around, walk towards him, and pass Erica, who stands and waits for me. Will he notice that I blushed?

"My little fawn," he smiles at me in the dark, placing his palm on my cheek and caressing it gently. His touch is warm and pleasant, even though his palm is so big. "Yes, Mr. Klimt," I raise my head to him, pressing my cheek to warm fingers.

"Red-haired Fuego, I want you to come tomorrow morning alone; he takes my hand and holds it, then takes out several coins from his pocket, placing them in my palm. I can feel the cool evening breeze touching my skin where his warm palm touched just a moment ago. "I want to get to know you better with my pencil."

"Thank you, Mr. Klimt," I gasp.

"You can call me Klimt," he smiles at me, but I don't answer him, afraid that I'll get my words mixed up, I turn around and run to Erica, who is waiting for me by the open iron gate.

"What were you talking about?" Erica asks as I close the gate behind us, and we walk down the dark dirt road toward the streetlamp that marks the main street.

"He asked if I liked the cat." I tuck my hand in my dress pocket, tightly holding the coins he gave me. I still feel the touch of his lips and his palm on my cheek. I smile to myself in the dark. He wants me to come to him again tomorrow morning, this time alone. But then I stop smiling. What will I do with my work at the Lady's house?

"Walburga, you're ready," Ms. Bertha says as she walks around me the following day. Her eyes check my dress and my carefully gathered hair. Will she notice that I'm lying to her? Can she read my mind? I cross my fingers with force until it hurts. I hope she won't notice how tense I am.

"Thank you, Ms. Bertha," I turn my gaze to the floral sofa in the entry room, feeling my heartbeat. My hand goes up by itself, trying to hold the ends of my hair, but it is gathered. A moment ago, Ms. Bertha arranged my hair into a bun. I can't remove the pins in front of her.

"Keep your hands behind your back. Behave yourself," her hand smacks mine away, and I straighten up and put my hands back behind my back. I can feel that I'm blushing.

"What are you waiting for? They won't wait for you all day. They are a respectable family," she turns away from me and goes to the second floor to wake up the other girls. I sigh in relief and rush out into the rainy, cold street in the morning breeze. She didn't suspect that I was lying to her.

Later, as I cross the wide boulevard and the passing trams, I deliberately choose a street far from the Lady's house and make a significant detour. Will they inform Ms. Bertha that I didn't arrive at work? They might start looking for a replacement, and I could lose my job. Every time I hear an automobile approaching, I instinctively avert my gaze, hoping it's not their vehicle and that the driver won't recognize me to report back to the housekeeper. I still have the option to change my mind and hurry to their house, explaining that I was delayed on the way. I spent the whole night awake, listening to Christina's breathing, wanting to seek her advice on what to do, but also fearing that she might try to dissuade me.

My fingers grip the collar of my coat, pulling it tight against the cold autumn wind. I observe a black carriage passing by on the gray street, and I continue walking towards his house. He expressed his desire to see me again. He's expecting me. I can't afford to disappoint him.

When I stand in front of the black iron gate, I pause for a moment, taking a deep breath and attempting to calm my nerves. My fingers fiddle with my tied-back hair, appreciating its smoothness. I mustn't mess it up; I need to keep it tidy, just as Bertha arranged it for me in the morning. Beneath my simple dress, I'm wearing a borrowed lace camisole from Erica. I informed her that I needed to wash my own and asked if she could lend me one.

My hand turns the gate handle, and I open it slowly, hearing the creak of the rusty hinges. I'm hesitant to walk along the path leading to his door, but it's too late for regrets. This is my chance to escape from Ms. Bertha's grasp.

"Cat," I murmur, walking down the path and whispering, as I search through the bushes, "Cat, where are you?" However, I don't spot him, and eventually, I find myself standing outside the door, scanning my surroundings. Should I keep looking for the cat? My fingers grip the collar of my coat once again. The smooth fabric of the camisole momentarily sends a shiver down my spine. But then the doors open.

"Come inside," Mr. Klimt says to me while standing at the door, holding the cat in his hands, and I hurry inside the warm house. Did he observe me from the window and see me walking in his garden? I stand in the center of the room and hear the door closing behind me. I realize that I've been impolite, not greeting him at the front door. I can sense his presence that fills the room, but I'm too shy to say anything.

Mr. Klimt also doesn't say anything but passes by me and walks inside, seemingly knowing that I will follow him. I remind myself to emulate Erica's demeanor, to act like someone experienced, so that he doesn't perceive me as a young girl.

"Mr. Klimt, like last time?" I say as I follow him into the studio. I already know what to do; I observed what she did when we were together.

Without needing instructions, I walk over to the large bed by the wall, sit on it, and take off my shoes. The warmth of the parquet floor envelops my feet. What did Erica do next? I stand up, approach him, and turn my back, saying, "Could you please help me with my dress?"

Through the fabric of my dress, I can feel his fingers touching my back, untying the laces that secure it to my body. With a subtle movement, he pulls them from the loops, caressing my back in the process. Despite the thick fabric, I sense the warmth of his fingers and his breath. He is so close to me. Mr. Walner also touched me in a similar way back then, but he slid his hand much lower and wasn't as gentle as Mr. Klimt. I clench my thighs tightly.

"Everything okay? You're shaking." Mr. Klimt asks me, his fingers continuing to touch my back.

"Everything is fine," I answer him. He's not like Mr. Walner who smelled of tobacco. He won't do to me what Mr. Walner tried to do. He will protect me.

"I'm done. Your body is free from laces and locks," he whispers to me and hugs my waist for a moment. I pull away from him and walk towards the bed that awaits me. Now I have to do it, like Erica did, without thinking.

With one movement, I roll up my dress and throw it on the floor, sitting on the bed in front of him, and start unbuttoning my camisole, exposing my breasts to his eyes. I look down and feel myself blushing, and my fingers have trouble opening the camisole's small buttons, but I don't stop. I won't stop now. I came to this house with a reason.

I hear his footsteps on the floor as he approaches, and the mattress shifts as he sits on the bed. He is so close. My hands freeze, and my gaze is fixed on my white thighs, which the short camisole does not cover.

"Slowly, my frightened fawn," he gently holds my chin with his warm fingers and forces me to lift it and look into his blue eyes and face. He is so close to me that I can hear his breathing. "Slowly, don't be afraid," he smiles at me, "one button at a time," he sends his fingers to my camisole and closes two buttons, leaving only one button open and my breasts covered. I keep looking into his eyes. Doesn't he want me? Does he prefer Erica?

"But I want to," I manage to whisper to him.

"I know you want to. You're *Fuego*, you're fire," his fingers caress my cheeks and go up to my hair, starting to pull the hairpins one by one, throwing them away as if he were a blacksmith releasing a horseshoe from a horse's leg. I can hear the gentle clicks of the hairpins when they hit the parquet, "Fire always waits for someone to strike a match, but fire also has the patience for the right moment," he leans so close to me. "Meanwhile, you shouldn't hide your flames," his hands spread my loose hair over my shoulders. I want him to get even closer and hug me. I haven't been hugged in such a long time.

"Thank you," I look into his eyes and grab the ends of my hair, wanting to put it in my mouth but refraining. I'm not a little girl anymore.

"Don't move," he slides his hand on my waist and touches my thighs, opening them a little. Mr. Walner touched me there. I shiver.

"Everything okay?" he asks.

"Yes, everything is fine," I try to smile at him and spread my thighs a little more, "Like this?"

"Yes," he smiles at me, "and lean back," he places my hand on the soft mattress and guides my palm at the right angle, "Don't move." He stands up and approaches the easel, puts light brown paper on it, and starts drawing.

I look at his eyes and watch how they shift from my body to the paper in front of him. His hand holding the pencil is in constant motion. Will he attempt to do anything with me when we're done? It's hard for me to stay so still for so long, and the cat that rubs against my back is also distracting, but I try to remain motionless and ignore it. I will show Mr. Klimt that I am mature and know how to be a good model.

"We're done, thank you," he says after a long while, bending down to pick up the cat to his lap, "you were good."

I remain in the same position for a moment. Should I stand up and get dressed now? What does he expect from me? What would Erica do? I open my thighs a little more, and my hand plays with my hair. However, he turns his back to me and busies himself with arranging his box of colors while the cat purrs at his leg. Finally, I rise from the bed and put on my dress and shoes, trying to tie the laces myself as much as possible, without asking for his help. Despite his kind words earlier, he didn't attempt anything with me. He didn't seem interested in me. I feel tears welling up at the corners of my eyes.

"Goodbye," I say as I walk towards the door, looking at the gray clouds in the window.

"*Fuego*, wait," he turns and approaches me, "you can't run like a deer in the meadow without letting me protect you from the hunters." He hugs me. I feel his warm hands wrap around me and pull me closer, his palm stroking my hair. He does care about me. I wipe my eyes and cling to him, not wanting him to stop. "This is for you," he says after a moment and moves away, taking out several coins from his pocket, "You were a good model today."

"Thank you, Mr. Klimt," I extend my hand and smile at him, taking the money and hurrying out, the cold coins clutched in my hand. He cares about me.

I am in no hurry to return to Ms. Bertha's hostel. I still have time until the afternoon. Ms. Bertha must not suspect that I did not go to work at the Lady's house. I stroll through the city streets. I don't care about the cold wind. I stop near the pawn shop and feel the coins in my dress pocket. Soon, I will have enough money to rebuy Dad's ring. But then I turn around and head back to the main street, walking quickly and looking at the shop windows. In front of a dress shop, I stop and gaze at the roll of loose fabric in a lavender color. It is so beautiful. Next to it hangs a modern dress. They never bought me dresses. I always received used dresses from my Mom or one of the neighbors. I look at the dress in the display window. Step by step, I approach, push open the glass door, and enter inside. I will be beautiful for him, and he will love and protect me.

⁂

"How does it feel to be a model?" one of the girls asks Erica a few days later, and I look down, wanting to cry. Since that day, he hasn't invited me again.

"It's different from being with the men who come here," Erica laughs, "Now I'm with an artist. I'm not just one of Bertha's girls anymore," she says. I lean against the wall of the hostel guest room and watch the girls sitting on the stained floral sofa. For the last few days, I've been walking around the city alone since morning, knowing I made a mistake by going to him that day. I lost my job at the Lady's house.

"Wally, why don't you join us?" one of the girls tells me, and I look down at her. She is standing next to the sofa behind Erica, holding a silver-colored hairbrush and combing Erica's yellow hair in slow motions, sliding it between her fingers until it ripples and shines like a cascade of sun rays hitting a silk curtain fluttering in an open window on a spring morning.

"Wally also knows him," Erica turns her face to the girl holding the brush and smiles at her, "We went to him once together. Come on, Wally, join us," she turns to me, her green eyes examining my simple dress, "Tell them what he's like."

"He's nice," I look for a place to sit. The other sofa, the one the men usually sit on, is empty now, but I don't want to sit on it, and none of the girls move to make room for me. I stay standing, looking at the vacant sofa on the other side of the room. Will he come here looking for me?

"Did he draw you naked?" one of the girls asks Erica.

"At the first time, no, when I went with Wally, we stayed dressed, more or less," she giggles, and the other girls around her laugh with her. I touch my hair that's pulled up in a bun, and begin to loosen the pins holding it tight. It has bothered me since morning when Ms. Bertha arranged it for me. My fingers unravel my hair by force, spreading it on my shoulders.

"Wally, why are you throwing away the pins?" one of the girls asks me. The small metal pins gently tap the stone floor as they scatter everywhere, but I don't answer her.

"Will he present your picture in an exhibition? Will you be famous?" another girl asks Erica. My fingers run through my hair, tucking hair ends into my mouth, and I suck on it.

"I don't know yet," Erica leans back between the girls, "for now, he's just drawing me, but he said he likes my hair. He said it's like waves of gold."

"You really do have golden hair," the girl with the comb says while continuing to caress it with the silver hairbrush. The taste of my hair in my mouth is bitter, and my fingers holding it feel clumsy.

"And does he let you see the drawings he made of you?" asks another girl. "Yes," Erica answers her. "Seeing my body drawn on the brown paper is very exciting. It's like he turned me into a character from a story."

Why didn't he show me my drawing? Why didn't I ask him to see it?

"Please describe it to us," the girl asks.

"I can't," Erica replies, "it's too bold," she laughs, "I wore my lace camisole, and that wasn't enough for him either."

"I wonder when he will come here again and choose one of us," says one of the girls. I look at her and walk away from them, going up to the second floor. He chose Erica, not me.

Our room is empty. I have no idea where Christina is. Maybe she is laughing with other girls in one of the rooms. I take off my dress, hold Christina's heavy iron scissors, and examine myself in front of the simple, dirty mirror. Why does he love Erica more than me? I'm so ugly.

With a quick movement, I cut the hem of the camisole I'm wearing, shortening it to expose my thighs, feeling the cold touch of the scissors on my pale skin.

"It's not enough. He chose her," I look down at my bare thighs. The pieces of cut fabric are strewn on the floor like scraps of paper blown here by the winter wind. I hold the ends of my red hair and look at myself in the mirror. She has hair of golden waves, that's what he said.

With a sharp movement, I cut the ends of my hair, let it fall on the wooden floor, covering it like pine needles scattered in the forest as I step on them in my old boots. One more cut, my hand grabs the ends of another hair and cuts it, ignoring the noise of the heavy metal scissors between my fingers, and one more cut, I close my eyes and just listen to the ticking of the cutting scissors again and again, I can't stop now.

A minute later, I look down, see my hair scattered around among the pieces of white cloth, and burst into tears. What did I do? My face stares at me in the small mirror with my short hair. It's still red and prominent but so short, almost like a boy. My tears are flowing down my cheeks. It does not matter anymore. Everyone will laugh at me.

I throw the heavy scissors on the bed, lie down, cover myself with the wool blanket, and continue crying. What does it matter what I do? He will never love me when I look like this.

Wally, what did you do to your hair?" Ms. Bertha asks me the next day as I descend the stairs. I can't explain to her. If I start talking, I'll start crying, and she'll find out everything that happened.

"I'm in a hurry, Ms. Bertha," I look down and continue walking towards the door.

"Young Walburga, stand where you are," I hear her command, and I stop, feeling my heart pounding. Does she already know that I stopped working there? I feel the tears threatening to burst from my eyes and breathe heavily, looking up at her.

"Wally, what happened to your hair?" she stands before me, her fingers firmly holding my chin while she examines me with her blue-gray eyes. Her touch makes me remember how Mr. Klimt held my chin gently, and I start crying. Why didn't I listen to her?

"Everything is fine," I manage to tell her, but the tears run down my cheeks.

"Very well, Walburga," she pulls out a handkerchief from her dress pocket and wipes my teary cheeks with strong movements, continuing to hold my chin and her face close to mine. "At my hostel, no one cries. There is no place here for weak women."

"Yes, Ms. Bertha," I wipe my eyes.

"And stand up straight when you answer me. You're a proud woman, not a rag, even though you cut your hair, and now you look like a boy." She smacks my hand that wipes away the tears. "What did you think, Walburga? That you could be a modern woman like these women who cut their hair?" She finally releases my chin and takes a few steps away, still examining my cut hair.

"I shouldn't have cut my hair, Ms. Bertha. I was wrong," I straighten up as much as I can and fold my hands behind my back, fighting the tears trying to break out again. How do I tell her I don't have work anymore?

"Walburga, there's no point in crying. Listen to what Bertha tells you. If you've made a mistake, then fix it."

"Yes, Ms. Bertha," I straighten up a little more.

"So why are you standing here like a useless broomstick? You have work to do. I don't want to see you here," she turns and goes back behind her counter, bends down, and pulls out her silver cigarette box. I rush out of the hostel before she fills the air with suffocating smoke. I have to fix what I did. I have to make him hug me again.

On the narrow street near the pawn shop, I avert my gaze and quicken my steps. I don't want to look at the shop's front glass and the bars protecting it. I still have enough time to retrieve my ring. Moreover, on the main street near the dress shop, I cross to the other side, walking behind a freight cart pulled by an old horse at a slow pace. I have a few more days until I have to return to pick up the dress and pay the remaining money for it. I can feel the few coins in my dress pocket rubbing against my thighs. Despite my long dress, my shortened camisole no longer covers my thighs, and I feel as if I'm walking naked in the street. I'll have to manage with it until I acquire enough money to buy a new one.

At the tram, I huddle among all the men, feeling their gazes fixed on me and my short red hair. It seems they can read my mind, knowing where I'm going. I try to ignore their staring eyes and concentrate on a bearded man with a beret standing in the tram, reading from the newspaper. I also ignore the man who gets too close to me from behind. I feel his body and the smell of his breath and want to scream, but I hold myself. I won't shout like I did at Mr. Walner's shop. If I do something, all the men around will look at me. Women should know how to hold back. I feel myself blushing and trying to get away from him and his hand while keeping my gaze on the newspaper headlines, which say that the emperor is sending another army to Serbia to restore peace against the rebels. Do the people looking at me notice that I'm blushing? I must not think about him. I will think about Mr. Klimt, who embraced me with his big arms, letting me feel his warm body. I breathe and count the minutes until the station. Finally, I get off the tram and breathe freely, enjoying the cold wind that hits my face. One day, women will be able to scream on the tram, and people will listen to them.

Near his place, I stop and stand frozen at the gate, my hand resting on the cold metal handle of the black gate. I hesitate, gazing at the garden and the house. What will he think of me? I came without an invitation. Respectable women don't just visit a man's house uninvited. I release the handle and remain standing, wrapping my arms around myself to shield from the cold wind. I shouldn't have come here, even though I'm desperate to find a way to earn more money. Maybe I should give up and return to the hostel, explain everything to Ms. Bertha. Perhaps she'll forgive me.

I search for the cat in the garden, and for a moment, I think I see the outline of Mr. Klimt standing inside the house, looking at me through the window. I quickly shift my gaze to the quiet street, so he won't assume I'm waiting for him. When I glance back at the house, the light inside goes out, and I can't tell whether he's still there, peering at me from the dark room, or if I just imagined it. The cold wind makes me tremble. I'll have to leave soon. The wind is getting stronger.

"Excuse me, Miss," a young man addresses me, "do you know where Kremsergasse Street is?"

I look at him. He's slightly older than me with a small mustache, the kind that young men grow but haven't fully matured yet. He's riding a bicycle, dressed in a simple coat, and stops beside me.

"I'm sorry, I'm not from here," I respond.

"I'm not from here either. I seem to have lost my way back to town," he gets off his bike and smiles at me.

"I am also on my way back to town," I say as I let go of the iron gate handle. I'm too cold to continue standing like this.

"Will the Miss allow me to accompany her to the city?" He removes his hat and bows slightly.

"With pleasure, Sir," I reply, holding the hem of my dress and returning the bow with a smile. The journey to the city is long, and it would be comforting to have someone to walk with and not be alone.

"I'm Ernest," he introduces himself, taking off the leather glove he's wearing and extending his hand.

"I'm Wally," I shake his hand, feeling his warm fingers.

We begin walking, but then I hear the sound of footsteps on the gravel, and the iron gate opens. I turn around and see Mr. Klimt approaching, wearing his stained blue smock. Without a word, he takes my hand and leads me towards the house, pausing briefly to nod at Mr. Ernest, who stands next to his bike, watching us without saying anything, unsure how to respond. Mr. Klimt holds my hand tightly, and I follow him, brushing against the flower bushes that line the path, but I don't mind. I don't look back at the young man who kindly offered to accompany me to the city, even though I probably should have. I simply breathe heavily as Mr. Klimt leads me into the house, closing the door behind us.

"*Fuego*, what have you done to your hair?" He runs his large fingers through my short hair. "What happened to the fire and flames cascading down your shoulders?" I feel his touch on the nape of my bare neck.

"I'm sorry," I say, moving a bit closer, hoping for his embrace. Will he appreciate me in this way? I'm struggling to hold back tears.

"You don't need to apologize, my lovely fawn. The fire is inside you, waiting to erupt. I can feel it," he hugs me, and I feel the warmth of his hands. His soft lips touch mine. They are soft and gentle, even though his beard scratches my face. No one has ever kissed me like that. I try to catch my breath as I breathe heavily and kiss him back. He wants me to be his.

"Wait," I whisper to him, "Wait," I'll be more to him than Erica. I free myself from his hug and take a few steps back, turn, and walk towards the bed standing in the studio. I know he is watching me. Even though I'm nervous about what I'm going to do, I remove my dress with one swift motion and stand in front of him, panting in my cut-out camisole. I didn't even take off my shoes. If I want him to love me, I have to give him what he expects to have.

We look at each other. My gaze examines the smock he is wearing. The spots of color that stain it look like colorful fireworks, as I saw once above the emperor's palace during his birthday celebrations. I watch his large palms, the ones that held me a minute ago. They are ready and waiting only for me. He will lead me in this way with his strong arms. I examine his broad shoulders, reddish-brown beard, and his blue eyes that look at me with a soothing gaze. I can notice the small wrinkles on the sides of his eyes. He will be gentle with me, I know.

My fingers reach up to open the buttons of my cut camisole, but he comes closer, takes my hands, holds them in his palms, and brings them to his mouth, kissing them gently.

"You are fire and flame. You are like a red fox that comes to a vineyard for the first time, asking for permission to eat from the grapes," he whispers to me as he lays me down on the bed and lies down next to me. I feel the soft mattress against my back and breathe slowly. I so hope he will be gentle with me.

While kissing my lips, his fingers caress my eyes, go down to my lips, feeling their softness, and continue down to my neck. I close my eyes and try not to move. I must trust him.

My breathing becomes heavy when I feel his fingers caress the thin fabric of my camisole. His lips kiss my bare skin as he opens button after button, his touch pleasant despite my tension, and I keep my eyes closed, trying to relax. I freeze when I hear him removing his smock, and for a moment, I shudder when I feel the weight of his body on top of me, but his fingers stroking my short hair calm me down. I'm ready for him. I will be the best for him. He will love me, just like I wanted.

Chapter Five

Pretty Girl

"Christina," I whisper to her later as we lie in our narrow steel bed at night. "Christina, are you awake?"

"Rusty, what is it?" I hear her from the darkness.

"Christina," I try to find the right words, "How pleasant should it be?" My body is still a little sore. The feeling down there is also strange to me.

"How should what be pleasant?"

"When you're with them," I'm ashamed to tell her what I did today with Mr. Klimt, "how pleasant should it be?"

"Pleasant in your thoughts or pleasant down there?" She asks me, and I keep silent, not knowing what to answer her. I can hear her breathing in the darkness and the creak of the bed as she turns, "Rusty, have you done this with anyone?" She asks me after a while.

"No," I answer quickly, blushing in the dark.

"You're still too young for this," I hear the bed springs creaking again, and after a moment, she turns and lies next to me, covering both of us, "Don't rush, even though there are girls here who will say you should do it already."

"How old were you when you first did it?"

"Too young, I didn't understand."

"What didn't you understand?"

"That there is a difference between pleasant thoughts and pleasant down there," she laughs a little, "When you feel comfortable with him and smile to yourself when you think about him, it doesn't matter if it's pleasant down there. It's just pleasant."

"I want to smile in my thoughts," I caress my thighs and smile in the dark. I felt comfortable when he hugged and whispered to me not to worry. I almost wasn't afraid when he lay on top of me, even when I felt the weight of his heavy body. I opened my eyes. I looked at his face so close to me and knew he'd protect me.

"For that, you will have to find a man who will respect you at the end of the night and not just compliment you at the beginning of it."

"And then it will also be pleasant down there?"

"Then you will miss him and want him to be on top of you again."

"I do," I look at the ceiling and remember his blue eyes looking at me as he did this to me, and I groaned in pain, seeing myself in his eyes.

"I thought you didn't have anyone. Was it the painter who was here? The one you went to with Erica?" She laughs and tickles me.

"No, it's not him. I don't have anyone," I try to tickle her back. I shouldn't have started this conversation. She'll tell the others.

"So you just went to him, and he drew you?" She holds my hands, not letting me continue tickling her.

"And what about you? Don't you want to go to a painter like him, have someone paint you?" I try to change the subject. I don't want her to keep talking about Erica, who said he invited her to his studio. He is with me.

"I don't have to search for someone like him. His kind come here to me," she laughs. "You're a child," she continues after a while, "You don't know yet that they don't mean all the nice words they say to you. They don't really want you."

"But he was nice to me," I answer quietly, "That time we went to him, Erica and I," I add, not wanting her to suspect that I was alone with him.

"He's not nice to you. He's a man. He's nice to what he wants to achieve, remember that the next time a painter like him invites you. We, women, think they care about us, but we are so wrong, and at the end of the night, we are left to cuddle in a place like this in a bed like this." I can hear the bed springs when she moves a little.

"I'll remember," I whisper in the dark and smile to myself. He was sensitive and cared about me. He didn't just say things.

"We have to be nice to what we want to achieve. That's the most important thing, not to their nice words." She adds.

"And what do you want to achieve?"

"Me?" She lets go of my hand, "I get it here in this place, my independence," She says quietly, "With the money they pay me at the end of the day."

"But that's not love," I whisper.

"Rusty, I don't believe in love and beautiful words," she says, "You see, all the men who come here and whisper nice words in our ears, call us whores when they close the hostel door behind their backs and walk back to their nice homes. But I don't care, I don't believe their words. I believe in coins with a pleasant ring, with the emperor's symbol stamped on them, and you should also grow up and believe in them."

"I'm already grown up," I answer and think about the silver coins he gave me today. She's wrong. With him, it's different, I was with him because I wanted to be, and even if he paid me before I left, I'm not a whore. I saw it in his eyes.

"Good afternoon, Ms. Bertha," I say to her a few days later and look down, hurrying across the entrance. I was with him all day, lying on the studio's bed, letting him draw my exposed body, listening to the rustling pencil on the drawing paper.

"Young miss Walburga, is there anything you want to tell me?" She stands behind her counter and watches me, the brown cigarette stuck in her mouth, a curling line of gray smoke slowly floating up until it dissolves in the air.

"No, Ms. Bertha," I stop and feel myself blush. Does she know? Did Christina suspect and tell her?

"Are you sure you don't have something to tell me?"

"No, Ms. Bertha," I look down at my shoes again.

"How's work at the Lady's house?"

"I apologize, Ms. Bertha," I look up at her and step back. Her blue-gray eyes are watching me, "I had no choice," I feel the tears rising, "He asked me to come to his place again." I straighten up as much as I can, like an obedient girl. What have I done? What choice did I have? I feel the tears falling down my cheeks. What will she do to me? I'm shaking.

"Walburga, you're not a girl anymore. Look at me."

"Yes, Ms. Bertha," I look up at her. Through the tears, I see her leaning back against the wall behind the counter with the small wooden shelves. She continues to examine me while she leisurely smokes her cigarette. I remain standing still with my hands behind my back, not daring to wipe away the tears. Will she throw me out of her hostel?

"You know, Wally," she continues to look at me, "The girls in my hostel can't read and write, but you can. I thought you were different," she crushes the cigarette in the silver ashtray on the counter, "Tell me, Wally, did you read fairy tales when you were a child?"

"Yes, Ms. Bertha, we had fairy tale books at home," I answer her and remember the Grimm Brothers fairy tale books that were placed in the small cupboard in our house before Dad died and we moved to Vienna.

"Maybe that's your problem; you've read too many fairy tale books about princesses."

"No, Ms. Bertha, that's not true," I wipe my teary face.

"You've been dreaming too much, about a glass slipper and a handsome red haired prince coming to save you," she turns and takes something from the wooden cabinet behind her, "And you haven't understood the main lesson of fairy tales." She turns back and looks at me with her blue-gray eyes.

"I don't understand," I answer her, my fingers tracing the hem of my dress. Mr. Klimt gently stripped it from me only a few hours ago.

"What you didn't understand, is that you pay for your mistakes, and you can't go back," She comes out from behind the counter and approaches me, "Follow me."

"I'm sorry, Ms. Bertha," I hold her hand and start crying again. Is she going to throw me out on the street?

"Wally, you're not a child anymore. It's not appropriate for you to beg," she shakes my hand holding her, as if she is kicking a stray cat that came too close to her in the street, asking for leftovers. Without changing her pace, she walks towards the stairs going up to the second floor, passing two girls sitting on the flowered sofa and looking at us, "It's time for you to move forward. In the real world, you can't go back," she climbs the stairs, and I follow her, wiping my tears. What could I have done differently?

"Christina," she stands outside our room door and knocks hard on it, "Christina."

"Yes, Ms. Bertha," Christina opens the door and turns her back to us. She goes and sits on the small chair, looks in the mirror and combs her hair.

"Young Ms. Wallburga wants to try new things," Ms. Bertha tells her as she walks to the little wooden closet, and I follow her, watching her open its doors. Once again, I get dumped, just like a few months ago, when my mother did the same. Why did I go to Mr. Klimt?

"She's still a child. Leave her alone," Christina replies as she starts to rub her lips with lipstick from a silver saucer, applying it with a brush, "She still believes in love and passion," She continues to speak without turning toward us.

"Passion costs money, and love is not given for free," Ms. Bertha answers her as she pulls my clothes out of the closet and slams them against me. I hasten to grab them so they don't fall on the floor. I won't beg this time. I won't give her this pleasure. She hates me anyway.

"Ms. Bertha, she will discover the pain on her own. You don't need to punish her," Christina answers her as she gets up from the chair and looks at me. Her lips are pink, and there is a blush on her cheeks. She will probably start working soon.

"She has already discovered the power of desire," Ms. Bertha answers and takes my carefully folded camisole from the shelf and tucks it between my arms, "She has also discovered the power of immoral behavior," she says and walks past me, forcing me to step back so she doesn't rub against my hands holding my clothes. How can I apologize to her? I start crying again. "Now she will discover the price of independence," Ms. Bertha says as she leaves the room and walks into the corridor, "Christina, from now on, you have a room by yourself again, and you," she looks at me, "For God's sake, stop crying already, follow me," she says and turns around, starts walking down the hallway. I follow her, but to my surprise, she doesn't go down the stairs.

She stops in front of one of the doors, takes a key out of her dress pocket, and opens it. 'The locked room,' all the girls call it. I never saw this door open. What is she going to do with me?

"Walburga, go inside. I won't wait for you all day," she says, taking a box of matches from her dress pocket. I enter the small room, which smells of mildew and dust, and look around as she lights the lantern and places it on the floor.

The room is even smaller than Christina's and contains only a steel bed and a small wooden bookcase, with no room for a chair or a closet. It's frightening in here.

"Welcome to your new room," she takes the clothes I'm holding in my hand and throws them on the bed covered with a woolen blanket, "From now on, you're alone, and you'll pay more," She extends her hand out and looks at me, her face like a mask of light and shadow in the yellowish light of the lantern placed on the floor.

"Thank you, Ms. Bertha," I hasten to take a coin out of my dress pocket and give it to her. I don't know how I'll manage the money, but I can't think about that right now. I'll find a way.

"Don't thank me. I'm not done with you yet. Leave the arrangement of your new palace for later and come," she leaves the room, and I hurry behind her. Erica and another girl are standing in the corridor watching us. Erica smiles at me, but I look down and follow Ms. Bertha. What is she planning for me? My hand climbs onto my head, wanting to grab the ends of my hair, but it's too short.

"Erica," she takes Erica's hand, "come with us. I need you. Young Miss Walburga needs some guidance. She wants to be mature." Ms. Bertha takes her by the hand and pulls her down the stairs as I follow them. What does she mean to do to me?

"Get up. You have a free evening," she says to Gitta and Monica, who are sitting on the floral sofa at the entrance, wearing matching camisoles.

"But this is our night, you promised me," Monica replies as she continues to sit cross-legged, and I look at her black garter socks with a pink satin ribbon tied at the top.

"When you run this hostel, you will decide on changes. Until then, I'm in charge here," she pulls her from the sofa, "And you," she turns to Gita, "I don't remember letting you smoke while guests are coming in."

"But they also smoke," Gitta answers as she gets up and walks over to Ms. Bertha's ashtray on the counter, putting out the cigarette she is holding.

"They are allowed to, because they are men, and you are not. It is immoral and makes a bad impression on the customers."

"But you smoke," Gitta replies as she takes Monica's hand, and they turn towards the stairs. She's wearing cream-colored silk garters and new leather boots.

"I smoke because I set the rules here. Go upstairs. If you're nice, I'll send you some gentlemen," She points towards the stairs and follows Gitta and Monica with her gaze. "Now you," she turns to us, "Erica, Wally, sit down. This is your evening," she orders us, and we sit silently on the stained floral sofa. I watch Ms. Bertha as she returns behind her counter, pulls out a black pad, and starts writing notes.

"What did you do?" Erica whispers to me after a few minutes.

"She's mad at me,"

"Why?"

"She thinks I was with someone," I whisper back, not wanting to tell her about Mr. Klimt. Will she be angry with me if she knows?

"Were you?" She comes closer and puts her hand on my thighs. I feel myself blushing and nodding my head. I'm already grown up. I'm allowed to.

The noise of the hostel entrance door makes me turn my gaze, and I see two gentlemen who enter, take off their rain-soaked coats, and go to talk to Ms. Bertha. She comes out from behind her desk and greets them. Will she send me to be with one of them? I feel an unpleasant sensation in the bottom of my stomach and close my thighs. I feel sick.

"I'll be right back," Erica whispers and gets up, disappearing up the stairs before I can say anything and leaving me alone, sitting on the couch. I turn my gaze to the men. They talk quietly with Ms. Bertha and, from time to time, look in my direction. One of them lights a cigar and smiles at me. The pungent smell spreads in the small space and makes me feel nauseous.

The other one also looks at me and turns to Bertha, saying something to her, which I can't make out. I place my palms on my thighs, ensuring they are covered, even though Ms. Bertha will probably be angry with me in a moment. She always orders the girls to seduce the guests. I look down at my clenched fingers. I'll be okay. I just need to breathe.

"It's okay, don't get nervous. They always talk to her first," I hear Erica. She comes back and sits beside me, lifting one leg up on the couch, revealing her toned thighs while holding a small mirror in one hand and a hairbrush in the other. In slow motion, she combs her hair while looking in the mirror, ignoring the two gentlemen.

I turn my gaze to them. One of them approaches the sofa before us and sits on it while Ms. Bertha stands beside him. The other continues to stand by the counter at the entrance, smiling at me and continuing to smoke his cigar.

"Ignore them," Erica whispers to me as she folds her leg and exposes even more of her thigh, but I can't. I miss Mr. Klimt's embrace so much right now. He hugged me this morning, and I felt so safe. The man with the cigar approaches and talks to Bertha again. I want to hug myself, but I dare not.

"She is very special," Bertha says to the gentleman, "There is a painter who is very interested in her,"

"Which of us does she mean?" Erica whispers to me.

"I don't know."

"Were you with him?"

"He asked me to come to his place," I hug myself. The gentleman continues to watch me. Ms. Bertha watches me too.

"He chose me, not you," Erica answers me as she smiles at the guest. She is no longer combing her hair.

"She's like a painting at a museum. You can only look at her right now, but who knows what will happen when the artist is done with her? Maybe then you'll get to be the first to peel off her plain dress," Ms. Bertha answers the gentleman who is watching me, "Walburga, go up to your room. You've been seen enough," She turns to me, and I hurry to get up from the sofa and walk towards the stairs, grimacing in pain when I feel Erica's fingers pinching my thighs vigorously.

When I reach the stairs I stop and look back, caressing my aching thighs. Erica leans back alone on the sofa, her legs crossed, her light camisole exposing her bare thighs. She continues to comb herself and ignores the two men sitting on the sofa before her. They watch her and laugh while Ms. Bertha stands beside them and lights herself another cigarette, looking at me, and I hurry to go up the stairs.

"I want to be somebody. I won't be a maid, on my knees all my life," I say to myself later as I kneel barefoot in my tiny room and scrub the floor with a cloth, cleaning the dust from the wooden floor.

From outside, I hear the other girls' laughter. Earlier, I heard Erica passing in the corridor, talking to one of the men. But I mustn't think about them. My fingers tightly grip the rag as I clean. I've never had my own room and my own bed. I've always had sisters sleep in the same bed, and then Christina.

I arrange my clothes on the wooden bookcase, lie in bed, blow on the candle, and wrap myself in the woolen blanket. I miss Christina's breaths and the conversations with her. I will make my way out of this hostel. Mr. Klimt will invite me to sleep with him and hug me all night long.

***

"*Fuego*, lean back," he says to me a few days later, and I lean on my hand, sitting on the large bed in his studio. Erica hadn't spoken to me since the day at Bertha's hostel. In the days that followed, she ignored me every time I saw her laughing in the hallway with the other girls and tried to talk to her and explain.

"Just a little further back," he tells me quietly, and I lay down on the bed and run my fingers through my short hair. Outside, it has started to snow, and I arrived at his place shivering from the cold, covering myself as much as possible with my ragged, plain coat. Even in my little room at Bertha's, I'm cold at night, but I don't dare ask her for another blanket. I know she'll ask me to pay for it.

"Open your legs a little," Mr. Klimt says, and I do as he asks, trying not to tremble. Even though his studio is heated, I'm still cold lying naked in front of him. But I don't care. I like being with him more than in Ms. Bertha's hostel. Last night I so badly wanted to go to Christina's room, not to be by myself, but she was busy with a guest, and I was left sitting alone on the chair in the corridor, listening to the sound of the bed springs creaking from within her room. Maybe she won't be busy tonight, and we can lie in bed together like we used to.

"Look in my direction, don't move now," I hear and turn my gaze to him, remaining steady. His hand holding the pencil moves as he concentrates on the paper, like the hand of the farmer that reaps the wheat while holding a sickle. Only occasionally does he glance at me, his blue eyes fixed on my body, before he returns to focus on the paper attached to the drawing board. He makes me feel secure, and his hug warms my body, like the big metal stove that was in our house when I was a girl, before we moved to Vienna. During the cold winter days, I used to sit beside the stove and read the books that Dad had brought me. I didn't care about Mom's complaints, and I wasn't cold at all, just like when Mr. Klimt is lying on top of me and covering my body. My hand reaches up and strokes my short hair again. I love the name *Fuego*.

"*Fuego*, don't move. Now you've ruined my drawing," He tears off the brown paper from the drawing board and throws it on the floor. I watch him as he goes and brings new paper. The unfinished drawing is on the floor, with sharp pencil lines of my body. It's strange to look at myself the way I'm reflected in his eyes. My bare thighs and breasts are so prominent. When will he draw me a real picture with my clothes on, like I saw him draw the Lady?

Her unfinished painting leans on the wall at the corner of the studio. It is large and almost reaches the ceiling. He's hardly made any progress since the first time I saw it here. Only the painting background got additions of yellow spots as if they were drops of gold.

I get up from the bed and walk barefoot towards the painting, approach and examine it closely, bringing my face close to the stretched canvas. The smell of fresh oil paint rises in my nose. I stroke the canvas with my finger, feeling the texture of the paint. He will draw me like that too. I know he will.

"*Fuego*, you need to go back to your place," I feel his arms wrap around me as he clings to me from behind and hugs me. I can feel the warmth of his body despite the smock he is wearing.

"Must we?" I put my hands on his.

"Yes, we must. The bed is waiting for you," He turns his gaze to the bed, and I go over and sit on it. Maybe he'll join me, and we'll hug? But he returns to the easel and attaches a clean drawing paper. He has not invited me to his actual bed yet, but

I know he will soon take me there, and we won't just be in the studio. He makes me feel special.

"How do you want me now?" I lie on my stomach and look at him. From the big window, I can see the gray sky. It has stopped snowing.

"Pretend you're reading a book," He leaves the room, returns after a minute holding a book with a yellow cover, and places it in my hand, "Open the book, lean on your elbows, as if you're reading," he arranges my hands in front of the open book and moves away to the drawing board.

I look at the first page and read the name 'Oscar Wilde,' then I flip through the pages.

"*Fuego*, don't move," I hear him but I don't respond. I'm reading the first poem written in the book.

"Tread lightly, she is near, Under the snow..." my lips whisper the words.

"You can read?" he asks. The studio seems quiet without the sounds of the pencil sketching.

"Speak gently, she can hear..." I read the second line.

"I didn't know you could read," I hear his footsteps as he comes closer, sitting next to me on the wide bed, "please go on, you have a beautiful voice. It's nice to listen to you."

"The daisies grow..." I continue reading the poem to him, as I feel his big, warm fingers caressing my back. I turn to him.

"Please, keep reading to me," he continues to hug me while I whisper the words to him until I can't take it anymore, and I close my eyes and cling to him, wanting him to hug me fiercely and do whatever he wants to me. But then I hear the doorbell ring and my eyes open, looking at him.

"Tell whoever it is that I'm not here," he whispers to me and smiles.

"I can't do that," I answer. Does he really want me to answer the door naked? Is he ready for other people to see me in his house?

The doorbell rings again.

"Don't run away," he says to me and gets up, hurries to put on his smock, the one he took off just a moment ago, and goes to the door.

I hear the door open, then talking. He's talking to a woman. I'm not sure, but it could be Erica's voice. I can't hear what they are saying, but I feel the winter wind that enters through the open door and reaches his studio, making me shiver as I lie naked on the wide bed.

What if he lets her in? What if she sees me like this? I want to cover myself with the bedspread or wear my dress, but I'm ashamed. What will he think of me? I am his model.

I sit on the corner of the bed, against the wall, and hug myself. The speaking voices continue, and with them, the cold wind that make me shiver. It's a woman's voice. I'm sure of that. The door closes, and the wind stops. Did he let her in? Will she enter the room in a moment, or has she left? I huddle in the corner and hug myself even tighter.

"Where were we?" I hear him and look up. He is standing beside the bed, wearing his smock, and watching me. He didn't let the woman in.

"You were just planning to draw me reading a book," I lay down on my stomach again and hold the book, but after a moment, I sit back. Who was the woman at the door? Is he drawing her too?

"*Fuego*, what happened?"

"The woman who was at the door, does she want you to draw her?" I can't help myself, even though It's impolite to ask.

"Does it matter?" He remained standing by the bed.

"No, it doesn't," I stay seated and look at the floor.

"It doesn't matter because I'm here with you now," he sits down next to me and puts his hand on my shoulder, hugging me, "and when I'm with you, it's just us here in this room, me and you, and not any of the women I've painted in the past or will paint in the future."

"Do you like to draw them?" I ask him, although what I really want to ask is whether he hugs them with his warm hands, the same way he hugs me.

"*Fuego*, I like to bring you in and draw you. That's the only thing that matters, not all the others," he approaches and kisses my cheek, "Do you like the touch of my pencil and my fingers over your body?"

"Yes, I do," I kiss him back. I mustn't think about if he kisses or hugs other women.

"So let's continue with these pleasant moments," he caresses my hair, "You are so special, with your pale body, contrasted with your red hair and delicate lips," he gently touches them with his finger, "that read poems to me."

"You wanted to draw me reading a book," I lie down on my stomach again, hold the book and open it, begin to read him a new poem. I won't think about the others. I will be the most special in his eyes with the poem I read to him.

The new dress I ordered is already waiting for me in the store. Next time, I will wear it for him.

❦

"Miss, could you turn around, please?" The saleswoman at the dress shop asks me a few days later, and I turn around and look at myself in the mirror. Then I spin quickly, feeling the hem of my dress rise as if I were a flower beginning to spread its petals in the spring. No one has ever treated me with such respect.

"It is so beautiful, thank you," I look at myself in the mirror again. The dress is light pink, with simple lines and a white lace collar. A thick waist belt replaces the uncomfortable corset. My fingers stroke the draped fabric over my thighs, feeling its softness.

"We're done, Miss," the older saleswoman smiles at me, "Shall we pack it for you?"

"No, thank you," I answer her as I continue to look at myself. He will be so happy to see my new dress. We haven't seen each other in a few days.

"Miss?" I hear and turn to her. She is standing behind the counter next to the register, waiting for me.

"Sorry, I forgot," I go to my small bag next to my old dress and take out my wallet, counting the silver coins. I'm almost out of money, now that Ms. Bertha takes more from me. He also hasn't paid me the last time I was with him. He just whispered pleasant words to me as he lays beside me on the big bed in his studio after drawing my naked body.

"Thank you," I count the money in her hand, watching as her fingers close over the shiny coins bearing the emperor's portrait. Mr. Klimt will pay me next time. There is no need to worry. My hand caressesthedress's smooth fabric before I wear my simple coat over it and hold my old dress in my hand.

"Enjoy your new dress," the saleswoman says as I leave the store, and I smile and thank her as I step out. Despite the sun outside, there is a cold wind, and I wrap myself in a coat and walk to the boulevard. I will save the tram ticket. Today I will be the most beautiful girl in his eyes.

Inside his garden, after I close the iron gate, I take off my plain coat and hold it in my hand, along with my old dress. I stand for a moment and look around, thinking what to do with them. Finally, I place them beside the small wooden shed at the corner of the garden. The cold that makes me shiver doesn't bother me as I walk to the front door. I hope he is looking at me from the window.

"Wally, come inside. You're almost naked," he hugs me and pulls me into the warm house.

"This is for you," I whisper to him, "this dress is for you."

"You are much more beautiful than any dress," he holds my hand and takes me with him to the studio, "The dress is just an unnecessary decoration that hides your delicate body's curves," he stands in front of me at the center of the studio and unbuttons the wide belt, throwing it on the floor. "Your body should be free of unnecessary fabric protection shields," his fingers open the dress buttons one by one, ignoring my breasts that are slowly exposed. "You don't need to hide from the world." He bends down at my feet, and his hands grip the fabric as he pulls it up. I lift my hands and he pulls the dress over my head, leaving me in my white panties, then his fingers remove those as well. "Now you are perfect, a Greek goddess with a fire in her hair and a clear blue lake in her eyes." He leads me to the bed and arranges me in the position that suits him. I look at my dress lying on the floor beside my panties. He doesn't want to hide me from the world. He will reveal me one day.

"This is how I want you, don't move," he caresses my hair, leaves me naked on the bed, approaches his easel, and starts drawing me.

Time passes, and I feel my body aching as I remain in the same position. I keep looking at the Lady's painting. It is almost finished. He is so talented. Soon he will paint me too, like the Lady, maybe wearing my new dress. But then, a bell ring makes me look at him. Is it Erica again, or the same woman who came to visit the last time?

"Just in time," he smiles at me, and I sit naked in front of him. What does he mean by 'Just in time'? Will he let someone in here? I feel myself blushing.

"Who is at the door?" I ask him.

"A friend," he answers. I get up from bed and go to put on my dress. Why didn't he tell me someone was coming?

"Wear this. It's more comfortable," Mr. Klimt takes a smock similar to his out of the wooden box, and hands it to me, "We wouldn't want to let the guest wait for us out in the cold," he smiles at me, "and please go back to lying on the bed, in the position you were in," he turns and leaves the studio, leaving me alone in the room holding the simple smock. I quickly put it on, ignoring my dress and panties that are thrown on the floor, and lie down on the bed again, trying to recover the position and looking at the Lady's face painted on the large painting that leans against the wall. Why did he surprise me like this? I hear their footsteps on the floor.

"Wally, meet Mr. Egon Schiele, the most talented young painter I know," he says, and I turn to look at him.

He is much younger than Mr. Klimt, only a few years older than me, and has thick quaffed black hair. His face clean-shaven, unlike all the men who usually flaunt their beards and moustaches, and he is wearing a white button-down shirt and a tie.

"Nice to meet you," I smile at him and look at his tailored brown pants, so different from the simple smock on Mr. Klimt's body. I, too, am now wrapped in such a simple smock. I know I should stand and shake his hand, but Mr. Klimt asked me to stay in the same position.

"Nice to meet Wally, the model of the great master," Mr. Schiele approaches the bed and climbs on it. I can feel the mattress move as he approaches me and does not shake my hand but instead kisses my cheek, as is the French custom. His aftershave smells like pine trees. "Don't tell anyone, but you are the most beautiful woman I have ever seen," he whispers to me before he gets up from the bed and walks to Mr. Klimt, who is watching us. I feel myself blushing and look down again, examining his polished leather shoes. Mr. Klimt's simple shoes step on my pink dress and panties that are thrown on the floor. He must not have noticed.

"Do not disturb yourselves. I am just visiting for a moment," he says to Mr. Klimt.

"I'm drawing her. It's a practice for a new big painting," Mr. Klimt replies.

"Can I see?"

"Certainly," Mr. Klimt invites him behind the easel. They are both standing behind it, looking at me and whispering. It embarrasses me that Mr. Schiele sees the drawing of my naked body. Does Mr. Klimt show my drawings to other people? I close my spread legs, even though the smock covers them anyway. The fabric's touch on my body is unpleasant.

"Can I try something?" Mr. Schiele asks him.

"Yes, of course,"

Mr. Schiele approaches and again gets on the bed next to me.

"May I?" he asks me, and I nod, even though I don't know his intentions. Mr. Klimt is watching us and protecting me.

Mr. Schiele puts his hand on my thigh and folds it. The touch of his hand is warm, and for a moment, I flinch. What does Mr. Klimt think of this? I look at him, but he is just standing by the easel with his hands folded, smiling at me.

"Give me your hand," Mr. Schiele says, and I hold his palm as he directs mine and places my hand on my thighs in the correct position. I already know how to free my body and let them shape it as they want.

"Your red hair is wonderful, like a fresh summer cherry waiting to be tasted," Egon quietly says before he gets off the bed, "Don't move, that's how I want you," he stands next to the easel, "Here, I can imagine her naked like this," he says to Mr. Klimt while he starts drawing me. How can he imagine me? I belong to Klimt.

"Her naked body is much more beautiful than your imagination," Mr. Klimt replies.

"Will you let me draw her in my studio?"

"You should find your own models. She belongs to me, at least until I finish learning every curve of her body," Mr. Klimt answers him while Mr. Schiele continues to draw, his eyes examining me non-stop.

"When is your exhibition?" Mr. Schiele puts down the pencil and walks towards the Lady's painting, examining it, standing with his back to me.

"In two months, I have more work to do on some paintings."

"Will the exhibition take place at the Vienna Secession?"

"I don't think so. All the artists there are pompous sticks in the mud who don't understand art," Mr. Klimt answers him, "They're all old men who refuse to retire, spending their time in cafés, arguing about art instead of creating it."

"Only you lock yourself here in your studio," Egon laughs and looks in my direction, "although I can understand why."

"Young Miss Wally is certainly a worthy substitute for boring conversations about art and what dress the duchess wore to the ball, and whether or not Mr. Freud's theories about psychoanalysis and dreams are real." Mr. Klimt says, "Or whether the emperor will send more army corps to threaten the Russians in the East," he says and turns back to the easel, continuing to draw me. "What about you? How are your paintings progressing? Aren't you thinking of an exhibition?"

"I'm waiting for you to give me your model, and then I'll have a muse for an exhibition."

"To have her, you will have to try harder than flatter her with those nice words you whispered in her ear," Mr. Klimt laughs, and I smile to myself. I like Mr. Klimt's compliment and the fact that Mr. Schiele desires me like that.

"Nice to meet you, Red Cherry Wally," Egon bows later and heads for the door, saying goodbye to Mr. Klimt as well.

"Wally, could you escort Mr. Schiele to the door and look for the cat? I haven't seen him since morning." Mr. Klimt asks me, and I get up from the bed and go with Mr. Schiele to the door.

"Would you escort me to the gate?" He asks me.

I can feel the cold, scratching touch of the gravel on my bare feet as I walk silently beside him on the path. "Cat, cat..." I whisper. I can still smell his aftershave but think of Mr. Klimt.

"Here you are," he says and walks over to the side of the hut, picking up the cat lying on top of my old coat and dress that I had placed on the ground earlier. "Take it." He puts the cat between my hands and continues to caress my palm.

"Thanks," I say to him, "It was nice to meet you,"

"I'm sure we'll meet again," he says and again brings his lips to my cheeks, kissing them as is the French custom, "Your Bohemian smock is beautiful," he whispers to me, "they always say that Bohemian women don't wear anything underneath," He kisses my other check. I feel the smock's simple fabric touching my naked body, "Welcome to Klimt's palace," he smiles at me as he moves away and opens the black iron gate, "You are the most beautiful representative of his harem."

Chapter Six

The Bohemian

"Christina," I knock on her bedroom door late at night, "Christina, are you awake?" I had been up for hours in my tiny room, turning from side to side. "Christina," I gently tap the door and look to the sides. The corridor is dark and quiet. All the clients who were here tonight have already left, wearing the coats they hung at the entrance and disappeared to the quiet street, and the girls who had sat on the couches on the entrance floor have slowly gathered in their rooms, leaving the hallway full of memories of their bare thighs and cigarette smoke. "Christina," I knock on the door again and sit on the floor in the dark hallway, leaning against the cold wall. I don't want to go back to my lonely room.

"What happened, Rusty? Is everything alright?" She opens the door slightly. I can see her silhouette in the dim light. What can I tell her that won't make her laugh at me?

"I wanted to ask you something," I get up from the floor and stand up.

"What?" She continues to hold the door opened to a crack.

"Can you let me in?"

"Come inside," she opens the door and walks in, and I follow her and close the door behind me. In the dark, I hear the creaking of the bed springs when she goes back to sitting or lying down in her bed, "Rusty, get under the blanket," she says, and I grope it with my hands, get into the bed and lie next to her. Her bed is warm and cozy, not cold like mine.

"Christina, what is Bohemia?" I ask her after I cover myself, feeling wrapped in the wool blanket.

"Is this to do with the painter, the one you're with?"

"No," I whisper, "I'm not with him. I heard two people on the street talking about Bohemia."

"I know you're with him," she laughs quietly, "He must be one of them. The Bohemians are strange artists. They call themselves modern and create new art unlike that which others painted before. They always sit in their cafés, arguing about art and allowing themselves to paint pictures that shouldn't be painted."

"What kind of pictures are not allowed to be painted?" I force my legs together. Is this what he's doing to me?

"Paintings of naked women. Surely you didn't see those at the lady's house. Ms. Bertha says you don't work there anymore."

"No, I don't work there anymore," I remember the large paintings in the lady's house. In her room, there was one of flowers painted as colored dots, but the wall of the main staircase was decorated with elegant paintings of men, looking at me with a scary look. "I stopped working there because the painter asked me to model for him," I say.

"Do you think he cares about you? Or whether you work or not?"

"He cares about me," I keep whispering. I don't want to tell her that he also pays me.

"He only cares about his art and that he can draw you any way he wants, all those pictures that shouldn't be drawn."

"He's not like that," I say, feeling myself raise my voice. I know he loves me even though he hasn't paid me in a while.

"Shhh..." she whispers to me, "You'll wake Bertha downstairs, even though the door is closed. She has rabbit ears. She hears everything."

"Sorry." I twirl the blanket with my fingers. I don't want Ms. Bertha to come and kick me out of here.

"So your painter is not one of Bohemia?"

"He's not like them. He's nice."

"I'm sure he's not asking you to undress," she laughs in the dark.

"I only do what I want in front of him. I don't have to. He cares about me."

"Of course, here at Bertha's hostel, we only do what we want with the men," She whispers to me and pauses for a moment. "As long as they pay and are satisfied, then Ms. Bertha is also satisfied."

"Are they allowed to do that? Are they allowed to ask for whatever they want?" I think of the large bed in his studio, imagine him standing next to the easel and looking at me and my spread thighs. My hands make sure the woolen blanket covers my thighs well.

"The men who come here or your painter?"

"Both," I answer after some time.

"They're men, so they're allowed."

"Why is it like this? Why are men allowed, but we're not?"

"Because that's what they've gotten us used to," she laughs bitterly. "They taught us that it's better for us to listen to them."

"But he also paints respectable ladies," I think about the bedspread's feel against my naked body as I lie there. Do ladies also come to his studio?

"They don't paint them like that. The ladies buy the paintings from them for a lot of money."

"And us?"

"We are the women of the forbidden art. That's why they come here, to Bertha's hostel, because they are allowed to do whatever they want with us."

"We're not whores," I whisper, knowing he cares about me. I'm not a whore.

"You're such a little girl. Even though you've already been with him, you still remain a little girl who understands nothing."

"They also talked about one called Freud," I say quietly, wanting Christina not to think I'm a little girl. I will show her that I am grown up and understand adult conversations.

"I haven't heard of him. Maybe he goes to someone else's hostel," Christina laughs, "Is he a painter?"

"I don't know. I don't think so. He's doing something called psychoanalysis. That's what I heard," I answer awkwardly. "Mr. Klimt said I was more interesting than him."

"Rusty, when you're naked in front of him, obviously you're more interesting than Mr. Freud, even though I have no idea who he is."

"Do you think psychoanalysis is an art?"

"Where are all these questions coming from? Don't you know we're women, and we shouldn't ask so many questions? You should know men don't like smart women. Neither does Bertha. They want us to know our place."

"Sorry, I apologize," I whisper into the darkness, "I'll ask fewer questions."

"You shouldn't upset her, but I assume you already know that."

"Yes, I know," It's warm here with her under the blanket. I missed talking to her. "Christina, can I sleep here with you tonight?"

"No, you can't sleep with me tonight."

"Please, I'll try not to move."

"Rusty, you're not a little girl anymore. You need to get used to being alone, like everyone else here at Bertha's hostel." She says, "We are prostitutes. We are left alone in bed at the end of the night."

I want to shout that I'm not a whore, but I'm afraid to wake Ms. Bertha. I hear the creak of the bed springs, and although she doesn't chase me away, I feel her turn her back to me.

Without saying a word, I remove the blanket and get out of her bed, groping with my hands in the dark and opening the door of her room.

"Good night," I hear her say to me, but I don't answer. Quietly, I return to my tiny room and sit on the steel bed. I'm not a prostitute. I'm a model he hugs and loves, even though he pays me money.

My fingers reach for something in the dark, searching for the small bag I hide in the closet, and I feel the silver coins, counting them. I only have four coins left. I need to ask him for more.

⁂

"Cat, good morning," I bend down, pick up the chubby cat, stroke its soft fur, and close the iron gate behind me. I don't know how to tell him I need more money. The gravel's sound under my feet reminds me of the horses' hooves carrying the rich carriages across the city streets at a gallop. Those carriages pulled by four or six horses. At the door, I stop and take a breath, as my hand continues to caress the purring cat. Mr. Klimt will give me money. I don't have to worry. My hand reaches out and presses the porcelain bell. He has an electric bell at home.

"Good morning. Can I help you?" A woman opens the door and looks at me. She is older than me, about thirty-five, has curly brown hair, and wears a smock similar to Mr. Klimt's, though hers is flowery and not full of colored flecks.

"Sorry, I must have the wrong address," I feel myself blushing. I was sure he was waiting for me.

"Emilie, who is that at the door?" I hear Mr. Klimt's voice.

"A young lady who got the wrong address," she replies loudly as she continues to watch me, her eyes scanning my hair and eyes.

"Excuse me, Miss, I apologize. Have a good day," I say and turn around, starting to walk on the gravel. The noise of my steps sounds like the screeching of the steam train as it stops before reaching the station.

"Miss," I hear her.

"Yes?" I stop and turn around.

"May I?" She points to the cat lying in my lap as she walks, reaches out, takes it from my hands, and hugs it. Her fingers caress the cat as she gives me a triumphant smile, and she turns and walks back towards the house's open door, her floral smock moving with every step, like a spring field in the wind. Why did I think he cared about me? I turn and walk to the gate, wiping my teary eyes and ignoring the sound of footsteps on the gravel. My fingers slip on the gate latch several times as I try to open it.

"*Fuego*, where are you going?" I feel his hands wrap around me while his big body clings to me from behind, "Don't run away from me." He continues to hug me tightly. I wipe my eyes and turn in his direction, hugging and resting my head on his chest, feeling the warmth of his body and ignoring the rough fabric of his smock. Who is this woman?

Gently, he closes the latch of the iron gate and holds my hand, taking me with him towards the house, and I follow him like a little puppy tied on a leash to his fingers holding my palm.

"This is Ms. Emilie Flöge. She's with me," he tells me as he closes the door behind us and takes me by hand to the studio. "I've been waiting for you and your red hair," he stands with me in the center of the studio.

"And what about her? Is she one of your models?"

"Emilie?" He caresses my cheek, but I turn my head away from his palm and look at the large paintings leaning on the wall.

"Yes," I nod.

"Sometimes I draw her too. I used to draw her more," he doesn't try to caress me again. Why did he ask me to come to his house?

"I want to go," I tell him, walking towards the door. I need him to ask me to stay. But he doesn't say anything, and I turn my back to him and approach the door. When I reach it, I stop and put my hand on the door handle. I'm afraid to go out. What if he doesn't chase after me? It's so cold outside.

"Wally, stop," I hear him and his steps approaching. I feel his hands wrap around me, but my hand continues to hold the door handle.

"I want to go."

"Don't go, my dear Wally," he hugs me tightly.

"You love a lot of women, not just me," I say. I need to know that he cares about me.

"My beautiful Wally," he kisses my neck, "I've met a lot of women. Emilie is one of them," he caresses my cheek, and again I turn to the other side, but he continues to caress me, and I feel the heat of his palm. "I know I have other women, and I know it's not easy for you," he continues, "but that's who I am. I'm a man who loves many women, and it doesn't mean I don't care about you."

"And what are you doing with them?"

"They're not important. What's important is that I'm hugging you now. That's what's important. You're now in my home. That's what's important,"

"Emilie is also at your house now,"

"Emilie is special in another way, but no other is like you. No one else has such beautiful red hair like you have. Please go inside to the studio with me," he releases me from his hug and holds my hand, taking me after him back to the studio. I don't want to walk the cold streets looking for work again. I want him to love and keep hugging me.

I look around in the studio—just him and I in the room. I don't see Ms. Emilie. The cat is not there either. I sit on the bed without him asking, remove my dress and underwear and lie back naked in front of him. I want to be the most beautiful in his eyes. My fingers caress my hair in gentle, seductive movement like I've seen the girls in the hostel do.

"Don't move. This is exactly how I want you," he says, hurrying to stand behind the easel, and I smile a little and close my eyes. I will be the one he loves the most.

"Have you decided what paintings you are taking to the exhibition?" I hear someone ask after a while and open my eyes. Miss Emilie is standing next to Mr. Klimt and talking to him while looking at my nude drawing. How long has she been standing like that, watching me? Why did I close my eyes for so long?

"I'll take the portrait of Fritza Riedler. She agreed to lend the painting to the exhibition."

"Don't you put paintings up for sale?" She places her hand on his arm, stroking it. I feel so exposed. She is deliberately caressing him in front of me.

"I have the painting of the pear tree. Wally, don't move. Keep your thighs open" his blue eyes look at me again. I want to cover myself with my hands or the black and white striped bedspread. Did she sew the bedspread for him?

"Maybe you should concentrate on finishing Adele's painting. It could be wonderful for the exhibition with its golden colors," she moves away from him and approaches the bed, standing over me, "They won't let you show your nude drawings there anyway, not after last time's scandal."

"The Secession's board are a bunch of gutless old men who want to please the emperor," he answers her, "They won't notice good art even if it's placed under their noses."

"After fighting with them last year, you should be glad they invited you to show your paintings in their gallery," she replies and bends down for a moment, sliding her hand over the bedspread before returning to stand beside him, "And besides," she smiles at him, "You're also a bit bloated and old yourself," she clings to him. Her fingers stroke his hair, "And you know the ladies like you to paint them for good money, much more than you like to draw nude young girls here at the studio," she kisses the back of his neck and laughs, "At least this one has red pubic hair, you have to paint it in color."

I blush, wanting to cover myself with my palm, but I can't. I must be professional. I'll show her that she can't hurt me. I close my eyes but can still imagine them both standing and looking at me and Miss Emilie's hand stroking his short brown curly hair, the way I used to stroke Daddy's hair when I was a child. My splayed thighs hurt, and I want him to stop drawing so I can get up and dressed, but I don't move. He didn't tell me he was done. She won't beat me.

"That too will come. Maybe I'll paint Wally, maybe even for an exhibition," I hear him answer her and open my eyes, looking at them. I don't care anymore that I'm naked in front of her and that I have strange colored pubic hair. "Maybe I'll combine it with other models. I'll call the painting 'Virgin'" he says to her.

"She's probably not a virgin anymore," Miss Emilie laughs, kissing him on the lips and leaving the room. I close my legs, covering my pubic hair.

"Wally, get back into position. I haven't finished drawing you and the red pubic hair that you're hiding now."

I lie back on the bedspread again and spread my legs. I won't let her hurt me. The main thing is that he said he might paint me. Maybe my painting will appear in the exhibition.

❦

"Miss, may I help you?" The salesman at the newspaper stand asks me. A woman shouldn't stand in the street and read a newspaper.

"I'm just looking around," I answer him and continue to read the newspaper headlines. In large black words, they state that the emperor will recruit more army corps to stand against the Russian, French, and English alliance. The next time I come to Mr. Klimt, I will talk to him about something that will make him more interested in me. That way, he will want to paint me in a real picture, not a simple drawing. My eyes scan the pile of books, looking for a familiar title, but all I know are children's books that my dad used to read to me. I can't find a book of poetry with the name of the poet Oscar Wilde, like the one Mr. Klimt read to me then.

"Miss?" The salesperson approaches and stands next to me. His black beard smells of cheap and stinky tobacco, "Is there anything special you are interested in?" I can also smell the sour smell of his sweat.

"How much is this?" I point to a green journal hanging between a newspaper reporting on the preparations for the Russian front and a magazine with a woman wearing a summer dress on its cover.

"This magazine? Are you sure, Miss? It's not for you," he holds and hands over the simple green journal while smiling at me, his palm trying to touch mine.

"Yes," I step back from him and look at the cover. I recognize the name 'Professor Sigmund Freud' printed on it.

"For you, Miss, this magazine is free," he extends his hand and touches my palm once again.

"Thanks, but I insist on paying," I move my hand away from his. I want only Mr. Klimt to touch me, "How much is it?" I pull out my wallet, even though I wasn't preparing to purchase the magazine. I don't have enough money, but I want only Mr. Klimt to be proud of me. I will read the magazine and understand what the bohemians talk about in their cafés. When he invites me to go with him, I can join their conversation.

Outside the hostel's door, I stop for a moment, placing my hand on the steel handle. From inside, I can hear the music emanating from the phonograph Ms. Bertha recently purchased for the visiting guests. She placed it in the corner of the room on a wooden table, and every evening the girls turn the handle before they sit, facing the gentlemen. Maybe I should continue walking the streets for a while? I was still holding on to the magazine I had just purchased. I will go straight up to my tiny bedroom and try to read; despite the noises the girls are making from the hallway.

"Good evening, Walburga," Ms. Bertha greets me as I enter, "What have you got in your hand?"

"Something I found on the street," I hide the magazine behind my back, not wanting her to know that I'm reading something that isn't meant for women. Still, she reaches out her hand while looking at me, and I hand her the magazine.

I watch as she reads the cover and opens the first page while her other hand holds the cigarette that emits a thin line of smoke into the room.

"Is that what you're interested in? Mr. Freud and his theory of dreams?" She closes the thin magazine.

"No, Ms. Bertha, I told you I found it lying in the street and happened to pick it up."

"Good thing," She looked at me, "You'd better be interested in your rent and not in modern ideas. You're already two days late in payment." She hands me the magazine and walks towards the entrance, probably to turn on the lamp outside the front door.

"Yes, Ms. Bertha," I hold the magazine and cross the waiting room towards the stairs, passing Erica, who is just getting up and approaching the phonograph to turn the metal handle again. I look at the reddish phonograph horn, which looks like a flower spreading its petals into the dim room, filling the air with soft music of a woman singing about her fiancé.

"Good evening, Copper," Erica turns from the phonograph and approaches me, standing in front of me.

"Good evening, Erica," I answer, trying to walk past her. We haven't spoken since that time she pinched me.

"You're hardly here. Have you found a better place to be?" She moves and blocks my way again.

"No, I live here," I stand up and answer her. It's not my fault that Mr. Klimt chose me.

"I think you took something that should have been mine. How is his bed in the studio? Are you comfortable lying on it?"

"I don't care about that," I look down even though I should have looked her in the eyes and told her it's none of her business.

"Because as I remember, you were quite shy the first time we went there together, and if I hadn't taken you with me, you wouldn't have gone at all." She comes closer to me, and I can smell the sweet rose perfume on her body.

"I wasn't ashamed, and the fact that you chose to undress in front of him is your problem," I finally answer her and try to get around her, but she moves and blocks my path once again.

"Really? And you don't undress in front of him?" She raises her voice.

"That is none of your business."

"It certainly is my business, because I should have had him, not you. You should have been here wearing a sheer camisole and garters in front of Ms. Bertha and the men who come here every night," she yells at me.

"I thought you enjoyed that. That's what you always say to all the girls, that you take care of men and make them happy," I yell back at her. She has no right to insult what's happening between me and Mr. Klimt.

"Really? Then come join me. We'll be here together," she grabs my arm and pulls me after her to the floral sofa, forcing me to sit down, "Come hang out with me and the men who will soon arrive instead of squatting with the famous painter for money, be a whore like us."

"I'm not a whore. I'm a model," I hit her with the magazine I'm holding. "Mr. Klimt loves me."

"You're just like us, even if you make yourself smarter," she grabs my short hair and pulls it, and I scream in pain, "What is this magazine?" She snatches it from my hand and gets up from the couch, walking away from me.

"Give it back!" I stand up after her.

"There you go, you can have it," She rips pages from the magazine and throws them at me, "Just because you can read doesn't mean you can look down at us," She screams at me and tears the remaining pages. I rush towards her, trying to pull the torn magazine from her hand, and we both fall on the stairs.

"What is going on here?" I feel a hand grabbing my hair and pulling me, and I scream in pain and get up from the floor. Erica screams, too. "What are you doing?" Ms. Bertha stands over us and continues to pull at our hair.

"She started it," Erica answers her, her face full of tears, "He chose her."

"That's not true," I reply to Ms. Bertha, my head aching, struggling to catch my breath. A few girls come out into the corridor and are looking at us from the top of the stairs.

"I don't care," She shouts, "You," she slaps Erica, "Go to your room and get ready. Look at yourself. Guests are coming here soon. And you," She slaps me hard and I scream in pain, "Pick up your papers from the floor and go to your room. I

141

don't want to see you downstairs; you still owe me money. And you," She looks up at the girls, "Return to your rooms immediately."

I hear pattering feet up in the corridor, but I don't look up. I get down on my knees and pick up the torn and crumpled papers from the floor, trying to straighten them out. I don't belong here. I belong in Klimt's world. In the background, the phonograph continues playing, and the singer sings a song about a lover who has abandoned her.

⁂

The next afternoon, I stand outside his garden, my hand resting on the iron gate, and I look at the path leading to the house. I need to ask him for money. I know he just forgot the last time, and there are no hidden intentions. He knew I needed to be paid when he arrived at Ms. Bertha's hostel to choose a model for his drawings. I walked around the city all morning and tried to look for work unsuccessfully. Although there are leaflets on the street message boards calling for men to enlist in the emperor's army, few do, and there is no need for working hands, not even in the market where I was sleeping that night.

I take a deep breath, open the black gate, and walk to the door. The gravel under my feet sounds like the squealing of the rats on the ground floor of our building before Mom threw me out. They would come out of their holes after dark and scare me. He didn't invite me today, but he is always happy to see me. I ring the bell and wait, breathing slowly.

"My *Fuego*," he comes out and stands close to me.

"I didn't know if it was okay for me to come today," I look up into his beautiful blue eyes.

"I'm always happy to see you," He reaches out and strokes my hair, and remains standing in the doorway.

"Shall we go in?" I'm holding his hand.

"No, my *Fuego*. Today's no good," He places his big palm on my cheek, and I feel his warm fingers, "I am dedicating myself to someone else this morning. She will be here soon."

"Sorry, I apologize," I take a step back and turn around, starting to walk towards the gate. I knew he had others. I knew he wasn't only with me. I knew this would come. I keep walking to the gate, my hand touching my cheek, feeling the place where he caressed me. I want to turn around, run, lay myself at his feet, and beg him to let me in.

"*Fuego*, wait..." I hear him and turn around. I'm so pathetic.

"What, Mr. Klimt?" I wait for him as he approaches me.

"Another day, my *Fuego*, just not today," He tries to reach out again and stroke my hair, but I turn and walk quickly to the gate, the gravel at my feet sounding like the croaking of frogs along the Danube on summer nights. I don't care that he's painting someone else. I don't care that she's lying on the bed in his studio. My hand slips on the gate handle, and I linger for a moment. Maybe he will run and stop me, invite me in, but when I turn back and look for him, the path is empty. He has walked back to the house and has gone inside. What was I thinking? He is waiting for someone else. Could he have chosen Erica over me? The cold afternoon wind hits my face.

"Pssss... Psssss... Cat..." I see its tail peeking out from under the bush and approach it, bending down on my knees, "Psss sss... Psssss... Kitty, come to me."

My hands caress its warm fur, and I gather it onto my lap, continuing to sit between the bushes. I'll wait for a few minutes, maybe the woman who should come today won't arrive, and Mr. Klimt will come looking for me. I know it won't happen, but it's nice to sit here rather than return to the hostel.

The cold wind doesn't bother me, and I bring my face close to the cat's fur, sliding my cheek against its softness when I hear the iron gate and raise my face in panic. I shouldn't be here. What if he has invited Erica, and she sees me like this and tells him?

It takes me a second to recognize her, it has been a few months since the last time I saw her, and even then, it was only for a brief moment. She walks down the path in new brown leather shoes with a small heel and wears a fashionable burgundy dress and jacket. Her hands are protected with black gloves, and there is a matching black hat on her head. I can still see the black automobile driving away on the dirt road, filling the quiet street with an engine rattle and the smell of gasoline. Will she recognize me?

She watches me for a moment as she passes, and I look into her brown eyes. When I worked at her house as a maid, I was not allowed to look at her.

She doesn't say anything and continues walking on the path toward the house. I don't think she has recognized me at all. Maybe she didn't even notice me. I crouch in the bushes on the side of the path and look down, pet the cat, and listen to the purr of the automobile driving away. I must get out of here.

She'll tell Mr. Klimt that she saw me. Maybe it's good he knows that I care and am waiting here for him to let me in. Someday I, too, will have such a noisy automobile and such a fashionable dress with black gloves. I keep petting the cat.

"Red Cherry, why are you hiding with the cat?" I hear a voice and look up and see Mr. Egon Schiele. I feel I'm blushing.

"I happened to be passing by," I stand up as I continue to hold the cat, my free hand adjusting the hem of my dress. Why didn't I hear him? "Are you coming to visit Mr. Klimt?" I look at his black quaff. He is wearing a white button-down shirt again, with a tie and a brown jacket, so different from Mr. Klimt and his stained painted smock.

"No, I just got out of his house," he looks at me and smiles, "I was on a social visit. He wanted me to meet one of the city's high society ladies."

"Did Mr. Klimt say anything about me?" I ask, even though I should ask if the lady said she saw me.

"Gustav wasn't talking about you."

"He must have been busy painting."

"He was busy entertaining a lady who is fond of the Bohemia and has plenty of money to buy paintings." Mr. Schiele caresses the cat I'm still holding, his brown eyes examine me, and his hand touches mine as if by accident.

"Why did she come here?" I ask. I have to leave this house and Mr. Schiele who is standing close to me and petting the cat. I should not have left my job at her place as a maid. Ms. Bertha was right.

"They are not like us. They have status and money that allows them to purchase whatever they want, and the more special it is, the more they want it." He reaches out and touches my hair, "You've got some leaves caught in your red hair." He hands them to me.

"Thanks," I take them from his hand, feeling embarrassed.

"I'm on my way back to town. Will you join me?" He continues to hold my hand, and even though I want him to leave me alone, I nod and let the cat go, walking with him to the gate. But I keep our distance. Maybe Mr. Klimt is looking at us from the window and is not busy painting the wealthy lady who is fond of bohemians and has money to buy whatever she wants.

"I like your courage," he tells me after a while as we walk in silence, side by side. In the distance, I can see Schönbrunn Palace.

"What do you mean?" I turn my gaze to him. He is slightly taller than me.

"You have the courage to cut your hair short and not cover it with a hat."

"Simple women don't wear hats." I look at the palace gates. They are wide open, but guards are standing by them.

"Brave women don't wear hats, they let everyone see their red hair, how it shines in the sun."

"I'm not brave enough," I answer him, knowing he only said those things to please me.

"Gustav Klimt doesn't know how to appreciate the special cherry that you are. He loves respectable women and money too much. Come with me." He says, and without asking for my permission, he holds my hand and takes me to a peddler beside the palace gate who is selling apples. "Those two," he points to the reddest ones and pays the woman standing by the cart, "I hope you like apples," he hands me one after rubbing it with the hem of his white shirt.

"Thanks," I take the apple from his hand, but he keeps holding my palm longer than necessary. I take a bite of the sweet apple. No one has ever bought me anything before.

We continue walking down the boulevard, leaving the big yellow palace behind us. I let Mr. Schiele walk closer to me, side by side until I can feel his fingertips sometimes touching mine. I must remember that I belong to Mr. Klimt, even though he prefers rich women and money.

"Thank you very much, Mr. Schiele. I enjoyed your company." I say to him and stop by the opera house. I don't want him to accompany me to Bertha's hostel and see where I live. He won't think I'm so special if he sees her place.

"This is where you live?" He points to the magnificent opera building behind us, "And please call me Egon."

"I live in the old city. You probably won't want to bother accompanying me all the way, Egon," I smile at him.

"Miss Wally, now that you call me Egon, it would be an honor to walk with you all the way," he theatrically bowed before me.

"Call me Wally," I answer him, but I refuse to let him hold my hand as we cross the wide avenue, hurrying to pass between the tram cars and the horses pulling carriages. I will let him accompany me to Ms. Bertha's hostel's door, and we will part there.

"Thank you for the escort," I stop at Ms. Bertha's hostel, placing my hand on the door's copper handle.

"So this is where Gustav found you? I must see what's inside."

"Please, no," I put my hand on his chest to stop him. I don't want him to see the other girls and understand, if he hasn't realized it by now. "Please, this is a hostel for women only. The landlady doesn't like men."

"I promise to behave myself. I will only politely introduce myself as the gentleman who has escorted a beautiful lady to her stately hostel." He puts his hand on my hand that is holding the handle and opens the door, placing his palm gently on my waist as he lets me in before him into the dim space. What would Mr. Klimt think of me if he knew that Egon had accompanied me?

"Good evening, Walburga. Good evening, young gentleman. How can I help you?" Ms. Bertha turns to Egon as she stands behind the counter, blowing smoke from the cigarette in her hand. Is this his first time here, or does he also come here to choose women for painting and bedding?

"Good evening, Ms." Egon smiles at her and extends his hand politely, "I escorted this beautiful young lady here." He turns his gaze to Erica and Leisel sitting on the floral sofa, waiting for the customers to arrive, dressed in pink camisoles.

"Well, young man, your task has been successfully completed," Ms. Bertha answers and does not extend her hand. "Have a pleasant rest of the evening."

"May I stay a moment and look around?" He asks her, and I look down. I shouldn't have let him accompany me. For a moment, I thought he cared about me.

"It's not a showcase. Looking costs money," I hear Bertha's voice.

"Then I'll pay." I look up and see him take a wallet out of his jacket pocket, pull out a silver coin and place it on the counter. Ms. Bertha motions to the girls, and Leisel lingers from the couch to the floor and sits down as if she were a pink satin fabric that slowly falls along the length of her body while Erica starts stroking her light hair. They both look at Egon and smile. I start walking towards the stairs, passing him without saying goodbye. Tomorrow I will try to go to Mr. Klimt's house again. He promised he would paint me.

"I want to look at her," I hear him and stop.

"You can't look at her. Find other girls to look at."

"I only want her." My hand rests on the railing. I belong to Mr. Klimt.

"She's not for sale," Ms. Bertha answers him.

"I don't want to buy her. She's too beautiful for me to afford. I want to buy the right to look at her." Egon answers her. I turn around and see him approaching the counter and whispering something to Ms. Bertha. Does he really think I'm beautiful, or does he want me because I belong to Mr. Klimt? My fingers stroke my short red hair as I watch him pull out his wallet again. Erica and Leisel also look at him as Erica slowly unbuttons her pink camisole, letting her big breasts burst out. I continue stroking my hair in slow motion. I hope he doesn't choose Erica.

"Let's go," he walks towards me and holds my hand, pulling me, to my surprise, towards the entrance door, "I've bought the right to look at you."

'Welcome to the Vienna Prater Amusement Park' The big sign above the entrance gate reads. Behind it, I can hear voices of laughter and see the world-famous giant Ferris Wheel lit by thousands of electric lamps in the early evening.

I've never been here. We never had any money, and no one ever invited me here. I stop beside a target shooting booth and let some ladies and gentlemen pass us. Is it okay if I hang out with him? What are his intentions?

"Wally, what's wrong?" Egon stops and holds out his hand to me, inviting me to walk with him. The lights behind him sparkle, as if a shower of stars has surrounded him.

"Please take me back to Bertha's hostel," I look at him.

"What happened? Did I say something I shouldn't have?"

"You'll tell him, I know," I turn around and start retracing my steps.

"Who will I tell?" He walks beside me.

"Him. Mr. Klimt. Don't you understand? You are friends, and you will tell him, and it will destroy everything between us." I try to walk faster towards the bridge that crosses the river, back to the old city. "He pays me, he's my livelihood, but that doesn't mean I'm like the girls you saw there. I don't do things like that." I keep talking non-stop as I walk, moving aside when a horse-drawn carriage passes us. Why did I even let him buy this time with me from Ms. Bertha? He will destroy everything I have achieved.

"Wally, I'm not," he runs after me, holding my hand and stopping me.

"You think you can buy my time, walk with me as if we were a couple, and be proud of it."

150

"No, I'm not. I'm sorry I did that," he continues to hold my hand, not letting me walk away.

"I'm not a whore. I'm not someone you can pass from one man to another," I wipe my cheeks from the tears.

"I know you're not a whore," Egon holds my other hand and looks into my eyes, "Wally, I won't hurt you."

"You will tell Mr. Klimt that we did all kinds of things, and you will make him jealous, and he won't want me anymore," I release my hand from his warm palm and wipe my eyes again.

"Wally, you're so innocent." He takes a handkerchief from his jacket pocket, his face illuminated by the street lanterns near the entrance gate, "Haven't you realized that this is exactly what you need with Mr. Klimt? You need him to be jealous." His hand holding a handkerchief gently wipes the tears from my cheeks. "Let me be your partner for an evening of fun at the world's grandest theme park and make him jealous." He whispers in my ear.

"I don't know," I look at him.

"Believe me, I know," He smiles at me, his eyes sparkling with the lights around, or maybe because of my tears. Should I trust him?

I place my hand on his palm that is stroking my cheek with the handkerchief, and turn around, walking with him past the gate. He is right. Mr. Klimt is with the Lady. He chose her. I am also allowed to choose someone else tonight.

On the roller coaster, I scream in fear and let him hold my hand, and on the carousel, he sits on the wooden horse closest to my horse. While the carousel spins quickly, I watch his brown eyes looking at me. Only he is on the wooden horse by my side while the whole world around us swirls in a jumble of colors and sounds of voices and music, as if it were a colorful kaleidoscope. But only in the Ferris wheel, do I let him stand close to me.

Evening has fallen, and the sky is black. Only the two of us are standing in the dark carriage that slowly climbs into the sky, moving slightly in the wind. I cling to the window and look at the city lights. They look like thousands of fireflies in the summer fields, coloring the dark with small dots of light. I have never seen such a beautiful sight. From above, I can hear the voices of the people at the fair and the music, but they are in the background, as if they belong to another world, and I can hear Egon's breathing. He is standing so close to me. I can smell his pleasant scent of pine tree perfume, different from Klimt's scent. I turn my gaze to him. He seems like a panther looking to pounce on me, while Klimt is like a full-grown bear peacefully sleeping through the winter.

"Amusement Parks are where imagination is made," I whisper.

"No, you're wrong," Egon whispers to me. I feel his finger touch my waist, "This is where imagination is created," he caresses my waist gently, "In the meeting of my fingers with the warmth of your body, a union that ignites the imagination and makes me want to paint you."

"Do you think he'll be jealous?" I turn towards him, feeling his palm resting on my waist.

"I think all the men in Vienna will be jealous of me, not just Mr. Klimt," I can see his smile in the weak light from the lanterns below. I have never kissed anyone other than Mr. Klimt, who is with the Lady.

His lips are different. At first, they are softer than Mr. Klimt's, but after a moment, he holds me tightly and hugs me as if he wants to conquer all my body, and I feel his tongue touching mine. I start breathing heavily while his hands caress me in the dark. I'm not allowed to do that. The carriage begins to move slowly, bringing us closer to the ground and the people patiently waiting for their turn on the Ferris wheel. I adjust my dress and stand up, reach out a hand to the guard in the blue uniform who opens the car door, and descend to the stable ground, thanking him politely. I don't care who Mr. Klimt hangs out with tonight. I hope Egon tells him that we went to the Prater.

"Can I invite you to a café? Maybe you'll meet some of my friends too," Egon asks me as we walk out of the park and cross the bridge leading to the city, over the Danube Canal.

"Yes, I would love to," I answer him as I let him walk by my side, but when he tries to kiss me again, I refuse. He knows I belong to Klimt, and I don't do such things.

"Egon, come join us," I see two men get up from one of the tables in a noisy café and invite us with their hands. Next to them, another two men and two women are seated. We make our way through the people filling the stuffy café full of cigarette smoke, sounds of laughter, and arguing. I can hear a piano playing on the other side of the café.

"Everyone, Meet Wally, a close friend and the most beautiful woman I've ever met." Egon announces as we stand next to the table. I feel myself blushing when the men bow politely and the women greet me.

"Please join us," one of them turns his chair to me and goes to get another chair for himself while Egon moves away and returns after a moment, carrying a chair.

"You are definitely beautiful and special," One of the women says to me, "It's no wonder you fell in love with her." She turns to Egon and places her hand on his thigh, "Have you already offered her to model for you?"

"I fell in love with her even without her modeling for me." He laughs and pours me a glass of wine from the bottle standing on the table. "You know me, my art must not have boundaries on love, or clothes; I am not like the old people who think there should be rules about what we can and can't do, I believe that everything is allowed." He stands up, holds a glass and announces, "May we live a life of breaking all boundaries."

"Cheers," Everyone answers and sips from the wine glasses, and I also sip from my wine glass, feeling its burn in my throat.

"How did you two meet?" One of the women asks me later.

"I happened to meet him in a bookstore," I say, not wanting to tell her about Mr. Klimt. The soft music is calming, and the cigarette smoke no longer bothers me. I have already drunk several glasses of wine. His friends are constantly talking about art and painting, and one of them is a photographer who describes the camera he has, with which he takes portraits.

"Egon, I see you found yourself an educated wife," the woman laughs with him, "I hope she's young enough for you."

"Everything about her is enough for me," he answers, "She just needs to love me back." He puts his head on my shoulder and pretends to cry, making everyone laugh and congratulate me for breaking Egon's heart.

"Where's my hostel?" I say in a whiny voice later as we both walk in the dark down one of the alleys. My head hurts, and I feel dizzy.

"We'll be there soon, my beautiful cherry," he says. It seems that his hands are supporting and helping me not to fall.

"I hate this place. I hate Ms. Bertha. She is mean to me," I whisper to a horse standing on the side of the dark street near a water trough.

"Then come live with me, my beautiful Wally. Klimt doesn't really want you, and I do," Egon says and tries to kiss me again, but I cover my mouth with my hand. He smells like wine, as do I.

"I don't want to live with you. I want to live with Mr. Klimt," I think that's what I say to him, "You promised not to hurt me," I whimper again, "I saw the woman put her hand on you. You're just trying to seduce me. You're like all the men who come to Ms. Bertha's hostel," I try to pull away from him but feel unsteady and lean back against his hands. Why is the street so crooked?

"Of course I'm trying to seduce you," I think he says. "Here we are," he puts my hand on the door's handle, "but you see, my lovely red cherry, even if you stay with Mr. Klimt forever, I'll still think you're the most beautiful woman I have ever met in my life."

"You have to ring the bell. It's locked," I whisper and try to remember the words he just said to me, repeating them in my mind.

"Good evening, Ms. Bertha," He says as she opens the heavy door, "I've brought her back as promised. I think she needs someone to hold her hand and take her to bed."

"Shame on you, Mr. Schiele." She scolds him while holding my shoulders.

"Thank you for a magical evening, Miss Wally, have a good night, Ms. Bertha." He bows to us both, turns, and starts walking down the street. I can see his silhouette walking away in the dark, until he disappears into one of the alleys.

"Come upstairs, you're drunk," Ms. Bertha says, closing the hostel's entrance door behind us.

* * *

"Klimt, I need you to measure the new tunic I made for you," Ms. Emilie walks into his studio a few days later, holding a folded bundle in her hands. She is wearing a black and white striped dress, like the bedspread I am currently lying on naked, my legs spread wide open.

"Just a second, my dear." He puts down the pencil and approaches her, takes the garment from her, and unfolds it. It's a dark gray-blue smock decorated with delicate golden embroidery, "It's lovely," he says as he approaches and kisses her lips, "It'll definitely be suitable for opening night, thank you." He kisses her again. It's been a long time since he kissed me.

"Try it," Emilie strokes his arm, "I need to know if it needs to be sent it in for repairs."

"Now?" He laughs and turns his gaze to me. I feel so exposed, lying naked in front of them.

"I don't think she'll mind." Emilie looks at me, "Ask her to close her eyes for a few minutes."

Without saying a word, he bends down, removes the smock he is wearing and stands in front of her, naked. I feel like a stray cat left outside. I won't close my eyes. I will not let them ignore me. I remain naked and show my breasts, staring at his fair body and the curly sparse brown hair on his back while he stands naked. What does Egon's back look like? Is he smoother?

Ms. Emilie holds the smock he removed and looks at him as he changes.

"Can you please not look?" She turns to me.

I don't answer her, but I close my eyes and lean back. It's been a long time since he's done it with me, although he continues to stroke my hair every time I come here.

"Don't move," she tells him, and I can't hold back any longer, and open my eyes. She bends down at his feet, arranges the hem of the new tunic, and sticks sewing pins in it from the pin cushion on her arm.

"You're tickling me." He laughs and reaches down, stroking her curly brown hair.

"I told you not to move." Her hand goes under his smock as she smiles. I lie motionless, feeling useless. I can hear them chuckling and turn my gaze toward my dress, which is placed on the chair at the side of the studio. I'll think about Egon and what we did on the Ferris wheel. I close my eyes again and continue stroking my hair slowly. Soon she will go and leave us alone again.

The screeching sounds of the pencil make me open my eyes and look at him again. Emilie is gone, and he's wearing his simple smock as he continues to draw me. It's as if she never walked into his studio.

"A few days ago, I was in the Prater," I tell him.

"Really?" He looks at me and smiles. "Did you enjoy it?"

"Yes, very much. We went in the evening."

"Evening hours are the most beautiful." He continues to look at me and the brown paper, "*Fuego*, don't play with your hair. You're moving."

"We got on the Ferris wheel to see the whole city. We were alone in the car, just the two of us in the sky."

"What about the Lady's painting, is it finished?" Emilie enters the studio again, holding a little red notebook and a pencil, "We need to inform them what paintings you are sending to the exhibition."

"Yes, it's finished. Add it to the list." I look at the large painting that is leaning against the wall. The lady looks at me from the painting. Yellow squares are painted around her and the gold coloring make her look radiant.

"What drawings will you show?" She writes something in the notebook she is holding.

"I'll choose three of them later." He removes my sketch from the drawing pad and places it on the side of the room, taking new paper and attaching it to the drawing board. I stretch my body and show off my breasts.

"What about the guest list for opening night?" She stands next to him and watches as he draws me. Will she try to insult me again?

"Please take care of it. You know all the right people in this town."

"Yes, they are already on the list, but are there any others you would like to invite?" She is watching me. Will he invite me?

"What about Mr. Egon Schiele? Is he on the list?"

"I can add him, but many are angry about his paintings. There will be gossip."

"These conservative old men will always find something to gossip about, whether it's a provocative painting or the taste of the champagne they're being served." He answers her as he continues to draw me, "Invite him."

"And what about the members of the Association of Psychologists? Freud and his friends?"

"Do you think the show would be of any interest to them? They are always busy with their theories and arguments about the conscious and the subconscious. Wally," he turns to me, "Put your hand on your thigh."

"There are many who like to listen to them. You should invite them."

"Then invite them," he says as I place a hand on my bare thighs. Will he remember to invite me?

"Anyone else?" She continues to write in her notebook.

"No, that's it. I think that's all." He says, concentrating on the drawing.

"Great, I'll send out invitations." She strokes his arm and leaves the room, and I close my eyes and breathe slowly.

"Just like that," I hear him say after a moment, "Don't move. I want to paint you with those tears," I continue breathing slowly, feeling a tear slide down my cheek, but not wiping it away.

Mr. Klimt brings the easel closer to me, and the rustle of the pencil scratches in my ears, like chalk on a wooden board.

"Great, you're great." He says to himself.

"You didn't invite me to your exhibition," I say with a trembling voice, "And I'm out of money," I continue, trying not to move.

"My *Fuego*, I'm so sorry." He puts the pencil down and approaches me, stroking my wet cheek. "Don't cry. Of course, you're invited to my exhibition. Don't be upset, I have a busy life, and don't always remember everything."

"It's okay. I know you're a famous painter. I shouldn't expect you to remember me." I place my hand on his large palm. Egon's fingers are more delicate than his.

"My Wally, don't be sad. With my hectic life, it's difficult for me to remember everyone." He kisses me, "I just forgot."

"What is my place, in your life?" I look at the paintings leaning on the wall. Will he prefer me one day, over those rich women who don't beg for money?

"You always have a warm place in my heart. Wait a minute," He gets up and walks out of the room, returning after a moment holding two bills of money. He stands over me for a moment while I lie naked, as if debating where to put them. Then he comes closer and places them on my thighs. "That's it, excellent, don't move. I'll draw you with the bills on you." He walks to the easel and holds the pencil again. I look at the turquoise bills lying on me, their touch like a spider walking on my skin, and I close my eyes, fighting the urge to cry. At least he invited me to his exhibition. Maybe I will see my drawings there.

❧

"Christina, please help me," I knock on her bedroom door a few days later.

"Rusty, what happened?" She opens the door and looks at me. I hear the gramophone's music downstairs and the laughter of one of the girls mixed with a man's voice.

"What should I do?" I'm standing in front of her, wearing the dress I bought for him. "Is it beautiful enough?"

"Where are you going with this dress?" She moves aside and lets me into her room.

"To him," I gasp and sit on her bed.

"To the painter?"

"Yes," I nod my head. I was up all night with excitement, tossing and turning in my narrow bedroom, afraid of what would happen.

"It's pretty enough for him." She sits beside me on the bed, "Don't worry."

"It's not just for him. It's for the exhibition."

"Did he invite you to an exhibition?"

"It's the opening of an exhibition of his paintings," My fingers fidget with the dress hem, "There will be many honorable people there, and I'm invited too."

"You've definitely moved on from this bed we slept in to-gether." She gets up from the bed, turns her back to me, and bends down in front of the small mirror hanging on the wall, examining her face.

"Christina, please."

"Stand up," she turns to me. In the yellowish light, I see her eyes sparkle a little. Was she crying?

"Christina, I didn't mean to." I get up slowly, hearing the creak of the bed springs.

"Belt," she places her hand on my waist, "You need a belt. Don't move." She turns and opens the door of her wooden closet, pulls out a modern wide belt, straps it around my waist, and moves back and examines me. Her gaze moves from my neck down. "And gloves," she turns to the closet again, "I have a pair to give you, just what you need," she takes out a pair of black gloves and hands them to me.

"Thank you," I hug her. Why is she so good to me?

"Wait, Rusty," She hugs me back, "You need to wear make-up. You can't be seen like this among all the respectable ladies. You need lipstick and some make-up." She leaves the room and returns a moment later, holding a cork in her hand.

"What is that for?"

"It's an old trick." She heats the cork over the candle until the tip blackens. "Don't move," She holds my chin and moves the cork's end above my eyes. I look in the mirror and see that she has created black shadows that make my eyes stand out.

"That's great," I smile at her.

"Now, a little Vaseline," She puts some on her finger and applies it to the black eye shadow soot, "It will make them shine. And now don't move," She holds the lipstick brush.

"Thank you, Christina," I search for the right words when she finishes.

"That's it, you're ready, and don't start crying now, you'll ruin your makeup." She says after a while, and I look at myself in the mirror and hold back the tears. My eyes have shiny black shadows, and my lips are plump with her pink lipstick. She also added blush to my cheeks. I have never looked so beautiful.

"Thank you for everything, Christina," I hug her again.

"Your shoes don't fit. They are too old," she steps back in the small room, and I look down at my worn shoes. Those are my only ones. "Take mine," she removes her new leather shoes and hands them to me, and I put them on. They have a modern low heel that I'm not used to, and they are slightly smaller, but I manage to tie the laces properly. "Go already, no more hugs," she says as I get up and walk carefully on the heels, trying to get used to my new height. I carefully wipe my eyes and walk out of her room. I wish she could come with me.

"Young Walburga, where are you going dressed up like this?" Ms. Bertha stops me as I pass her counter on my way out. "Have you been invited to a ball?"

"I've been invited to Mr. Klimt's exhibition of paintings at the Vienna Secession Gallery." I stand and proudly smile at her.

"Do they know you're coming?" She watches me, examining my dress and pink lips.

"I've got an invitation. He invited me." I glance at her. "A drawing of mine will be hanging on the wall, and people will look at it."

"My innocent girl," She smiles at me, "Just because they invited you doesn't mean they will accept you."

"Who are they?"

"You'll see on your own. You're a big girl," She pulls out a cigarette from the small silver box, lights it, goes to the stairs, and shouts, "Come on, girls, come down. More guests will be arriving soon. Dress nicely. "

"Have a good evening, Ms. Bertha," I say to her as I hold the door handle, but she doesn't hear me. The noise of the girls laughing and talking from the second floor fills the entrance, and I walk out to the street. I must hurry. I lingered too long when Christina was dressing me.

Outside it is dark and cold, and I walk as fast as I can to keep warm. The street lanterns illuminate with a weak light, and I must look down so I don't stumble. I turn onto the main street toward the boulevard, carefully walking on the smooth cobblestones. I have a long way to go to the gallery, and already feel my legs ache. They are not used to the small heels on me. If I keep walking like this, I will start limping. How will all the people look at me at the exhibition then?

"How much to the Vienna Secession Gallery?" I gasp and ask a coachman standing bored beside his horse-drawn carriage. I can't walk anymore with the tight shoes.

"Half a krone." He says, holding out his hand.

"Here you go. Please. I'm in a hurry," I take out the coin, hand it to him, climb into the carriage, and sit on the soft leather seat. I never rode in such a carriage, but I can't walk anymore. The coachman climbs onto his seat in front of me, clucks the horse, pulls the reins, and drives the carriage down the street. The sound of the horse's hooves hitting the cobble-stones rhythmically creates a pleasant sound that relaxes me, and I lean back on the soft leather seat, close my eyes, and let my cheeks feel the cool night air. One day I will have a carriage like this with a coachman that will politely open the wooden door for me, give me a hand when I climb in, and take me from place to place.

"Miss, we have arrived." I hear the driver and open my eyes, looking around.

Two gentlemen in suits and top hats are standing, talking to each other while smoking cigars on the entrance steps of the white building. Further down the street are several new black automobiles parking with their drivers next to them, probably, waiting for the guests who have entered the exhibition.

"Please, Miss," The driver opens the carriage door for me, and I give him my hand and jump to the sidewalk. I can still hear the carriage driving away as I begin to climb the steps leading up to the gallery. I look up. In the light of the street lanterns, I can see the large golden dome on the roof of the building. It is made of hundreds of sparkling gold leaves connected to each other like a crystal ball. The walls are also decorated with curled golden lines.

"Good evening, Miss," The two gentlemen stop their conversation and greet me, bowing politely.

"Good evening," I smile awkwardly at them as I cross the cloud of their cigar smoke and proceed to the lit entrance, walking into the bright white hall full of people.

I stop at the entrance and look around. Where is Mr. Klimt? The hall is full of men in suits and women in evening dresses.

My eyes move along the crowd gathered in small groups talking to each other, but I can't see him. His large paintings and drawings are hung on the surrounding walls.

"Excuse me, Miss," A woman who had just arrived turns to me, and I apologize and move away from the front door, letting her in. She is wearing a fancy green evening dress and black leather gloves. Not simple ones like mine. Where is Mr. Klimt?

I approach one of the large paintings hanging on the wall and pretend to be looking at it. It depicts a few women lying side by side in different positions. Did they also lie on the same bed in the studio while he lay or leaned on them? I try to recognize myself among them, but I can't. My shoes hurt.

The next picture hanging on the wall is of the lady with gold squares around her. The lady is standing next to the picture with her hair up, wearing a black evening dress, and is talking to several men and women, but Mr. Klimt is not among them. For a moment, it seems to me that she notices my presence, and I smile at her, but she ignores me. I blush, hurrying to the other side of the hall, pretending to be looking at a hanging painting of a naked girl lying down. But this one is not of me either.

"Good evening, my beautiful Cherry," I hear a voice and turn around, seeing Egon Schiele standing next to me, holding a glass of champagne, and looking at the drawing hanging on the wall. "You are much more beautiful than her," he looks at me and smiles. He's wearing the same brown jacket, button-down shirt, and thin black tie. I can smell his pine tree cologne.

"Thank you," I return his smile and search the audience for Mr. Klimt.

"He's over there," he points with his hand holding the champagne glass to Mr. Klimt, who is standing in the corner of the hall. Next to him, Ms. Emilie is standing. They are both dressed in their smocks, the ones I saw that day, and they are talking to a lady in a blue dress and golden hair. "Do you want us to approach them together?" He asks after a moment, still standing close to me.

"No, thanks, I'll go to him alone." I answer and move along the wall in their direction, stopping to look at the next drawing, which is also not mine, and neither the next nor the one after that. Could it be that Mr. Klimt did not bring any of my drawings to the exhibition? I try to signal to him with my hand, but he continues talking to the lady and does not acknowledge me. Neither does Ms. Emilie, even though I think she has noticed me. I turn back and look for Egon, but I can't see him anymore. Maybe I should have accepted his offer. Perhaps I should have walked hand in hand with him in Mr. Klimt's direction.

"My lady?" A foreign man dressed in a black suit approaches me.

"Yes, sir," I look up at him. What does he want from me?

"You have been asked to leave the exhibition. You are causing discomfort to one of the respectable women here." He continues to stand close to me.

"But..." I try to answer him, feeling myself blush.

"With your permission, my lady, I will escort you to the door."

"But..." I look in Mr. Klimt's direction. This is wrong. He will explain to this man that I'm invited. But Mr. Klimt is standing with his back to me, talking with two gentlemen in brown suits.

"Will you join me?" The man is still standing in front of me, his eyes like a viper in the field.

Step by step, I walk to the gallery door, feeling all eyes are fixed on me. The voices around grow quiet as they talk only about me and the man in the black suit who accompanies me to the door. They all look blurry to me, but maybe that's because of the tears in my eyes.

"Have a pleasant evening, Miss," He says when we reach the front door , but I don't answer him and start going down the stairs to the street.

"Good evening," The two gentlemen from before at the stairs greet me again and bow, but I keep walking down the stairs and turn into the empty street, starting to walk back to the hostel. No horse-drawn carriage is waiting for me, and even if there was, I don't have the money to pay for it. In the quiet street behind me, I can still hear the waiting car drivers talking to each other. I quicken my steps despite my sore shoes, wanting to escape from the white building with the glittering golden dome. The small room in Bertha's hostel is waiting for me.

"Wally," I hear a shout and stop, turning back. Is that Mr. Klimt? "Wally, stop," I see Egon running towards me, calling my name, but I turn again and continue walking, "Wally," he catches up and starts walking beside me, "What happened? Why did you leave?"

"They don't want me there," I answer him and start to cry.

"Who doesn't want you? Those ladies?" He holds my hand and takes out a handkerchief, gently wiping my cheek with it.

"Him too," I continue to cry.

"You don't need him. He's too old for you. You need someone who sees how beautiful you are."

"I'm a simple girl. They'll never accept me."

"You don't have to care if they accept you or not. They are all from the old generation, even Mr. Klimt, who thinks himself a rebel. He has become accustomed to the wealthy people's money and has long forgotten how to rebel." Egon smiles at me in the dark. "I'll always accept you." He continues to wipe the tears from my eyes, and his lips come closer to mine. I think he's going to try and kiss me, but I can't. Not now. I can still imagine Mr. Klimt talking to the lady wearing the giant diamond necklace and ignoring me.

"Could you please accompany me to the hostel?" I turn away from him and start walking slowly.

"Is everything okay? You're limping." He walks beside me.

"My shoes are tight," I answer him and continue walking.

"Can you stand up for a moment?" He asks me, and when I do, he bends down on his knees at my feet and takes off my shoes, his fingers gently caressing my sore feet. "You'll be more comfortable this way." He stands back up, holding my shoes, and I walk barefoot down the street, feeling the cool cobblestones under my feet.

"Come with me." He holds my hand after a while as we walk between cafés.

"I don't want to. I can't go inside like this," I show him my bare feet.

"It seems to me that you haven't drunk champagne yet today. You deserve to celebrate. Do you think the honorable gentlemen inside will mind you being barefoot?" He pulls me into the café after him, approaches the waiter, and orders us a table, the whole time, still holding my shoes in his hand. The people around are looking at us, but Egon doesn't seem to care at all.

"Have you been drinking again?" Ms. Bertha asks me later when she opens the hostel entrance door. It is late, and the dark street is empty.

"Good evening, Ms. Bertha," Egon bows.

"Thank you very much, young man, for bringing her here. Good night, you may go." She opens the door slightly, lets me in, and closes it behind me.

"Good night, Egon," I say to him, "Good night Ms. Bertha," I answer her and walk slowly towards the stairs, careful not to fall. One hand holds Christina's shoes, and the other gropes the railing in the dim light.

"Is that what you're going to do with your life? Continue hanging out with young men and drink?"

"No, Ms. Bertha," I stand and look at her. My head hurts. My legs too.

"Listen to Ms. Bertha, you won't achieve anything in your life that way." She continues to scold me, "Is this the kind of life you plan for yourself? Returning to my place drunk?"

"You're right," I answer and drop the shoes from my hands, hearing them fall noisily on the floor, breaking the silence in the quiet hostel. Quickly, I walk past her, open the front door, and run barefoot to the street. Far away in the darkness, I can see Egon.

"Do you still want me? Like you asked me back then in the Prater?" I shout at him. He stops, and turn around to face me.

"Always," he shouts back to me from the end of the street.

I run back to the hostel, close the door behind me, and walk towards the stairs.

"Walburga, you can't continue behaving this way," She stands by the stairs while holding Christina's shoes, handing them to me.

"You're right. I wasn't meant for such a place." I take the shoes from her and rush to the second floor, placing them near Christana's door. In my bedroom, I tuck all my clothes into the canvas sack and go down to the entrance floor, placing the two bills that Mr. Klimt put on my body on the counter in front of her. "This is my payment," I say as I walk away. My fingers force the door latch open, and I go out into the street, hearing the door slam behind me, hoping he is still waiting for me.

Chapter Seven

Egon

An apartment in Vienna, autumn 1911.

I open my eyes and look at the gray ceiling. The bluish morning light enters from the small bedroom window. I can hear the rain falling outside. My hand pulls the thick blanket to cover my bare shoulders, and I turn around and reach out, caressing the smooth body of the man who agreed to let me into his house and bed.

Egon is lying in bed with his eyes open, watching me intently. How long has he been awake, watching me like this?

"Good morning," I whisper and smile at him. His face rests on his hand, and his brown eyes look at me closely.

"Your hair is like a flame of fire waiting to flare up." He reaches out and strokes my short hair that is scattered on the pillow. "And your blue eyes are like a clear lake on a hot summer day, the kind that just makes you want to take off your clothes and jump into it naked, diving into its coolness." He runs his finger over my eyes, and I close them and smile. The touch of his finger caressing me feels so good. "And your eyelashes," he continues to speak to me quietly, "Are like a rowboat in which I sail on the lake between the mountains, sailing leisurely."

"Cover me with your words," I say to him, keeping my eyes closed. Can I trust him? Will he hold me when I need to be held?

"And your nose," His finger touches my nose, "Is like a snowy mountain that I can climb in the winter, and feel its softness under my heavy shoes."

"And my lips?" I continue the game between us. I should trust him.

"Your lips are like a soft and warm loaf of bread that just came out of the baker's oven, waiting to be eaten. Out of all the women I've met, you have the softest lips." He laughs and bites my lip, making me shudder. How many women was he with before me? Did he also say those mesmerizing words to them, showering them with compliments and making them feel safe?

"Come to me." He continues to whisper, his lips kissing my neck, but I keep my hands at my sides and don't hug him. I must not think about other women. I was also with Mr. Klimt. I close my eyes and feel his lips kissing my body. "You will be my muse, the goddess of my painting." His hands caress my breasts, but I don't move or squirm like the girls at Bertha's hostel were teaching each other to. I need more time to trust him.

"Please, keep doing that," I say and reach out, stroking his wild dark hair, but I don't spread my legs, not yet. I try to breathe. He is good to me. I chose him.

"I see Klimt didn't teach you too much." He says, "I've already taught women to have fun with me." I shiver for a moment, probably because of the cold in the room.

"Draw me, please. I want you to draw me." I want to change the subsect. I don't want him to explain how I should behave.

"Let's do it," he gets up from the bed and walks, naked, into the other room. I watch his smooth back while he is walking and get up after him, but the room is cold, and I wrap myself in the thick blanket and carry it with me to the other room. Egon sits on his knees next to the fireplace, places a log inside and lights it. "Sit on the chair," He orders as he brings the easel near the chair I sit on, wrapped in the blanket. I watch him as he sits on the plain wooden chair and begins to draw me, ignoring his nakedness in the cold room, which is slowly warming up with the fireplace's heat. His brown eyes look into mine the whole time, as if trying to dive into my soul and swim in me, just like he whispered to me earlier. I'm going to be his muse. That's why I came to be with him. I will adjust.

"Wally," he stops drawing and comes near me.

"Yes?" I keep looking in his eyes.

"I'll peel you bit by bit and swallow you like a delicious summer cherry." He reaches under the blanket that wraps my naked body. I feel his cold fingers caressing my warm thighs and close them tightly over his fingers, but after a moment, I spread them, letting him touch me.

"You are a contrast of blue eyes and an orange flame," He whispers as he lays on top of me on the parquet floor near the fireplace.

I hug him tightly and close my eyes, letting him teach me. All other women will become his history, and I will be his muse

174

from now on, the one he will love and cherish. We will be perfect together.

⁂

Since he took me into his apartment two months ago, Egon has been preparing for an exhibition in Munich that is coming up, and I am helping him. We live in a small apartment that overlooks the gardens of Schönbrunn Palace. From the window of the large room that Egon turned into a studio, I can see the wall surrounding the gardens and the trees that look like a small patch of forest behind it. Two months ago, when it was still winter, the trees were bare, and in the distance, I could see the lake in the center of the garden and the elongated yellowish palace behind it. Sometimes I could also see ladies walking in the garden. They looked to me like black ants in their heavy winter coats. But now, the trees surrounding the garden have begun to bloom, and I can no longer see the palace and the ladies.

I stop watching the two guards standing by the side gate leading to the garden as I bend down again, get down on my knees, and continue cleaning the room's parquet floor. I have never seen this gate open. Still, the guards always stand there like it is their duty to keep it closed. I hold the stiff wooden hand brush as I scrub the wooden floor. He is busy with his paintings for the exhibition, and I need to help him as much as I can. Together, we will succeed.

I get up from the floor and grab the bucket with the water and the hairbrush, moving to another corner of the room. On the way, I stop beside him, gently kissing his bare back.

Egon stands naked and motionless next to the easel and paints himself while looking at the large mirror leaning against the wall. It's getting warmer now, and we don't need to buy wood to heat the house or shiver while he paints himself or me.

I look at Egon's back. Unlike Mr. Klimt, he has almost no hair on his back or chest. Since that evening in the gallery, I have not met Mr. Klimt, nor do I have any idea whether he tried to look for me at Ms. Bertha's hostel. Egon doesn't mention him, although I know he meets with him occasionally. His studio is not far from the house where we live now, on the other side of the Schönbrunn Palace gardens.

"You have a smooth back," I run my fingers all wet with soap and water over his back.

"Your fingers are wet," he moves away from my caressing hand, "And you are ruining my concentration. I must keep working," he turns and kisses me quickly, returning to the position he was in before and looking at himself in the mirror. He could have been nicer to me. For several days now, he has been focused only on himself, painting all day and going to the café to meet his friends in the evenings. I watch him. He holds one hand in the air while his other hand clutches a brush and applies red and black stripes of gouache paint on the brown paper hanging on the painting board. It's strange for me to watch him draw himself naked like that, his tool so prominent. Is he planning on showing this painting in the upcoming exhibition? I stroke his back with my finger again. I don't mind disturbing him a bit.

"Enough, Wally, you're bothering me, stop clinging to me."
He recoiled from my hand again.

"Sorry," I pull away from him, feeling a lump in my throat.

"Is there anything to eat?" He continues to paint with rapid
strokes, "I'm hungry." his hand holding the brush moves like a
wasp, and the thin brush creates swirling lines of black around
his pubic area on the brown paper. Will people like to look at
such a painting?

"I'll prepare something for you right away," I answer as I
bend down, grab the wooden bucket again, take it, and place
it next to the pantry cabinet in the corner of the room. There
are only a few potatoes in the basket. I can go down to the
market and buy some sausage and cabbage. I hurry to remove
the apron I'm wearing and wipe my hands.

"Egon, could you give me some money?" I approach him,
holding the straw basket I usually take to the market. The
money he gave me last week has run out. I used it to buy food
and a pillow for our bedroom.

"Didn't I give you money last week?" He answers without
turning his head.

"I bought food with it," I stand by the door.

"You spend too much." He continues to paint, "And I must
concentrate on the paintings for the exhibition. I can't stop to
get money right now. Make me dinner with what we have."

"Yes, Egon," I put down the empty basket and go to the
pantry, taking the potatoes. Why does he treat me like this?

I hold the potatoes and begin to peel them, but after a moment, I stop and place them as they are on the plate, uncooked
with the remains of the peel.

"Dinner is ready," I walk over to Egon and noisily place the plate with the uncooked potatoes on the floor next to him, throwing a knife and fork on the floor next to the plate. I ignore the sharp noise they make when they hit the parquet and turn and go to the bedroom, ignoring the tears on my cheeks. I lie down on the bed and cover myself with a blanket, not bothering to undress. All I want is to hide myself from the world.

"My bright red cherry, I'm so sorry." I hear his muffled voice after a while and feel the weight of his body above the blanket, but I don't answer him, just wipe my tears. I so badly want us to succeed together. "I shouldn't have talked to you like that. It's the exhibition, and all the paintings I have to prepare for it." He whispers to me, "I want to break boundaries, to paint as no one has painted before. I don't care what others will say." He continues talking, "I'm so sorry," he removes the blanket covering me and kisses my face. "We'll get along, you'll see, I promise, I'll take care of you." He gets up from the bed and holds my hand, pulling me to him, "Come with me, please forgive me."

In the studio, he goes to the corner where the canvas boards and the paint boxes are stacked onto each other. Swiftly, he moves the paintings, drops some of them on the floor, and pulls out a drawing that is leaning against the wall. "Here, I'll sell this drawing. I'll get us some money," he walks over and places it by the door. I look at the painting of a woman wearing a hat and smiling at her painter.

"Who painted this woman?" It isn't Egon's style.

"It's his."

"Your friend?" I don't want to say his name.

"Yes, It's Gustav Klimt's painting."

"How did it get here?"

"He gave it to me. We made an exchange," Egon turns around and returns to the easel, standing in front of the mirror and recreating the position in which he painted himself, "I gave him my drawings, and he gave me his. He suggested this exchange out of pity for a young and unknown painter." He approaches and hugs me, "I'll sell it, and I'll take care of you." He says before returning to the center of the room, grabbing a brush, and continuing to paint himself.

"Are you sure? This is a gift from him."

"He gave me these paintings out of pity. It's time we use this pity to buy us food." He continues to draw, not looking at me. Is he ashamed that we are poor?

I lean down, pick up the potatoes from the wooden floor, take them to the table, and start peeling them. But after a moment, I stop. I'm used to eating them boiled as they are. It is healthier that way.

I fill the pot with water and look at Mr. Klimt's drawing leaning against the front door. I examine the woman in his painting, the one with the hat. Egon needs me.

"Draw me. You haven't drawn me in a long time," I put the pot on the stove and approach Egon, starting to undress, "I'll help you become the most famous painter in Vienna," I roll up my dress and panties and stand in front of him naked. I chose him, not Mr. Klimt, and we will succeed together.

"Put your hand down, don't cover your breasts," he tells me after a while, standing over me and drawing with quick movements, "Place it between your breasts."

"Are you sure?" I ask him, blushing, "Is that what you need for the exhibition?"

"You're used to being naked, aren't you?" He watches me for a moment with his dark eyes. What did Mr. Klimt show him from his drawings of me? I turn my gaze for a moment to the painting next to the door. Did Mr. Klimt also exchange my drawings with other painters? I shouldn't think about that. This is my new home, with Egon, the man I chose. I close my eyes and, in slow motion, open my legs. I know that with him, I am doing the right thing. He is my man, and I should trust him.

"Just like that." I hear him say, "Artists shouldn't have limits of law and morality, and if there are any, they should shatter them."

Even though I feel red with embarrassment, I smile at him, keeping my eyes closed. He will draw great pictures of me, and we'll have enough money to buy us bread, sausage, cabbage, and wine. We won't have to use Mr. Klimt's paintings. I'll be better than his paintings.

The house is quiet while I walk through the rooms, my bare feet feeling the parquet's roughness. I stop and look out the window at the trees in the emperor's garden, and at the guards who stand by the closed gate. It's been a few months since he started painting himself and me in those provocative paintings. It's been two weeks since he went with them to the exhibition in Munich, trying to sell them. Apart from a short letter he wrote me, saying he arrived at the hotel and settled in, I haven't heard anything from him. He left only a few paintings and drawings scattered on the floor, the ones that he decided were too plain and boring.

I go to the wooden cabinet near the entrance door, take out his letter from the drawer, and read it again. The words are written in black ink on the cream-colored paper. He writes as he draws, with sharp lines connected to short, clear words. Does he go out to cafés with friends in the evenings, like he usually does here? Does he think about me? Who is Mr. Arthur Roessler who invited him to show the paintings in his gallery?

I carefully fold and tuck the paper into the envelope, return it to the drawer, put on my shoes, and leave the house. His train from Munich will be arriving soon.

I see the grand station building in the distance and hasten my steps. Marble statues of women stand on the roof, over-looking the broad street and the steps leading up to the station, as if watching over the horse-drawn carriages standing in front of the entrance square and the porters carrying luggage and wooden boxes. Several modern, black automobiles are parked in front of the carriages, their drivers waiting. I stop and watch a woman in a gray cape holding the hand of a girl in a burgundy dress. The girl stands and strokes the rubber tires of one of the cars parked near the entrance. One day I, too, will have a child like her. I smile to myself. I must choose a name for my girl.

I hear a muffled whistle and go up the wide entrance stairs. The big clock above the station doors shows three minutes to twelve. His train should be arriving now.

Inside the station, the hustle and bustle replace the street's quietness. Portes's voices mixes with the shouts of the vendors standing at the side of the hall, small baskets of berries in front of them. Next to them is the sausage stand with a line of people waiting. The newspaper boy runs onto the platform while waving a newspaper and announcing that the emperor was going on an important political visit to Bavaria. The conductor whistles, and I see the train enter the station. It advances slowly, like a massive black and tired horse that blows clouds of steam and smoke into the hall while ambling before stopping to rest. The screeching of the brakes is barely heard over all the noise and people, and I walk onto the platform and look at the opening doors of the wooden carriages. What car will he be coming from?

The people exiting the train pass me by while I wait for him. A gentleman in a black suit and hat bows to me politely, but I ignore him and continue looking at the carriages' open doors, waiting for my man.

"Excuse me, ma'am," Two porters carrying a large wooden box ask me to move a little, and I see the girl in a burgundy dress politely approach and bow to a gentleman who just got off the train. Perhaps he is her father? The woman who held her hand also bows politely to him, and they walk towards the exit, passing me. The girl smiles at me, having a pink apple in her hand. Egon finally comes off the train.

I straighten my back and increase my steps as I advance toward him, stopping myself from running. He hasn't noticed me. He is wearing his brown jacket and talking to someone still on the train. For a moment, I think he is talking to a woman, and I slow my steps, but when I get closer, I see that he is holding a large wooden box, and one of the porters helps him get it and his suitcase off the train. Did he fail to sell the paintings?

"Egon," I stand close to him, patiently waiting for the porter to take down the box and place it on the platform.

He looks at me and doesn't smile, but after a moment, he holds me and presses his lips to mine firmly, kissing me passionately and ignoring the porter who is standing beside us with his outstretched hand, patiently waiting to receive the payment he deserves. His lips investigate mine for a long moment, and I feel hot, knowing I'm blushing. "My red cherry," He whispers in my ear, "Munich was gray without your flame. I've missed you. Thank you," he turns and places a coin in the hand of the porter, who looks at me curiously. "Please take the box and the suitcase to the carriages at the entrance," He says to him and again turns and kisses me, his hand stroking my body under the cape I'm wearing, lightly caressing my breasts. "I've missed you. Let's get away from all the smoke and these noisy people." He hugs me, and we walk towards the exit, following the porter.

"The train to Linz will leave in three minutes," The announcement sounds. "The Emperor will require the Germans to sign an alliance of mutual defense." Shouts the newspaper boy who runs past us waving a newspaper, but I don't listen to the voices around me, I just feel Egon's hand hugging me as we leave the dark and stifling station towards the sun outside.

"Which carriage would you like to ride in?" He asks me as we stand in front of the horse-drawn carriages line in front of the station.

"I thought we'd walk," I say quietly. What happened to the paintings? Did he sell them, giving us money to ride in a carriage? If so, why did he return the box?

"I'm tired from walking today. Do you have any money on you?"

"Yes," I take a coin from my dress pocket, placing it in his palm. I planned to buy good pastries and a bottle of wine so we could celebrate tonight.

"We deserve to celebrate." He tells me, approaching one of the coachmen and giving him the money. "Let me help you, my Wally." He offers me his hand as I climb onto the carriage while the coachman loads the box and the suitcase. I sit down on the comfortable leather seat and feel his hand caressing my back while the coachman clucks at the horse, and we start moving.

"How was the exhibition?" I ask him after a while, but he ignores me. His eyes are fixed on the gentlemen walking down the street wearing top hats, and the elegant ladies wearing colorful spring dresses holding parasols.

"I'm tired of this city." He declares as we pass the opera house, "I'm tired of the people in top hats and suits who understand nothing." He points at three gentlemen standing in the street talking to each other.

"Did you sell any paintings?" I ask him again, placing my hand on his thigh.

184

"People don't understand me, my cherry." He turns and looks at me with his brown eyes, "People don't understand art, don't you get it? They suffocate me with their criticism. How can I be creative when everything here is so clean and fair?" He spreads his hands to his sides and speaks loudly. What about the coachman that sits in front of the carriage? Is he listening to what he is saying? He can surely hear him. I look at the back of his head, but he does not move and only occasionally waves his whip gently, leading the way.

"So the paintings weren't sold?" I caress the back of his neck.

"No, Wally, the paintings weren't sold. People didn't like them. I don't even know why Mr. Arthur Roessler invited me to show in his gallery." He leans back on the carriage seat and looks up at the sky, "People said it was pornography and walked out." He whispers, "Do you understand? People thought that mine and your bodies were pornography." He continues talking non-stop, and I keep caressing the back of his neck. I want to hug him but am embarrassed to do so out here, in front of other people.

"You'll sell your paintings, I'm sure."

"I sold two, two paintings of you to Mr. Arthur. He must have bought them out of pity."

"That's great," I answer him and close my thighs. A stranger will look at my naked body. I feel nauseous, even though I should be happy.

"It's not great," He laughs bitterly, "There a town of conservatives there, and a town of conservatives here, and one man who feels sorry for me. That's all there is. Got any more money?"

"No, I gave you all I had."

"Too bad, I wanted to stop and buy me a bottle of wine."
He continues to lean back and look at the sky as the carriage
approaches the house.

"May I offer you a painting for sale?" Egon asks the coachman when we are standing next to the entrance to the house,
but the coachman ignores him and pulls the reins of his horse.
I look at the carriage moving away and the coachman sitting
upright in his seat, glad he didn't want to look at the paintings
tucked in the wooden box. He would not understand Egon's
art.

"Wally, let's go pack." Egon tells me as he bends down and
grabs the wooden box.

"Pack for what?"

"We're leaving this city. I need to live somewhere quieter,
where there are nice people. They don't understand my art
here." He walks to the front door and starts climbing the stairs,
panting.

"Where shall we go?" I follow him, holding the suitcase.

"To my mother's hometown."

"And they will understand your art there?"

"I don't care. The people there won't care what I do,"

"Is it really that simple? We just pack and leave Vienna?"

"Yes, as simple as that."

"And where is this place? You've never talked about your
mother." How will she treat me? I look down at my plain dress.

"Krumlov, South Bohemia." He answers as he continues to
climb the stairs. He places the box on the floor next to the door
and opens it. "I don't want to be in this city anymore. It has
the smell of crumbling imperial death."

"And we won't come back here?" I place the suitcase in the center of the room, looking at the trees surrounding the palace garden.

"This place depresses me. What do we have in this apartment?"

"Nothing," I answer as I look at my nude paintings that remain on the floor, the ones he chose not to take to the exhibition.

"Then let's get out of here," he goes to the bedroom, opens the closet, and starts throwing his clothes on the bed.

"Don't you want to think about it for a moment? You're used to living in Vienna. Your friends are here, the cafés you like." I stand at the entrance to the room, watching him. I don't want to leave.

"I don't have to think." He turns to me, "I'm an artist, I have to create art, and in this city, I can't create anymore." He turns to the closet again, taking out his neatly folded white shirts.

"Please, Egon, let's stay here. This is our city," I approach him and put my hand on his arm. How can I leave again? I have left too many homes over the last few years.

"Is this what you want? To be here in Vienna with a poor painter whose paintings interest no one?"

"No, I don't want that. You will succeed here."

"Don't you understand that my soul here is dead?" He moves away from my caressing hand. "My soul is not like you, who undresses anywhere in front of anyone. My soul needs its freedom, and that is not here in Vienna."

"It's not easy for me to undress either," I feel a lump in my throat, but I try to get closer to him again. I take one of his shirts out of the closet and fold it, "I'll help you find inspiration again. I'm your muse," I need to appease him. That's a woman's job.

"You will be my muse, but not here. I've decided, Vienna is not the place for us." He puts the folded shirt in the suitcase, "You will be my muse in Krumlov, with my childhood friends and my mother."

"Please, Egon."

"I've decided, and so that's what we are going to do. Unless you don't want to be by my side anymore." He puts his underwear in the suitcase and doesn't hug me.

"Then let's get out of here," I start taking my clothes out. I'm a woman. I must do what my man tells me to do.

Slowly, I arrange my clothes on the bed. I'm used to moving houses, and he wants me to come with him to meet his mother. He cares about me.

"Wally, do you have any jewelry that we can sell? To finance the trip and our stay there?" he asks as he rolls up his brown ties, and I remember Dad's signet ring and the pawn shop. How long has it been since I put it there?

"Wally, is everything alright?"

"Yes, Egon, everything is fine," I kiss him swiftly. How did I forget it?

The house is quiet in the morning as I get out of bed, careful not to wake him up. Egon is sleeping and snoring lightly. He's still wearing the white button-down shirt he wore yesterday, which is now wrinkled. He didn't bother taking off his tie, either. As the evening approached, he found some money and went to the café to say goodbye to his friends.

I pick up the empty wine bottle thrown on one of the drawings scattered on the floor and look at the drops that have stained the paper. I must hurry before he wakes up and wonders where I've gone.

I approach the pictures leaning on the wall, examining them one by one. Which one will fit? I recognize Mr. Klimt's signature on two of them, but finally, I choose two drawings that Egon painted of me and left lying on the floor when he went to the exhibition in Munich. He probably won't remember them. I don't have the courage to take the nude drawings in which he painted himself. I roll my pictures carefully, put on my plain summer dress and walk out the door, closing it quietly behind me.

"Good morning, how can I help you?" The pawnbroker raises his head from the jewelry placed in front of him on the table in his small shop. An iron-bar separates us. Does he recognize me from that time?

"I have two paintings I wish to sell," I place the rolled paintings on the counter.

"Sorry, Miss, I don't buy things. I'm a pawnbroker." He doesn't untie the simple thread binding the paintings.

"Please look at them. They are made by a young painter who will one day be famous. You can sell them for a lot of money."

"There is no money in paintings. There never will be." he pushes the rolled paintings back towards me, "Have a good day, Miss." He gets up from the chair and turns his back to me, facing the drawer cabinet behind him. Which one is my ring in?

I turn and face the door, put my hand on the handle, and stop. I don't know any gallery owner or art dealer, and I have to sell these. I also must get my ring back.

"Please, I also have a ring here." I turn again and return to the counter and the iron-barred window. "I will give you one painting in exchange for my ring and one painting for eight Kronen." I untie the thread that binds the rolled-up paintings and unfold them. He must look at them. He must see how good they are and how talented Egon is. "He'll be a very famous painter one day, I know it." I say to him again as I stand in front of him in the small shop, holding the paintings.

The salesman remains standing behind his counter and looks at the drawings. he examines the lines written on the brown paper, then he turns his eyes to me and begins to examine me, focusing on my red hair. He keeps looking at my blue eyes and slowly glances down at my breasts and legs. I feel my cheeks reddening. Egon painted me lying almost naked with my legs spread apart while my hands cover myself and my breasts are exposed. I don't move, but my hand holding the papers is shaking. He continues to look at my breasts and no longer looks at the painting.

"It's obscenity," he says in a low voice, "Pornography." He looks into my eyes with anger. "What sort of promiscuous woman agreed to be painted like this?" He continues to stare into my eyes, and I remain silent. "I will pay you, but not for the paintings. You must know what I mean," he says after a moment and smiles.

I freeze, unable to move. My legs seem to be welded to the floor with iron rivets. *Breathe slowly, breathe slowly.* I manage to tear my feet from the floor and walk out of his shop, hearing the door slam behind me as I walk quickly down the street. Only after a few steps do I notice that I'm still holding the paintings spread out in my hands, and the passers-by on the street are looking at them, moving their gaze from the paper to me. I roll and crush them between my hands. I feel my eyes burn, and the tears want to burst out and flood me.

Near Ms. Bertha's hostel, I stop and look at the front door and the sign above it. I haven't been here since that night. I take a deep breath and start walking towards the main street. I should have chosen a different way. But when I get closer, the hostel door opens, and I notice Erica coming out. I quickly turn around, walk to a side alley, and hide in it, turning my back to the street. I don't want her to mock me or ask what I'm holding in my hand. I cling to the stone wall in the small, dark alley, listening to the footsteps of those passing on the nearby street and looking around. Only me and a skinny, dirty cat stand there. It watches me apprehensively as it chews on the remains of a silver fish. But when it realizes that I don't intend on attacking it, it continues its meal in quick movements, making sure to occasionally turn its gaze to me. Has Erica already crossed the street? Can I turn around and leave the alley?

I wait a few moments longer and only then do I look from the alley to the street. She is gone. I must get rid of the two paintings, now a lump of crumpled paper in my hand. I can no longer hold them. They feel heavy, like a pair of weights that

191

prevent me from walking, making everyone stare at me. Can they see what is drawn on them even though they are wrinkled?

"Excuse me, Ms., do you have a match?" I ask a woman in a plain dress who is passing by on the street carrying a large basket, but she shakes her head no and continues walking. The other women I approach do not have a box of matches either, and finally, I turn to a man in a blue suit walking down the street smoking a pipe.

He examines me for a moment, takes a box of matches out of his jacket pocket, lights one, and hands it to me. What must he think of me? Does he think I smoke? Does he know that I am the one drawn naked inside the crumpled piece of papers?

With a trembling hand, I hold the match and bring it closer to the drawings, looking at the bursting flame that eats away at the brown paper. The man who gave me the match stands for a moment and watches me, as if debating whether to say something to me, but after a moment, he turns his back and continues walking down the street, leaving a small cloud pipe tobacco behind him. My eyes are fixed on the flame of the paper in my hand until I have no choice, and I drop it onto the cobblestones, watching the fire until it dies out, leaving behind only a few black crumbs. What have I done? What will I say to Egon if he asks where the paintings are?

I could return to the pawn shop. If I manage to get the money, I can tell Egon I sold them. I could go back to him. He will give me money for what I can offer him. For a moment, I feel like I want to throw up, and my mouth fills with a sour taste, even though I haven't eaten yet this morning. I must get away from here, from this pawn shop and Ms. Bertha's hostel. I must find someone who can give me money before Egon wakes up and wonders where I've gone.

I close the black iron gate behind me and walk on the gravel path, looking for the cat in the bushes, but I can't find it. The last time I was here it was winter, and the bushes were bare of any leaves. Now, they are full of red and pink flowers. I will knock on his door and ask him. He is the only one who will give me money.

At the door, I panic for a moment. What if Erica was on her way here, and she opens the door? I take a few breaths and ring the bell. I have no other choice.

"Hello, *Fuego*," he says as he sees me. He hasn't changed in those months we haven't seen each other. He is still wearing the same gray smock, and he is still looking at me with his blue eyes.

"I need money," I tell him immediately, "We're about to leave Vienna," I keep talking, unable to stop myself, and blurt the words out. "Egon mustn't know I'm here. I love him."

"Come in," he gives me a smile that suddenly seems malicious and turns and walks towards his studio, leaving the door open.

I remain standing on the doorstep. What if there's someone there that he's painting right now? But after a moment, I go inside. I have no other choice. I shouldn't have told him I love Egon.

He stands in the center of the studio, and I follow him, entering the room. If there's someone else there that he's drawing naked, I'll turn around and run away. But the big bed in the corner of the room is empty. Only the black and white striped bedspread is laid on it.

"We are together," I stand before him and look into his eyes.

"I'm happy to hear that." He smiles at me again and sends his hand to my cheek. I feel his warm palm caressing my cheek, and I freeze, unable to move, just breathing slowly.

With a gentle, slow movement, his fingers go down and caress my neck, slide further down to my breasts, and he runs his hand over them. All the while, he continues to look into my eyes and smile a little while I am frozen and unable to move, still looking into his blue eyes. *Breathe slowly.* I have to do something. Why did I come to ask him for help?

His palm caressing my breasts stops, and he turns around, goes to his pants which are lying on a plain wooden box at the end of the room, bends down, and takes out a wallet. I feel tears running down my cheeks, but I remain standing, frozen. Why did I come here?

"Take it," he approaches me, holding my hand and placing some bills in it. "Keep this innocence. It will save you," He continues to say and caresses my wet cheek with his large palm. Finally, I manage to move. I turn and run away from the room, opening the house door and quickly fleeing, the noise of my footsteps on the gravel path like the hooves of galloping horses. When I get near our house, I stop for a few minutes to catch my breath. I look at the wall surrounding the palace garden and the guards guarding the locked gate. I'll wait out here for a few minutes and then go home. I shouldn't have let him touch me. I should have stopped him. Next time I'll be brave enough.

"Wally? Where have you been?" I hear Egon when I close the door quietly.

"I got money," I approach him and put the bills on the bed, "For the trip. Let's make a new start."

"My red cherry, you are wonderful." He is still lying in bed and reaches out, caressing the bills.

"I had a ring. I sold it," I tell him, unable to tell him what I did with the paintings or Mr. Klimt.

"You are indeed my protective muse." He rises and hugs me tightly, "Don't cry, everything will be alright." He caresses my hair, "Outside this gray city, we will start a new life, you will see. We will be free when we leave Vienna, please stop crying." He runs his fingers over my wet cheeks.

Chapter Eight

Krumlov, South Bohemia

A s we walk down the boulevard on the way to the train station, we stop to rest for a few minutes. That's when I see them.

They march in straight columns wearing blue-gray uniforms, holding guns in their hands, barrels resting on their shoulders. Every one of them also carries a large backpack on their backs. I put the heavy suitcase on the ground, let my aching hand rest, and watch them.

An officer mounted on a horse rides at the front. He sits upright on the saddle in his clean uniform. His red collar is decorated with gold stars, and his wide mustache sticks out from under his visor hat, almost hiding his eyes. He does not turn back but rides leisurely on his horse, ignoring the marching soldiers following him. Behind him, the junior commanders walk proudly, looking like a proud mother goose leading her chicks.

"Long live the Empire," a worker in blue work clothes shouts at them and raises his hand in a fist motion.

"Long live the Austro-Hungarian Empire," a woman in a yellow dress throws flowers at them, and the officer on the horse stops for a moment, smiles at her, and salutes before continuing down the boulevard towards the city's exit.

"Long live the emperor," I shout at them.

"Return home soon, after defeating the enemy," an older woman in a gray dress, shouts beside me.

"Like us, they are embarking on a new journey." I smile at Egon.

More people stop at the sides of the boulevard and look at them, waving goodbye. The carriages also move to the side, making way.

"May God protect you." An elderly woman in a black dress says, crossing herself as they pass her.

"Don't worry," another woman answers her, "the emperor will take care of them." The people around her nod in agreement. I watch the old woman who continues to cross herself, her lips muttering a silent prayer.

"I'm so happy we are going together," Egon hugs me, even though I'm sweating from the long walk in the sun I wipe my sweat away, bend down and lift my suitcase again, giving the soldiers one last look. Some of them look at me and smile, and one even slightly moves his hand as if he wants to bow, but after a moment, he turns his gaze forward and smiles at other women who are waving goodbye.

"We'll have a wonderful time in our new place. It doesn't matter if war breaks out. We have each other." I grab hold of Egon's hand. One girl runs to the soldiers, quickly kisses one of them, gives him a flower, and hurries away before the soldier stops and disturbs the marching order. Another moment passes, and they move away down the boulevard, looking like a large gray flock of sheep moving slowly to a different world behind the blue mountains, on the horizon. Once they have gone, the street is once again filled with horse-drawn carriages and noisy automobiles.

In the distance, I can already see the train station with the marble statues on its roof, as if waiting to greet us.

As we enter the train station and walk under the big clock, I look at all the men carrying suitcases and the women accompanied by porters carrying luggage boxes, but this time it is different. For the first time in my life, I am going to travel by train.

I silently look at the locomotive that has entered the station and stop to rest on the side of the platform. We never had money to travel by train to faraway places, like the ones I read about in books in our little kitchen in the village, back when Dad was still alive.

"Wait for me here, my cherry. I'm going to buy us tickets." Egon places his suitcase next to mine on the platform, "Is everything alright?"

"Yes," I smile at him and wipe my tears. "I'm just excited."

He kisses my lips hard, his hands caressing my waist, ignoring three older ladies standing beside us. "Don't go anywhere without me." He smiles and walks away.

I watch him as he walks to the ticket office, but feel the stares as the three ladies glare at me and whisper. How is it that men can behave impolitely and kiss a woman, but that same woman will be gossiped about? I turn my back to them and ignore them. At least I'm dressed as elegantly as they are. In honor of this trip, I wore my beautiful dress, the one I bought for Mr. Klimt. Now I am wearing it especially for the meeting with Egon's mother.

"Your ticket," Egon returns from the register, and hands me a cardboard ticket with our destination written on it.

"Thank you, my Egon," I hold him and kiss his lips, feeling their softness.

"Let's go, my cherry. The train is waiting for us." He takes my hand, and we walk onto the platform. I make sure to pass by the three ladies with my chin up as I smile. I will kiss him whenever I want to.

Inside the car, Egon places our luggage on the shelf above our heads, and I sit down on the wooden seat, caressing the smooth mahogany wood and looking at the copper lamps on the ceiling. The car's interior looks like the café where Egon goes to meet his friends, only smaller, like the wooden candy boxes in the shop near the palace, decorated with delicate brown and gold ornaments. More and more people enter the car and take their places around us, and I press my face to the window's glass, looking at the big clock that hangs on the station wall repeatedly, waiting for the conductor's whistle.

Precisely on time, I hear the whistle, and the locomotive starts to blow like a big dog after a long run in the field. I look out the window at the platform moving away from me and at the station disappearing from my sight. The city houses remain far behind, and are replaced by green fields and snowy mountains on the horizon. I watch the cows graze in the meadow, ignoring the train. Occasionally, I notice a horse carrying a large cart loaded with hay.

"Tickets, please." The conductor walks in the car wearing a black uniform and a visor, and I hand him my ticket.

"Put your head on my shoulder. Try to sleep" Egon hugs me, and I lean on him, looking at the newspaper held by the gentleman sitting in the seat across from us. 'The emperor signed an alliance with the Germans and will enlarge the army.' The title screams in black letters. But I'm a woman, I shouldn't care about politics. I close my eyes and try to sleep. We are traveling together as a couple to a new place. Soon I will meet his mother. Everything will be alright.

"Wally, wake up," I feel the touch of his hand and open my eyes. Where am I? I look around at the dark brown wooden carriage. The train is still rocking, like a boat moving leisurely on waves, and the afternoon sun sends long rays that paint the carriage with golden colors. The gentleman who sitting in front of us earlier, reading a newspaper, has gone, and an older woman in a dark purple dress is sitting in his seat. Where are we? "Wally, we're almost there," Egon pats my arm, and I get up and look out the window.

Green trees surround the railroad, and it seems I can reach out my hand through the window and touch their branches, which are moving in front of me. I open the window and peer up at the cloud of black smoke coming out of the locomotive's chimney. In the distance, I see several yellowish buildings. The conductor passes in the car and announces: "Krumlov, Bohemia, Krumlov, Bohemia. The train will stop for fifteen minutes for a refreshment break and then resume." The gasping locomotive begins to slow down as I continue to look out. On the platform, there is only a man in uniform, a black and white shaggy dog, and a woman, older than me, in a black dress with a white lace collar. Is that Egon's mother? I smooth the fabric of my dress. I need to make a good impression on her. The black locomotive blows a loud breath and stops in front of the station building while the dog accompanies it by barking and running along the train.

"Wally, let's go." Egon extends his hand to me. We have arrived.

"Mother, meet Miss Walburga, Wally, the one I wrote about in the letter." Egon introduces me when we get down to the platform and walk towards her.

"Very nice to meet you, Mrs. Schiele." I bow politely and shake her hand. Her black hair is decorated with streaks of silver, and is carefully gathered. Her skin is white, her lips are thin and pale without lipstick, and she has a pointy nose, like a vulture.

"Nice to meet you." She surveys me with her eyes. Her gaze examines my short, red hair, down to my eyes, my bare neck, and dress. "Will you be comfortable here in a dress like that?" She continues to look at it. "This is a place of simple people, not fancy evening dresses."

"Yes, Mrs. Schiele," I answer as I reach out and straighten the fabric of my dress, even though I did it before we got off the train. She hasn't asked me to call her by her first name, Marie.

"All passengers are requested to get back on the train." The man in uniform announces on the platform while blowing his whistle, and the shaggy dog runs towards me, wagging his tail and sniffing my palm.

"Shall we go?" Mrs. Schiele asks as she puts her hand in Egon's, "We haven't seen each other for so long. You rarely write to me." They walk towards the station's exit and onto the dirt road leading to the village. I stroke the shaggy dog's head one more time before grabbing my heavy suitcase and walking after them. We've finally moved away from the city that has suffocated us.

❦

I watch the red dusky sky as we walk between the village houses, crossing the central square and the several shops surrounding it. The houses here look similar to those in the village where I was born, two or three-floored, cream-colored buildings carrying a triangular tiled roof. I look at a girl in a gray dress running around the square chasing a chicken, her brown hair fluttering everywhere as she laughs while the chicken runs away, clucking and flapping its wings. I smile to myself. I was like her once too.

"Wally, are you coming?" Egon calls me, and I follow them into one of the alleys, feeling the houses on both sides protecting me. The village is quiet in the early evening hours, with no noise from automobiles or tram clangs. Only in the distance can I hear the whistling noise of a train passing through the fields.

"I've found you a place." Mrs. Schiele says and pulls out a large key from her dress pocket, opens a wooden door, and we climb the stairs to a small room on the second floor. "You will be comfortable here." She takes out a box of matches and lights the gas lamp in the room. I enter the room after them and place my suitcase on the floor, looking around. The room is simple but pleasantly furnished. There is even a colorful curtain on the window and a jar of flowers on the small table. In the corner, there is also a place for Egon's drawing pages and the white canvases Mrs. Schiele brought for him.

"Thank you, Mrs. Schiele." I smile at her.

"I prepared dinner for you. Refresh yourself after the long journey and come eat."

"Thank you, Mother," Egon says to her, placing his suitcase next to the easel, opening it, and taking out the wooden box of paints he brought with him. There is an enamel water pitcher jug next to the bed. I can refresh myself after the trip.

"Come with me, Wally." She turns to me, "I'll show you where you will be sleeping." She turns to leave the room and talks with her back turned as she walks down the stairs. "In our village, it's not customary for unmarried people to stay together in the same room."

I stand at the entrance to the room and look at Egon, but he just turns to me, making a gesture of helplessness and smiles, saying nothing. I pick up my suitcase and follow her quietly. I'm a guest here. I have to respect her rules. She is the mother of the man I am with. But at the door, I look back at Egon. I want him to fight for me, just like he knows how to kiss me impolitely whenever he desires. But he has already turned his back on me and is busy arranging his painting color tubes.

"Here, this is your room." She goes down to the basement and lights a candle, placing it on the large, plain wooden table in the center. "I'm sure you'll get along here, even if you were used to better conditions in Vienna." She turns to me, "This is not Vienna. Here, we are committed to family values and morality. We believe in marriage." She walks to the corner of the basement and lights another candle. "To be honest, Egon surprised me when he informed me in the letter that he was coming with a companion. I thought he was coming to visit me and his friends here by himself."

"We've been together for several months, Mrs. Schiele. Egon is devoted to me," I can't help myself and tell her, even though I have to behave according to her rules.

"I'd appreciate it if you keep that information for yourself. The whole town needn't know about it." She looks at me for a long moment. In the dim light, her eyes look black. "Refresh yourself and come to dinner. You must be hungry from that long day."

"Thank you, Mrs. Schiele." I answer quickly, wishing for her to leave me alone so I can get organized, even though what I truly want is to go back to the train station and take the next train to Vienna. Egon shouldn't have let her separate us. Breathe slowly, breathe slowly. If I want to succeed here, I must obey her rules.

I wait until I hear her footsteps going up the stairs, and only then do I place the suitcase on the stone floor, sit down and look around. The tiny room in Ms. Bertha's hostel was much smaller. She doesn't scare me. I smile at the dusty wine bottles lying in the corner next to the large glass jars of preserved fruit and sausages hanging on thin ropes, waiting for the cold winter. They smell good.

"Wally, are you ready for dinner?" Egon appears at the basement door. He's combed his hair and changed into a clean shirt.

"Get out of here. I'm getting ready." I kick him out and close the wooden door behind him, locking the bolt. I haven't forgiven him for not protecting me in front of his mother yet, but I know I must be nice to her. She mentioned the word marriage.

I open the suitcase, take out one of the plain dresses I brought with me, and put it on. I also make sure to comb my hair so that it is neat. At first, I apply a slight blush but then I wipe it off. I must be simple, not stand out. I need her to love me.

"Thank you, Mrs. Schiele, for hosting us here." I say politely as we sit around the table at her house, and she serves us a meat stew.

"Thank you, Mother, for finding us a place on such short notice." Egon smiles at her. He sits between her and me, and the tablecloth hides his hand, which is touching my thigh. "Thank you also for hosting Wally." He adds.

"I'm always happy when you come here. Your friends ask about you every time I see them." She pours some stew onto his plate, "But I tell them you are busy in Vienna."

"Yes, I was very busy in Vienna." He continues stroking my thighs, and I look down and smile.

"Wally, is everything alright?" Mrs. Schiele asks as she pours stew onto my plate.

"Yes, thank you." I answer her, blushing. My hand moves his from my leg. I will make her love me.

"So, what paintings are you drawing these days?" she asks Egon.

"I draw buildings, Mother. I like to draw the beautiful architecture of Vienna." He answers, and I look down and concentrate on eating the delicious meat stew. I wonder what she would think if she saw his real paintings.

"My cherry," I later hear a knock on the door. I sit up in bed, dressed in my nightgown and comb my hair.

"Good night, Egon." I get up and stand close to the closed basement's wooden door, whispering to him.

"My cherry, Wally, open the door. I have something important to tell you."

"What?" I bring my ear close to the door.

"I can't say it to the door. I must see you."

I open the latch and the door. "What did you want to tell me?" I look at him. I still haven't forgiven him.

"The more I am away from you, the more I desire you." He gets inside and starts kissing me forcefully while trying to remove my nightgown.

"Egon, no." I break away from him, "I thought you really wanted to tell me something."

"Isn't what I said good enough?" He unbuttons his shirt, revealing his smooth chest.

"It's good, but not here." My fingers grip his shirt, and I start to close its buttons.

"It's perfect here, in your dark basement." He laughs and holds my palms, not letting me pull away from him.

"No, the people here are different."

"No one will know." He laughs. "It's a simple village. Every-one has already gone to sleep."

"But we're not married."

"Who cares?" He tries to kiss me again.

"Egon, no." I move my face away from his face, wanting to tell him I care that we are not married.

"I won't tell anyone." He bends down and removes his brown shoes.

"No, Egon, you have to go." I pull away from him, "I love you, but you have to go." His mother will never forgive me if she knew he came to stay with me at night.

"I need you. I'm a man. I don't care what the people of this place think about me or you." He approaches me again, trying to hug me, but I forcefully push him away.

"They will hate us. We must hold back for a while. Think about me." I come closer and stroke his quaff. I miss him too.

"They will not be the first to hate me. It's okay."

"No, it's not okay." I continue stroking his hair, sliding my hand over the back of his head.

"I thought you were different." He pulls away from me angrily, his eyes black with rage.

"I am different. You know me. You know exactly who I am. But not here."

"No, you're no different. In the end, you're just like every-one else." He bends down, grabs his shoes, gets up, and contin-ues talking to me angrily. "I thought you were a revolutionary, like me."

"I am a revolutionary like you. I let you paint me in poses no other woman would agree to, but they won't accept what we did in Vienna here." I move closer to him, but he pulls back and stands at the door, his button-down shirt still open.

"I'm ready to pay the price, and whoever I'm with should also be ready to pay it."

"Egon, please, I'm with you. I love you." I say quietly, wanting to tell him that I've already paid the price to the man at the pawnshop and to Mr. Klimt, but I can't tell him that. What does he want me to do? Does he wish for his mother to hate me? For the people in this town to hate me? They will blame his inappropriate behavior on me.

"You may love me, but a revolution needs more than love." He says and slams the wooden door in my face, leaving me standing alone in the basement in my nightgown. Why must women always feel guilty?

⁂

The following morning, I climb the stairs to his room and knock on the door. I want to explain myself so that he may understand, but there is no answer.

"Egon," I knock on the door again and push the handle. To my surprise, the door is unlocked, and I walk in. "Egon?"

The sunlight from the window illuminates his jacket which lies on the chair, the sheets on the bed are made up, and the room is empty. Where could he be? The box of paints he brought with him is also gone. I leave the room and start walking through the town, looking for him.

The locals watch me curiously as I pass the village's main square, looking around. In the center of the square, a few children play with a hoop on the cobblestones; they roll and run after it, laughing while holding a stick. In the corner is a café with metal tables outside, occupied by several gentlemen sitting and enjoying the summer sun. On the other side of the square, a few women are selling apples and pears from wooden crates, and a cart of hay tied to a horse patiently awaits its owner, who has entered the post office. I cross the square and continue to look around, walking through the village streets. I came here for him. I want us to make up and be together.

After a long time, I see him in the distance. On the other side of the stream that crosses the town, he is lying on a picnic blanket, and next to him are two men about his age. His easel is standing unused on the grass far away from them. Why didn't he invite me to join? I wave at him, but he doesn't notice me. One of the young men takes a bottle of wine from a straw basket on the grass and sips from it, passing it to the others. I want to call out loud to him, but on the path next to me, three women are talking to each other, and I don't want to draw attention. I will look for the bridge that crosses the stream.

"Wally, come join us." He calls me and waves his hand when he notices me, "These are my friends," he points at them, but he doesn't get up to hug me. He doesn't make room for me on the blanket, either. "Everyone, this is Wally. She's with me." He introduces me, and I politely smile at them, remaining standing next to the picnic blanket.

"We apologize for stealing him from you." One of them says to me with a smile. He has dirty blond hair that falls over his eyes, and he's wearing a white button-down shirt with one of its buttons open. "Nice to meet you, I'm Klaus." He holds out his hand, and I shake it.

"Nice to meet you, my name is Bernhard. You have Egon all to yourself all the time. We also deserve some of him." The other laughs and sips from the bottle, raising his hand and offering me wine. He has slightly darker hair than Klaus, and his face is full of freckles."

"Thank you." I shake his hand and take the bottle from his hand, sipping it and ignoring the bitter taste of the wine in my throat. I don't want them to think I'm a little girl who can't hold her drink.

"Come, join us." Klaus moves a little on the blanket and makes room for me. Why didn't Egon offer me to sit with them? I sit down next to Klaus and sip from the bottle again as I watch Egon. He remains lying on his elbows on the blanket, examining me.

"You have good wine in this village. This place is beautiful." I smile at Bernhard.

"Beautiful indeed," he takes the bottle of wine from my hand. "Egon, why didn't you tell us how beautiful she is?"

"It's because he likes to keep me all to himself in my small basement." I answer him, wanting Egon to get a little jealous and intervene, but he remains silent and just continues to watch me.

"Then it's lucky you managed to escape this horrible basement and find us." The dirty blond haired Klaus butts in. "That way, he can't just blame us for wasting his time and getting in his way of becoming an artist."

"What are you drawing?" I ask Egon. I want to sit next to him on the blanket.

"A landscape." Egon finally answers me, "I like to paint landscapes."

"I would like to see it." I hold the bottle of wine and get up from the blanket, approaching the easel that is standing in the grass in front of the townhouses on the other side of the stream. Egon gets up and comes with me. I can smell his body odor which is so familiar to me. I miss him, but I don't want to hug him in front of his friends. I want us to make peace.

"At home, you draw people, not houses." I say while looking at the painting. He painted the town's houses as if they were colored cubes connected in shades of yellowish brown. Why didn't he paint such paintings in Vienna? Why did he paint me in such blatant nudity there? I recall the pawnbroker's look and sip from the wine.

"I paint what I feel I want to paint." He answers, taking the bottle of wine from my hand, sipping it, turning his back to me, and returning to sit among his friends.

I remain standing next to the easel, looking at the colored spots painted on the canvas. He painted white, red, and yellow clothes hanging on ropes to dry between the houses. Only the people are missing, although the three ladies still stand on the side of the stream talking to each other.

I go back to sitting among them on the blanket. I want him to tell them that at home he draws me, that I am his muse and the one he loves, but they keep silent, and only freckled Bernhard takes out a pipe and a pipe cleaner from his pocket, slowly fidgeting with it while Egon and Klaus watch him. I feel my presence bothers them.

"See you in the evening," I rise from the blanket and say goodbye, not before taking another sip of wine. Distanced from them, I think I hear them start talking again, but maybe it's just the sound of the stream flowing nearby.

The grass beside the stream moves gently in the autumn evening breeze. I return to my basement, go down the stairs and wait for him. I miss the conversations we had at the beginning, when we walked to the Prater in the evenings. I also miss being his muse. The hours tick by, and I sit on the bed and wait for him. Now and then, I hear footsteps on the street above and look up at the small window tucked near the basement ceiling facing the street, hoping I will hear his steps on the stairs. But he doesn't come down and knock on the door like he did yesterday, asking me to open it for him. Was I wrong to kick him out of my room? After all, he is my partner, not his mother.

Another hour goes by, and another one, and he does not come to be with me. There is no point in sitting here and waiting for him. I will go to his room. I get out of bed, open my suitcase and take out my small rounded makeup box. Quickly, I apply lipstick, put on some blush, do my hair, spray myself with perfume, and stand in front of the mirror. For a moment, I hesitate whether to wear my beautiful dress for him, but it doesn't really matter. He will probably try to undress me right away anyway, just like he did yesterday.

At the top of the stairs, I breathe deeply before knocking on his room door. What if his mother sees me with him? Will she think me immoral?

I press my ear to the wooden door, trying to listen, but I don't hear any noise, and I knock on the door, like I did that morning. This time the door is closed and locked. He isn't in his room.

I go down the stairs and turn to go back to my basement, but in the distance, I hear music, and I walk in the dark between the buildings, following the sounds. In the center of the square, between the closed shops, I stop and watch the light coming from the café.

Like the flames of a campfire, the yellow light invites me to come closer, and the sounds of laughter and music draw me in.

Step by step, I walk until I am standing in the doorway and stop, searching for him among the people sitting inside. When I see him, my breath stops.

He is sitting with his two friends, but another girl sits on his lap while everyone laughs.

Egon is wearing his fine clothes; brown pants, and a white button-down shirt, while Klaus and Bernhard are wearing the same outfits they wore that morning, when they all talked to each other enthusiastically. On the table in front of them is a bottle of wine and full glasses, and on his lap is the girl with wheat color hair, wearing an orange chiffon dress.

I freeze in my place, unable to go inside and throw the bottle of wine at him, but also unable to step back and disappear into the darkness of the square. My eyes are fixed on the girl in the orange dress, who looks younger than me. She is sitting with her back to me, but I can hear her laughing as she touches his hair before she gets off his lap and sits between him and dirty-blond haired Klaus, who turns his gaze and notices my presence.

He turns to Egon and whispers something in his ear, but I'm no longer there. The movement of his lips as he starts whispering is like magic that frees me from the chains that bind me to the café's light, and I turn around and start walking quickly through the dark square. I must get to my basement. I must get away from here.

"Wally, wait," I hear a shout, but I start running. I don't want to see him.

"Wally," I hear him yell and gasp. Then I feel his hand grab my shoulder as he tries to stop me.

"Get off of me." I shout at him, "Go to her."

"You don't understand, it's nothing." He is breathing hard, "I've been waiting for you." He stands in front of me in the dark and stops me, not letting me walk away.

"She was on your lap." I shout, trying to hold back my tears.

"It's not what you think," he tries to kiss me, "I tried to make you jealous after you didn't want me. She's nothing to me."

"That's not true, you want her," I wipe my eyes. In the dark, I can feel his hands holding me in place.

"You're imagining. I love only you, and no others." He hugs me forcefully, "But you can't imprison me with moral chains. I'm an artist. You know that. I need thrills."

"I'm trying to listen to your mother," I move away from him, "I'm trying to listen to the people of this town." I start walking again in the dark, towards my basement, "I didn't tie myself up with the shackles of morality for no reason."

"I am not my mother." He remains standing and does not follow me. "You knew who I was from the first moment you met me." He says, and I stop and watch him, seeing him as a silhouette while the café lights shine behind him like a beacon spreading light in the darkness. "You knew, and you followed me." He continues, his silhouette as black as the night.

I stand and watch him, saying nothing. I want to believe him, but I can't.

"I'll be waiting for you in a café." He finally says and turns around, and I watch him walk away from me until he disappears inside the café. I can hear music and laughter from inside. Why did I choose his mother's demands and not him?

I stand for a few moments in the deserted square, looking at the café, but I am unable to go inside. Finally, I turn and walk to my basement. I want to talk with someone who is not from this place so badly right now.

In the basement, I take a piece of paper and a pencil from my bag and write a letter to Ms. Bertha, though she probably won't answer it and probably doesn't want to hear from me at all. I'm interested in how she's doing, how she feels, and how all the girls are doing. I can't tell her what I'm going through.

Then I go to bed, ensuring the door's latch remains open. Maybe he will regret what he said and come back to me. I remain lying in bed, looking at the lit candle and fighting to keep my eyes opened.

The following morning, when I wake up, I see that the candle has burned out. Egon didn't come at night to my basement and did not try to get under the blanket with me.

When I go out and look for him, I find him again on the river bank painting the village houses, and I sit down next to him all day long, even though we barely talk to each other.

In the following days, I sit by his side and sometimes walk alone through the fields, enjoying the summer sun. We sometimes meet his mother in the evenings for dinner, but I make sure not to go out with him to the café. I also don't look for him in his room anymore. I know he won't knock on my basement door again at night and try to enter.

"How are you adjusting here?" Mrs. Schiele asks me one day when I return alone from a walk in the fields. She is holding a straw basket with sausages she bought from the butcher in the village square.

"I'm enjoying myself here, Mrs. Schiele, thank you." I stand in front of her embarrassed, stroking my short hair and pulling out straws. Earlier, I lay in the field and looked at the clouds, searching for shapes.

"Fall is coming soon. Have you made any plans?"

"What do you mean?" I look at the basket she's holding in her hands, her fingers clutching it as if they were the claws of a bird of prey.

"Each of us has a summer vacation when we are young. I had one too," she looks at me.

"And what happened at the end of your summer vacation?" I look her in the eyes. Is she trying to scare me?

"My parents found me a man that befitted my status, not the one I dreamed about while I was lying in a field or a haystack, doing things young girls are not supposed to do." She reaches out, pulls out another straw from my hair, and hands it to me.

"Egon loves me." I answer her, feeling myself blush.

"Egon needs the right woman for his status, not the one he turns his head after." She answers indifferently. "Besides, from what I've seen since Egon arrived here, I don't think you're right about that either."

"I'm a polite and educated girl." I answer, but I want to yell at her that Egon doesn't want me here because I'm trying to follow the rules. The same rules she set.

"What did you do before you met my Egon?" She continues to stand in front of me on the street.

"I worked in a rich woman's house." I answer her, not wanting to tell her about Ms. Bertha's hostel or Mr. Klimt. Could Egon have told her how he met me?

"So you understand what I mean," she smiles at me. "Egon will not marry a servant woman. Have a nice day." She passes me by and continues walking down the street toward her house. I follow her with my gaze, feeling my face burn. Why did I behave the way she expected me to if there was no point in doing so?

"By the way," She stops after a few steps and turns to me, pulling out a small package wrapped in brown paper tied with a rope, "The postman brought you a small package. It's not customary for you to write your name next to my address." She returns, places the package in my hand, and walks away again, disappearing at the street corner.

I grab the package and rush to my basement. I want to get away from this village and the people who live in it. I go down the stairs and close the heavy door behind me, close the bolt, and light a candle. Then I look at the return address. Ms. Bertha's neat handwriting is written on it. With trembling fingers, I untie the rope that wraps the package, peel off the brown paper and notice a note that falls onto the floor. I pick it up and read the words: *'Why do you care how I am? I thought of something that suits you. Listen to what Ms. Bertha tells you. It's time for you to decide what kind of heroine you want to be.'*

I open the paper and see that she sent me a book; 'Little Women'. I run my fingers over the book's title, then over the name of the author I've never heard of, 'Louisa May Alcott.' I sit on the bed, open the first page, start reading, and begin sobbing after a few pages.

I lie in bed and read from the book until the evening hours., Then I put it on the small chair and get dressed. I comb my hair forcefully, apply strong pink lipstick, put on some blush, and wear my beautiful dress.

Without stopping, I walk through the dark square to the café, like a moth drawn to a flame. At the doorway, I stand, looking for him. It takes me a moment to spot him among all the people in the café. He is with his two friends, Klaus and Bernhard, and with two women. They are all sitting around a table and looking at Egon, who is talking and describing something with his hands. The men smile, and the women look at him admiringly.

"Good evening, my Egon." I approach the table and smile at everyone.

"Come, join us." Freckled Bernhard says, rising from his seat, hurrying to bring me a chair.

"Thanks, but there is no need." I smile at him and sit on Egon's lap, kissing his lips passionately. I don't care what everyone says. I know how to be a rebel too.

At first, Egon closes his lips, but after a moment, he opens them slightly and lets me feel his warmth while I continue to kiss him and caress the back of his neck. After a while, I turn to his friends and smile at the girls looking at us, "Now you can bring me a chair." I say to Bernhard and get up from Egon's lap, patiently waiting for him to return with the chair while my hand continues to caress Egon's black hair.

⁕

"Egon, there is someone there," I say to him a few days later.

We are both in a field outside the village. He is standing over me next to the easel, and I am lying in the grass wearing only my camisole rolled up over my thighs.

"He won't notice us," Egon continues to paint.

"Egon, he is coming down the path in our direction." I say, wanting to reach out and put on the summer dress I removed and threw on the ground at his feet.

"Wally, don't move." He laughs and approaches me, bends down and kisses my lips before returning to paint.

219

"He'll see me like this."

"What do you care? We are artists."

"They will talk about us."

"So, it's a sign our art interests them." Egon doesn't stop painting even for a moment.

I watch the farmer who walks along the path holding a pitchfork and approaching us. Although we are a little far from the path, if he looks in our direction, he will notice Egon painting me lying on the grass, almost naked. I reach for the dress but change my mind and return to my pose for Egon. We are artists, and artists create art that not everyone understands. I don't care if he notices us.

I look at Egon and his hand holding the brush, trying to ignore the farmer. However, only after I notice him moving away from us down the path leading to the village, do I breathe a sigh of relief. We are rebels, and we will change the world with our paintings. I lean back on the grass, ignore Egon's complaints, and close my eyes, letting the pleasant sun warm my body.

A caressing sensation awakes me. Who is touching me?

I open my eyes and notice Egon sitting near me, his face close to my body.

"What are you doing?" I smile at him. The caressing feeling continues with a touch of wet material.

"Nothing, my Cherry." He smiles and puts on his serious expression, looking at me.

"What is it?" I raise myself on my elbows and look down. "You're crazy," I look at him, not knowing whether to be angry or hug him. His hand holding a brush, is drawing lines and colors on my exposed body, turning it into a painting.

"You are my muse, and art has no limits."

"And how exactly will I go back to town like this?" I look up at him.

"I'm sure you'll find a solution," he laughs.

"I think you'll have to find a solution for this, too," I reach for the color palette he's holding, dip my finger in the mixed colors and apply it to his nose and cheeks, starting to laugh.

"You're an immoral woman with red hair." He applies a line on my face with the brush.

"And you are an arrogant, handsome man who is going to be a famous painter," I stand up and look at myself, "And I am a mermaid who is going to clean herself." I run to the stream that flows nearby, feeling the soil clods under my feet. I remove my camisole while walking, and enter the cool water naked. I don't even care if his mother walks by and sees me like this.

"Wait for me, my cherry," I hear him walking behind me as he carries the easel and paints with him, and I'm already waiting for him in the water, seeing how he takes off his clothes and jumps in naked after me. With strong movements, he swims to me and hugs me in the water.

In the evening, we meet again at the café with his friends, and Egon orders a bottle of wine for the table.

"Wally, you're one of us." Klaus says as he sips the wine.

"She always was," Egon hugs me, "She just didn't know what to do in order to be accepted."

"Now I know," I kiss him, sip from the glass of wine and take a piece of the rustic bread and the sausage on the table. We haven't eaten anything since morning. I watch two girls sitting at a nearby table with an older woman. They are twelve or thirteen years old and dressed in light lilac and lavender dresses, their blond hair gathered in braids decorated with colorful ribbons. I smile at them. They look to me like delicate flowers that will unfold their petals in all their glory in a moment. Despite the food on their table, they do not eat but rather look at us, and their blue eyes wander from Egon to me and back.

"Good evening, young ladies." Egon smiles at them from his place at the table and raises the glass of wine he is holding.

"You drank too much, Mr. Painter," I lower his hand holding the glass, take it from him and sip the sweet wine.

"I drank just the right amount." He answers and continues to smile at the two girls.

They smile back at him and continue to watch us, but then the older woman notices them smiling at Egon, and gets up from her seat at the table and slaps them both hard.

I watch them both, unable to look away, even though it's impolite. They are no longer smiling, and their big eyes look with fear at the woman who accompanies them. She takes a bill out of her purse, throws it on the table, grabs the girls' hands, and marches them out of the café. On the way out, she quietly says something to Egon as she passes by him, but I can't hear what she says. Did other people in the café notice what happened? I look down at the table and continue to hold my glass of wine, sipping it all. I'm not hungry anymore.

"Egon, I think we should go home." I say to him and get up.

"But we just sat down. I'm still hungry."

"I'm dizzy. I think I drank too much." I answer him, even though I want to drink more.

"Shall we help you?" His friends ask us.

"No, we'll manage on our own." Egon finally gets up from the table, "See you tomorrow." He says goodbye to them, and I let him lead me out of the café, lowering my eyes as we walk among the people.

By the stairs, I let him lead me to his room. Since that conversation with his mother, I go up to his room at night or let him come into the basement and into my bed.

"What did she say to you?" I ask as I turn my back to him and undress.

"Who?"

"The woman, in the café, with the two young girls."

"I didn't hear. There was a noise." He answers me, "Are you coming to bed?"

I turn off the gas lamp and lie beside him, wondering if he's lying about what that woman said to him.

The sound of shattering glass wakes me up. What happened?

"Egon?" I call him in the dark, reach out my hand and feel his warm body beside me.

"Perverts," I hear a muffled call from the street, followed by a thump and more shattering glass.

"Egon, wake up." I yell and shake him.

"Wally, what is it?"

"I think they threw a stone from the street," I search for my nightgown in the dark, feeling the cool night breeze.

"Who threw it?"

"I don't know," I put my nightgown on and get out of bed, searching for the table. A moment later, I feel something stab into my leg and scream.

"Wally, what happened?"

"I'm hurt," I lean on the table, manage to find the box of matches, and light the gas lamp. In the yellowish light, I notice the glasses scattered on the floor, along with two black stones. Why did they do this to us? My injured foot drips dark blood droplets on the parquet floor, but the bleeding is not heavy.

"Thugs," Egon gets off the bed, steps carefully between the glass shards, and goes to the window, cursing into the night.

"Is there someone outside?" I ask him. Will they throw more stones at us?

"No, I don't see anyone. They ran away. I should go down and show them." He turns to me, "Are you okay? You're injured."

"I'm fine, it's not bad," I wrap the wound up with a handkerchief.

"Let's go back to bed." He comes near and hugs me, "These are just brutes. They won't come back. Put out the candle, and go back to sleep."

I wash the wound and tie it tightly with a handkerchief, and we return to bed. He hugs me, but I can't fall asleep. I feel the night wind coming in through the broken window as it blows on my face. We shouldn't have done what we did.

The following day, I walk to the square and enter the small delicatessen. I want to buy cheese for dinner.

"Good morning," I greet the salesman, but he just looks at me and returns to his work, ignoring me.

"Good morning," I say to him again.

"I don't have any goods today, come another day." He answers and turns his back to me. I look at all the cheeses spread out on the table and want to say something to him, but I change my mind and leave the store. What harm have we caused him? Is it because that farmer saw us in the field? We were alone in the meadow and did not disturb anyone.

I cross the square over to the bakery, but when I go inside, all the customers waiting in line stop talking and look at me. I smile awkwardly and walk out after a minute. I don't want to be refused service here as well. Are they gossiping about me behind my back? I walk away from the square and head towards Egon's room. He will tell me what's going on.

I knock on his door, but he doesn't answer me. Maybe he went out looking for a glazier to fix the broken glass? I don't want to walk in town without him, and I head to my basement and go down the stairs, but then I freeze.

'Perverts' is written in ugly black paint on my basement door. The black color drops look like a poisoned stew thrown on the door.

I breathe quickly, open the door, and go inside. Why did he bring me to this place? Why did I believe this could be a good place for both of us? I'll stay here, in the basement. I won't go out among the people who think we're perverts. Why are people so bothered by our freedom?

I hold a piece of cloth, dip it in the water pitcher beside my bed and go outside the basement to clean the ugly word. I forcefully rub the black paint with the wet cloth to get it off. They will not tell us how to live. We are artists and free people. But even though I rub the door until my fingers hurt, the letters are not erased, and only turn into an ugly stain of black paint, covering the whole door. This is exactly what the people of this town look like, I think to myself before entering my basement, slamming the heavy wooden door, closing the bolt, and wiping my tears. I don't need their acknowledgment of how we live. There will always be those who are opposed to different people, like us. I sit on my bed and try to read from the book Ms. Bertha sent me. Could it be because of what happened yesterday with the girls at the café? I try to concentrate on my reading.

"Wally," I hear a knock on the door after a while, and put the book down from my hand. I've been reading the same page for a long time, repeating the same line over and over.

"Who is it?" I approach the heavy wooden door, putting my ear next to it. Have they come back?

"It's Egon. Open the door."

I open the door and want to go out and show him what they did, but it's clear that he saw it. "Are you okay?" He walks in and hugs me.

"I'm fine, and I don't care about them."

"Wally, we need to leave." He pulls away from me as he holds my shoulders and looks into my eyes.

"We don't have to give in to them."

"We can't stay here," he replies, and I notice that he is holding a crumpled piece of paper in his hand.

"What is that?"

"It's a telegram. My mother found us a place to live not far from Vienna."

"Your mother?" I take a step away from him, "Your mother is the one who decides about us? I thought you were a rebel."

"We're both rebels, but we can't stay here," he answers me, "The people in this place don't understand us."

"Is it because of what you did at the café yesterday?"

"It doesn't matter."

"Is it because of me? I must know."

"It's not because of you. We're together." He looks at me seriously, "And we will be together in the new place. The rent prices there are not high, we will get by," he hugs me, "You are the only one who understands how much my art is a part of me."

"We don't need them," I hug him back, "We'll start over. You'll paint, and I'll find a job there." I feel his warm hands.

"And be my muse," he kisses me.

"I will always be your muse." I kiss him back, "Go pack, let's get away from this place and these people." I hate this place.

As we arrive at the small train station, a pleasant afternoon sun warms us. His mother did not come to see us off. He must have said goodbye to her when I packed my things, but I don't ask him about it. She doesn't love me anyway, and thinks I don't deserve to marry her son. But I don't care.

Her son chose me, and he is hugging me now as we stand on the platform waiting for the train, and with her son, I will go to a new place, and we will have a new beginning there, far from her and this town.

Another woman and a girl are standing on the platform at a distance, but they don't look at us. Neither does the station manager in his black uniform. He strolls along the platform, occasionally glancing at his watch. Only the shaggy dog with white fur and black spots runs happily in my direction, wagging its tail and sniffing my fingers.

I pet it and look at the cloud of black smoke approaching us. Our train is coming. I'm sure that we will be happy in our next home.

Chapter Nine

Wandering

Moving West of Vienna

'Neulengbach' is written in black letters on the white sign mounted on the station building's wall. We get off the train, along with several other passengers, onto the deserted platform. In the cold wind, I watch the train speed away with a shrill whistle. The carriages rattle as a black cloud of smoke blows into the morning sky.

"Let's ask the station manager." Egon says, walking toward the building. We have been on trains for two days already, and all I want is a tub of water to clean myself, and a bed to lie on that is not the hard wooden bench of a train seat.

I look at the village houses outside the station; everything looks similar to the previous place. Only here, no dog runs on the platform and wags its tail happily at my petting hand, and a brown castle stands on a hill overlooking the village. For a moment, it seems its windows are like eyes, examining me. Will they banish us from here too?

"Wally, come," Egon calls me from outside the station building, and I pick up my suitcase and walk along the platform in his direction. "Our house is outside the town," he tells me, "But there is someone who will take us there." He takes the suitcase from my hand and walks over to the cart standing outside the train station.

It is a simple country cart drawn by a brown old draft horse, different from the black Viennese carts covered with shiny lacquer and carried by young, black horses.

"Good morning. Are you the coachman?" Egon turns to the young man lying in rest under the tree outside the station.

The man mumbles something and gets up, takes the suitcases from Egon, and puts them in the back of the cart. Then he gives me his hand and helps me up to the wooden seat. He is slightly older than me and has wild, sandy hair that is hidden by a simple beret hat. His clothes are also plain looking.

"Thanks," I smile at him when I settle onto the rough wooden seat.

"I'll manage," Egon says as the coachman reaches out to help him, and he climbs up and sits next to me. The coachman takes his place on the wooden bench next to Egon, pulls on the reins, and the horse begins to walk slowly on the dirt road out of the village, to our new home.

"This is the place," the coachman says to Egon as the horse turns down the dirt road, and I look at our new home. It is a small, one-floor house with a triangular roof. It stands a short distance from the town, surrounded by a field of yellow grass. From the outside, I can see the floral curtains peeking out at me through the closed windows, and on the side of the house, there is a small plot of ground for vegetables and a clothesline between two trees that is waiting for me to hang our clothes on, after I wash them. I have never lived in my own house, with a garden, a gate, and a mailbox at the entrance, where I could write our names.

"Wally, is everything alright?" Egon asks me.

"Yes, everything is wonderful," I answer and wipe my eyes. "The house is lovely." I smile at him and look back at the distant townhouses. They won't stop us from being who we are, like they did where we previously lived.

"We have arrived," the coachman stops the horse, gets off the cart, unloads our luggage, and places it in the house's entrance. I go down and sit on my suitcase, watching the cart slowly move away while the coachman sits upright with his back to us. In front of him on the path, a woman in a gray-green country dress walks toward us. She stops to greet him and continues walking.

"That must be the woman who owns the house," Egon says, and I nod and rise to greet her.

"Mr. Egon Schiele?" she stands in front of him.

"Yes, Ms., nice to meet you," he shakes her hand.

"And I assume you are Mrs. Schiele," she turns to me and smiles.

"Yes, Ms., I'm Wally," I nod, not wanting to correct her mistake. Maybe it's better that way. I look at Egon, but he doesn't correct her either, and I smile at him.

"I'm glad you came," she tells me as she takes out a large steel key from her dress pocket and opens the door, ushering us into the house. "You will find the house pleasant and welcoming," she continues talking as she shows me the rooms while Egon stands and watches the fields outside from the doorway. "We have one bedroom here, but if you want, I can get you another bed in a separate room, if you wish to have some privacy. I know there are married couples who live in separate rooms." She smiles at me.

"No, it's fine, we'll manage like this." I smile back at her, not wanting to tell her about the basement I slept in. This is a new beginning. I need to forget everything that happened in that place.

"I wish you a pleasant stay, Mr. Schiele," she stands beside Egon in the doorway after she finishes showing me the house and patiently waits until he takes out his wallet and pays her. "Have a pleasant stay, Mrs. Schiele." She says and walks to the dirt road, back towards the town, leaving us alone at the house. Our new home.

"Come here, my cherry," Egon walks up to me and removes his shirt.

"Not now," I push him away and close the door, "I'm going to clean our house, and you're going to town to find a carpenter who will make you an easel, so you can be a famous painter."

Only after I see Egon's back as he walks away towards the townhouses do I allow myself to run to the bedroom, jump on the bed and laugh. I haven't laughed in such a long time.

A few days later, I walk into town. The house is clean and smells of flowers I picked and put in the China jar in the kitchen, but I must find a job. Soon, we will run out of money again.

"Excuse me, do you have a match?" a young girl asks as I walk down the dirt road near the village school.

She stands outside the schoolyard, leaning against a stone fence with a defiant look in her brown eyes. I stop and look at her. She has brown hair, just like Antonia, my young sister, and she wears a plain, cream-colored dress and torn black shoes. Antonia also had a dress like that.

"Why do you need a match?"

"Are you new here?" she asks me.

"Yes." I answer her. The schoolyard behind her is empty of pupils. They must be in class right now.

"Where are you from?" she continues to lean against the wall nonchalantly, but examines me with her eyes as if she were a stray cat ready to escape if I start to moralize her.

"I'm from Vienna."

"The emperor's city?"

"The emperor's city." I smile at her.

"And you live here?" she investigated me.

"Yes, in the yellow house with the green shutters outside of town."

"I know it," she remains standing, seemingly wanting us to continue talking.

I take an apple out of my dress pocket. "You hungry?"

She steps towards me, reaches out, grabs the apple from my outstretched hand, and goes back to lean against the stone wall, taking a greedy bite of it.

"Do you have more?" She asks after a moment, her mouth full of apple.

I take a pear out of my dress pocket for her. I planned on eating those for lunch, but I will buy others. This time she

233

approaches slowly, takes the pear, and puts it in her own dress pocket, but still moves away from me. "Why aren't you in class?" I ask her.

"It's not like anything good will become of me anyway," she shows me her fingers, and I notice the red marks of the ruler's blows on them. I also had those when I didn't know the correct answer.

"Those go away in the end," I show her my fingers. No red marks are left on them, although the memory of the pain is still etched in my flesh.

"What is your name?" she asks me.

"Wally,"

"You're a good woman." She says, throwing the apple core to the ground and walking back towards the gray school building. I follow her with my eyes until she opens the metal door with the glass windows and disappears inside the building. She didn't tell me her name.

❧

A few days later, I hear a knock on the door. Egon is in his studio, and I'm cooking potato soup in a copper pot, stirring it gently. I look out the window at the gray afternoon sky. It started to rain early in the morning, and the dirt road leading to the house is filled with puddles. I wipe my hands with my apron and open the door.

Two girls are standing at the door, both wet from the rain, wearing plain dresses soaked with rainwater. It takes me a moment to recognize the young girl I gave the apple to near the school that day. Beside her, stands another girl, about her age, twelve or thirteen. Their faces and hair glisten with raindrops.

"Hello, Ms. Wally," the apple girl says to me. "Perhaps you are looking for someone to help you with the housework?"

"Are you looking for a job?" I ask them, even though I cannot employ them. I barely managed to find a job in one of the houses in the village for myself.

"Yes." they both nod.

"After school hours." The other girl adds. She has wheat-colored hair.

"And if necessary, we can even come in the morning sometimes," the apple girl smiles at me.

"I'm sorry, but I don't need help." I smile at them awkwardly. The cold wind passing through the fields enters the house.

They say nothing, just turn around and start retracing their steps back on the muddy path. I look at their wet dresses clinging to their skin, and their old shoes as they try to avoid the puddles.

"Wait," I call them, "Do you want some soup?" They must be hungry. There is enough in the pot for them too.

They turn to me, nod, and walk back to the house.

"Wait here," I tell them as they stand again at the entrance, and I rush into the house. First, I collect three drawings that Egon drew me yesterday and was left on the living room floor, and take them to the studio. "Egon, we have two guests for dinner," I tell him and place the drawings on the wooden table standing at his studio.

"They are welcome," Egon answers me without turning around, while he sits on a wooden chair, his back turned to me. He's wearing only his underwear and is painting himself in front of the mirror, "I'll join you soon," he continues talking as if to himself, his hand holding the brush, painting his smooth chest in shades of brown and cream. Even though the room is cold, he doesn't move or shiver. He's completely focused on the painting.

"Don't be long," I take the shirt hanging on a top back of a chair and place it on his back. I don't want them to see him like that, even though I'll take them straight to the kitchen. I hug him from behind, give him a small kiss and go open the door for the girls who are shivering outside, still waiting in the doorway.

"Come in," I lead them to the kitchen, bringing two chairs closer to the hot stove we use for both cooking and heating, "Have a seat."

They sit silently and look around, their eyes scanning the small, simple kitchen. I bend down and add another log to the stove, enjoying the roar of the fire inside as I open the iron door. They just look at me and say nothing, waiting for me to do something or ask them questions.

"Are you cold?" I ask as I pour soup from the pot and place it in front of them, along with a few slices of the plain bread I baked yesterday.

"No, we're comfortable," The apple girl smiles at me as she eats hungrily, though it seems to me that she is still shivering. She has beautiful eyes.

"Did you come here right after school?" I sit down next to them, feeling like their big sister.

They nod their heads as they eat.

"Don't you have a home? A place to go to?"

"We do," The other girl answers.

"Isn't someone waiting for you at home?"

They shrug their shoulders and continue to eat silently, not answering me. I look at their wet dresses that cling to their shivering bodies, and I get up from the table, leaning next to the stove, and put another log into it. Later I will ask Egon to bring some more logs from outside.

"Good afternoon," Egon walks in and sits beside me, dressed in simple khaki pants and a tank top.

"Good afternoon, sir," the fair-haired girl answers. She stops eating for a moment and looks at him.

"Good afternoon, sir," The apple girl also says to him, and I realize that I didn't even ask them for their names. "Your wife invited us to come in and eat with you. Thank you." The fair-haired girl looks at me and then returns to her bowl.

"You're welcome," I get up from the table, go to the pot, and pour Egon and myself some soup.

Egon watches the two girls for a moment, then he leans back, reaches out, and hugs my waist. "She's the best woman a man can ask for." He smiles at them.

"Careful, I'll accidentally spill soup on you," I release myself from his embrace and place the soup plate before him.

"Thank you, my wonderful Wally." He caresses my thighs as I turn my back to him and go over to pour me some soup, feeling myself blush. I can hear the girls giggling.

"Young ladies, may I ask for your names?" Egon asks them.

"Frieda, sir," replies the golden-haired girl.

"Astrid, sir," says the brown-haired apple girl.

"Nice to meet you, I'm Egon." He stands up and reaches out, shaking their hands as if they were ladies, and they smile at him.

"They're passing through the houses because they are looking for work," I say, taking my place at the table. I start eating my potato soup.

"Only in the nice people's houses." Astrid says.

"Doesn't the rain bother you?" I ask, but they shrug.

"And what job are you looking for?" Egon asks them.

"Whatever we can find," Frieda answers him. "Thanks for the soup, Mrs. Wally, it's delicious."

"Do you want some more?" I ask her, and she nods. I pour her some more and slice some more bread for the table.

"Wally, do we have any wine?" Egon asks me.

"Yes, in the pantry," I get up.

"I'll bring it," He stands up and kissed me on my cheek. I watch him walk to the pantry and notice the girls are looking at their soup bowls and smiling. It embarrasses me that he hugged me like that in front of them.

"I hope you will manage to find jobs." Egon returns to the table with an open bottle of wine, pours himself a glass, and raises it in the air. "To your jobs, girls." He proposes a toast, and I stop eating and look at the girls. They watch him, and I think Astrid blushes a little.

"We will find one, sir. We are hard workers." Frieda answers him. I remember the two girls in the café and get an uneasy feeling in my stomach.

"Have you finished eating?" I ask them after a moment.

"Yes, thank you, Mrs. Wally, it was delicious." They answer almost simultaneously.

"You should go," I get up from the table. "Your families must be waiting for you at home."

"Not really, Mrs. Wally," they get up from the table.

"Thank you very much for your hospitality, Mr. Egon." Frieda says.

"You can call me Egon." He finishes the wine and gets up from the table, accompanying the girls to the door with me.

"Goodbye, girls," Egon says and passionately kisses me in front of them at the door. "We were happy to host you," he says, and we both remain standing in the doorway, watching them as they walk towards the town on the muddy path. At least the rain has stopped, and they won't get wet.

"Wally, I want to draw you now." He closes the door and takes my hand, taking me to the studio.

I sit in front of him on the chair but remain dressed.

"I'm waiting." He stands behind the easel, holding the brush and watching me.

"Maybe you'll draw something more decent today?" I ask him.

"What's that supposed to mean?"

"Not a nude. A painting that people will want to buy. You paint so beautifully, and people don't buy your paintings."

"I'm not ready to paint something that people want to buy. I'm an artist." He says angrily, "I paint what exists in my imagination."

"And that's all you have on your mind? Just naked women?" I answer him angrily. He shouldn't have smiled like that at the girls.

"What I have on my mind right now is wine." He throws the brush and the palette on the floor and walks into the kitchen.

I look at the stain of paint that splattered on the parquet floor, but I remain seated on the chair, still wearing my dress.

⁂

"Have a nice day. You must go to school now." I say to Frieda and Astrid.

They've come to visit us from time to time, sometimes in the afternoon and sometimes in the morning. They usually arrive without warning, stand in the doorway and knock, patiently waiting for me to open.

The second time they arrived, I was surprised and wanted to get rid of them, but they stood trembling in the doorway, their hair covered in snow, and I couldn't bring myself to turn them away. I brought them inside and gave them hot soup and some sausage, letting them warm up by the stove in the kitchen. They reminded me of Hilda and Antonia, my two young sisters. I hope they are not cold now in the Viennese winter.

Sometimes they come when I'm not at home, and Egon lets them in. I find them waiting for me in the kitchen while he's busy with his paintings in the studio. I gave them my old coat, and I see them sharing it when they come to us, passing it between themselves. I have no more clothes to give them. I have already saved some money this month and will buy new shoes soon. I will give them my old ones, but they will also have to share those.

"You have to hurry. You will be punished for being late." I tell them as we stand at the door. Frieda is wearing the coat I gave them.

"We don't mind. The teacher at school punishes us either way." Astrid proudly shows me the red marks on her fingers, "We're used to it. It doesn't really hurt anymore." She smiles at me, "Neither do the strikes on our backs with the cane."

"He hits your backs?" I ask her, feeling chills.

"He doesn't like us." Astrid answers, "He thinks that because we're girls, nothing will come of us."

"Is he the only one who hits you?" I feel like hugging her. Her back must hurt so much.

"There are girls he likes, but not us." She indifferently says while putting on her scarf. It's Frida's turn with the coat today. "It's okay, Mrs. Wally. I don't really mind when he hits me." She added.

"Thanks for the bread, Mrs. Wally." Frieda says as she puts on her gloves and a scarf.

"Goodbye, girls," Egon appears from the bedroom. He walks barefoot on the wooden floor, wrapped in the thick blanket we usually sleep with. He slept in.

"Goodbye, Mr. Egon." They smile at him and wave their glove-clad hands. I can see their white fingers through the holes.

"I hope the marks on your back disappear soon." Egon says as he approaches, clings to me in the doorway, giving me a morning kiss. The cold wind penetrates our warm home.

"We promise to behave." Frieda answers him, and they turn away and start walking toward the village. Their steps on the path look like black dots in the snow that painted the fields around us and the distant mountains on the horizon white, until it blends in with the gray sky.

I close the door and look at Egon when he returns to the bedroom. He usually sleeps in, gets up only around noon, and then starts painting. I must hurry and get dressed and go to work. Something feels wrong to me, like I felt back at the fabric store with Mr. Walner, when I knew something was wrong even before he started touching me. Still, I hurry to arrange the kitchen and get ready for work. I can't be late. I can't think about other things right now.

The winter wind blows in my face as I walk down the path toward the village. Frieda and Astrid's footsteps are already blurred by the snow that has started to fall again. Spring will begin soon, but now it is still very cold. Despite it being morning time, the gray clouds hide the sun, and the windows of the townhouses sparkle at me in the distance, like stars. I work as a maid here, at one of the wealthy families' homes. They treat me well, and Egon has also been painting a lot lately, planning an exhibit in the coming summer. I tighten the collar of my coat and smile. We will succeed together.

"After you finish cleaning here, go to the guest room," the lady tells me later and leaves the room. I nod and look at the rag I'm holding. What did Egon mean when he talked to the girls about the marks on their backs? I continue to polish the family photos carefully. How did he know they had marks on their backs? I grip the photo forcefully, watching the picture of the whole family looking happy and smiling until my fingers turn white, and I think the glass may shatter. How did he know about the marks on Frieda and Astrid's backs?

"Wally, are you okay?" The lady enters the room a few minutes later.

"Yes, Ms.," I breathe deeply, "I was momentarily dizzy," I carefully place the picture back on the cabinet, supporting myself with my hand.

"I hope it's for the right reason, and that you're expecting a baby." She smiles at me.

"No, it's not that," I smile her tiredly. Could it be they were at our home when I wasn't there, instead of going to school?

"So, when you're done cleaning the room, move on to the guest room." She goes into another room, and I sit down for a few minutes before returning to vigorously scrubbing the cabinet, gripping the rag so tightly my fingers hurt.

The way home seems never-ending. My throat burns with every breath I take in cold wind. I walk as fast as I can. The snow has stopped falling, and the white field stretches to the horizon under the gray sky, dotted with trees that seem speckled with patches of snow and distant farmhouses that glisten like little fishing boats in the middle of a gray lake.

In the middle of the path leading to the house, I stop and look at the ground, examining the foot tracks in the snow. Some people have walked and retraced their path since morning, leaving patches of mud in the white snow. Maybe Egon has left the house? Or perhaps the postman or a neighbor came to visit? Am I imagining things? Maybe I'm wrong?

The door handle is cold and wet, and my trembling hand slips on it as I enter the house, hurrying to close the door behind me. Is Egon alone?

The kitchen is empty and cold, the iron stove is not lit, and it seems that no one has been in it since I left the house that morning.

"You are early," Egon comes out of his studio wearing only a shirt and socks. He walks over and hugs me, "You are cold."

"Yes, the lady let me leave early." I go to the bedroom. It's also empty, there's no one in it. I open the closet and look under the bed.

"Will you make us something to eat? I haven't eaten since this morning. Wally, is everything okay?"

"Yes," I answer and enter the studio. It is also empty. Only me and Egon are in the house.

"Are you looking for something?" He hugs me, but I pull away from him.

"Where are they?" I turn to him.

"Who?"

"The girls."

"Frieda and Astrid?"

"Yes, Frieda and Astrid." I walk into the kitchen again. Perhaps they're in the pantry. I look, but they're not there.

"They left this morning. You were here, don't you remember?"

"And they didn't come back later?"

"No..." he continues to walk after me. "Are you okay? Are you feeling well?"

"I'm perfectly fine," I return to the studio and look around, then I see the large pile of paintings leaning against the wall.

"What are all these questions? I don't understand." He says in an angry voice.

"Do you draw them?" I go to the pile of paintings.

"I'm an artist. I draw people." He tries to hold my hand, but I pull it away and start looking at the paintings.

"Wally, what are you doing?"

"Did you draw them?" I ask him with teary eyes as I bend over the pile, moving several of his nude paintings. I hope I don't find their painting there, that I'm wrong. Another drawing and another one of him naked, one of me with my red hair, and one of me naked touching my breasts. Maybe I'm wrong?

"Wally, you're my muse. That's the only thing you should care about." He tries to keep me away from the paintings. "You need to rest. You're sick. You're sweating. Come to the kitchen. I'll turn the stove on and warm the house."

"Just a moment," I move the painting of houses he painted in Krumlov, and then I see Astrid.

She looks at me from the page with her young face, standing naked in her childish body that has not yet begun to develop. I touch the painting with my fingers, feeling the roughness of the paint on the brown paper. My fingers run over her slim thighs. The garter stockings she wears make her look like a child who went through her mother's lace drawer and took them out, playing a game.

I bend down on my knees, feeling nauseous. I need to vomit, but I can't. My fingers keep flipping through the paintings and can't stop. Underneath this painting is another painting of hers, another of Frieda, and another one, painting after painting.

"Wally, are you okay? You're sick."

"Why?" I raise my face and shout at him.

"What is the problem?" He yells back at me, "You should thank me."

"Thank you?" I shout and get up from the floor, take one last look at those horrible paintings, and go to the bedroom.

"Yes, thank me." He follows me and continues to shout. I open my drawer near the bed and throw all my underwear on the floor until I find them, the black garter socks. "You are the one who brought them to this house, and they ate my food in this house. And I did them a favor." He stands close to me.

"What did you do to them?" I walk past him, move away so he doesn't touch me, and go to the kitchen. I take scissors out of the drawer, and cut the garter socks into pieces.

"I did them a favor, and you did too. They were looking for a job, and I helped them." He stands in the doorway and continues to shout at me, "You should be the one apologizing. I'm an artist. You knew I was an artist when you met me. No one forced you to come with me from that whore house you were in. What did you think? That I would draw only you?" He shouts as he stands at the entrance to the kitchen, "I'm going back to my studio." He says in a harsh voice and turns around, and I feel nauseous again and need to vomit.

I wash my face and breathe deeply. Then I go to the studio, and stand before him.

"Wally, I thought we were done with this conversation." He sits back in his chair and prepares to go back to painting.

"They're just girls. They're twelve years old." I scream at him, "They don't even have breasts yet. They haven't gotten their periods yet." My fingers unbutton my dress, and I move the straps, letting it fall to the floor along with all the scattered paintings. "Aren't my breasts pretty enough?" I keep yelling at him as I release the camisole I'm wearing, almost forcefully tearing it off and throwing it to the floor, "Isn't my body nice enough?" I stand before him naked, "Am I not young enough for you?" I ask in a choked voice.

"That's just how it is with artists. I won't ask for your permission to paint someone, or who to is allowed to strip for me." He answers me dryly, turning his back to me and returning to concentrate on the painting of himself he has started. "We artists paint our passions wherever we find them, you should know that. You must have known that from Klimt." He turns and looks at me for a moment and I shiver in the cold room. "Now, please make me dinner, and turn the stove on in the kitchen." He returns to his painting, "The house is cold, I'm hungry, and I have a painting to finish."

"I'll make you dinner right away," I answer him quietly. I bend to the floor, collect my clothes, and leave his studio.

"Thank you." I hear him say to me.

In the bedroom, I sit naked on the bed, still holding my clothes. I make sure not to look at the mirror on the side of the room. The memory of their nude paintings still makes my throat tighten. I must think of something else. I must do something. The gray sky peeks at me from the window. Soon, the sun will set. I must hurry. I can't be in the same house with him.

I get dressed and go to the kitchen, open the small jar where I hide some of the money I receive from work, take it all, and shove it into my small handbag. I quietly put my coat on, along with my wool hat, scarf, and gloves. I leave the house and close the door with a gentle click. It will take a while for him to realize I left. I must hurry.

※ ❧ ❧ ❧ ※

In the distance, I can already see the train station, and I accelerate my steps. The sound of my feet in the snow reminds me of an old dog struggling to walk. I gasp, and the cold air hurts my lungs. I must get away from him and make it to the train.

The young coachman who took us on his cart when we arrived here is standing at the station entrance, wrapped in a long wool coat. His horse is also covered with a blanket as it is patiently stands and eats from a sack of barley attached with a rope to its neck.

"Excuse me, sir, has the train come through yet?" I ask him, although I don't think he's used to being called sir.

"No, you still have half an hour or so." He answers me without turning around as he continues to care for the horse and stroke its neck, "Ask the station manager. He has a watch."

I thank him and enter the station, searching for the manager.

The station manager is standing on the platform dressed in the railway company uniform, wearing leather gloves, and holding a watch attached to a thin silver chain. He looks at it and at the big clock on the station's wall, as if comparing them. "You have another seventeen minutes." He says, putting the watch back in his uniform pocket, "Are you traveling without any luggage?"

"Yes, sir," I smile awkwardly and try to calm my breathing. Does he know I ran away? I go to the ticket office and buy a ticket, looking apprehensively at the entrance of the station. Has he already noticed I left the house? Will he search for me? Maybe my tracks in the snow will lead him.

I walk to the far end of the platform and look into the distance, at the point where the tracks disappear between the snowy fields, searching for the black cloud of smoke that will herald the train's arrival. Every now and then, I look back, hoping Egon is still busy with his painting.

Finally, I see the smoke approaching and the locomotive panting like a faithful dog that runs and collects the sheep in the pasture.

"The train to Vienna is now entering the station." The station manager announces, blowing his whistle even though it is just me on the platform. He stomps his feet and moves slowly, trying to warm himself while he waits for new passengers who might arrive.

Inside the car, I sit in the wooden chair opposite an older woman in a black dress and a black hat that covers almost her entire face.

"The train to Vienna is now leaving." Whistles the station manager, and I feel the slow movement of the carriage. The station platform is empty now. He didn't come looking for me. He must have continued to draw, not even noticing that I walked out on him.

In Vienna, I will go see how my sisters are doing. Even if Mom hates me, I shouldn't have disappeared on them like that. They must have grown so much. I tuck my hand into my coat pocket and feel my money. I'll give them some of it. I'll postpone buying new shoes. Maybe Mom will let me sleep with them for a night or two until I decide what to do.

Despite the early evening hour, the train station in Vienna is full of people. I hurry to walk out into the cold street, pass the carriages and the automobiles waiting outside and rush towards the old town and the alleys where I grew up, where we came after Dad died.

Although the streets remained exactly as they were, they suddenly seem so different and foreign to me, as if I were a guest here. I watch two girls playing hopscotch at the entrance to one of the alleys. They jump between the squares drawn on the stones, argue with each other, and ignore the cold air. A brown horse tied to a metal ring attached to a building wall watches them indifferently. I approach them and stop, looking at them, but they are not my little sisters.

I continue walking down the alley and stop at the entrance to the building, breathing deeply, feeling the cold air enter my lungs. I need to go in. I didn't come this far to stand on the street. The gas lamp is dimly lit in the stairwell, and I can hear the chirping of the rats living in the cracks under the stairs. I don't care if Mom kicks me out again. I just want to say hello to my sisters. She doesn't scare me.

I climb the wooden stairs to the third floor, hearing the wooden boards creaking with my every step. Do they still live in this apartment? The landlord often threatened to throw us out. The neighbor was also threatening us. I stand before the wooden door and breathe slowly, pressing my ear to the door. I can't hear anything. My hand hits the door, quietly at first, then forcefully, and I call, "Mom, open the door, it's me." Do they still live here? The door remains closed.

"Mom, Antonia, Hilda," I shout and knock hard on the door, but no one opens it for me. Were they evicted from the apartment? I feel my hand shaking.

"Mrs. Steiner," I go to the neighbor's door and knock, "Mrs. Steiner."

"You, what are you doing here?" She opens the door to a crack and looks me.

"Mrs. Steiner, where are Mom and my sisters?"

"They're not here. Why did you come back?" She keeps peeking at me through the crack.

"Mrs. Steiner, please, where are they?"

"They left. She didn't pay the rent. He kicked them out." She examines my dress, "Why have you come? Do you need money?"

"No, Mrs. Steiner, do you know where they went? Please."

"No, and I don't care. The house is quiet now without all the yelling and crying that was coming from your apartment. Nothing good came of you." She slams the door in my face and leaves me standing in the hallway before the closed wooden door. I breathe heavily, unable to move and go down the stairs. They were kicked out because of me. Because I didn't help with the money.

I must get out of here. I can't stay here. I go down the stairs, my beating feet against the wood sound like the thunderous sounds of cannons in the distance, and I go out into the street, breathing heavily. What am I going to do? How can I find them?

Next to the two girls playing hopscotch, I stop for a moment and watch them. They are about my sisters' age, and they laugh while jumping in the street with their dirty dresses and wild yellow hair.

"Do you know Antonia? She is your age." I ask them.

They stop playing and look at me, nodding their heads.

"Where did she go? Do you know where they went?" I approach them.

One of the girls shakes her head. No.

"And you? Do you know where they went?" I bend down towards the other girl. She has blue eyes and a red face from the cold.

"Over there," she points down the street. "With a cart and a horse." she stands and watches me.

"Where? Do you know the name of the place they went?"

"Over there." she continues to point. What am I going to do?

"Thanks." I stroke her hair and turn around, starting to run in the direction the girl pointed in. Even though I know I have no reason to run, I still can't help myself.

I quicken my steps near Mr. Walner's store even though I'm already panting. Two women standing near and looking at the fabric rolls displayed in the window turn their gaze to me, but I ignore them and continue running as I pant. Keep running, just get away from his shop, just get away from those streets. I have no idea where my feet are leading me.

When I see the three golden balls of the pawn shop hanging above his door, I stop and catch my breath. Despite the late hour, there is still a light in the store, and I approach the door step by step, but then I stop. There it is, my dad's ring, displayed in the shop window.

I press my hand against the cold glass as if trying to touch my ring. My mouth creates a cloud of steam on the window. The pawnbroker is still there, inside the store. He leans over the table, holds a magnifying glass, and examines jewelry by the light of a lantern placed on the table. Will he recognize me? Very few people are walking in the dark street.

I cover my hair as much as I can with my woolen hat, making sure there are no ends of red sticking out, and take out the note of paper he gave me a year ago. I must go in. He will close the shop soon. It's already late.

"Good evening," I enter the darkened shop.

"Good evening." He looks up at me shortly and then tucks the jewelry he's holding in an envelope, placing it inside the table drawer.

"I've come to cash it." I place the crumpled paper on the table, making sure to stay in the shadows, away from the lantern's light.

He outstretches his hand through the iron bars, holds the paper, brings it closer to his eyes, and examines it.

"It's expired. Are you aware? It's not valid anymore." He looks up at me.

"Yes, I know," I look back at him from the shadows. "It's in the shop window. I saw it. I have the money."

He looks at me for another moment as if trying to remember where he has seen me before, and I take a step back, feeling myself blushing.

"We'll see," he mutters as if to himself while holding the paper and walks over to the display window, holds the ring, places it on the counter, and looks at me from the other side of the bars. Why is he looking at me like that? Soon he will remember me from the paintings. I take the money from my wallet and put it on the counter. The ring is more important than my new shoes.

"There you go, fifteen Kronen."

He doesn't take the money and continues to look at me, "That's not the price."

"It's the price written in the note you gave me a year ago." I say quickly.

"True, it was a year ago when you pawned it, but now it's mine, and its price has gone up." He places his hand on the ring. "They say there's going to be a war, people are buying jewelry, the prices have gone up."

"What is its price?" I approach the counter from the darkness. I need my ring, I must get it now, before it is sold.

"Thirty-five crores." He whispers.

I open my wallet and pull all I have. I don't have that much money.

"Please, it was my father's. I must have it. I'll pay you twenty." I place another bill on the counter.

"I'm sorry." He returns the note to me through the bars, pushing the bills towards me. "The ring will find another father to wear it."

"But it's mine." It's hard to breathe.

"Sorry, over a year has passed. After a year, I put the things in the shop window and sell them. It's mine. That's the law."

"Keep it aside for me. I'll get more money," I hold the bills. I have no idea how I am going to get such a large amount of money.

"Then you better hurry. This ring won't wait for you. Before a war, people buy every piece of jewelry they can lay their hands on." He fixed his gaze on me, "You look familiar," he says, "Do I know you?"

"I'll be back. Good evening," I say and rush out of the store, closing the door behind me and walking down the street.

A few minutes later, I stop running in the cold street, drop to my knees and start crying. I have lost my sisters and will soon lose Dad's ring. I have no way of getting money. What am I going to do now? My fingers caress the finger I wore the ring on, trying to remember the feeling of the heavy metal. I close my eyes tightly and think of him sitting in the kitchen with me when I was a child. His face is no longer as clear as it used to be in my memory, but the scent of his body when he hugged me makes me smile, even though I'm still crying.

The sound of horse hooves makes me open my eyes. A man leading a horse tied to a cart passes by, and I hurry to move aside and cling to the wall, hiding my tear-stained face. The horses' hooves sound like the ticking of a clock, which is interrupted only by the sound of a coin striking the rain-slicked cobblestone and splashing in my direction, left lying at my feet, shiny from water and the light of the street lantern. I hold the coin and raise my head, wanting to shout at him that I don't collect alms, but the man was already walking down the street while holding the horse's reins until he disappeared behind the alley. I need to get up, keep walking.

In the distance, I see the large wooden door of Ms. Bertha's hostel and stop, catch my breath, and wipe my tears. They will laugh at me, the girls, and Ms. Bertha too. I can already see Erica standing in front of the other girls and imitating me reading a book, tearing the pages, and stuffing them in her bra to the sound of their laughter, explaining to them that this is the proper use of books and even a whore that can read, will always remain a whore.

I should have stayed here. Why did I think I could do better?

I hear footsteps in the dark street and turn around, seeing a gentleman in a suit and a top hat approaching. In the dim light of the street lantern, I see how he surveys my body and smiles before walking to the big brown wooden door. There, he removes his hat and goes inside. Snow starts falling again, and it gets dark. I wait a few minutes, look around, waiting for the gentleman inside to choose the girl he wants, and go up to the second floor. Despite my gloves and coat, I'm cold, and I rub my hands together. The falling snowflakes hit my face, and I start to shiver. Finally, I walk towards the door waiting for me and enter. I have nowhere to go. When I ran away from Egon, I didn't think about where I would spend the night.

The hostel's interior hasn't changed, the gramophone at the end of the room is playing, and the air is dense with cigarettes and cigars smell, but at least it's warm and pleasant inside. I look at the reception desk, but Ms. Bertha is not there. I step in. I'll search for her.

"Look who came to visit us," Erica sits on the floral sofa and blows smoke in my direction from the cigarette she is holding. "What happened? Your painter dumped you?" She smiles at me and crosses her legs. She is wearing a black lace camisole.

"Who is she?" Another girl I don't know asks her and looks at me curiously. She is about my age and has curly brown hair and brown eyes, and she wears a plain white camisole and garters.

"She's the one who thought she was better than us and has now come back begging for mercy." Erica says and continues to smoke nonchalantly.

The new girl says nothing. She just keeps looking at me, and I touch my cheek, feeling the wetness of the tears, and look around. Where's Ms. Bertha?

"You can go," Erica tells me. "If you've came to look for your painter, he's not here today." She smiles at me, "Although he does come to visit us from time to time." She speaks to the new girl, and I breathe heavily. Does she mean Mr. Klimt or Egon? "I think you already know him." She continues to speak to the new girl, making sure I hear. "You like him. Although he hasn't been around lately. Maybe he's found another hostel." She turns to me again and smiles. "You should probably know when he runs away from you."

I turn around and face the door. There is nothing for me here. They all hate me in this place anyway.

"Young Walburga, where do you think you are going?" I hear a voice and turn around, seeing Ms. Bertha coming down the stairs from the second floor.

"To the street," I whisper and wipe my eyes. She must still be mad at me.

"She said she was going to look for men on the street," Erica tells her.

"Erica, go upstairs and change," Ms. Bertha tells her, "You know I don't like the color black. It's a color for death. And you, come with me." She approaches, and holds my hand, taking me to the small room behind her counter.

"Sit down," she says, pointing to a small wooden chair against the wall. I've never been in her room before. It stifles cigarette smoke and has a mahogany cabinet with drawers and a small bookcase behind a plain armchair in the corner. Bertha goes to the cabinet, takes out a bottle of wine, pours it into a glass, and hands it to me, "Drink."

"Thank you, Ms. Bertha," I sip the bitter drink, feeling it burn my throat.

"Walburga, what happened?"

"I was passing by, so I popped in to say hi." I wipe away my tears. They must be from the drink.

"And that's why you're crying?" She pours me more of the wine.

"I letFrieda and Astrid into my house. They trusted me," I sip the wine and burst into tears as I speak, forgetting that Ms. Bertha doesn't know who they are. "They trusted me, and he drew them, and I'm to blame for everything that happened." I continue to speak in a sobbing voice, unable to stop, "I ran away from him, and I have nowhere to sleep. He drew them because of me, and now my sisters were evicted from their apartment, and I have no idea where they are, and my dad's ring is for sale at the pawnbroker's and I don't even have the money to buy it back." I can't stop speaking, shaking and crying.

Ms. Bertha doesn't say anything. She just pours herself some wine and lights herself a cigarette, blowing the smoke into the air.

"Walburga, it seems to me that you have more troubles than the emperor." She finally says.

"So what do I do?" I whine.

"There's not much you can do. Women who don't stay to work for Bertha have to depend on a man. You'll have to go back to him, no matter what he did or who he painted." She inhales from the cigarette once again, "That's how the world has always been. No woman will change it."

"I lost Dad's ring. I'll never have enough money to buy it back," I whisper, even though it's none of her business.

"Walburga, you're not a little girl anymore. That's life; sometimes you have to say goodbye to the past and move on." She takes the glass of wine from my trembling hand and places it on the cabinet, "I think you've had enough for one evening."

"Thank you, Ms. Bertha," I wipe my eyes and get up, "Good night."

"Where are you going?"

"I don't know."

"Come with me." She grabs my hand again. "I don't have a room to give you, but we will find a solution, and tomorrow you can go back. You can't just walk around the streets like this." She takes me to the stairs. We pass the young girl and

Erica, who has changed into a transparent white camisole. When I pass her, she tries to pinch me, but my body is so tired from this whole day that her nails trying to hurt me don't affect me anymore.

"Christina," Ms. Bertha knocks on the door of her room. "Open up. I brought you a guest for the night."

"Why in my room, Ms. Bertha? Let the guest sleep with one of the young women." I hear Christina's nervous voice, but when she opens her door and sees me, she hugs and pulls me in. "Good night Ms. Bertha. She will be fine with me." She tells her and closes the door behind us.

"I missed you, Rusty," Christina whispers to me later when we're both lying together in bed, covered in her wool blanket. The room is dark, and the corridor is quiet.

"Me too," I whisper back, "I will ask Ms. Bertha if maybe she'll agree to take me back."

"No, don't."

"Why not? You're here, and Ms. Bertha doesn't hate me that much, and I can get along with Erica."

"Because you managed to get out of here," I hear her breathing, "And you met a man who wants you, and girls who meet men who want them don't come back here."

"But you're here, and it's a good place for you." I can't tell her what he did with the young girls.

"That's right, I'm fine here, and I'm used to this place already, and I'll probably stay here forever." She holds my hand, and I feel her warm fingers, "But don't you think I envy you for having the courage to slam the door in Ms. Bertha's face and run away, and go after a man?" She laughs a small laugh,

"The next day she smoked more than she usually does. Even Erica, who hates you, envies you. You know, all the girls here at the hostel would switch places with you if they could, me included."

"It's not always that simple out there," I look at the ceiling in the dark room.

"It's not always simple here either, to lie alone at night or to wait for the next customer to lie on me and then disappear, leaving a bill of money on the dresser."

"Thank you for letting me sleep with you tonight," I want to hug her, but I don't have the courage.

"Rusty, don't get used to my bed. I'll throw you back to your man tomorrow. You don't belong here anymore." She strokes my hair slowly until I fall asleep, imagining that she is my older sister.

The next afternoon, I return from Vienna and get off at the small train station in the village. A warm sun is shining, and the snow has begun to melt, leaving dark mud spots and yellow grass in the surrounding fields.

"Can you take me home?" I ask the coachman. He nods in silence and climbs on the cart's seat. I've got a headache from the wine I drank yesterday.

"Thank you," I say as he reaches out and helps me get up, and I sit next to him on the wooden bench.

On the way, I want to ask him if he has a wife waiting for him at home at the end of the day. But it is not polite for a woman to talk to a stranger, and I just watch his hands wearing woolen gloves as they hold the reins. Egon is waiting for me at home. I look at the house as the path turns from the main road.

The snow that was here yesterday has melted and left behind puddles of mud.

"Thank you," I pay and say goodbye to the coachman, walking carefully towards the stairs. I will prepare something for us to eat. I also must apologize to Egon because that is what I should do: the woman must apologize, no matter what her husband did.

I turn around and take one last look at the coachman. He is sitting upright on the cart. I take a slow breath and approach the door, but when I get close, I see that there is a piece of paper attached to the door with the empire's symbol.

'To Mrs. Walburga Neuzil,
You are requested to appear at the police station of Neulengbach for an investigation of the moral crimes of Mr. Egon Schiele, for which he was arrested.

Mr. Eberhard Brunner
Neulengbach Police Station.'

Chapter Ten

Prison

"Name?"

"Walburga Neuzil."

"Age?"

"Nineteen."

"Marital status?"

"Single."

The police officer, Mr. Eberhard Brunner, stops writing and looks up at me. I lower my gaze and focus on his thick fingers emerging from his blue uniform like the roots of a tree beside a stream, gripping the muddy ground tenaciously. Only his black police hat and a sheet of paper rest on the plain wooden surface between us. The silver police emblem on the hat gleams in the dim light of the interrogation room.

"Are you not married?" he asks, his blue eyes fixed on me, as if awaiting a carefully considered response.

"No, we are not married," I finally say, studying his face. He appears to be in his forties, with a thick brown mustache and a small scar near his right eye. Should I have lied to him?

"How long have you lived together?" he resumes writing on the paper, his large fingers clutching the yellow pencil so tightly that it seems it might vanish between them any moment, ending my interrogation. I keep my hands in my lap, clasping them together. I need to remain calm. I am not accused of anything. Only he is under scrutiny.

"We have lived together for about a year and a half."

"And during the time you were with him, did he used to draw obscene pictures?" the police officer pauses in his writing again and fixes his gaze on me once more. I feel myself blushing. What should I answer him? Will he even listen to me? I'm a woman. He might not listen to me. He might not understand either.

"He only drew me," I answer quietly, my fingers painfully intertwined beneath the table. Could it be that he painted other young girls before we arrived, and I am unaware of it? I think of two young girls in the café in Krumlov and glance around at the room's yellowing walls. Is this what a police interrogation room looks like? Two wooden chairs, a table, and yellow, peeling walls? Will they also blame me for bringing the girl to our home?

"Miss Walburga?" I hear and look at him again.

"Sorry, Sir."

"How did the girls get to your house? Did Egon invite them?"

"No, they knocked on our door, looking for a job," I answer him quietly, and I want to shout that they came because of me, because I gave Astrid an apple. They came because of an apple.

"And Egon suggested to draw them?"

"I offered them soup."

"Were you also an accomplice?" he stops writing and looks at me, and I look at the sheet of paper under his hand. Why is it so full of words? Why are they blaming Egon? I am to blame. They trusted me. They trusted the cozy house they visited. He should arrest me.

"I didn't know about the paintings," I place my hands on the wooden table, as if awaiting the placement of metal handcuffs. Where is Egon? Is he imprisoned in this building?

Earlier in the morning, I arrived at the village police building and stood outside, hesitating to enter, even though I knew I had to. I observed the two-story building with its triangular roof, painted with remnants of white snow. Near the entrance, next to a pile of firewood, stood a black carriage drawn by two horses, while two policemen waited as a prisoner disembarked, his wrists bound in metal chains that clinked with each step. Would the officer handcuff me for complicity in the crime?

"Miss Walburga, wait here a moment, please," the officer says, rising from his chair, leaving the room. I am left alone with my hands on the table, gazing out of the window. The sun's rays illuminate the snowy mountains on the horizon. Spring will soon arrive.

"I apologize for the wait," he returns, carrying a large leather bag over his shoulder, which he places on the table. His large fingers deftly open the leather buckles and remove a series of drawings that Egon has painted. These are his artwork.

"Do you recognize these paintings?" He spreads them out on the table, and I shake my head, trying not to look at them. I feel nauseous and have the urge to vomit.

"Thank you very much, that's all, Miss Walburga," he returns the drawings to the leather case, carefully closes the straps, and jots something down on the paper on the table.

"May I go now?"

"Yes, you can go," he rises from his chair and shakes my hand, "but for the next few days, please do not leave Neulengbach. I may have more questions."

"And what about Egon?" I ask for the first time.

"Egon is arrested. For now, he will face trial for these paintings." He escorts me to the door.

I search for something to say but can't find the words. All I want is to leave this place and step into the cold air outside.

"Miss Walburga," he says as we stand in the hallway, "Mr. Schiele has requested to see you. He's being held here at the building."

But I shake my head, declining the offer, and walk out the door. I can't bear to see him.

I slow my steps only when I reach the house on the dirt road, marked with small puddles of melting snow. My lungs ache from the cold air. I open the door and enter his studio for the first time since that day.

The studio is quiet. Egon's chair remains in the center of the room, waiting for its owner to return. The easel is empty, devoid of canvas or brown paper, and the brushes are neatly stowed in a wooden box beside the chair. The police have taken the paintings I scattered on the floor, leaving only his and my nude paintings in a tidy pile against the wall. What do the police officers who see them think of me? Does Mr. Eberhard Brunner see them too? I go to the stove and light a log. The fire sends a cheerful flame toward me, and for a moment, I fight the urge to take all of Egon's paintings and throw them into the fire. At least the police have confiscated all the girls' paintings, and the house no longer feels tainted.

I go to the kitchen, fill a stainless steel bucket with water, and begin scrubbing the entire house. I must clean it.

* * *

A few days later, while I stand at home and look out the window, I see him walking on the path. He walks in a brisk gait typical of soldiers or policemen, as if they are on a parade or a march to some distant battle. On his shoulder hangs a small leather bag, and he wears the blue police jacket and the black hat he placed on the wooden table when he interrogated me. Why has he come?

I move away from the window, rush to the bedroom, open the closet, and put on a simple dress instead of my nightgown. For several days now, I stay at home all day, only occasionally going outside to bring in some logs for heating.

I hear a knock on the door and go to open it. I didn't have time to fix my hair.

"Miss Walburga," police officer Eberhard Brunner removes his hat and bows to me, "Good morning."

"Good morning Mr. Brunner. How can I help you?" I look at his well-groomed mustache. Has he finally come to arrest me?

"I'm glad you're home," he remains standing on the doorstep, and I don't invite him in.

"You know how it is," I give him a bitter smile, "rumors travel fast in small places."

"I'm sorry to hear," he answers, not even asking what the rumors are about. He surely knows that I was fired from my job and that people cursed me when I went to buy potatoes. He has been a policeman for many years. He must know these stories. I'm probably not the first woman this has happened to.

"Ms. Walburga, may I come in for a few minutes?" he asks with a kind smile.

"Yes, please," I open the door, and he enters and stands for a moment at the entrance, looking around at the clean and tidy house. I've been cleaning the house for a few days now. I only don't go into his studio.

"May I take your coat?" I ask him and hang it on the hanger at the entrance.

"Shall we sit?" Mr. Brunner points towards the kitchen table, and we sit facing each other again, like the day he interrogated me. I put my hands in my lap, not wanting him to see my folded hands. I'm tense.

He opens the leather bag he brought with him, takes some papers and the yellow pencil, and places them on the table.

"Miss Walburga," he says and looks at me, "Mr. Schiele's trial will take place in a few days."

"Yes, Mr. Brunner, I understand."

"And I need to submit your pre-trial investigation report," he looks at me.

"You've already questioned me, Mr. Brunner," I grip my fingers tightly. What does he want from me?

"True, but I haven't submitted the report yet," his blue eyes continue to stare at me. "You understand, Miss Walburga, you are not married, and this isn't Vienna. It isn't customary here." He takes a pipe from his uniform shirt pocket. "Do you mind if I smoke?"

I shake my head. What does he expect me to do? I told him everything I knew. Will he punish me for not being married? I'm nauseated.

I watch his thick fingers take out some tobacco from the leather pouch he places on the table. Gently, he pushes the tobacco into the pipe and lights it, breathing in pleasure. "You understand, Miss Walburga," he continues to speak, "It isn't customary for unmarried people to live together. If the judge hears about it, he will punish Egon severely."

"So, what do you want me to do?" I ask him, confused.

"There are two options, Miss Walburga," he takes the pipe out of his mouth. "Either you get up and leave this house and disappear as if you've never been here," he pauses for a moment and continues to watch me.

"I have nowhere to go," I look at him. I can't go back to Ms. Bertha's. I've come so far. I'm not going back. I will not become one of her girls.

"Or you should act as a woman should," he says, putting the pipe back in his mouth. "And what do you mean?"

"Support your husband, even if he made a mistake; the wife must help him."

I look at him, not exactly understanding what he means but nodding. I can't go back to Vienna on my own.

"Ms. Walburga," he speaks to me with the pipe still in his mouth, "I'm questioning you again, are you married to Mr. Egon Schiele? Please, think again about your answer."

"Yes sir, we are married," I say after a moment of silence, nodding.

"Good," he holds the pencil and fills the paper with dense lines. "Mr. Egon Schiele is begging you to visit him," he says as he finishes writing and returns the papers to his small leather case, carefully closing it with his thick fingers. "I think you should."

"Yes, Mr. Brunner," I reply, knowing I have no choice.

"I'll wait here while you get ready," he looks at me, and I get up from the table and go to the bedroom to get dressed.

While I'm getting dressed, I occasionally peek at him from the bedroom door, wanting to make sure he's not trying to enter the room, even though I know that if he does, I won't be able to do anything. He's a police officer, and I'm a woman. No one will believe me. But he just sits in the kitchen, lost in thought, with the pipe in his mouth, which releases grayish smoke into the kitchen space, filling it with the warm smell of pipe tobacco. I hurry to comb my hair and go to the kitchen. His presence scares me.

"Shall we go?" he asks me and approaches the door, and I hand him his coat and take my coat that hung next to his.

We walk side by side on the muddy path, and I want us to get to the police station already. The silence makes me nervous.

"How did you find out about his paintings?" I ask after a while.

"The girls talked about it at school. You know how it is with young girls," he says. "One of the fathers came to the police to complain, and we went to investigate."

I continue walking beside him in silence, not knowing what to say. Did he see my paintings when they came to arrest Egon? What does he think of me? Why does he even want to help Egon? Is it because he is a man, and men help each other?

"I wanted him to succeed, to become a famous painter," I say after a while, unable to stand the silence.

"You are his wife now. You should want him to succeed," he answers as we bypass a mud puddle on the path.

We keep silent for the rest of our walk until we enter the village and the small police station. He leads me inside, accompanying me down the stairs to the basement.

"He's here," he stops next to a heavy brown wooden door with the number twelve engraved on it, "You have ten minutes," he says, "when you want to leave, knock on the door and shout, and one of the policemen will come down and open it for you."

"Why are you helping us?" I don't resist asking him.

He turns and looks at me under the dim light of the hallway, examining me for a moment before he answers, "Miss Walburga, we are a quiet town, hardworking people. We go to church every Sunday morning, law-abiding citizens," his blue eyes, which appear black in the dim light of the gas lamp on the wall, continue to study me. "We don't want newspaper headlines, scandals; this isn't Vienna," he speaks to me quietly as his big fingers pull the iron bolt, making a high-pitched noise, "When this is all over, you'll take him, and you'll leave my town and never come back."

"Yes, Mr. Brunner," I whisper and enter the cold holding cell. Egon is sitting on the wooden bench and looking up at me.

❦

Egon is wearing a simple linen button-down shirt and brown trousers, but his black quaff is gone. They cut his hair, maybe to prevent lice, and his hair, which I loved to caress so much, is now short. He is also unshaven, looks tired, and appears thinner. I look around at the small holding cell containing a simple wooden bench with a mattress, a blanket, a wooden chair, and a stainless steel bucket.

The sound of the heavy door slamming and the bolt locking makes me jump, and I look back at the closed door with a small barred window in the middle.

"My Wally," Egon gets up from the bench and walks towards me, hugs me with his arms, and clings to me so tightly that I can barely breathe. "I miss you so much," he brings his lips to my ear and whispers, starting to kiss my neck. But I cannot hug him back. My hands remain frozen. Although he doesn't smell of sweat or dirt, I can't identify his scent, as if another unfamiliar smell has replaced the one I knew and loved.

"I can't," I say quietly. I feel suffocated, as if his hands that once warmed me have become the branches of a climbing plant that are imprisoning me.

"What's wrong? My Wally," he continues kissing my neck with tiny pecks.

"I need air," I whisper and forcefully push him away, turning around and knocking on the heavy wooden door. "Guard, please get me out of here."

"Please don't go," he clings to me.

"Goodbye, Egon," I breathe heavily, turn to him, and step back until I feel the door's metal rivets through my dress.

"Please don't go," his whole body leans against me.

"Is everything okay? Do you want to go out?" I hear the guard's voice outside.

"Everything is fine, just a few more minutes," Egon presses his face to the barred window and speaks to the policeman. "Please don't go," he turns to me, his forehead sweaty. He gets down on his knees on the concrete floor, hugs my legs, rests his head on my stomach, and starts to cry.

"Miss, is everything alright? Shall I let you out?" the guard asks me again from the other side of the door, and I look down at Egon kneeling at my feet and crying. What do I do? I've never seen him cry like this.

"It's okay, officer, thank you," I answer him and reach down my hand, caressing Egon's short hair, running my fingers through it and trying to get used to the new feeling at the tips of my fingers.

"Please don't leave me," he sobs, his body trembling. "You're the only one I have left," he slowly whimpers, his warm hands hugging my legs as he kisses them. "I wrote them letters, but no one arrived. They apologized that they were unable to come."

"To whom did you write?" I ask him.

"To my friends in Krumlov, Klaus, and Bernhard," he gets up and walks away from me, sits on the wooden bench attached to the wall with metal chains, wiping his eyes. "And to my mother and Mr. Roessler from Munich," he looks at me. "They are not like you. People don't want to be beside people who go their own way and fail. Only if I succeed, they are happy to get on the train or a carriage with fast horses and arrive," he wipes his eyes again, looking like a little child who needs a hug.

I hesitate for a moment before asking, "and what about him?"

"Who?" Egon is watching me.

"What about Mr. Klimt," I say finally.

"I didn't write to him," Egon sighs. "If they knew in Vienna what happened here, I would never be able to set foot in a salon or an exhibition there. He must not know."

"Did your friends write back why they can't come?" I ask. What do his friends know about me and his paintings?

Egon retrieves a few letters from under the simple mattress on the bench, waving them in front of my eyes and tearing them, scattering the paper pieces on the floor. "I've been here for eighteen days, and they don't come simply because they're like everyone else," he says, looking at me. "You know?" He continues talking non-stop. "You don't choose me because I'm like everyone else. You choose me because I'm different. We're the same; you can be a servant all your life and not complain, and you choose to be different."

"I chose you," I answer him, "and I followed you from Vienna, to Krumlov, and now here, no matter what they say about you or me." I pause for a moment, searching for the right words. "I take off my clothes in front of you, undress, and let you paint me as no one else has ever seen me." I look down at the torn papers on the stone floor. "But not everything is permissible. There are boundaries that must not be crossed, even if you're a man who believes he can do anything in the name of art." I take a deep breath. "Drawing these young girls is forbidden. Believe me, as a woman, I understand how forbidden it is, and you will never understand as I do."

"My trial is in two days," he remains sitting and watches me.

"I know," I can't approach and hug him.

I can hear the door latch moving, and the guard opens it, "Mrs., you need to leave."

"Please testify for me at trial. Just do this for me, and then you can leave me forever," he looks at me and doesn't try to hug me.

"Mrs.?" the guard stands and waits.

"I'll think about it," I answer him and go outside, tears welling up in my eyes.

The guard slams the door and closes the bolt with a loud click.

"Wally wait," he calls out to me from inside. I stop by the door and see his fingers gripping the small barred window with his face showing through the bars. "Please, officer, will you allow me to say one last thing to her?" he presses his face against the bars.

"Can you please?" I turn to the guard, and he nods before moving a few steps away, standing near the stairs leading up from the basement.

"Wally, you were right," Egon whispers, "and I was so wrong. You brought them into our home. I should have treated them as if they were your little sisters, not models for painting."

I don't respond; I simply gaze at his face disappearing from the small window, and his fingers slowly release their grip on the metal bars. The only sounds are those of his footsteps inside the cell and the creaking of the iron chains as he sits down on the wooden bench.

"Mrs.?" the guard calls to me, and I turn away from the locked wooden door, walking toward the stairs. What should I do?

"All rise," the court clerk announces loudly, and we all stand. The wooden courtroom pews rustle, and the murmurs fall silent as the judge enters, wearing black robes.

"Everyone, please be seated," he says, and I can hear the pews rustling as we all take our seats in the small courtroom within the town hall.

The wooden benches are filled with spectators, most of whom I don't recognize. However, I can spot some familiar faces among the crowd, those I've seen during the months we've spent here: the woman from the bakery, the postman, the milkman, and perhaps a few more. None of them greets me, and despite the crowd, no one chooses to sit beside me. No one wishes to be associated with or seen as supporting me.

None of Egon's friends, to whom he sent letters, have shown up either. It's just me here, dressed in a simple blue gown.

Egon sits at the center of the courtroom on the defendant's bench, his white shirt standing out against the judge's black robe and the dark wooden benches filled with spectators who have come to observe the proceedings. He is clean-shaven and looks better than when I last visited him in the holding cell. However, it will be a while before his hair grows back, and his distinctive black quaff returns. I shift my gaze to the judge's stand.

Next to the judge sits another man in a suit who is taking notes, and to the side, Police Officer Brunner sits in a clean blue uniform, his police hat resting on his lap. I turn my head back to the entrance door. Perhaps one of Egon's friends will come in and sit beside me? But the door remains closed, and only a policeman in uniform stands nearby, his helmet securely in place. I glance at the gun in the brown leather holster he's wearing. What should I do? Should I believe Egon's claims of regret for his actions, or should I let justice take its course and send him back to prison?

"The accused, Mr. Egon Schiele," the judge reads from the paper on his desk, "you stand accused of kidnapping two thirteen year-old girls, forcing them into your home and engaging in immoral activities with them. Do you confess?"

"No, sir, I did not engage in anything immoral," Egon responds, attempting to sit up straight. I hear murmurs of anger from the audience in the pews behind me.

"Sir," the judge turns to Officer Brunner, "do you possess the testimony of the two girls?"

"Yes, Your Honor," Officer Brunner puts on his visor cap and rises, holding a piece of paper. The audience falls silent. "I have the testimony of the girls. Due to their young age, we did not summon them to court." He approaches the judge and places the paper in front of him, and the judge reads it. I scan the silent courtroom, where everyone's eyes are fixed on the paper resting on the judge's table.

"Could you provide a summary of your findings?" The judge looks up at the police officer.

"During their interrogation, the girls stated that they came to the house of Mr. and Mrs. Egon and Walburga Schiele of their own free will. They reported being treated kindly and denied any involvement in a kidnapping," the police officer says, and I can hear murmurs of anger from the crowd.

"Is Mr. Schiele's wife present in the courtroom?" The judge inquires of Officer Brunner.

"Yes, she is here," he answers, indicating me. I feel the collective gaze of everyone in the room directed at my back, searing my flesh like red-hot iron. My entire body is tense with anticipation.

"Did you also question Mrs. Schiele?" The judge watches me from his seat on the stand.

"Yes, sir," the police officer answers, "she confirmed the young girls' testimony." I feel myself blushing, my face burning. I'm afraid to turn around and meet the eyes of the crowd, unable to look them in the eye.

"As his wife, doesn't Mrs. Schiele want to sit by her husband's side?" The judge asks the police officer. But is he asking me?

"Mrs. Schiele can sit next to her husband," the police officer responds, and the judge looks at me. What should I do? Should I stand up? I glance around at the people surrounding me. Everyone is looking at me, seemingly waiting to see how I'll react. I have to be the supportive wife they expect me to be. But I'm afraid that if I stand, my legs will betray me, and I won't be able to take a single step.

I rise carefully, step by step, and sit next to Egon on the bench, making sure that our thighs do not touch. We are both in the center of the courtroom.

"I hereby declare the cancellation of the attempted kidnapping charge," the judge announces, turning again to the police officer. "Do you have any further findings?"

"Yes, sir," Mr. Brunner turns to the leather briefcase by his side, and the audience falls silent. His large fingers undo the buckles, and he pulls out several drawings. Even from a distance, I can tell that these are the girls' drawings. He walks over and places the drawings in front of the judge. I look down at my plain shoes, my gaze fixed on them. Behind me, I hear some people shouting, and I believe they are cursing us.

"Order in the court," the judge strikes his wooden gavel, and the courtroom falls silent, but the murmurs of anger persist.

"Did you paint these immoral images?" the judge turns to Egon.

"I painted them, but they are not immoral. It is art," Egon stands up and responds, "No one can judge art. Art should be free from any morality and judgment," he finishes speaking and sits down, and the audience becomes noisy again.

"Quiet," the judge raises his voice and strikes the gavel again. "This is not art. This is obscenity. Bring me a candle." He roars and turns to the court clerk, who leaves the room and returns after a minute.

"Is that what you call art?" the judge shouts at Egon and shows the audience one of the nude paintings. I can't bring myself to look at the painting. "It's an abomination, and this is what should be done with an abomination," he places the edge of the paper over the flame, and in an instant, the fire consumes the painting. I watch as the lines on the brown paper turn into flakes of black ash while the crowd behind me cheers.

"Sir, you are not allowed," Egon shouts and stands up, "you will not judge my art. Only the world will judge it, even if it takes years."

"Sit down immediately," the judge thunders at him, "I am the judge, and therefore I will judge it. This is profanity, silence in the court."

Egon remains standing, trembling. I look at him for the first time since I sat down next to him. He has lost weight during the three weeks he has been in custody. I notice tears on his cheeks and place my hand on his palm, caressing him. He turns his gaze to me, "they are burning my paintings," he whispers to me, two tears running down his cheeks.

"It doesn't matter," I whisper to him, "they will never understand you and your art, no matter what you paint," I keep caressing his hand, and he sits down next to me, his whole body shaking. He is sweating.

"Is there anyone else you want to call to testify before I deliver the verdict?" The judge turns to the police officer. Mr. Brunner surveys the courtroom, his gaze lingering on me for a moment. "No, Your Honor," he says, looking back at the judge.

"Is there anyone else in the audience who wishes to testify before sentencing?" The judge asks the audience, and the crowd falls silent as if waiting for something.

I look at police officer Mr. Brunner and shift my gaze from the glittering Empire emblem on his hat to Egon, who rests his head in his hands. Do I want to be the wife he thinks I should be?

"I wish to speak," I say weakly and stand up. My legs are shaking. In the courtroom's silence, I can hear the scratching of the ink pen on the paper as the court clerk records my words, hunched over as he writes.

"The court is listening," the judge says, leaning back.

"Your honor," I look at the judge.

"Speak louder," someone shouts from the crowd behind.

"Your Honor," I begin, swallowing my saliva, "I know these paintings are inappropriate, and Mr. Egon Schiele should not have painted them. Egon is an artist. He wants to paint everything he sees—houses, people, and even me," I look at police officer Brunner. He must have seen the pictures he drew of me, "And Egon was wrong. He saw these girls and wanted to draw them, too, just as he wants to draw anything he sees. But he was wrong about that." I pause for a moment, hearing murmurs of agreement from the audience, "But I want to assure you of one thing: I was with him the whole time at home, along with the girls, and I was also wrong not to stop him," I catch my breath, trying to clarify my words, "but he did not engage in anything immoral with them. I witnessed it, I swear to God, and Egon confessed to me that he regrets what he did." I finish my words and sit down.

People continue to mutter angrily, but I watch the police officer examining his thick mustache. He gives me a small smile and ignores Egon with his gaze. It doesn't matter if they're angry with me; we'll have to leave this place soon.

"Is there anyone else who wishes to speak?" The judge asks, and I look down again, hoping fervently that this trial will soon be over, and I can disappear from the courtroom.

"The accused, please stand," the judge hits his gavel, and Egon stands up. I remain seated and touch his hand, feeling him grasp my palm tightly. "I declare," the judge continues speaking, "that although the crime of kidnapping was not committed, a crime of moral indecency did occur," he pauses for a moment, and I hear the audience nodding in agreement, "Therefore, you have spent twenty-one days in detention. I sentence you to an additional three days of detention, totaling twenty-four days in prison. The trial is concluded." He hits his gavel once more.

"All rise," the court clerk announces, and we all stand as the judge exits the courtroom. I hold Egon's hand and stand beside him, feeling embarrassed knowing they are looking at us.

We remain standing as the audience slowly leaves the hall. Police officer Brunner also passes by us but ignores Egon and me, going to talk to the policeman who stands by the door, and disappears with the crowd.

"Thank you for pretending to be my wife. I don't know why the officer didn't say you were lying," Egon whispers to me, still holding my hand. I watch the policeman approaching us, waiting patiently for the audience to leave the hall. "I'll be released in three days, and I'll make it up to you," Egon continues to whisper to me, "I'll return home, and we'll continue to be here like before, just you and me, inside this house, far from the town. I promise you, we'll be happy together."

"We have to go back to Vienna," I say, suddenly feeling tired. When I get home, I'll start packing. They aren't open-minded enough to accommodate an artist like you," I don't tell him what the police officer said to me.

"You know, Wally," he tells me when the policeman is already holding his arm, just before he is taken back to the holding cell. "Thank you for being with me. You were right. I don't feel punished, but cleansed."

Chapter Eleven

The Return to Vienna, a City at War

S pring sun spreads morning rays over the fields outside the house, and I take out my leather suitcase, placing it on the doorstep, and sigh.

"Are we ready to go?" Egon comes out after me, carrying his luggage and placing it next to my suitcase.

"Yes, I've packed everything," I lock the door for the last time and go to the mailbox, placing the key inside. Later, the landlady will come to collect the key. She didn't want to say goodbye to us.

I look at Egon; his hair has started to grow, but it's still short. It will take some time for it to return to its original form.

"Are you cold?" Egon asks me as he stands next to me.

"I like the morning chill," I smile at him and look at the distant mountains and their snowy peaks. The snow in the valley had already melted, and the fields were filled with small white spring flowers. At the end of the path, I can already see the brown horse carrying the cart to take us to the train station. I'm tired of wandering. I want a home.

"You'll see that moving back to Vienna will be good for us," Egon takes my palm with his gloved hand. He is still thin and weak from being in detention. It will take time for him to return to his previous weight.

"Whoa," the coachman says to the horse and stops the cart at the foot of the house, and we take the suitcases and approach him.

"Where's the young man? The one who always takes us?" I ask the older coachman when he gets down and takes the suitcase from my hand.

"What does it matter to you who takes us?" Egon also gives his suitcase to the coachman.

"They recruited him for the army," the coachman answers and holds out his hand, helping me climb up to the wooden seat. I think of the young man and hope that war will not break out. The newspapers in the village are talking about the tensions between the powers.

"I wish him good luck in the service of the empire and our great emperor," Egon says to the older coachman in an ironic voice. I don't think the coachman notices, he silently pulls on the reins and clucks to the horse. As we begin to ride along the dirt path toward the train station, I turn and take one last look at the house that I first loved and then hated.

"Next stop on the way to Vienna is Pressbaum," the conductor announces later that afternoon as we sit side by side on the busy train, "the train will stop for five minutes and continue on its way," he continues to announce as he moves through the car. As the train approaches the platform and stops with a long puff, I look out the window toward the small townhouses and the pointed church tower.

"The heir to the Austro-Hungarian throne was murdered in Sarajevo. The heir to the Austro-Hungarian throne was murdered in Sarajevo, read now," a young boy shouts as he runs along the platform waving a newspaper.

Two gentlemen in suits standing on the platform stop the boy, place a coin in his palm, and take a newspaper from his hand.

"What happened? What happened?" I hear murmurs in the car.

"Pressbaum," the conductor announces, and the doors open. I see a few gentlemen getting off the train and rushing to the newsboy.

"Wally, wait here. I'll be right back," Egon says and joins the crowd on the way to the car door.

I rise from my seat, open the car window, stick my head out, and gaze at the platform. Several other women also follow suit, and together, our heads turn towards the gathering of gentlemen surrounding the newsboy. Among them, I spot Egon.

"The train to Vienna is departing," the conductor announces on the platform and blows his whistle. The locomotive chugs, and men scramble to abandon the newsboy, hastily making their way back onto the train. Slowly, the train starts to move, and a few men are left running after it, clutching their top hats and newspapers.

"An assassin shot the heir to the throne, Franz Ferdinand, during his visit to Sarajevo," Egon says as he sits beside me, panting. "I couldn't get a newspaper. They ran out. Apparently, his wife was also murdered alongside him."

"Duchess Sophie was also murdered?" the woman sitting on the bench in front of us asks Egon. She wears a fashionable blue dress with a matching hat and gloves. I observe as she wipes her teary eyes with a handkerchief.

"How did it happen?" another passenger asks.

"They were shot while driving through the city streets in an open car," someone answers.

"Why weren't they guarded?" asks an elderly woman with glasses.

"The Serbs will pay for this. The empire will not stay silent," proclaims a middle-aged gentleman in a suit, waving a newspaper.

"We will go to war against them. The Austro-Hungarian empire will uphold its pride," a man wearing a cap and a thick mustache asserts.

"You can have the newspaper," someone offers us a newspaper, and Egon opens it while more passengers from the car gather around us to read the scant lines describing the events in Sarajevo.

"Will there be a war?" a young woman in a spring dress asks the man next to her.

"If war does break out, we will easily defeat them. We are an empire," he replies, holding her hand and offering a reassuring smile.

"The train is pulling into Vienna station," the conductor announces. I rise from my seat, sticking my head out of the open window, watching the locomotive as it enters the vast station, disappearing into a cavernous black space. What will become of us if war indeed breaks out? Suddenly, everything that happened in Neulengbach seems so distant, as if from another era.

"Wally, let's go. We must hurry if we want to find a carriage," Egon takes my hand, and we gather our luggage, rushing to leave the train.

The train station, as usual, is bustling with people. However, unlike our last visit, most men are clutching newspapers, and newsboys are darting along the platforms, loudly repeating news of the assassination.

"The Ministry of Defense has issued an ultimatum to Serbia. Germany supports the empire, while the English and French are opposed," announces one of the newspaper boys. Although women shouldn't be interested in politics, I feel unwell. Suddenly, it seems to me that the train station is closing in on me with its iron beam-ed roofs, the noise of the people, and the stifling smoke from the locomotives. Only when we depart from the station and Egon goes to find us a carriage do I start to breathe again, gazing at the spring afternoon sun. Maybe this city will be pleasant for us after all.

However, as the carriage drives down the main boulevard and nears the Ministry of Defense building, I notice the crowds outside blocking the boulevard. They surround the statue of the emperor riding his horse in front of the building, as if awaiting the bronze statue to begin speaking to them. I notice numerous police officers guarding the entrance to the building.

"They are waiting for the Ministry of Defense's decision. It will take some time. The street is blocked," the coachman turns around and explains to Egon. "We'll have to take another route or wait."

"We'll wait a few minutes," Egon answers him and stands up, observing the people from the top of the open carriage. I glance around at the people walking down the boulevard, joining the crowd surrounding our carriage until it seems like we're a small boat in a sea of gentlemen in dark suits and top hats.

"Welcome to Vienna," an elderly florist, dressed in a ragged dress and holding a basket of flowers, approaches us. She offers a bouquet of flowers to Egon.

"Thank you," Egon pays her and takes the bouquet of roses from her hand. "Wally, the world is changing before our eyes," he declares, "it's time for us to change too." He hands me the bouquet and kisses my lips. He had never bought me flowers before.

I transfer the flowers from the simple glass to the water jar that I bought this morning at the market and gaze out from the window of our new house on Hietzinger Hauptstrasse, overlooking the avenue below. We live on the third floor in a pleasant apartment with a view of the street. In the center of the road, a tram passes like a red worm, and the windows of the buildings on the other side of the street seem to smile at me. Luckily, we were able to find this apartment for rent. Since the murder of the to the Austro-Hungarian throne's heir a few days ago, the city seems to have gone crazy. All prices have risen, and every street is filled with billboards calling on men to enlist in the war to restore the empire's honor. The tranquility of Neulengbach's countryside is gone. Perhaps it's better this way, to be anonymous in the big city.

"Wally, I managed to find one," Egon enters the apartment carrying a large easel, "I was at Klimt's, and he gave it to me as a gift along with a few tubes of paint, so we won't have to buy any." He places the easel in the center of the room and the leather bag next to it, saying, "I can get back to painting."

"Shall we begin? How do you want me?" I go to the bedroom and take the blanket from there, placing it on the studio floor to have a comfortable place to lie down. I want him to succeed.

I unbutton my shirt and remove it, as well as my skirt and underwear. I lie naked on the blanket and look at the ceiling, patiently waiting for Egon to take off his jacket, freshen up and join. I want him to draw me. I don't want him to search for other women.

From outside, I hear a faint noise, a continuous rattling. What's happening on the street? I get up and approach the window, but after a moment, I return and put on my shirt. Perhaps someone on the street would look up and see me through the window.

A column of soldiers marches down the avenue toward the city's exit. At the column's head are commanders on horses, and behind the marching soldiers are horses carrying supply carts. As long as Egon is not drafted into the army, he must paint and sell paintings; otherwise, we will run out of money.

"Wally?" I hear Egon and turn to him.

"I'm ready," I walk past him and remove my shirt again, lying down on the blanket. We haven't been intimate since what had happened with the young girls. I couldn't. However, I have to forgive him.

"I want to draw you differently this time," he brings a chair from the kitchen and positions it behind the easel, sitting down. "I want to draw you clothed. I want to capture the intricate folds of the fabric," he looks at me.

I offer him an awkward smile and suddenly feel vulnerable in his presence. I reach out and pick up the shirt strewn on the floor and start to put it on, my cheeks reddening, even though I should feel relieved. What else has changed?

⚜

The warm sun of late August caresses my face as I leave the house and walk down the avenue. We've been living here for over a year, and I hardly think about what happened in Krumlov and Neulengbach anymore.

The war also seems far away. It exists in another world in the east, where the sun rises on the Russian front or sets in the west on the English-French front. But little by little, it seeps into Vienna as well, causing me an unpleasant feeling that I try to ignore. Like back then, before this all started; when Mr. Walner from the fabric store would talk and smile at me, and I would freeze, sensing that something bad would happen.

I stop at the market. I need to buy cheese, bread, and some cabbage. There is still almost no food rationing, and the markets are brimming with goods as usual.

"Give me three hundred grams of this cheese, please," I ask the female stall-owner, pointing to the block of cheese on the stand while I stand with the other women nearby. Most male sellers in the market have vanished, replaced by young women. When the war began, the streets were plastered with posters calling for young men to enlist, promising they would return home in a few months. But almost a year has passed since then. The posters are gone, but the war has persisted into the fall. Now it's reflected in newspaper headlines and the large sheets of paper hanging on the Ministry of Defense wall, filled with long lists of the dead in black letters. Only the men in suits and top hats continue to sit in the cafés, reading newspapers, and talking to each other as if almost nothing has changed. Instead of discussing Freud's new theories, they talk about the course of the war and explain to each other that we should have won a long time ago.

"One Kronen," the seller in the market holds her hand out, and I place the silver coin in her palm. Food prices keep rising. Lately, I hardly buy meat and sausage. The price of firewood in the winter has also increased, and there are fewer carriages on the streets. Many horses were recruited for the war.

Further down the market, I see an elderly woman selling old household items. She has scattered kettles and utensils on an old blanket spread on the cobblestones. Many people are selling their jewelry and silverware to buy food. I mustn't dwell on Dad's signet ring. I need to heed what Ms. Bertha told me. I should forget about it and move on. Someone must have already bought it. I will never have enough money to get it back.

I turn around and head home with the groceries, placing them in the pantry. Later, I will prepare our meal. Egon will arrive soon. For several months, he has been searching for a gallery that will agree to exhibit his new paintings. At least he hasn't been drafted yet, unlike many other men his age.

I sit down in front of the window, open the book Ms. Bertha gave me, and find dried petals of the flowers Egon gave me on the day we returned to Vienna. Now and then, I look at them, waiting for him to take the next step that a man should take for a woman who has been with him for so long.

I hear the noise of the key turning in the door lock and hurry to close the book and put it back. I must have been daydreaming. I didn't have time to prepare Egon's meal.

"Wally, we made it," he walks through the door, holding a bottle of wine and a fine sausage.

"Did he agree?" I take the items from him and head to go to the kitchen, but he stops and kisses me passionately.

"He agreed, and he wants to present my paintings, and I'm going to be famous," he whispers in my ear as he caresses me. "Here in Vienna, in the center of the empire, and during a war, people will come to see my paintings," he tells me as he takes the bottle of wine and the sausage from my hands, placing them on the chair in the living room next to my closed book. Then he takes my hand and leads me to the bedroom.

Later, I stand in front of the window dressed in a nightgown and gaze out at the boulevard, watching the people walking along it. Suddenly, I notice some army cavalry passing by the street, instructing people to move to the sides. I shift my gaze and spot a group of people following behind them.

They resemble a long, dark snake slowly crawling from the end of the street, all clad in dirty green uniforms. Only when they draw closer and pass beneath my window do I manage to discern their faces. Some sport wild beards, while others are unshaven with unkempt hair. None of them carries a weapon, and for a moment, I wonder if they are soldiers or laborers forced into uniforms and sent across the city to reinforce the army. However, many of them wear grimy bandages, and some walk with difficulty. The bystanders who have moved to the sides of the street stand and watch them. I witness a woman approaching the group, offering a water pitcher to one of them. He eagerly drinks from it, thanks her, and then passes it on to his friends.

"Russian prisoners of war from the eastern front," Egon whispers and embracing me from behind, his arms wrapped around me. "They're on their way to a POW camp."

"They're just like us," I whisper back to him, observing two of them supporting a friend who hobbles on one leg, the other covered in bandages. They place their arms under his shoulders to help him walk, ensuring he doesn't fall behind.

"Yes, they're just like us: fighting for their empire for no reason."

"I hope they don't recruit you to fight for our empire for no reason," I place my hand on his arm, feeling his warm body close to me. He hasn't dressed since we went to bed.

"You and I have nothing to do with the war," he begins caressing me again. "I don't want to be a soldier of an emperor. I don't belong to anyone. I belong to my art." He kisses me once more. "Do you feel the window?" He guides my hand to the cool glass. "The window is our shield from the outside world."

"When is your exhibition?" I kiss him back. At the exhibition, we will break that shield.

"In two weeks. I have a few more paintings I want to finish. They accepted me to exhibit at the Wiener Secession Gallery," he continues speaking, and for a moment, I shudder, recalling the last time I was there. "They promised that tomorrow the invitations to the exhibition will be ready." Egon releases his embrace and moves away, heading to the studio. "Can you go there to collect the invitations and deliver them to the addresses I'll provide?"

"Sure, I'll do it tomorrow. Are you hungry? I'll prepare us something to eat," I continue to watch the never-ending line of Russian prisoners in the street below, feeling an urge to go down and offer them the expensive sausage that Egon bought specifically, but I know he wouldn't agree. He has worked for years to achieve success. Tomorrow, I'll go to the Secession Gallery again, as expected of someone who aspires to be a wife. I despise that place and am afraid of it.

❦

The following day, it takes me a while before I dare to climb the stairs of the white building and enter. I had stood on the street for a long time, gazing at the famous gallery's golden leaf dome. They had expelled me from here last time. I take a deep breath, ascend the stairs, and step into the Wiener Secession Gallery.

In the daylight, the gallery appears larger than I remembered. I walk along the white walls, some of which are adorned with art painted directly on them. I recognize Mr. Klimt's style, similar to the paintings I saw in his studio. I stand and observe them, breathing slowly. He belongs to the past. I have moved on. My fingers grip my purse. His name is also on the guest list that Egon gave me this morning.

"Good morning, Mrs., may I help you?" a man in a suit approaches me, bowing slightly, and I startle a bit. He caught me by surprise.

"Good morning," I reply. "I came to pick up the invitations to Mr. Egon Schiele's exhibition." Did he notice how nervous I am?

"Please, follow me," he gestures, and I walk alongside him towards the office in the back of the gallery.

"If I may ask, who is the lady?" he says as we walk, "You look familiar."

"I don't think we've met before," I smile at him nervously. How does he know me? Did he see how I was expelled from here at Mr. Klimt's exhibition? Did he recognize me in Egon's nude paintings? Or maybe he once saw me at Ms. Bertha's hostel? I want to turn around and leave this building, the pristine white walls looming over me.

"I apologize, Mrs.," he opens one of the doors, and we enter a neat, simple white office, "you just look familiar to me."

"I will soon be Mrs. Schiele," I breathe and tell him. I see the stack of white invitations on the wooden table. Egon's name is engraved on them in black letters in a square script.

"Mrs. Schiele," he hands me the invitations, "we are so excited to host him in our gallery. His paintings are groundbreaking; if I may say so, so are you." He looks at me and smiles. Is he just being polite? Or is he like Mr. Walner from the fabric store? I freeze for a moment in my place.

"Thank you, sir," I pull myself together after a moment and take the invitations from his hand, hurrying out of the gallery. It's only when I descend the stairs to the street that I stand in the shade of one of the trees and breathe again. I must remember that I'm not sixteen anymore, like I was back then. I've been through a lot since that day.

However, when I approach Mr. Klimt's house, I stop, unable to enter through the iron gate. What did Egon tell him about what happened in Krumlov and Neulengbach? Did Mr. Klimt tell him about when I came to ask him for money? What if he tries to touch me again? How will I react this time?

My hand caresses the handle of the black gate repeatedly, but I can't bring myself to enter, and I remain standing, looking at the garden and the house, searching for the cat, but it's nowhere to be found.

The sound of a door opening startles me, and I hurry away down the street. In the distance, I see Mr. Klimt coming out of the gate and walking towards the city. Did he notice me from the window? He didn't turn in my direction.

Only after he disappears further down the street do I approach the gate again and open it, heading toward the door. I'll ring the doorbell and then leave the invitations in the mailbox, informing Egon that Mr. Klimt wasn't home.

I ring the doorbell and wait, clutching the invitation in my hand. To my surprise, the door swings open, revealing a tall, curly-haired woman in a loose light blue dress adorned with decorations. Could she be one of the women he's painting?

It takes me a moment to remember that I met her here already. It's Ms. Emilie Flöge, who is with Mr. Klimt. "Good morning, Ms.," I say to her.

"Good morning," she continues to look at me, examining my red hair and eyes.

"My name is Walburga Neuzil. I've brought you an invitation to Mr. Egon Schiele's exhibition," I hand her the envelope.

"Don't I know you?" she asks me. "Weren't you here with Mr. Klimt?"

"Yes," I blush.

"And now you're with Egon?"

"Yes," I reply curtly, although I want to tell her I'm not like her. I'm Egon's only woman.

"Does he also paint you naked? I remember your red hair and blue eyes," she doesn't invite me inside or take the envelope from my hand.

"Yes, he only draws me," I finally answer her.

"We'd love to come to the opening," she finally takes the envelope from my hand and smiles at me. "We'll see who painted you better. Mr. Klimt or Mr. Schiele."

"We'll be happy to see you there. Have a good day," I answer and turn around, walking to the gate, feeling my face redden.

I stand outside the gate for a few minutes before I walk back and breathe. Even though she tried to insult me, I stood firm in front of her and didn't get confused. I'm a rebel just like Egon. I shouldn't be embarrassed by her or the gentleman in the gallery I met earlier. I shouldn't be embarrassed by anyone. I start walking back towards the city and smile to myself.

On the avenue near my house, I stop to admire the display window of a lingerie shop. I've never purchased stockings for myself; the ones I have were a gift from Christina. I washed them thoroughly in the stainless steel tub in our shared bathroom and have been using them ever since, except for the black pair I cut after the incident in Neulengbach. My eyes linger on the beautiful camisole and silk stockings. I feel the desire to celebrate, just as Egon did when he bought a bottle of wine.

"Good morning," I enter the store and look at the selection.

"Good morning," the saleswoman replies, and I explain what I'm looking for, observing her as she disappears into the back room.

"Good morning," two young ladies enter the store.

"Good morning," I respond awkwardly. They appear to be around my age, perhaps a year or two older, in their early twenties. They both have striking blue eyes and stylish, slightly curly brown haircuts. They are dressed in modern morning dresses in cream colors and bear a striking resemblance, suggesting they might be sisters.

"You're not the saleswoman here, are you?" they giggle.

"No, she went to get me something for me from the back room," I smile at them.

"We recognize you," one of them remarks. "We've seen you several times walking here on the street."

"Yes, I live here, at number one hundred and one," I reply.

"So do we, right across the street from you," one of them says with a smile.

"So you're the girl who occasionally stands at the window and watches the street or reads a book," the other one comments.

"Yes, that's me," I respond, feeling a blush creeping up. Did they catch me naked?

"Nice to meet you, I'm Edith Harms," the lighter-haired one shakes my hand.

"Nice to meet you, Adéle Harms," the dark-haired woman extends her hand.

"Walburga Neuzil, Wally," I shake their hands, and we all sit down.

"Here you go," the saleswoman reemerges from the back room with a cardboard box, takes out the silk garter socks, and delicately presents them.

"They're lovely," I say. "May I try them on?"

"Go ahead," the sisters encourage me while the saleswoman nods in agreement.

I slide the garter socks over my thighs and stand in front of the mirror, feeling so feminine.

"They are beautiful," says Edith.

"Try the black ones. They'll suit you," Adéle suggests.

"Shall I bring you black ones?" the saleswoman asks.

"These are for an opening of a painting exhibition," I explain to the women around me.

"Then black it must be," Edith and the saleswoman concur. I remain standing in front of the mirror, watching my reflection while the saleswoman heads back to the back room. Black would indeed be more fitting for the occasion.

"Whose exhibition is it?" Edith inquires.

"A talented painter, Egon Schiele; we are together."

"You should consider buying more items here," Adéle whispers to me, "with the war who knows when the prices will rise, and it will be impossible to get good products. Your talented painter will probably be happy if you wear beautiful intimate accessories to the exhibition," she smiles at me and giggles.

"I'd also like a new camisole," I tell the saleswoman when she returns with the black garter socks, and I try them on, encouraged by the approving looks from Edith and Adéle.

"Come to the opening," I bid them farewell, and give them an invitation. I've never had female friends who've spent time with me.

The exhibition hall seems much less threatening in the evening than during my previous visits.

Despite the war, there is no blackout, and the boulevard's lanterns across from the gallery bathe the street in small points of light, resembling fireflies scattered in a field, guiding the way for arriving visitors. I position myself at the building's entrance atop the staircase, observing black automobiles pulling up to the curb and men in suits and top hats stepping out. With graceful gestures, they open the car doors and extend their hands to the elegantly dressed women accompanying them. Pair by pair, they ascend the stairs, resembling guests at a grand ball in the Imperial Palace.

"Good evening," they greet Egon, who stands beside me in his perpetual brown jacket and white shirt, his slicked-back haircut glistening.

"Good evening, this is Wally," he introduces me, and I shake their hands while beaming with excitement, making a concerted effort to remember everyone's names. I manage to do so, and together, we stand at the top of the stairs, welcoming the guests.

"Mr. Arthur Roessler," Egon hurries down the stairs and warmly shakes the hands of a gentleman in his thirties getting out of a carriage who has stopped by the entrance.

"Wally, meet Mr. Arthur Roessler from Munich, the man who exhibited my paintings when everyone thought I was a pervert," he introduces him to me, "Mr. Roessler, let me introduce you to Walburga Neuzil, Wally, my muse, the red-haired woman who kindles my imagination."

"Nice to meet you," I smile at him and shake his hand. His face is round and decorated with a well-kept black mustache, and he smiles at me in a friendly way.

"Flaming Wally, this great artist's inspiration," he holds my hand. "Egon, will you forgive me if I take this beautiful lady to escort and show me the wonderful paintings inside?" he asks him, and I laugh.

"Of course," Egon caresses my arm and turns to greet a woman ascending the stairs. She is wearing a blue dress glistening with diamonds.

"Lead the way, red-haired princess. Let me see your creations," Arthur puts his arm in mine and leads me into the crowded hall. I look around at the pleasant waiters with trays of champagne glasses. It's as if the war stopped at the entrance of this hall.

"My dear, every artist needs a muse like you," Mr. Roessler tells me as we stand before one of my nude paintings. "This art is so groundbreaking."

"Thank you," I reply, feeling a blush creep up despite having seen my own nude portrayal on the brown paper so many times.

"I noticed that some of the paintings Egon exhibited in Munich weren't included here, the more daring ones," he remarks as we move from painting to painting. "Did he manage to sell them? That's fantastic."

"No," I reply and look at one of the paintings where I'm clothed. "Egon was looking for a more reserved image."

"He's just wonderful. One day, he'll be a famous painter. I'll talk to him about another exhibition next year if the war allows it," he continues, standing beside me while I smile. His art will succeed. He will break into the world.

More people approach to look at the painting, talk amongst themselves, and I introduce Mr. Roessler to them. Then I walk away and mingle among the guests. From the other side of the hall, I see Egon talking with Mr. Klimt and Ms. Emilie Flöge, and I feel a small tremor of discomfort. I don't want Mr. Klimt to notice and approach me. I blend into the crowd, hiding behind two ladies wearing colored dresses and talking loudly about the latest summer fashion.

"Mrs.," someone addresses me, and I turn, seeing a waiter in a black suit in front of me, freezing. Does someone want to banish me from here again?

"May I offer you champagne?" he holds the tray with the glasses in front of me, and I smile awkwardly at him, taking one of the tall glasses and sipping from it to relax. The drink is sweet and makes me smile again.

"Congratulations," Ms. Emilie Flöge walks towards me, holding a glass of champagne, raising it slightly. Where did Mr. Klimt and Egon go? I search for them with my eyes but can't see them.

"Thank you," I smile at her and sip the champagne.

"Your paintings here are very impressive. You are definitely the center of the exhibition."

"Thank you, Egon is the center. I'm only his muse. We're together."

"So you got what you wanted?" she watches me and sips the champagne in her hand.

"Yes," I look around at several gentlemen who are conversing in front of my nude painting. "I'm here talking with you now," I answer her, "and no one is kicking me out." Is she the one who demanded that I be expelled last time at Mr. Klimt's exhibition?

"My dear child, you're wrong," she says to me as she looks around at the people, "please show me your left hand." She turns to me, and I hand it to her. Why is she asking me to see my left hand?

"You don't have a ring," she gives me a little smile, "not even an engagement ring." She continues after a moment, "you're wrong, no one has accepted you for this exhibition or high society, they just smile at you," she sips from her glass of champagne, all that is left. "There is now a war, so everyone thinks that the world will change, but believe me, the world will not change so quickly. As long as you don't have a ring on your hand, you are the mistress." She finishes speaking, continuing to hold her empty glass.

"You're wrong, Ms. Flöge," I also sip my champagne and look up at her. "I'm here to stay. No one will take my place."

"Good luck to you," she gently raises the empty glass she's holding, and I can't help but notice the absence of a ring on her fingers.

"Have a pleasant evening," I reply with a polite smile, slowly stepping away from her. I'd managed to respond.

Approaching the waiter, I pick up another glass of champagne. No need to dwell on what she mentioned about Egon not proposing yet. He'll propose when the time is right.

"Wally, there you are. We've been looking for you," Edith and Adéle Harms, sisters dressed in stylish summer evening attire adorned with exquisite pearl necklaces and matching pearl earrings, approach me.

"Here I am," I smile at them, feeling rather plain in their presence.

"Your man has very impressive paintings," Edith remarks.

"You're quite daring," Adéle giggles, "I wouldn't have the courage to expose myself like that."

"Nor would I. You're certainly a liberated woman," Edith adds, "and very brave."

"I've chosen to embrace my freedom," I reply while taking a sip from my champagne glass. I don't want to disclose that my motivation was simply to succeed and avoid staying at Bertha's hostel as one of her girls. They probably haven't seen such places from the inside.

"It takes a lot of courage with all these men around," Edith observes, casting a glance at the men in suits surrounding us and the paintings I appear in.

"Why should it require courage?" I hear Egon's voice and turn my gaze to him as he approaches, standing beside me.

"Egon, meet the ladies, sisters Edith and Adéle Harms," I introduce them.

"Pleasure to meet you," he hugs my waist, drawing me closer, his fingers softly tracing my waistline as he kisses their extended hands.

"Nice to meet the talented artist," Edith smiles as he kisses her hand, while her other hand lightly caresses her pearl necklace.

"The pearl necklace around your neck is truly exquisite, contrasting beautifully with the whiteness of your skin," Egon compliments her.

"The necklace is a family heirloom, but my skin color is uniquely my own," Edith smiles, "during the summer, I make sure to avoid sunbathing in the village."

"We were just telling Mrs. Wally how courageous she is to let you paint her like that," Adéle informs him.

"Wally is wonderful. She's willing to follow me down every path I take as an artist," Egon replies.

"Were there times when you walked too far?" Edith asks him, her eyes fixed on his fingers caressing me. What will he answer her?

"Being an artist is about exploring boundaries," Egon replies, "but an artist also needs to know when to stop and mature."

"That sounds fascinating," she touches her pearl necklace again, and I notice the absence of a wedding or engagement ring.

"Misses Edith and Adéle are our neighbors," I say, wanting to change the subject of the conversation. Suddenly his fingers caressing my waist feel right uncomfortable.

"Really?" Egon asks. "Then, how have we never met you?"

"Definitely surprising. We live right across the street, at number one hundred," says Adéle.

"Perhaps because you're always holed up in your studio painting. You need to step out into the sunlight more often," Edith adds with a laugh.

I place my palm on his hand embracing me, feeling the absent ring on my finger.

"Well, I'm sure we'll have the chance to meet again. Excuse me, I'd like to show the paintings to more guests," he nods to them, kisses Edith's hand, and leads me away.

"We will surely meet again," Edith assures him, and I smile at her as Egon and I leave them and walk towards more gentlemen. I know she notices Egon's hand around my waist.

Chapter Twelve

The Sister Across
the Street

A few weeks later, I walk to the house from the city center. Many men and women gather around the Ministry of Defense, all looking at the large white pages on the wall, listing all the casualties. Thank God they haven't recruited Egon yet. A woman in a white shirt and a summer brown hat decorated with flowers walks away and bitterly cries while two women rush to hug her. A gentleman in a beret also approaches, takes out a handkerchief and hands it to her as she stops to lean against a tree on the boulevard. Despite the noise of the automobiles driving down the road, I can hear her crying.

I look away and walk away from the building. I can't dwell on it. I so badly want this unnecessary war to end. Why do men go to war and leave us women to deal with the consequences?

Near the Secession Gallery building, where Egon's exhibition was held, I stop and gaze at the convoy of horses pulling carts covered with white tarps, positioned near the entrance.

A large Red Cross is painted on each cart's tarp, and a new Red Cross flag waves above the building. Did they convert the building into a hospital? I pause next to one of the horses and gently stroke its nose. What's happening at the front? Are there so many casualties that there aren't enough hospitals? And what about doctors and nurses?

I take an apple out of my basket and offer it to the horse, extending my fingers as it sniffs it with its delicate nose before taking it from my hand. I'll stop by the butcher's and purchase more cured meat. Since Egon's exhibition, we have more money, and who knows when food shortages might begin.

"Wally, how are you? We've been talking about you lately," Edith and Adéle greet me when we meet outside the butcher's shop. I haven't met them since the exhibition.

"We were thinking of inviting you," Adéle adds. Both are carrying straw baskets.

"Invite me where?"

"To a gathering at our home," she replies, lowering her voice.

"A home gathering?"

"We've seen your drawings. You have courage. We believe our movement would resonate with you."

"A protest movement," Edith adds, glancing around as if to ensure no policeman is eavesdropping. However, police officers are seldom seen in our neighborhood. They are usually stationed near the emperor's palace or in the city's impoverished areas.

"The suffragists," Adéle explains, "have you heard of them?"

"No," I answer awkwardly, feeling rather ordinary compared to them.

"Come, listen to us. I'm sure it will pique your interest," Edith tells me. "It's in two days, at eight o'clock in the evening. It's a women-only gathering."

"I'll come," I promise them, happy that they want me to join them.

"Goodbye, we'll be expecting you," Adéle says.

"Don't forget, and give our regards to Egon," Edith places her hand on my arm for a moment before she joins her sister, who has already begun walking down the avenue.

"I won't forget," I reply, watching them as they depart. I can still feel the touch of her left hand on my arm, the one without the ring. I caress my bare fingers and enter the butcher's shop. I shouldn't dwell on it. I'm becoming too suspicious.

"Where are you headed?" Egon asks me two days later. He is drying himself after washing in the large stainless steel tub in our bathroom.

"The sisters Edith and Adéle Harms invited me," I respond while examining myself in the mirror, debating which dress to wear: my fancy one or a simple everyday dress. What is the appropriate attire for such gatherings?

"Our neighbors?" he asks as he puts on his shirt.

"Yes," I follow his reflection in the mirror. Did he change his tone of voice when inquiring about them? Or am I just being paranoid? "It's a women's gathering," I add.

"Have a good time," he says, turning away from me, bending down to put on his pants. "By the way, you could use this opportunity to invite them to our place. Perhaps they'd be interested in purchasing a painting. They seem to have money and property," he suggests, approaching me. "You look beautiful," he kisses me briefly and leaves the room.

"But apparently not beautiful enough," I whisper to myself, removing the simple dress and tossing it on the bed. I opt for my fancy one and begin applying makeup.

"Good evening, I'm so glad you could make it," Adéle greets me at the door and lets me into their house, "the other women are already here," she accompanies me to the guest room, and I look around.

Their house is larger than ours, adorned with numerous landscape paintings on the walls. In the guest room, luxurious armchairs surround the living room table, although the women are seated on mahogany chairs in a circle.

"Please meet Mrs. Walburga," she introduces me, and they do the same. I sit on a chair, and examine the teapot and the tray of sweet cookies on the table.

"Please, call me Wally," I smile at them.

"We invited Wally because we believe she'll fit right in," Edith explains to the other women.

"For the demonstrations?" one of them asks.

"We haven't mustered the courage to demonstrate yet," another replies.

"We must demand our rights through demonstrations," someone else chimes in. "They will never grant us rights if we don't insist on them."

"Remember what happened three months ago when a group of women dared to demonstrate?" another woman adds indignantly. "They were branded as traitors. The minister accused them of undermining the war effort. Men hurled insults at them."

"They tore up the signs they were carrying and yelled that women didn't need the right to vote," other women contribute.

"Men think we're foolish, and they always will," another concludes, and the discussion about women's suffrage continues. They sit there in their modern dresses, sipping tea from delicate cups, and enjoying *Cremeschnitte* cake served on porcelain plates with silver forks. I listen intently to their conversation about the demonstrations. It feels good to be a part of this.

"So, what can you bring to our cause?" one of the women asks me after a while, and a hush falls over the group as they all turn to me. I can hear the clinking of forks on the tea plates, and I feel myself blush. My fingers trace the fabric of my dress.

"Wally is a model, and she's married to an artist. She poses for him in the nude. She's brave," Adéle offers. They continue to look at me in silence.

"To be honest, we're not married," I admit, gazing out the window. In the evening darkness, I can spot our house across the street, with the light from our apartment glowing. But I can't see Egon. He must be in the studio, painting.

"Are you living together without being married?" Edith asks.

"Yes," I turn my attention to her. "He hasn't proposed to me yet." I keep my fingers in my lap, not wanting the women to scrutinize them.

"That's precisely the issue," one of the women interjects. "We're expected to wait for a man to propose to us. Without men, we're considered nothing. We're denied the right to vote, a bank account, and a say in anything beyond the color of our dresses."

"We need to assert ourselves more with men," another woman joins in.

"We certainly need to be more assertive with men," Edith concurs, smiling and glancing at me. The discussion among the women resumes as they debate the protest measures they're planning to undertake.

"Please come and visit us. Egon would be pleased," I say to Edith and Adéle later as we part ways, wondering if I made a mistake by inviting them.

"We promise to come," Edith responds, shaking my hand before bidding farewell. I quickly cross the street, gazing up at the brightly lit window of our house as though it were a guiding lantern. Why hasn't he proposed to me yet?

 ❦

A day later, as the rain patters outside, I'm sitting on the chair next to the window reading a book, while the raindrops gently tap against the window. Occasionally, I glance up at the city's gray rooftops and the few people hustling down the avenue. A smile creeps across my face when I spot a couple strolling beneath a large black men's umbrella, drawing closer to our house. Egon owns such an umbrella.

I place the book on the small cabinet by the window and stand up, pressing my face against the glass. Is it Egon? Who is he with? The man's pants are brown, like Egon's, but who is the woman with him?

My breath fogs the glass, and I wipe it with my hands, but I can't be certain. For a moment, I think I might be mistaken, just imagining things. But then they approach the entrance of our building disappear from view. Is it Egon?

I rise from the chair and walk to the wooden door, pressing my ear against it. I hear footsteps in the stairwell, and I hurry back to my spot by the window, adjusting my dress and trying to steady my breathing. Is she the woman I suspect?

A key enters the keyhole, and I take a deep breath.

"Wally, you won't believe who I ran into near the wine shop," Egon enters, dripping wet from the rain. He hangs his umbrella by the door, and following him, Edith Harms comes in, shaking off the rain from her coat.

"Good afternoon, Wally," she greets me with a smile. "Egon is a true gentleman, holding his umbrella for me so I wouldn't get wet," she turns her back to Egon, and he helps her remove her wet coat. She holds a bottle of wine in her hand.

"I invited her up to see the studio and my new paintings," Egon hangs her coat next to his. "I hope it's all right that I bring a guest without notice." He takes the bottle of wine from her hand.

"It's perfectly fine. I'll make you some tea," I smile at them and walk to the kitchen, though I want to scream. I place the kettle on the metal stove, my hands trembling. What should I do? Why did he bring her? While they talk quietly to each other, I strain to hear their conversation. Why is she here? I will not give him up. I am the woman he loves.

I walk to the studio with a tray of tea cups. They are both standing by the window, looking outside. I place the tray on the cabinet and hand them the tea cups. "There you go," I hug Egon, stroking the back of his neck and his hair, "What do you think of my man's studio?" I ask Edith with a smile, even though I want to ask her to leave our home.

"Your man is incredibly talented. Thank you for the tea," Edith holds the cup, trying to warm her hands, and blows gently on the hot liquid. "And where do you stand when you draw?" she asks Egon.

"Usually right here," he walks away from me, goes to the corner of the room, holds the easel, and places it in front of the chair against the wall.

"Is this where the model sits?" Edith puts her teacup next to the one Egon placed on the cabinet and approaches the chair. "May I?" she asks me.

"Yes, of course," I smile at her politely. Why won't she leave already? I watch her as she sits on the chair before Egon.

"Just like that, raise your right hand a bit," Egon instructs her, and it seems to me that in an instant, he bends down, opens the wooden paint box, and begins to paint her; they both completely ignore my presence.

"Let me show you," I approach her and stand in front of the chair. She smiles at me and gets up. "You sit down and lean back," I instruct her, "and let down your hair," I take out the hairpins that keep my hair neat and throw them on the floor, "and lean your head against the wall," I lean back, pushing forward my chest. "And if you have the courage," I look at her and smile, "you strip."

Later, after she leaves and night falls, I get ready in the bathroom. I wash myself in the large stainless steel bowl, vigorously rub my skin with the sponge until it turns red and pour on my body warm water that I heated on the stove. I will not give up on him.

Careful not to tear them, I wear a garter belt and garter stockings with nothing underneath, just like some of the girls do at Bertha's hostel. I heat a cork over the candle, burn its tip, and gently apply the ash over my eyes as black eyeshadow, following Christina's instructions. Carefully, I apply Vaseline over my eyeshadow to give it a shine, apply a little pink lipstick, and I'm ready. I blow out the candle and head to the bedroom.

But when I get under the covers next to him, he is already asleep.

The knock on the door two days later surprises me.

I find myself in the kitchen during the afternoon, peeling apples to make apple strudel and placing them in the heavy metal pot on the stove. The air carries the pleasant scent of cinnamon, which I purchased earlier at the market. As the knock sounds, I turn around quickly, inadvertently cutting my finger with the knife and letting out a small shout.

I look at my bleeding finger and the small dark red spot that continues to spread. Another knock echoes from the door, prompting me to wrap a kitchen towel around my injury before making my way to the door.

"Good afternoon Ms. Wally," Adéle stands at the door.

"Good afternoon," I smile at her. Why did she come?

"Sorry to come like this without an invitation," she gasps, likely due to the climb up the stairs. "Is Edith here? I'm looking for her."

"No, she's not here. Please come in," I open the door. Why is she looking for her here?

"Mom and Dad came unannounced to visit, and I don't know where she is," she walks in, looking around as if not believing me.

"Why did you think she would be here?" I ask her after a moment. Egon left in the morning. He said he had a meeting with someone interested in his paintings.

"Because she told me she visited you a couple of days ago," Adéle says after a moment, continuing to look around the apartment. Is she telling me the truth? I am ashamed of our simple apartment compared to their modern and luxurious one.

"Sorry, she's not here. I haven't seen her since," I continue to wrap my injured finger in a towel. It hurts.

"Sorry, I disturbed you," she looks at the towel in my hand for the first time. "I apologize; I'll keep looking for her. Mom and Dad are very strict when they come to visit," she turns towards the door and bids me farewell.

After she leaves, I lean against the door, remove the towel, put my injured finger in my mouth, and taste the blood. It has a metallic tang, reminiscent of rust. Are Egon and Edith together?

I approach the window with my finger in my mouth, look down at the street, and search for them among the passersby, just as I saw them two days ago. But I can't find them among all the people walking down the avenue. I need to go back to the kitchen, but I can't. My face stays glued to the window, and I look at every man and woman who walks down the street.

Only when it gets dark do I notice Edith walking on the other side of the street. She is momentarily illuminated by the street lantern as she approaches their house. I break away from the window, go to the pot, and look at the peeled apples that have turned to pulp. I didn't have time to make the dough.

The sound of the key makes me turn towards the door. Where has he been until now?

"What a wonderful smell," Egon closes the door after him, puts his jacket on the chair, and walks into the kitchen, coming to hug me. "I'm so hungry," he kisses me passionately. Am I just suspicious? I stop kissing him and smell his neck, noticing the scent of perfume.

"Where were you?" I ask him directly, unable to hold myself.

"I told you in the morning I would meet someone interested in purchasing one of my paintings," he continues hugging me.

"Is it her?" I push him away from me.

"Who do you mean?"

"You know exactly who I mean."

"No, I don't know," he moves away from me and gets out of the kitchen. "I'm trying to make a living for us, and you're being suspicions, and now I'm hungry." He returns to the kitchen and sits before the dining table. The legs of the wooden chair creaking on the parquet floor sound like the squealing of a rat. Could it be that I suspect him for no reason?

"She was here," I say quietly.

"Who?" He quickly looks up, examining me with his dark eyes, his wild quaff looking like a fighting rooster's comb.

"Her sister, Adéle, she was looking for her," I turn my back to him, looking at the iron pot and the applesauce inside.

"Yeah, so I met her for coffee," he raises his voice, "what's wrong with that?"

"You should have told me. You shouldn't have lied." I speak to the black iron pot, feeling tears welling up in my eyes.

"What's wrong with me meeting her?" he says angrily, "She's from a bourgeois family, they have money, and she can buy from my paintings. Don't you want us to have money?"

"Not through the bedroom," I turn to him and shout. I no longer care if he sees my tears.

"Walburga, you're confused. This house isn't Bertha's hostel where you came from. She's from a respectable family, and not every cup of coffee ends in the bedroom," he shouts back at me.

"Bon appétit," I lift the metal pot with the applesauce from the oven and forcefully place it on the table before him. The pot hits the table with a thud, and some pulp splashes out. "Enjoy the apple strudel I made today, especially for you. I didn't have time to make the dough because I was worried," I throw a spoon into the pot, walk to the bathroom, wash my face, and start crying.

"Don't cry," he whispers to me, and I feel his hand caressing me a few minutes later. "So what if I met her, it's just to sell the paintings. There's nothing more to it than that," he hugs me, and I'm trying to relax. "You're just imagining that I have other intentions," he kisses me gently on my neck.

At night, when I hear his peaceful breathing, I quietly get out of bed and go to the kitchen and light a candle. Barefoot, I walk into his studio while holding the candle and start checking his stacks of drawings. I go through them one by one, bring the candle flame closer, and search for Edith's face in them, but I can't find her. Finally, I blow out the candle and return to bed, lying beside him. Maybe I'm wrong after all, and it's my imagination.

"Have a nice day. I'll be back later. I love you," Egon says to me a week after our fight and hugs me.

"Good luck with the paintings, whoever you meet," I answer him and hug him back, "will you paint me when you come back?"

"I will be glad to. You are my only muse," he pulls me for a passionate kiss, his tongue trying to penetrate my lips, but I keep them closed.

"Goodbye, my red cherry," he walks out the door. Since the fight, he has been trying to treat me more lovingly. He also didn't mention Bertha's hostel again, though he didn't apologize.

I look out of the window at the black clouds arriving from the west and then turn to the kitchen, noticing he forgot his jacket lying on the chair.

I hold the jacket and open the door, "Egon, you forgot your jacket," I call after him. But he's already out on the street and doesn't hear me. I hope he doesn't get cold.

I take the jacket to the bedroom and feel something in the inner pocket. Even though I'm not allowed, I tuck my fingers in and pull out a letter, holding it in my hand.

'Arthur Roessler,' is written on the envelope, the gentleman from Munich who complimented me on the paintings. I'm breathing quietly, it's not a letter from Edith, but even so, I have a bad feeling. Maybe with the way he called me Cherry this morning after going so long without using that name, perhaps I'm just imagining. But the letter is already open. Why does Egon keep it in his jacket pocket?

I open the envelope with trembling fingers, unfold the paper, and begin reading the words.

Line after line, my eyes skim over the text until they come across one sentence, and I tear up, **'Regarding your decision about the right woman for marriage, I agree with you, Ms. Edith Harms is more suitable for you than Wally.'**

I sit on the chair and wipe my eyes, noticing one tear that falls on the paper and wets some written words, turning them into an indistinct ink stain. I didn't imagine it.

Go away, get out of this house. The room suffocates me, and I can't bear to be in it anymore. I grab my coat and leave the house, slamming the door behind me without bothering to lock it. The tear-stained letter remains discarded on the floor.

What does it matter if he finds out that I know or not? I can't change a thing. I never could

I stop only by the river to catch my breath, standing on the bridge. I hold the railing and gaze at the green water. Two soldiers stationed on the bridge look at me curiously. Since the war started, they've been posted to guard the bridges, not allowing people to pass without permission.

What if I were to fall into the water? Would he care about me? He's going to choose someone else. I can't imagine it.

I pick up a stone, lean against the railing, gently release it from my hand, and follow its descent until it hits the water with a pleasant thump, as if returning to its rightful place. My eyes fill with tears again. It's so hard for me to breathe.

"Miss, can I help you?" one of the soldiers approaches me. I look at him through my tears. He is much older than me and is wearing a simple green uniform. "Miss, are you alright?" he asks me again, looking at me with his blue eyes. His brown beard moves slightly in the wind on the bridge. He must be too old to be sent to the front.

"Everything is fine," I answer him and turn around, running back to the bank. Even though I would like him to hug me right now, I need someone to hold me.

While running, I pass a couple holding hands as they approach the bridge. They must be on their way to the Prater, the amusement park. Maybe they will also ride the giant wheel to see the city lights, and he will whisper tempting words about war and love in her ear. But I don't warn the woman not to trust the man holding her hand. This is their story, not mine.

In the evening, I sit down in a café. I'm tired and thirsty, but I don't want to go home and see him. I also don't want to go to Bertha's hostel and cry.

Only men are sitting around me at this hour, and the place is stuffy with suffocating pipe and cigar smoke. The women who were here in the morning hours have already gone home, leaving the hall for conversations about the war and the fate of the empire.

The waiter stands at a distance from me, waiting for the man accompanying me to arrive, and the other gentlemen around look at me suspiciously.

"Waiter, a jug of red wine, please," I gesture to him after some time has passed, and he didn't approach me. I'm tired of being a polite woman.

"Maybe the lady would like to sit outside? You would be more comfortable," the waiter suggests.

"No, I'm comfortable here," I answer him, looking at the men around in suits and top hats. Everyone falls silent and watches as the waiter brings me a jug of wine, and I pour myself a glass and sip it to the brim.

"You can continue your conversation. I won't interrupt," I say to a gentleman with gray hair and a well-groomed beard who has a thick cigar in his mouth.

"These are not suitable conversations for a young lady like you," he answers me politely while the big cigar is held in his mouth like a carrot in a horse's mouth.

"Why?" I pour myself another glass of wine and sip it, ignoring my burning throat. "Is it because women are not allowed to decide who goes to war and who dies? Is it only men who have that privilege? I've seen people looking at the blacklists posted outside the Ministry of Defense. It seems to me that in the end, only the women are left to cry," I continue to drink more wine, unable to stop. "You sit here comfortably in your leather seats and organize the empire, while we women are left to cry," I empty the wine glass.

"Miss, you are slandering the empire," the man takes the cigar out of his mouth and speaks angrily while holding it in his hand. "It's against the law," and all the gentlemen around him nod in agreement.

"It's because you create the laws," I show him my bare fingers without a ring. "Do you all see?" I display my bare hands to the gentlemen around. "You also create these laws," but I don't think they understand what I'm talking about.

"Miss, you're drunk," says a man about forty years old, smoking a pipe, and dressed in a black suit.

"No, I'm not drunk. I'm a woman," I answer him and pour myself more wine. "I'm not even allowed to vote in elections or save money in a bank on my own without a man to support me."

"Women should stay at home, cook, and raise children, and you are not in the right place. This is a men's café," the man with the cigar answers me, putting it back in his mouth.

"We women are definitely not in the right place," I try to continue arguing with him, but the smoke suddenly suffocates me. It feels like the café is closing in on me with all those men who look alike. "For all of you men, it's much more convenient that we stay in boarding houses where you come to visit in the evenings. I can recommend Bertha's hostel to you; you'll receive excellent service there," I say without thinking and see his face turn red. "Maybe you know me from there," I add and get up, leaving a coin on the table, and walk slowly to the door, being careful not to stumble.

The cool air refreshes me, and I stroll through the cobblestone streets back to the house, stopping now and then to lean against the wall of one of the houses and rest.

I slowly take out the house key and struggle with the keyhole, but then I realize the house is open, so I enter. I don't remember if I locked it when I left in the morning. In the moonlight shining through the window, I see that the letter is still on the floor, but Egon is nowhere to be found.

I carefully return the letter to the envelope and place it back in his jacket pocket, then get into bed and go to sleep without waiting for him.

The late morning sun wakes me up, and I sit up in bed, Egon not by my side. My head hurts so much.

I get out of bed and see that the jacket and the letter are gone. I also notice that he left me a note, asking to meet me at Café Eichberger at noon.

Chapter Thirteen

Café Eichberger

1⁹¹⁵

I enter the café and scan the room, searching for him. The waiter at the counter briefly looks my way, his eyes noting my red hair, before returning to his task. Around one of the tables, three women in vibrant morning dresses lean close, engaged in conversation while delicately piercing Sacher Torte cakes with their forks. Nearby, two men in suits are engrossed in reading the newspaper. My attention is drawn to the headline, reporting the failure of the attack in the west against the French and the English. Finally, I spot him. Egon sits at a corner table, his backdrop a painting of a serene lake and mountains hanging on the brown wall. In front of him, there's only a cup of tea, and he leans over a sheet of paper, either writing a letter or sketching something. He hasn't noticed me yet.

I stand still for a moment, wondering what he has to say to me, even though I think I already know. I have a feeling he may have confided in his friends, especially Mr. Arthur Roessler from Munich, who once said that every artist needs a muse like me.

The women at the Sacher Torte table pause their conversation and give me a curious look, as if wondering if I'm part of their group. I walk over to Egon's table, determined to stay strong, no matter what he tells me.

"Good morning, my cherry," he rises from his chair as soon as he notices me and moves to kiss my neck. However, I take a step back, stopping him. He returns to his chair and says, "Come, have a seat." He gestures for me to sit next to him. "Shall I order you some tea and cake?"

"No, thank you," I respond as I sit down across from him. I didn't come here for cake, even though I'm hungry and my head still aches. I won't break down, and I won't cry in front of him.

"Wally, we need to talk. I have something to say, and I'm not sure how to say it," he looks down at the paper in front of him, filled with sketches of the people at the café.

"I don't think eloquence has ever been a problem for you."

"I wrote you a letter. I'd appreciate it if you read it after I leave." He places an envelope on the table between us.

"I don't understand," I look at the envelope but don't touch it. "For years, you whispered words in my ear that made me blush. Now, you can't speak to me?" I reach for the teacup, tilt it over the letter, and pour the yellowish tea onto it. The envelope turns transparent, and the paper inside becomes a mass of shapeless black ink. "Waiter," I raise my hand, signaling to the man in a uniform near the entrance counter, "I've spilled some tea." The waiter hurries over with a clean towel and does his best to absorb the liquid. "You can throw the letter out," I tell him. "It's ruined." All this time, Egon remains silent, as if afraid to draw the attention of the people around us.

"I'm listening," I say at Egon after the waiter leaves. I must stay calm, even through tears threaten to roll down my cheeks.

"Wally, I'm going to marry Edith Harms," he runs his fingers through his hair, adjusting his quaff, and places both hands on the table. Although I anticipated these words, they hit me like a blow to the stomach by a horse, just like when I was a child, before we came to Vienna. The pain in my ribs is palpable, and breathing becomes difficult. I want to collapse on the café floor and clutch my stomach.

"Is there anything I can do that will change your mind?" I manage to ask. My eyes well up even though I promised myself I wouldn't cry. But he shakes his head.

"I've been with you for four years," I continue, breathing heavily. "I know everything about you; how you break down, how you get angry, how you strive for success," I wipe my cheeks. "For four years I've been undressing in front of you, letting you paint me however you wished, I let you display my nude paintings to strangers," I can't stop the words from pouring out. "I followed you and your artistic rebellion everywhere – to Krumlov, to Neulengbach. I stood by you when you did things that shouldn't have been done. I didn't abandon you when you sat in prison, begging me not to leave when no one else was there for you. I saw you on that wooden bench after they sheared your hair. I defended you during your trial. And now you're telling me that the rebellion is over, and you don't want me anymore? What must I do to make you want me?" I beg him even though I shouldn't. I struggle to breathe.

"We can't turn back time. I'm sorry," he says, still looking down. He takes out a sheet of paper from his leather bag, places it on the table, and starts sketching something vague.

"Is that all? Is it too late? Have you already decided?" I wipe my cheeks again, my thirst unquenched.

"Yes," he nods, continuing to sketch a woman from the café on the paper.

"So she already knows?" I ask, my stomach churning.

"Yes," he nods.

"Does she have an engagement ring?" I barely say the words. I want to puke.

"Yes," he nods.

"So, I'm the last to know that the sword hangs over my neck? The woman loyal to you is the last to receive the fatal blow?"

"I warned you when we last returned to Vienna that the world had changed, and we had to change with it," he says softly, still not looking up.

"What has changed? Am I too bold for you now, or do I not meet your expectations in terms of class and money?" I can't stop myself.

"You know how it goes."

"Yes, the world you men have created. You smell money and status and change the rules to suit your convenience," I grab the pencil from his hand. "Perhaps you should start reading newspapers about your macho war and smoke cigars. That scent would befit you." I continue speaking while drawing rough lines on the paper, marring his delicate sketch with black lead stripes.

"What?" he raises his dark eyes and looks at me for the first time since he said those hurtful words.

"Never mind," I break the pencil and toss it onto the table.

"Maybe you should also look for a wealthy man, not someone poor as me,"

"I chose you so we could be together and achieve greatness together. But I will likely never have the status you desire. You're right; I should look for wealth elsewhere. Goodbye, Egon." I stand and leave the chair. There's nothing left for me here. I need to leave this café.

"Wally, please don't go," he rises and takes hold of my hand. "There's something else I need to share with you," he gazes deeply into my eyes. "I wrote it in the letter you tore apart," he smiles warmly. "Please, have a seat."

"What?" I sit down and look around. Several other women dressed in black are seated at a nearby table, engaged in hushed conversations. The men who were reading newspapers earlier have left, and a woman in a floral hat sits in their stead.

"I love you. I want you to stay a part of my life," he tells me, still holding and caressing my hand.

"I don't understand," I watch his fingers stroking my palm. Do I stand a chance? Does he want me after all? He has just told me that he proposed to Edith. Maybe I misunderstood?

"Edith doesn't like to expose herself to the sun, so in the summer, she doesn't leave Vienna for a vacation by the lakes," he takes the broken pencil and gently draws with it on my palm.

"So? You're marrying her, aren't you?" I move my hand away, placing it in my lap, not wanting him to touch me.

"I want you to be my muse and lover. I want us to meet every summer for a vacation, just you and me, and during that time, I will be only yours."

"How will that work?" I get up from the chair and speak to him while standing. "How will the arrangement work between us?" I ask him. "You will support me with her money, and once a year, I will see you for two weeks without her knowing? Is that how it will work?" Again, my stomach churns like stormy sea waves crashing over me, one after another.

"You know that's how the world works; we didn't invent it, and we certainly won't change it," he stands up and tries to hold my hand again.

"No," I firmly reply, "don't touch me," I step back. "You know, Egon," I look into his eyes, "you will get what you want—status, money, and the right to draw others, but your punishment will be that in your thoughts, you will always think of me," I tell him and turn around, leaving the café, feeling his gaze and the gazes of all the people in the café fixed on me, stabbing at my back.

❦

I wipe my tears only when I arrive at our apartment. It doesn't matter that I managed to answer him. It doesn't matter that I got up and left, preserving my dignity. I failed. I will forever be that poor sixteen-year-old girl thrown out of her home. I can never do better than a small room in Ms. Bertha's hostel.

I throw my clothes on the bed, stuffing them haphazardly into my suitcase. I want to hurry in case he returns home before I leave.

I place the suitcase by the door and do a final sweep of the house, taking the money hidden in a jar in the kitchen. I have worked hard for it, and Miss Edith will provide him with money from her class. My eyes scan the rooms to ensure I haven't forgotten anything. I avoid his studio. I don't want to look at my paintings anymore. It's not me who is painted there. It's a different red-haired girl who once believed she could overcome and move forward.

I hang the door key on the hook next to the entrance, pick up my suitcase, and close the door behind me for the last time. I only have one place left to go. That's where I belong.

"Young Walburga, what brings you here?" Ms. Bertha emerges from behind her counter, and it seems like she wants to hug me, but she stops herself at the last moment.

"I've come for good," I tell her and place my suitcase on the hostel floor. I hope she accepts me; I have no other place to be.

"What do you mean, for good?" She walks back behind the counter, retrieves her cigarette case, and lights a cigarette, coughing dryly.

"Ms. Bertha, are you all right?" I ask her, looking at the cigarette in her mouth emitting bluish smoke in the stuffy room.

"I'm perfectly fine. No cough will kill Bertha," she removes the cigarette from her mouth. "What do you mean, for good?"

"You were right," I say to her quietly. "This is the right place for me. I'll never do better than this. I'll never be able to climb the ladder. He chose to marry someone else."

"Walburga, I'm not going to pity you. He's like all men." She exhales cigarette smoke.

"I don't want your pity. I came to be here," I wipe away my tears.

"So, I take it you finally want to be one of Bertha's girls?" She smiles at me and takes another puff of the cigarette.

"Yes," I take a coin from my purse and place it on the counter. "This is for the next week's rent. I'm no different from any of your other girls, and I'm already old enough. The floral sofa is the right place for me. I already know the right moves to seduce men." I glance sideways at the hall, where only one unfamiliar girl sits on the sofa, smoking a cigarette, preoccupied with her own business.

"Young Walburga," Ms. Bertha puts down her cigarette and coughs again before turning her back on me and entering her back room. The coin remains on the counter. Would she throw me out? "Listen to Ms. Bertha, and I'll tell you what we'll do," I hear her from her room, but after a moment, she comes out and stands in front of me. "Take this money and leave. I don't want to see you here anymore," she places a stack of bills in my hand.

"Ms. Bertha, I don't understand," I hold the bills.

"Walburga, you are wrong. You are special. You always saw the opportunity to climb the ladder. And you tried, unlike my other girls," she points her eyes at the girl sitting on the floral sofa. "You just didn't understand that you climb the ladder to gain control over your life, not for someone else to control you. You've already reached the top. You just have to look at it differently." She crushes the cigarette in the ashtray. "Now take this money and never come back."

"Ms. Bertha, I won't be able to repay you," I feel tears welling up again.

"Listen to Ms. Bertha. You have a ladder to climb. Now, get out of here. And stop crying already."

"Thank you, Ms. Bertha," I go behind the counter and hug her, feeling her warm body.

"Get out of here. I don't want to see you anymore," she gives me a small hug back, immediately breaks away, and turns her back on me.

"I promise I'll come back and give you your money back," I tell her, but she doesn't answer me. I watch as she walks through the hall to the bottom of the stairs and calls out, "Come on, girls, get organized and come down. Customers will be arriving soon."

I wipe my eyes, take one last look at the floral sofa, grab my suitcase, and walk out into the street, gently closing the heavy door behind me.

On the main boulevard, on the wall of the Ministry of Defense, next to the never-ending white pages with the blacklists, I see a poster that reads, "Be a nurse and help save lives." I approach the poster and begin reading the small letters.

Chapter Fourteen

Death and the Maiden

Six months later, spring 1916, the war is still raging

    I step off the tram onto the main boulevard and begin walking toward the old city. It's been six months since I last visited. I gaze at the familiar streets, feeling like nothing has changed yet also sensing that a lifetime has passed since that day.

The stores still have their products, but the shop windows display a reduced selection. There's less traffic on the streets, and although the trams continue as usual, the horses pulling carts have almost disappeared, likely sent to the front. I walk down the main street. The cafés are still full of old gentlemen sitting and reading the morning papers, but the young men have almost disappeared. Several women are standing outside the butcher shop, most wearing black dresses. I look ahead to the rest of the street. So many women wear black. I pass a young woman in a black dress and smile at her encouragingly, but she ignores my smile and continues walking forward as if staring into the air, looking for something that doesn't exist.

An older man smoking a pipe scrutinizes me critically, as though he wants to say something but ultimately remains silent as I walk by. I hold my head high, ignoring him, even though I still feel somewhat out of place in my green uniform and army beret.

On the street near Bertha's hostel, I stop for a moment next to a girl in a ragged dress who is stroking a dirty cat, holding it in her lap and looking at me with her big blue eyes.

"Are you a soldier?" she asks me.

"Yes," I reply, "I am a military nurse."

"One day, I will be a military nurse too," she tells me, hugging the stray cat. I smile at her and head to the hostel, enter, and gently close the heavy wooden door. I came to repay my debt.

"Wally?" someone calls my name, and I see Christina standing behind the counter.

"Christina?" I ask her and look around. The entrance looks cleaner and is lit by electric lamps instead of the old gas lamps. The upholstery of the floral sofa is also new, and the smell of cigarettes is gone.

"Wally? Is that you?" She comes out from behind the counter and approaches me, hugging me tightly. "How much you've grown," she moves away from me and examines my uniform. "What is this uniform? It fits you so well. You look so mature and serious. I'm glad you came to visit."

"I've just completed nursing school, and I have a few days off before I board the train to report to a hospital near the front," I say. "You look more mature, too. Where's Ms. Bertha?" I look at the counter. The ashtray is missing too.

"Haven't you heard?" she returns to stand behind the counter.

"Heard what?" What happened to Ms. Bertha?

"Oh, Wally," she seems to be searching for the right words. "She was sick and wouldn't listen to the doctors' advice. She passed away during the winter, from tuberculosis," Christina says slowly. Despite the bright lights, the room suddenly seems darker.. "Many people contracted tuberculosis during that harsh winter," she continues, "Wally, are you alright?"

"Yes, I'm fine," I approach the counter and place my hand on it. "I'm fine," I repeat. Many people have died since this damn war started. I shouldn't be so emotional about it. I'm a nurse.

"I'm so sorry, it was a difficult time," she again approaches and hugs me. I try to hold back my tears. What will I do without all her annoying sayings?

"Have you taken her place?" I finally ask.

"Yes, she left me the hostel when she was quite sick," Christina says slowly. "She wanted me to change the name, but I want to keep it 'Bertha's Hostel.'"

"I came to return the money she lent me," I pull out an envelope from my uniform pocket and hand it to her.

"I know," Christina looks at me. "She knew you wouldn't listen to her and come back. She told me not to accept the money from you," she smiles and hands me back the envelope with the money. "So I won't take it. She also left something for you," Christina heads to the back room and then places a sealed envelope on the counter.

"What is it?" I feel the envelope. There's something solid inside.

"I don't know. She told me to give it to you if you ever came back," Christina shrugs.

I quickly tear the envelope. My Dad's signet ring falls on the counter, glinting in the yellowish light. Next to it lies a small note.

I slip the ring onto my finger, feel its weight, and wipe my tears. Then I read the note, which contains only one line:

'Young Miss Walburga, you must leave the past behind to move forward into the future. But having a small memento is always good.'

"What is it?" Christina asks me.

"It's something from her, a keepsake from the past," I reply and smile through my tears. I need to sit down and collect myself.

"By the way," Christina adds, "there was a man who came looking for you several times. He said it was important, that if I saw you, to tell you to come see him in his studio. I think he's the painter you were with. I didn't allow him in to see the girls."

"What did he look like? Was he young or old?" I ask, looking up at her. Was it Mr. Klimt? Egon? What could he possibly want from me?

"He's a little older than you, and he had a black quaff and a troubled look in his eyes. Do you know him?"

"Yes," reply. "I do," although I'm no longer certain he'll recognize me.

I stand in the street in front of the address Christina gave me, debating whether to knock on the door or give up. He is a married man; he made his choices, and I made mine too.

I knock on the door and wait. I hear the latch click, and he opens it—my heart races.

He stands at the door and watches me. He hasn't changed. The same white button-down shirt, brown pants with shiny leather shoes, the same black hair, and dark brown eyes that look at me like they want to devour my body. Exactly the same look he gave me the day we first met.

"My cherry..." he starts to say but stops, steps back, opens the door for me, and says, "Please come in."

I still stand at the door for a moment before I walk in and look around. His studio is larger than the rooms he used when we were together. But other than that, everything looks the same. The easel stands in the center, the wooden box containing the paints and brushes, and the chair by the wall on which I sat so many times. Only the paintings leaning against the walls are not mine. I don't belong here anymore. This studio belongs to other women.

"You were looking for me," I tell him. It seems like he's searching for something to do with his hands.

"You disappeared. I searched for you all over the city," he approaches and hugs me, "I even looked for you in that hostel where you once lived. I've been there several times. But the elderly landlady drove me away. Even after a younger woman took her place, she didn't tell me where you were." He clings to me forcefully, his arms wrap around my body, and I feel like he's hanging on me, but I don't hug him back.

"You're married," I say. His scent suddenly seems strange to me.

"So what," he whispers to me, "You used to be a rebel just like me. You didn't care what other people thought of us. That's what made us so special," he brings his lips to mine and tries to kiss me, but I turn my face away.

"No," I forcefully push him away with my hands. I gasp. I shouldn't have come here.

"You've changed," he remains close to me, "the uniform you wear is like a wall between us. Thick and rough fabric I can't caress and can't penetrate your soul."

"No, what you did is the wall between us, not the uniform I'm wearing."

"Why are you even in uniform?" he asks as if its presence bothers him.

"I'm in the army now, I'm a nurse. I graduated from nursing school."

"I thought we were rebels, that we were against the empire, the emperor, this war," he tries to approach me again, "Why did you suddenly become one of them?"

"Goodbye, Egon," I turn and head for the door. Suddenly, he seems like a stranger to me.

"Wally, please don't go," he runs and grabs my hand, "please," he begs.

"You don't need me here. You have the life you chose for yourself," I answer him and pull my hand away.

"Please, I want to show you something. Please, just a few minutes. Don't go,"

"What?" I stay standing near the door. The feel of the uniform on my body gives me confidence.

"After you left, I drew this," he approaches the paintings placed by the wall and starts removing them one by one, "I had to. I couldn't stop," he reaches the last one, which is covered by a sheet, "you were in my thoughts the whole time. I couldn't stop thinking about you." He removes the sheet, revealing a painting of a young woman embracing a dark green, gray figure. Both are kneeling and supporting each other.

"What is this painting?" I ask him, feeling a wave of coldness.

"Death and the Maiden," he looks at me with his dark eyes, "You're the maiden, I am Death," he once again tries to move closer to me, but I step back. "I drew you from memory," he speaks without stopping, "at night, every time I closed my eyes, I saw your face. You were right. Without you, I died. You're my woman. You've always been my woman."

"No, I'm not yours anymore," I answer him. I hate myself in this painting.

"Please, you must return to being my lover and muse. My wife will understand. She can never be you. I want to return to what was between us. I need you," he sits on the wooden chair in the room, looking up at me.

"But I don't need you anymore," I look at him. I used to go over to him and give him a hug—no more.

"You are nothing without me. You will never be who you want to be. No one will remember you. Only my paintings will be remembered," he gets up from the chair and stands before me.

"It doesn't matter to me who will remember me; even if he's a simple man, and not someone who paints me with Death," I yell at him.

"No one will draw you anymore. If you leave me, we'll both die. I'm already dead now. It'll take you a while to understand, but eventually, you'll see that I'm right. We're both meant for each other," he says in a trembling voice and arranges his quaff with his fingers. "Don't go. You mustn't leave us."

"I'm not afraid of dying. And I wasn't meant for you. I was meant to live for myself." I answer him in a quiet voice, regulating my breathing, and placing my hand on the door handle, "I'm afraid of dying without having lived for myself, and now I'm going to go live for myself. Goodbye, Egon," I open the door and go out onto the street, feeling the breeze on my face, and I smile.

Chapter Fifteen

Epilogue, The Last Portrait of Wally

A year and a half later, Croatia, near the Adriatic Sea, the Austro-Hungarian Empire's south border, December 24, 1917

The day death met the maiden.

Written by Alfred, a coachman in the Austro-Hungarian army.

"Walk," I click my tongue, releasing the reins to the two brown horses pulling the cart down the winding street inside the small town. My other hand holds tightly to my green military woolen coat, closing it to protect myself against the cold and snow that's slowly falling on the ground, covering the road with a white blanket.

Occasionally, I catch a glimpse of the snow-capped mountains encircling the distant valley, but most of the time, they remain concealed by gray clouds. "Go," I coax the horses once more, attempting to ignore my numb fingers. My gloves are torn, and I couldn't afford to replace them. In recent months, all the good supplies have been dispatched to the soldiers fighting at the front, while we, the soldiers stationed in the rear, are compelled to make do with worn-out clothing. The coat I wore is also tattered.

"All right," I guide the horses at the fork in the road; even though they don't heed my words, they respond to the tug of the reins as they plod slowly, pulling the wagon along the muddy, snow-covered road. It took me a while to find someone in town who could show me the correct way.

A few minutes ago, I stood in the town square, beneath the city hall clock, which indicated noon. It seemed as though the town had been emptied of its inhabitants. Maybe they rushed home before darkness fell, or perhaps it was due to the approaching holiday tonight. There might also be a shortage of men left behind, as so many of them had been drafted into the war that had been raging for three years now.

Finally, I spotted a woman hurrying out of the post office. She paused briefly, paying no mind to the snowflakes adorning her hair with white specks, and provided me with directions before hurrying away, vanishing into one of the narrow streets leading away from the square.

"We've arrived," I murmur to the horses as we pass through the gate in a white wall at the end of one of the streets, encircling a large building, and proceed under the sign that read "Military Hospital of the Austro-Hungarian Empire." Next to the gate, there is a sizable wooden sign that read 'Caution, Epidemic,' but I pay it no mind. I need to get supplies.

"Whoa," I bring the cart to a halt near the entrance, engage the brake to prevent it from moving, and hasten to retrieve old woolen blankets from the cart to cover the horses. I must keep them warm after their strenuous journey. In a moment, I will release them from their harnesses and take them to the horse stable situated on the side of the yard. We will spend the night here.

"We've been waiting for you," a nurse wrapped in a military wool coat emerges from the main building and strides toward me. As she walks briskly, I notice her white uniform peeking out from beneath the hem of her trench coat with each step, her boots emitting a creaking sound on the frozen ground.

"I couldn't find the place," I say, rubbing my frozen hands and hastily removing the tarp covering the crates behind the cart, revealing them carefully arranged.

"Haven't you been here before?" she asks me.

"No," I respond, looking around. In the corner of the hospital courtyard, several tarpaulin-covered carts for transporting the wounded are parked, those arriving from the Russian front, and beside them stands a new gasoline green lorry, emblazoned with the Empire's emblem on the driver's door. These new trucks had only recently been introduced to the army.

"Place the boxes in the main hall; follow me," the nurse instructs, then turns and ascends the hospital entrance steps. I grasp the cold metal handles of a box and hurry to follow her. Afterward, I will set the box down and seek out the person responsible for the horse stable to attend to the horses.

The beds of the wounded are arranged in neat rows in the grand hall, all covered with white sheets. I pause for a moment, allowing my eyes to adjust to the dim light emanating from the oil lanterns that illuminate the room. However, the nurse who had greeted me earlier does not stop and continues walking through the passage between the wounded beds. I hurry to catch up with her at the end of the hall.

"Place the boxes here," she instructs, pointing to a corner next to the fir tree, which is awaiting the upcoming holiday tonight. "Once you're done, head to the kitchen. They'll provide you with a meal. You can also spend the night over there by the stove; it's warm and cozy," she smiles at me.

"Thank you," I smile back, but she has already turned away, returned to her rounds in the hall, removed her coat, and approached one of the wounded.

I set down the wooden box and stand, gazing at the fir tree. I can still detect its pungent scent, as if it had been freshly brought from the forest in the past few days. Despite the holiday tonight, only a few decorations have been placed on it, glistening faintly in the lantern light. Coughs and sighs emanate from all directions, prompting me to cross the hall between the wounded individuals who are groaning in pain and make my way in the cold toward the cart filled with crates of medical supplies. I will search for the stable manager and expedite the unloading of the crates. Afterward, I can have dinner and rest.

"Nurse," I hear someone sigh after I place another crate at the end of the hall and pause, watching her.

She lies on the side of the hall, isolated and away from the others, covered with a white blanket, and coughing a shrill cough, "Nurse."

I scan the area, but the three nurses in white uniforms are tending to other wounded patients in the hall.

"Nurse," she coughs again.

"I'm not a nurse," I approach her slowly. I must continue unpacking the boxes; that's my job. She looks small in the white bed, her head resting on the pillow, and her short red hair scattered over it, shining in the lantern light and the pre-sunset gray light coming through the window. She looks oddly familiar with her short red hair. Was she a nurse at another hospital I was at?

"May I have water?" she looks at me, and I meet her blue eyes. For a moment, she gazes at me as if recognizing me too, but after a second, she closes her eyes and coughs a dry cough again.

"There you go," I quickly pour her a glass of water from the enamel pitcher beside her bed. "Drink it."

"Thank you," she opens her eyes and reaches out, holding the glass. Her fingers tremble as they touch my cold hand. On one of them, I notice a silver male signet ring.

"I apologize," I rub my hands to warm them as she sips slowly. Her face and hands are dotted with small red marks.

"It's fine," she continues to look at me while holding the enamel cup, but I sense she may be confusing me with someone else. Perhaps I'm also confusing her with someone else.

"Soldier," I hear a voice, and I turn around, spotting one of the nurses approaching us, "Don't get too close to her. She has Scarlet Fever; you'll get infected." She stands next to the patient, takes the enamel cup from her hand, and places it on a small cabinet beside her bed.

"I'm sorry," I say to the nurse and watch the red-haired woman lay her head on the pillow again. She keeps her blue eyes on me as I walk away, hurrying towards the exit. I have more boxes to unpack, and it's getting dark.

Later in the night, I stand at the door of the wounded hall, looking at the row of dark beds filled with injured people groaning in pain. The medicine boxes are arranged at the end of the hall. I've already had dinner, the horses are in the stable, and soon I will sleep in the corner of the kitchen next to the large baking oven that emits warmth. The windows at the end of the hall are dark, and I can't see through them due to the snowfall that has been ongoing since the morning hours. Only a few candles on the side of the fir tree continue to twinkle in the dark hall, filled with the sounds of breathing and coughing. I slowly approach the tree, gazing at the candles.

"Soldier," I hear a faint voice from the woman's bed on the side of the hall.

"I'm not allowed to get close to you. The nurse doesn't allow it," I take a few steps towards her, stand at a distance, and whisper to her.

"Please"."

"What do you need?"

"Please sit next to me, just for a few minutes."

I glance back, looking for the nurses. I plan to call one of them, but I can't see them in the dark. "Please," she whispers again and coughs. I walk to the corner of the hall, fetch a chair, bring it to the side of her bed, and sit on it.

"Thank you," she whispers as I hand her a glass of water. Her hand gently touches my outstretched hand, her fingers warm.

"You'll get better soon, don't worry," I reassure her in the dim light. In the dark hall, her red hair appears almost black, and her blue eyes, which previously seemed to recognize me, also look dark now.

"I won't get well," she sighs and coughs weakly, "I won't get well anymore."

"Shall I call a nurse?" I rise from the chair.

"No, please don't call a nurse. Just sit next to me." She extends her hand as if trying to stop me.

"Can I do something for you?" I return and sit in the chair, moving a little closer to her, despite the nurse's warning. In the dim light, I can see her chest rising and falling slowly under the white blanket, and the outline of her breasts. "Are you comfortable?"

"Yes, I'm comfortable. Now I'm comfortable with you sitting next to me."

"Do you need something?"

"Please draw me," she whispers with her eyes closed. It seems she might be hallucinating. Perhaps she's confusing me with someone else.

"Do you want me to write to someone? Do you have someone at home to write to?" I ask her.

"No, I don't," she whispers, shaking her head.

"Don't you have anyone?" I place my hand on her hand lying on the bed, feeling her warm fingers.

"It doesn't matter anymore. It's too late," she turns her head towards me and coughs weakly. Then she opens her eyes, as if examining me again.

"Do we know each other? Do you know me?" I ask her, "You look at me like you know me. You looked at me like that before too." I have a feeling that I know her from another life before the war.

"Where did you grow up? Before you came here," She asks, and I think she's trying to smile at me.

"I was a coachman in Neulengbach, west of Vienna. People always need coachmen. Even here, in the war, officers always have to transport things or soldiers from place to place," I tell her. She continues to gaze at me with her open eyes, as if trying to remember.

"I was once in Neulengbach," she pronounces the name slowly, "but you probably won't remember me," she finally says. Her fingers gently squeeze my palm, closing it.

"I remember," I feel the warmth of her fingers, "the girl with the red hair from the train station," I remember the time she arrived at the train station with a man in a black blazer, and the time she arrived at the train station alone in the snow. The day after, she returned by train from Vienna, and she looked so sad to me. What happened to that man who was with her? I want to ask her, but I'm too shy. "Are you scared?" I finally ask her.

"No," she coughs again, "I succeeded in doing what I wanted and saved many lives. I'm no longer afraid to meet death."

"Shall I call a nurse?"

"Do you have a wife at home, someone waiting for you?" she asks me.

"No. I don't."

"Would you like to have a wife?" I feel her warm fingers.

351

"Yes, I would like to live a simple life with her, to love only her," I whisper to her and move a little closer to her, despite my embarrassment.

"Please draw me," she gasps.

"I don't know how to draw."

"It's not important," she speaks quietly until I have to bring my head close to her lips, "Please draw me," she continues after a moment, "I need you to be the one who draws me for the last time and not him."

"Who is he?" I ask her, but she doesn't answer. She just breathes slowly and closes her eyes. Is that the man with the black quaff who was with her?

I hear the sounds of coughing and sighs all around, and when I turn my head, I can see the silhouette of a nurse approaching one of the wounded. She must not have noticed me when I bent over her bed. I have to go to the kitchen and sleep by the stove.

I quietly get up and approach the medicine boxes placed in the corner of the hall, next to the fir tree adorned with pictures of the saints and the emperor. I gently open the top medicine box and take out a cardboard covering the rolled bandages.

"You're back," she sighs as I sit down next to her again, holding the cardboard in my hand. I take a pencil out of my military shirt pocket and look at her.

My fingers holding the pencil pass gently over the hard cardboard, drawing her pink lips, which are dark in the dim hall, her small nose, and her big eyes looking at me. I close my eyes for a moment and imagine them blue and bright, as they were when she looked at me for the first time this morning.

Then I draw her short red hair scattered on the white pillow, appearing black in the dark.

"Thank you," she says when I finally put the pencil down, knowing I didn't manage to draw her as well as I would have liked.

"Shall I show you the drawing? I'm sorry, but it didn't turn out well," I get up from the chair and prepare to leave. Tomorrow, I have a long day on the snowy road.

"No need, thanks," she holds out her hand, and I take it, even though I'm not allowed to. "Please sit next to me a little longer. I'm afraid to be alone in the coming darkness."

"Imagine you are my girl," I return to sit in the chair next to her, gently caressing her fingers while my other hand holds tightly to her sketch.

I continue to sit and watch her for a long time, holding her hand and hearing her breathing, which slowly grows quieter and quieter. And all that time, I stroke her hand and gaze at her.

The End

On December 25th, 1917, the day after Christmas, Wally Neuzil died of scarlet fever in a military hospital in the town of Sinj in Sarajevo at the age of 23.

Her last painting has never been found.

Chapter Sixteen

Author Notes, Pieces of History

Vienna, in the summer of 2022, at the Belvedere Museum, early in the morning.

My 23-year-old daughter, Dana, and I stood in line to enter the museum. We had ordered tickets online for the opening, wanting to be among the first visitors of the day before the rooms became crowded.

The gate opened, and we validated our tickets, hurrying to follow the signs that pointed to a single room and a specific painting: Gustav Klimt's "The Kiss."

There was a special feeling standing alone for two or three moments—just the two of us in front of this large painting. We stood there silently, observing this masterpiece and enjoying every brush stroke before the moment was gone and other visitors arrived. They chatted excitedly, pulled out their cell phones, and began taking pictures of themselves with the painting.

Later, we separated in the museum and agreed to meet later. She likes classical art, and I prefer impressionist paintings.

While walking through the rooms, I suddenly came across one of Egon Schiele's famous paintings, "Death and the Maiden," painted in 1915, depicting Death embracing a red-haired woman.

I stood looking at the painting. Honestly, I didn't like it. In my opinion, it was too dark and depressing. I much preferred his other paintings. But what caught my attention was the small note beside it. It mentioned that the model for that painting was Wally Neuzil, who had also previously modeled for Gustav Klimt.

At that moment, I knew I wanted to write Wally's story, the story of a young girl who'd wandered between these two great artists. I knew dozens of books had been written about Gustav Klimt and Egon Schiele, but I wanted to tell Wally's story, letting her be the hero of her own life for once.

Later that day when we arrived at the hotel, I started reading about her life. I learned that this was the last painting Egon Schiele had ever painted of her. I also discovered that her life was much more fascinating than I had initially thought. I sat at the small table in the hotel room and began writing the first lines of her story.

This book is based on the life of Wally Neuzil, but in writing it, I took a lot of literary freedom, and many times, I did not stick strictly to the facts. I didn't want to tell a purely historical story. Instead, I wanted to narrate the story of a girl who believed she could overcome the constraints of social class.

Wally's story is set at the beginning of the twentieth century, before the First and Second World Wars broke out, forever changing the course of humanity. The early twentieth century was a period of dramatic change as the world modernized. Inventions like the airplane and automobile replaced horses and carts, and electricity became widespread, supplanting candles and gas lanterns. The old Europe of nobility, with counts, dukes, and kings, was giving way to emerging labor organizations and mass movements advocating for equality. Thinkers of socialism and communism were gaining prominence, alongside extreme right-wing militaristic movements. Women were also raising their voices, demanding equality in suffragist demonstrations against male conservatism.

In Central Europe, this era marked the twilight of the Austro-Hungarian Empire. Within a few years, by the end of the First World War, it would cease to exist. In the meantime, however, Vienna was a significant cultural center before the outbreak of war. Amidst the grand palaces and the Emperor's extravagant balls, Sigmund Freud developed psychoanalytic theory in Vienna, establishing the first associations of supporters in the study of the human psyche. Art also flourished in Vienna during these years. Groups of artists and architects embracing modern art in painting and design dared to create bolder images and simple designs with straight lines, replacing the flamboyant styles that had dominated architectural design.

Wally was born in 1894 in a small town in Austria as the second of five girls. Her mother was a simple worker, and her father was a primary school teacher. After her father's death, the family moved to Vienna.

Wally held various jobs and, in 1910, at the age of 16, she left home. There are speculations that she may have been involved in prostitution, but this remains unclear. It is known that at some point, she became a model for Gustav Klimt and was possibly one of his many lovers.

At that time, Gustav Klimt was a famous 44-year-old painter, and wealthy Viennese women lined up to have him paint their portraits. Rumors suggested that many of them also had romantic involvements with him. He was considered one of Vienna's famous bohemians but did not often socialize with them. He lived a life of ease in his house in Vienna's suburbs, while painting the wealthy women who supported him financially. During this period, he had a cat named 'Cat.'

Among Gustav Klimt's many lovers, there was one constant companion, Emilie Louise Flöge, a pioneering fashion designer who, contrary to the fashion of the time, designed wide and comfortable dresses with strong lines and prints for women. Although less famous than Klimt, her influence on his paintings, particularly in fashion, is evident. In this book, Emilie Louise Flöge is mentioned as a side character through Wally's eyes, but in Gustav Klimt's life, she held significant influence.

In 1910, Gustav Klimt also acted as a mentor to Egon Schiele, a talented young painter of 23. While Klimt painted nudes and even explicit scenes, Schiele pushed the boundaries further, creating paintings that were not well-received by conservative art critics of the time.

Gustav Klimt and Egon Schiele exchanged paintings, which helped Egon Schiele financially. Around the same time, Gustav Klimt introduced Wally Neuzil to Egon Schiele, and in

1911, Wally moved in with Schiele, becoming his mistress and the primary model for his paintings.

During these years, Schiele struggled to exhibit his paintings, one of which was in Munich, where he met Arthur Roessler, a gallery owner mentioned in the story. Arthur Roessler greatly appreciated Schiele's paintings, and a friendship developed between them.

In the spring of 1911, Wally and Egon moved to Krumlov, Egon's mother's hometown, which was then part of the Austro-Hungarian Empire and is now in the Czech Republic. In Krumlov, Egon had friends, and they stayed there for a few months. However, due to their permissive behavior, local residents forced them to leave the town and find a new place to live.

In the summer of 1911, Wally and Egon moved to Neulengbach, a small town west of Vienna. There, Egon became even more entangled with the law.

Egon and Wally hosted girls from lower economic classes in their home, and Egon painted them. In April 1912, he was arrested on charges of kidnapping and creating obscene paintings of young girls.

In reality, Wally and Egon went to Vienna with one of the girls who wanted to visit her grandmother, and they returned with her after two days. During her absence, the girl's father reported a kidnapping. In this book, I have slightly altered the story.

Egon spent twenty-one days in prison before his trial. Indeed, at his trial, the judge accused him of creating obscene art and burned one of his paintings. He was ultimately sentenced to three more days in prison before being released. In May 1912, Wally and Egon returned to Vienna.

In the story, the First World War breaks out on their way back to Vienna. Historically, the war began later, in June 1914, with the assassination of the heir to the throne in Sarajevo. However, for the sake of the narrative, I have placed the outbreak of the war earlier in the story to create the appropriate atmosphere.

The First World War, which occurred from 1914 to 1918 and was often referred to as the 'Great War,' is widely regarded as one of the most unnecessary conflicts in history. It erupted due to complex alliances between nations, monarchies, and kingdoms, which drew one after another into the largest war of its time. The immediate cause of the war was the assassination of the Austro-Hungarian heir, Franz Ferdinand, in Sarajevo. This event set off a chain reaction of threats and declarations of war, ultimately leading to exhausting trench warfare across Europe, lasting for four years. The consequences of the war were devastating, resulting in the loss of 16 million lives and plunging Europe into a period of instability that ultimately paved the way for the emergence of Nazism and the onset of World War II.

World War I also marked the end of the era of European empires, giving rise to republics and socialist movements. At the war's conclusion, both the German Empire and the Austro-Hungarian Empire were dissolved and replaced by republics.

Following Egon's arrest in Neulengbach and his return to Vienna, his paintings took on a more moderate tone. During this time, he crossed paths with Edith and Adéle Harms, who resided across the street from him. The Harms sisters belonged to the bourgeois class, and in a letter to his friend Arthur Roessler in 1915, Egon announced his decision to marry Edith.

He later met with Wally at Café Eichberger and informed her of his choice. During that meeting, he proposed that Wally become his mistress and meet with him once a year during the summer vacation.

Wally declined the offer and left the café; historically, this marked the last time they would see each other.

After she left, Egon painted the famous painting 'Death and the Maiden' in which he depicted himself as Death and Wally as the Maiden. He used his previous drawings of her as a reference.

In the story, I introduced an additional scene where Wally encounters the painting, making it the final time they meet. Following their separation, Wally enlisted as a nurse in the Austro-Hungarian army.

The Wiener Secession Gallery and the Secession Society were established in 1897, a few years before the story's beginning, by Gustav Klimt and several other artists, including sculptors and architects, as a rebellious movement against the conservative art currents of the time. The members of the movement erected a building for exhibitions in Vienna, which featured murals by Gustav Klimt. However, in 1905, differences of opinion emerged among the association members, leading to Gustav Klimt's withdrawal from the group.

I used this magnificent building to describe the artists' exhibitions, even though historically, Klimt did not exhibit there after he retired from the association. During various periods of the First World War, the building was indeed used as a hospital but was later returned to its original purpose for hosting exhibitions. Egon Schiele exhibited his paintings there in 1918 and even designed the exhibition poster.

What happened to the heroes of the story:

Egon Schiele

Egon Schiele married Edith Harms in 1915 and was immediately recruited into the Austro-Hungarian army. He was stationed in Prague, where he guarded Russian prisoners of war, and his commander even allowed him to paint them. In 1917, Schiele was released from the army and returned to Vienna, but in 1918, after the end of the war, the Spanish flu epidemic broke out in Europe. Egon and Edith died from the epidemic three days apart.

Gustav Klimt

Klimt was too old to be drafted into the army. He died in 1918 at the age of 56 due to complications from the Spanish flu epidemic.

Emilie Louise Flöge

After Klimt's death, he bequeathed to her many of his paintings. Unfortunately, some of them and most of her fashion creations, were destroyed in the Allied bombings of Vienna during World War II. Emily died in 1952 at the age of 77.

The Wiener Secession Gallery

The Secession Building was severely damaged in World War II by bombs and remained deserted for many years. In recent years, it has been renovated and reopened in its original structure.

Wally, Walburga Neuzil

Wally served as a military nurse in a hospital in Sarajevo, but on December 25, 1917, she died from Scarlet Fever and was buried there.

This book's heroine is a woman struggling against social norms forcing women to depend on men and live under discriminating conditions. We were born into such a world, but we have to remember that this world is not self-evident and was created mainly by people; people, women and men, must act to change it. I believe that we are able to accomplish this goal.

I would like to end this book with a quote from the United States Supreme Court ruling by Judge William J. Brennan Jr. in the case of Frontiero v. Richardson (1973)

(Future Justice Ruth Bader Ginsburg, representing the ACLU as amicus curiae, was also permitted by the Court to argue in

favor of Frontiero. It was her first time giving an oral argument in front of the court.)

Judge William J. Brennan Jr.:

"...Moreover, since sex, like race and national origin, is an immutable characteristic "determined solely by the accident of birth, the imposition of special disabilities upon the members of a particular sex because of their sex would seem to violate 'the basic concept of our system that legal burdens should bear some relationship to individual responsibility'."

Thank you for reading this book
Alex Amit

Made in the USA
Las Vegas, NV
11 October 2023

78945956R00215